NOBLE RETRIBUTION

JACK NOBLE BOOK SIX

L.T. RYAN

LIQUID MIND MEDIA

THE JACK NOBLE SERIES

For paperback purchase links, visit:
https://ltryan.com/pb

For paperback purchase links, visit:
https://ltryan.com/pb

PART I

EPISODE 6

1

JACK NOBLE REACHED OUT AND GRABBED THE THIN HANDLE OF THE WHITE MUG
on the edge of the table. He brought it to his lips and blew into the cup, sending
a cloud of steam into his eyes and nose. The smell of strong coffee invaded his
senses and alerted his body to the rush of caffeine that would soon come. He
placed his lips to the cup and pulled a half mouthful of the hot liquid in, letting it
cool under his tongue before swallowing. He watched the morning sun crest
over the Libyan Sea in the Mediterranean. Orange, red, pink and purple colored
the sky and sea, making it impossible to tell where one ended and the other
began.

He knew that the cropping of white buildings behind him changed colors
with every passing minute as if they were part of a laser light show. Some morn-
ings he walked on the beach and watched the town during sunrise. Other morn-
ings he sat on the small cafe's patio and woke up with the sea.

The small town of Palaiochora on the Greek island of Crete had turned out
to be the perfect hiding spot for a man who was now a ghost. Small. Quiet.
Quaint. Tourists came through daily. Some stayed overnight. Most didn't. Only a
few of them ever came into the cafe. The cafe with the apartment above it. The
apartment that Jack lived in with Alik, the Russian.

"Good morning, Jack."

Jack nodded, keeping his eyes fixed on the sea and his coffee mug in front of his mouth.

"Beautiful morning." Alik's Russian accent had started to take on a Greek quality over the past few weeks.

"Just like every morning the last six months," Jack said.

Six months. The most peaceful six months of Jack's adult life. After sixteen years of non-stop action, Jack's now thirty-six year old body welcomed the respite. But the itch had returned. The calm and quiet of Palaiochora had started to wear on him. He missed the city. He missed the action and the thrill of his job. In addition to that, there was too much unfinished business. Professionally and personally.

Jack held the mug to his face with both hands. He took a sip. When he exhaled, his breath turned to steam as it met the cool morning air. A breeze blew in from across the sea. The air bit at his face with the promise of a mild spring day. He set his mug down on the table. Pushed the sleeves of his blue sweater past his forearms. Grabbed a napkin and wiped droplets of coffee away from the hair on his upper lip. He rubbed his face, feeling the coarse hair that covered his cheeks and chin. His hair, uncut for six months, hung over his forehead, past his eyebrows. He used both hands to part it in the middle and brushed it back.

"Have you heard from Frank?" asked Jack.

Alik shook his head. "I'll try him today." He cut a piece of danish with a butter knife and stabbed it with a fork. "You are a ghost, Jack. They want to keep it that way. If it takes a year to get you off this island, then it takes a year."

Jack sighed. He arched his back and stretched his arms high in the air. A ghost, he thought. Frank did Jack a favor when he had Alik temporarily kill him while he was imprisoned in the Russian hell hole nicknamed *Black Dolphin*. Jack still had no idea how they pulled it off. Alik wouldn't tell him and Jack hadn't talked to Frank yet. Not one to dwell on such things, Jack had almost forgotten all about it.

Jack pushed back in his chair, stood and walked to the green painted metal railing at the far end of the patio. The railing could use a fresh coat of paint. He leaned over and looked down into the blue sea. Then he turned around and leaned back against the long cold strip of metal. He reached into his pocket for a cigarette. There weren't any there. Hadn't been for three months. Old habits die hard, he figured.

"I'm sure it will be soon," Alik said.

"You said that three months ago."

Alik shrugged. "What do you want me to say? Quit asking."

Jack waved him off and leaned his head back. Over the top of the cafe he could see a few of the houses built into the hillside. The sunrise color show was ending and the buildings were fading from orange to white.

"What about me? He tell you what is going to happen to me yet?"

"Jack," Alik paused a second. "There isn't anything that I can—"

"Anything that you can divulge to me at this time. Yeah, I know." Jack crossed the patio and leaned against the cool exterior wall of the building. His eyes shifted from Alik to the vast openness of the empty sea. "I wish you would quit this act and tell me. You said yourself, I'm a ghost. They wouldn't care about that if they didn't have plans for me. Well, let me tell you something, Alik. I have plans for me. I have some unfinished business that I need to attend to."

Jack stood there shaking his head for a minute before sitting down at the table, across from Alik.

The Russian placed both hands on the table and leaned forward. "Jack, yes, you are correct. They have a plan for you. I'm not privy to all the information, though. I promise you that."

An hour passed and they sat in silence. Jack drank two more cups of coffee and had a breakfast of eggs and fried kalitsounia, a sweet cheese pastry. The locals filed in and out of the cafe, grabbing the coffee and pastries they required to start their morning. A few of the old timers took regular seats on the patio, nodding at Jack as they passed. He thought he could get used to the life here. Not now. But someday. Someday when he had someone to share it with.

"What was that?" Alik asked.

Jack shrugged.

"Listen."

Jack leaned forward. Closed his eyes. He blocked out the chatter of the locals and honed in on a single voice. A voice that stood out from the rest. Similar to Alik's, but with a harsher tone. The voice rose and fell as it interrogated outside the cafe. And then inside.

"Russians."

Alik's eyes widened and he nodded in agreement.

From inside the cafe a voice called out in English, "Jack Noble. Present yourself now."

2

"TELL THEM TO LEAVE." JACK POINTED AT THE LOCALS SEATED AT TABLES ON THE patio.

Alik spoke in Greek and then repeated in English, "Get off the patio. Through the cafe. Leave now, your lives are in danger."

Six older men looked around in confusion.

"Now," Alik shouted.

The men stood and staggered back through the door into the cafe. Coffee and coats and smokes in hand.

The patio offered Jack and Alik little in the way of cover or protection. Walled on three sides and open to the sea on the fourth with only the green metal railing separating the men from the water below. And with the air temperature at fifty degrees, the water would be too cold to offer a suitable means of escape. Besides, it was too shallow.

Jack scanned the tables. He grabbed two serrated edged knives and flipped them in his hands so that the blades pressed against his forearms. He nodded to Alik and flattened himself against the wall, a few feet from the door. Alik moved to the far end of the patio so that he would be the first man the Russian would see. Only just then Jack heard a second Russian voice. Possibly even a third. His eyes widened and he tried to get Alik's attention, but the man appeared to have already seen what Jack had heard.

Alik reached behind his back. Was he armed today? Both of the men had reached a point where they felt there weren't any real threats in the small town. Hell, on the entire island, for that matter. The chance of something happening seemed *less than* slim-to-none. Who would look for Jack, a man believed to be dead, at the southernmost point of Crete?

A voice called through the door. His voice sounded close, perhaps just past the threshold. Jack held the knives tight. One back against his left forearm ready to defend. The other pointing out ready to strike and attack. He thought about swinging his body around and launching himself through the door, attacking the first person he saw. He quickly shook the thought from his head. He felt rusty. No action for six months had dulled his responses and reflexes, and his senses were now overwhelmed. He closed his eyes and let the cool air rush in through his mouth. Lungs expanded and oxygen flooded his bloodstream. His mind calmed as he tensed and relaxed his muscles.

The first man stepped through the doorway. He focused on Alik and started toward him with his arms slightly extended.

Alik spoke in Russian. Jack didn't know what he said, but it obviously caught the other man's attention because he didn't even seem to notice Jack.

The second man stepped through. Jack wasted no time. He turned and brought his right arm across his body with the blade of the knife extended. The man reacted and took a defensive position. He must have seen Jack in his peripheral vision. Unfortunately for the man, his reaction left the soft spot of his neck exposed. Jack adjusted his aim in a fraction of a second and plunged the knife deep into the man's neck. The sharp point combined with the force of Jack's blow allowed the knife to penetrate through the tangle of skin and muscle and blood vessels and finally into his spinal column. The blade severed the thread that linked the man's brain to his body. He dropped to the ground in a lifeless heap.

The first man through the door spun on his heels and reached inside his coat. The jacket fell open, revealing a pistol, most likely the Russian Army issued Makarov PMM. Jack couldn't be sure as he only saw the weapon for a split second. The moment the man's hand hit the handle of the gun, Jack leapt into the air. He swung his left arm in an arc. The dull side of the blade of the knife pressed against the side of his forearm. The serrated edge faced out. Jack timed the swing of his arm so that the knife sliced across the man's throat. The cut wasn't clean, but it did the job.

The Russian dropped his gun and brought both hands to his neck. It muffled, but didn't stop, the arterial spray. He backed into the center wall and slowly slid down it and into a seated position. Two thin lines of blood left an extended outline of his neck on the wall.

Jack allowed his momentum to carry him through his jump. He hit the ground and rolled on his back and then over onto his hands and knees. He got to his feet and rose to a standing position. He faced the open doorway between the cafe and the patio.

A third man yelled from inside the cafe. Jack scanned the room and saw the man aiming a gun in his direction. Jack quickly moved out of the man's sights. An explosion ripped through the air. A flash of light that lasted barely a second brightened the opening between the cafe and the patio. The bullet hit with a thud.

Alik groaned loudly and fell back into the wall. He shuffled his feet and fell to his left, trying to stay low and out of range of another shot.

Jack rushed toward the door. He was greeted by the sight of pandemonium inside the cafe. That told him that the third Russian would not be able to get a clean shot at him or Alik. But it also meant that he could possibly kill an innocent bystander with another shot. Jack blew through the open doorway.

Two older men had the Russian by his arms. A third older man had his thick arms wrapped around the Russian's neck. The Russian pushed back and tried to crush the older man on his back against the glass display case. They had not managed to get his gun from him, though, and he struggled to aim it in Jack's direction.

Jack continued toward the group of men and slammed his right fist in the Russian's jaw. The man went slack in the arms of the Greek men and his gun fell to the floor. Jack scooped the gun off the ground. Tucked it in his waistband. He grabbed a fistful of the man's hair and started pulling him toward the patio.

"That'll be enough," he said. "Thank you, gents."

Jack dragged the Russian onto the patio. He dropped him on the ground and then turned and slammed the door shut.

Alik had propped himself up against the wall. Blood poured from a bullet hole in his chest.

"Christ," Jack said. "Alik, you with me?"

Alik nodded slowly. He tried to speak.

"Save your strength."

Jack turned to the Russian. Kicked him in the stomach. The man rolled over and opened his eyes.

"Who sent you?" Jack said.

"Screw you," the Russian said in English.

Jack kicked him again.

"Who? Tell me or so help me I'll put a bullet in your head."

The man spit.

Jack knew this was a wasted effort. He needed to attend to Alik before he bled out. He knelt down and placed the barrel of the gun to the man's forehead.

"Last chance."

The man said nothing.

Jack cursed at the man. Pulled the trigger twice. The bullets ripped through the Russian's skull, tearing his brain apart.

Jack got up and went to the door. He opened it and yelled into the cafe.

"I need help out here."

The three older Greek men responded and came out to the patio. Two went to work on Alik. The third turned to Jack.

"We are all experienced medics," he said in English. "From the war."

Jack didn't ask which war. "Is he going to be OK?"

"We need to take him somewhere."

"Hospital won't be safe. There could be more of them." Jack gestured toward the three slain men on the patio.

"I know a place." The older man turned to his two friends and waved at Jack. "Come. Help. Get him to the truck."

THEY DROVE through town and into the country. Fast and steady. Paved roads gave way to packed dirt. The truck slowed down. They turned onto a gravel driveway that jutted out between two lines of trees. A small stone house sat at the end of the driveway.

Jack turned to the man in the back of the truck sitting opposite him. Alik lay between them.

"Where are we?"

"My mother's house."

"She a doctor?"

"No." He paused a moment and looked toward the house. "I am, though."

The truck stopped near the house. The two Greek men in the cab got out and rushed to the rear of the vehicle. The four of them lifted Alik from the bed of the truck and carried him to the house. An old white haired lady with a slightly hunched back stood by the door, holding it open. They brought Alik inside and into the kitchen. Placed him on a long wooden table that looked to be over a hundred years old. The table was covered in white sheets. Several stainless steel medical tools were laid out neatly at one end.

The man who had declared himself a doctor grabbed a pair of scissors and cut Alik's shirt down the middle. He pried the blood-soaked garment from Alik's chest. The doctor wiped away blood from the site of the wound and inspected the damage.

"I think he's going to be OK. He's severely injured, but will heal."

Jack nodded and took a few steps back. He wanted to get out of the way. The doctor knew what he was doing and the men appeared to have worked with him before. Jack, on the other hand, was useless in this situation.

Jack said, "His pocket. The phone."

The doctor nodded to one of the other men who reached into Alik's pocket and pulled out a cell phone. The man tossed it to Jack.

Jack snatched the phone mid-air and turned to the front door. He passed the white haired lady and stepped through the open doorway. He worked the phone. Pressed a button and scanned through a list until he found Frank's number. He highlighted the number and pressed send.

Frank answered midway through the third ring. "Hello?" His voice was soft and deep. He had been sleeping. Jack looked at his watch and calculated it was two in the morning on the east coast of the U.S.

"What did you do?"

"Huh? Who is this?" Frank's voice trailed off. Jack figured he was looking at his caller ID.

"Alik, huh? Jack, is that you?"

"What did you do, Frank?"

"Jack, what are you talking about?"

"God dammit, don't screw with me. I'll end you if you don't tell me the truth."

"I've been working to get you moved. I have it all set up for—"

"How did they know?"

"—two weeks from now. There's gonna be a guy...wait. How did who know what?"

Jack said nothing. He held the phone to his ear. He exhaled fast and heavy.

"Jack, what happened?"

"We were ambushed. This morning. At the cafe where we've been staying."

"Who?"

"Russians."

The line went silent and for a moment Jack thought Frank had hung up.

"This is bad, Jack. Very bad."

"No kidding, Frank. Alik's been injured. What are you going—"

"Hold on. I'm thinking."

Jack turned around and looked past the old woman in the doorway. Two men held Alik down while the doctor worked on his chest. It looked like he had forceps inserted into the wound in an effort to retrieve the bullet. Jack lowered his eyes toward the white haired woman. She held up a cigarette. He shook his head, shrugged and then held out his hand. The old woman lit the cigarette and handed it to him. The first drag tasted like the street after Mardi Gras and the smoke burned his lungs. He nearly coughed. But he took a second drag, and then a third. The rush of nicotine excited and then calmed him all within a period of twenty seconds.

"Christ," Jack muttered under his breath, disappointed in himself for accepting the cigarette.

"What?" Frank asked.

"Nothing," Jack said.

"Jack, call me back in five minutes. I need to wake someone up."

Jack looked around, through the trees, toward the dirt road leading in. Five minutes wouldn't be long enough to get someone else here to finish the job the three Russians failed to complete.

"OK. I'll call back in five."

He hung up the phone, took a final drag off the cigarette and dropped it to the ground where he crushed it with his heel. He walked past the woman in the doorway, nodding with a smile as he did so.

"How is he?"

The doctor looked over his shoulder. His hands continued to work, sewing shut the hole in Alik's chest.

"He'll live. The bullet lodged in his rib. The rib is broken. Shattered. But had it not stopped the bullet, your friend would be dead."

Jack stood next to the table. Looked down at Alik. The man's eyes fluttered as he passed between states of consciousness and unconsciousness. The doctor had given him some type of anesthetic, but Jack questioned its effectiveness.

"He'll be OK," the doctor said. "He should be in the hospital, though."

"Can't. You saw what happened at the cafe. He checks into a hospital, he won't check out."

"Then he can stay here," the old woman said.

The doctor nodded. "I'll keep an eye on him over the next few days. Administer pain meds so he isn't suffering. In a few days he should be in much better shape."

Jack looked at his watch and pulled the phone back out. He dialed the number as he walked toward the front door.

Frank answered after the first ring.

"Jack, OK. We're getting you out. I'm sending one of my guys."

"Just me," Jack said.

"What do you mean? Is Alik dead?"

"No, but he's in no condition to travel."

"Dammit. OK, I'm sending an extra man to stay with him then."

Jack looked back at the three Greek men and the old woman. "Probably a good idea."

"Where are you?"

"About ten miles outside of town. Get your men here and call me. I'll send a car."

"They'll be there by nightfall."

3

A CLOUD OF SMOKE LINGERED JUST BELOW THE CEILING OF THE SMALL apartment. Pierre sat in a stiff wooden chair, a cigarette pressed between two fingers and hovering an inch or so from his lips. He rested his elbows on a small square wooden table. The only furniture in the apartment. His cell phone next to him on his left. His Glock 17 with a fully loaded magazine opposite him, just out of reach. A large round glass ashtray sat in the middle of the table with a few dozen stubbed out cigarette butts strewn about the crushed black and gray ashes. The smell of stale cigarette smoke filled the air.

The apartment was dark. It wasn't that Pierre didn't want to turn the lights on. He couldn't turn them on. The power had been cut off earlier in the week. He had run out of belongings to pawn and that meant he had run out of money to pay his bills. Soon he'd be evicted from the apartment. His eyes glanced at the gun. Pawn it or use it, he thought.

He stubbed out his cigarette and walked to the fridge. He pulled the door open and a wave of foul odor from spoiled milk filled the surrounding air. He quickly slammed the door shut. How stupid, he thought. He'd done the same thing at least half a dozen times the past few days. He sidestepped along the counter and grabbed a tumbler from the cabinet. A nearby bottle of whiskey promised to erase his pain for one more night. The bottle had at least a few pours left, and there was one more unopened bottle in the apartment. He filled the glass three-quarters of the way and stopped himself from opening the freezer for a cube of ice. There was no ice in there, only rank meat.

He returned to the table, sat down and lit another cigarette. Two more in the pack. Two more packs until he ran out. Quit smoking or steal more, he thought. He blew a thin line of smoke toward the ceiling and sighed as he watched the smoke billow out into a cloud. He took a sip from his glass. Placed the glass down. Dragged his thumb along his stubble covered jaw line.

It had been over three months since he left his job at the agency. The pain he faced had become unbearable. His lack of focus had caused problems for him and for his team. He knew that it was no longer prudent for him to work there. Not only was his life on the line, but the lives of the men and women who worked on his team, as well as the innocent civilians they protected. It would only take one misread communication to lead to Pierre doing something very stupid. Or nothing at all. Either of which could result in consequences he didn't want to face. Consequences he could be forced to face in a court of law. Or in a funeral parlor. So he left. Told his boss that he was done. Left his gun and badge on his desk and walked out the door.

In most cases, that would be enough for an order to terminate. But Pierre had given everything he had to the agency. His boss hesitated to let him go, but stepped aside. Even walked him out the door. Told Pierre he could call if he ever needed a hand. Needed help. Pierre thanked his boss, never imagining that he'd need to take him up on the offer. He knew that he could never return to the agency, but his boss could put in a good word for him wherever Pierre decided to go next.

He had figured that he had enough money in the bank to last until he got through his bout of depression. He just never imagined that the depression would last this long. Three months since leaving his job. Now, with the money gone he had nowhere to turn. Well, almost nowhere. His eyes moved about the room and settled on his Glock 17. He leaned over and reached out for the gun. Stopped and grabbed his cell phone instead.

Pierre pushed a button and slid his finger across the screen of his cell phone. He scrolled through a contact list and stopped on the name Alonso, Charles's right hand man. Six months ago Pierre had told Charles that he would work with him. Charles hadn't called, though, and Pierre had forgotten all about the offer. But now he'd reached the end of his rope and working for a crime boss didn't have the same sting it once held.

Surely Charles would have work available. A man as highly trained as Pierre could be in demand among the right crowd.

His finger lingered over the green send button. He nearly pressed it when a single old fashioned chime rang through the apartment. His doorbell. He pushed back in his chair, took a quick drink and stood up. Walked across the apartment to the door and flipped back a small square panel, revealing a peephole. He looked through and saw the back of a head full of dark hair. He reached down and opened the door.

The young woman spun around and greeted him with a smile.

"Kat."

"Hello, Pierre." She reached out and took his hand in hers. "Can I come in?"

He stepped back and gestured her through. She coughed as she entered. He caught her face shift to a look of disgust, but she quickly masked it with a forced smile.

"What's happened here?"

He hiked his shoulders a few inches and frowned.

She turned to him. Reached out and brushed strands of his unkempt hair away from his forehead.

"Pierre, you have to get over this."

He shook his head and turned away. Walked to the kitchen, past the table. He stopped in front of the large window that overlooked an empty city street. He stared at a collection of trash cans on the curb. He inhaled deeply as the pain of confronting his feelings welled up inside.

"I tried. I can't. A man died, a friend of mine died. It was my fault."

He felt slight vibrations in the floor as she walked toward him. Her hand pressed against his shoulder, the touch warm against his clammy skin.

"It's not your fault. It is what it is. You knew the risks of your job. He knew the risks of his."

Pierre shrugged his shoulder and her hand fell to the side. They'd had this conversation several times during the three months they dated. He wasn't sure why she would even bring it up again. The last time they spoke, the night before he quit the agency, this exact conversation had led to him pulling his gun. First he aimed it at her. Then at his own head. He had almost pulled the trigger. Kat left that night but not before shouting several hurtful parting words. Pierre didn't blame her.

She squeezed against him from the side and wrapped her arm around his waist. She rested her head on his shoulder. Her hair brushed against his ear and the side of his face, getting caught up in the stubble.

"I'm here, Pierre. We'll get through this together."

Pierre closed his eyes and took a deep breath. "Maybe we can get away. Go somewhere. Italy or Greece. Hell, the U.S., maybe."

"That would be nice, Pierre." She let go of his waist and took a step back. Reached up and turned his face by his chin. "Why don't we start with my apartment? Wouldn't you like to get out of here?"

He smiled. "I think that would be—"

His cell phone rang.

Pierre glanced at the cell phone and held up a single finger to Kat.

He looked at the display. It read "restricted." He answered.

"Hello, Pierre. My name is Alonso. I am a business associate of—"

"I remember who you are. What do you want?"

"We'd like to offer you a job."

"I'm listening."

"Good. I'll call you in a few days. Be ready to meet us at a moment's notice."

Pierre hung up the phone. A twinge of excitement passed through his body. It started in his stomach and spread through his chest. Traveled down his arms and legs. He felt the heavy skin on his face relax and loosen. For the first time in months he felt alive.

He looked back at Kat and said, "Let's go."

4

FENG LEANED BACK IN THE OVERSIZED LEATHER SEAT. LEG ROOM WASN'T A problem on his private jet. One of the benefits of buying new and being able to select a custom seating arrangement. The rest of the seats were empty. He liked to imagine the ghosts of those who had fallen victim to him traveled with him. Ready to welcome him to Hell should his plane crash.

This was a business trip, and by the definition of his business, not the type of trip he should take alone. Technically he would not be alone, though. He had a team in place in Chicago and four of his best Chi-town men were meeting him at the small commuter airport west of the city.

One of the flight crew had just come back to inform the old man that they would be landing on time. He should expect the approach to begin in twenty minutes.

He shrunk into his seat and continued reviewing the documents in his lap. The documents that had caused so much trouble and put the final strain on his relationship with Charles. Perhaps he would have been better off taking out Jack Noble to appease his right hand man. Things had been smoothed over, though. Jack had died in that Russian prison, and Charles had been sent to France to oversee European operations.

And Charles had done quite a good job so far.

Feng didn't find much of interest in the documents. It told of weaknesses that could be exploited. A foreign country might be interested in the information. Feng had no intent to try to overthrow the U.S. government, and didn't think any terrorist organization really had a chance. Therefore he didn't have any interest in using the information for any gain other than monetary. It didn't take long to find a buyer, either. A small terror cell hidden in the heartland of America had a keen interest. A seven figure interest. They offered one million dollars. Feng countered at seven million. They settled on five million. A tidy sum for very little work. In the end he didn't even have to pay Jack for the job.

The sudden drop in altitude signaled to Feng that it was time to lock the documents in his briefcase. He then turned his attention to the window. The setting sun turned the sky shades of pink and purple. The ground was littered with browns and greens, signaling the end of winter and the beginning of spring. Small patches of snow lingered on the northern side of houses in areas where shadows remained throughout the day, waiting to rejoin the night.

The plane landed and Feng remained seated until one of the flight crew emerged from the cockpit and told him it was time to depart.

THE CO-PILOT OPENED the plane's door and dropped a set of stairs. Feng nodded at him as he passed and then stepped through the opening into the blustery cold evening. The high in New York that day had been sixty. He figured it was in the low thirties in Chicago. He pulled his coat tight with one hand and held the briefcase in the other. He scanned the area and spotted one of his men. The old man took the steps one at a time until he reached the bottom.

Feng crossed an asphalt parking lot to meet Reynolds, the most trusted member of his Chicago team. Halfway across the lot he saw a group of men appear. He did not recognize them.

"Who are these men?" he asked.

Reynolds shook his head.

"Reynolds, who are they?"

"Sir," Reynolds said.

One of the other men reached out and placed a hand on Reynolds. Pulled him back. The man stepped forward. He had blond hair and blue eyes. Pale, prematurely aged skin. He spoke with a slight accent that Feng couldn't quite place.

"Mr. Feng, please come with us." He extended an arm and gestured toward a parked limousine.

The old man narrowed his eyes and looked at each man individually.

"I don't know if you are aware of who you are dealing with. I can buy and sell each of you fifty times over. I can kill your families in their sleep and force you to watch."

The blond haired man smiled and nodded. "We know. Let's go." He grabbed Feng by the elbow and led him to the limo. Another man opened the door. Reynolds stepped in first, then Feng, followed by the blond haired man. The other three men got in and blocked the exits. All four men unbuttoned their coats, revealing pistols in holsters.

Feng studied each man individually and then turned to Reynolds.

"What happened, Reynolds? Where is your team?"

Reynolds looked from Feng to the blond haired man. "I think you should—"

"That's enough," the blond haired man said. "Mr. Feng, all your questions will be answered by my boss."

"This is not how we arranged this, young man. I don't do business in this manner." He held up the briefcase. "You can tell your boss he can forget all about the contents of this briefcase if I don't get answers now."

The blond haired man smiled.

"My name is Jeremy. Jeremy Fletcher. I am your liaison for the next forty-eight hours. Everything will go as planned. Our plan, that is. You just sit back and relax and nothing will happen to you or your associate here."

The old man turned his head and looked at the man at his side. Reynolds cast his eyes down to the floor and shook his head.

"Where is the rest of your team?"

"They…I…" Reynolds couldn't finish.

Fletcher said, "Neutralized."

"Any damages suffered to my organization will be paid back threefold. Understand? You can tell your boss that, too."

Fletcher smiled. "Understood."

No one said another word for the next half hour. Finally, when the limo pulled into a parking lot, Fletcher spoke.

"We're here."

"Where is here?" Feng asked.

"The hotel. We are going to stay here until my boss is ready for you."

Feng resisted at first, but then decided he had no choice. He was cut off from everyone in his organization at the moment. For now, he would remain in survival mode.

"I know what you are thinking, sir," Fletcher said. "Don't worry. We're working together here. No harm will come to you or your men as long as you cooperate."

Feng stepped out of the car. Walked up to Fletcher. He opened his mouth to speak, stopped and waved the man off.

"Show me to my room," he said as he turned toward the hotel entrance.

5

Jack's plane departed Athens, Greece at 12:55 am. The flight took just over eleven hours, landing in New York's JFK Airport at five in the morning. He passed through customs without any problems, thanks to the fake passport Frank had arranged for him. The name on the passport said John J. Martin. He wondered if that was his new alias. For the past six months he had been known simply as Jack. The Greeks he had befriended needed no last name.

He made the trans-Atlantic journey with two men. Both early thirties, close cut hair, dark suits. Anyone with an eye for such things would have labeled them as Feds without giving it as much as a second thought. The men didn't talk much other than to introduce themselves as Coppa and Shipley. They sat in front of and behind him on the commuter flight from Crete to Athens. On either side of him in the middle row on the flight from Athens to New York. Jack tried to make small talk. They said nothing. Typical of the agents in the SIS.

Jack had spent two years as an agent in the SIS after his stint with the Marines. Frank had been his partner for the majority of those two years. He never got to know many of the other agents on a personal level, despite it being a relatively small group. They spent little time in the office.

Jack and the two agents stood next to the taxi line. Coppa scanned the artificially lit road and pointed toward a black sedan.

"There. Let's go."

They stood on either side of Jack and led him toward the idling car. Coppa took the front passenger seat. Shipley sat in back with Jack.

Jack stared out the window, wondering where they were heading. The street lamps along the airport's roads gave way to the headlights of cars stretched out in columns along I-678. It was almost six a.m. and the eastern sky showed the first signs of sunrise.

"You guys trust me now?"

"No," Shipley said. "Try something and we'll shoot."

Jack smiled. "Where're we going?"

Coppa and Shipley said nothing.

"Last I checked the SIS was based out of D.C. That where we're headed to?"

Shipley turned his head and nodded once.

Jack took that as an affirmative response to his question. They were looking at a five to six hour drive to reach D.C. depending on the traffic around New York City and Philadelphia, which they would reach during the peak of morning rush hour traffic. He kept his focus on the road until they merged onto I-95 southbound. Satisfied they were heading to D.C., Jack closed his eyes and fell asleep.

THE CAR SLOWED TO A STOP. Nothing unusual, probably traffic. Then one of the car doors opened and slammed shut. Jack sat up and looked at his watch. Barely seven am. He looked around. They were in a parking lot. In front of the car and off in the distance were two basketball courts. Behind them were four tennis courts. To his left was a baseball field. He turned in his seat and saw a brick building

"Where the hell are we?"

Shipley opened his door and stepped out. The only remaining person in the car was the driver.

Jack reached forward and grabbed the man by his shoulder. The driver leaned forward and shrugged out of Jack's grasp.

"You can get out of the car now," the driver said.

Jack took another quick glance around. The sun was high enough in the sky that the park posed only a limited risk of agents lurking in the shadows. He placed his hand on the door handle and pushed the door open. Got out of the car and walked around back to where Coppa and Shipley were standing. He glanced across the parking lot. On the other side of the road was a line of houses. He figured they were somewhere residential outside the city.

"Where are we?"

"Walk with us," Coppa said.

Shipley touched Jack's elbow.

Jack pulled away and started walking. Jack and his two escorts passed the building and the ground under them transitioned from parking lot to a paved walkway that cut through the park. A few people walked in pairs and walked their dogs along the network of pavement throughout the park. They passed through a grouping of trees and then headed toward a football field with a track circling it. On one side of the field was a single four row aluminum frame bleacher. On the top row, a lone man sat facing the field. His back was turned to the approaching men. He wore a dark overcoat and held a cup of coffee in his right hand. There appeared to be a second cup of coffee on the bench to his left.

Coppla and Shipley stopped. Shipley pointed at the man sitting atop the bleachers.

Jack kept walking. He approached the bleachers from the side, entering the man's peripheral vision slowly and cautiously. Out here, in this environment with no weapon of his own, he was a sitting duck. Best to take his time and avoid surprising the man.

The man turned his head and Jack instantly recognized him as Frank. His short, dark hair was neatly groomed. Same as it was eight years ago when they were partners. His face had aged some and there were slight lines etched into his forehead. But his face remained strong and cut with muscular jaws.

"Glad to see you, Jack."

"Frank. Wish I could say the same." Jack climbed the bleachers and sat to Frank's left. "Where are we?"

"Newark. West Side Park."

"This where you're based now?"

"No." Frank took a sip of coffee and motioned to the steaming cup in between him and Jack. "I figured if you didn't like what I had to say, then it was best you didn't know where our new office is."

"What is it you have to say?"

Frank nodded toward two middle aged women wearing oversized red and blue coats and spandex pants. The woman were walking moderately fast along the brown track circling the field. After they passed, Frank spoke.

"Alik was going to come work for me. He's been providing intel for some time and I thought... Hell, you know the score I'm sure. Anyways, there's a cell, probably more than a cell, that we've identified. Near here, Jack." He waved his hand in the air for emphasis.

Jack said nothing. His eyes focused on the two women who were now a quarter of the way around the track.

Frank continued. "From the intelligence we've gathered and had shared with us, the group is Russian. Possibly with ties to your friend, Ivanov." He glanced sideways and made eye contact with Jack. "We're not sure what they are planning, but we've gotten word that a set of highly classified documents were intercepted and fell into a certain old man's hands."

Jack shrugged. Said nothing.

"And now that old man is selling those classified documents to another cell in the terrorist organization. We now believe that we are dealing with more than a small group of terrorists. We have reason to believe that this is big, Jack. And I mean big as in huge. Alik would've been our in. He still might be, but I'm guessing it is going to be a month, maybe two, before he'd be fit for this kind of work. And with the recent intelligence confirming that this group is getting those documents, well, we just don't have the time to waste."

"Get to it. Ask me."

Frank stood and stretched his back. The ladies were passing in front of the bleachers again. The one closest waved at Frank. He waved back.

Jack looked away.

The women passed. Frank sat down and looked at Jack.

"I need you to come work for me, Jack."

Jack didn't answer. He looked across the field, beyond the park at the row homes across the street. The sun peeked over the long shared roof line. He felt the temperature rise a few degrees as the first rays of sunlight hit his face.

"You're in an envious position, Jack. The intelligence community believes you are dead. The SIS can give you everything you need. Multiple identities. We can get the funds you have stashed in private accounts transferred to new accounts in any number of names. You can start over. Get out of the private contractor stuff you started doing after you left us." Frank paused. "Like stealing those documents. For Christ's sake, Jack. If the right people got wind of that you could be tried for treason."

"There are people high up in the government that do far worse than what I did. Besides, I didn't know what they contained. I had a name, a date and a location. Simple as that. I took a job and completed it. Don't insinuate anything about me, Frank. You and the rest of the SIS certainly aren't a bunch of choir boys."

Frank held his hand in the air. "Sorry, Jack. I didn't mean to go down that path."

Jack took a deep breath. Rolled his head side to side.

"I need your help, Jack. Forget everything else. Help me out now and I'll help you after this job is finished."

"How long are we talking about? Until Alik can join?"

Frank shook his head. "Once you're in, you're in until it's done. Plain and simple. It might require you to go undercover. I can't wait for Alik."

Jack placed his hands on the cold aluminum bench. He leaned his head back. Did he really have a choice? Frank had told him without telling him that he had Jack by the balls. Tried for treason. Wouldn't that be a kick in the nuts after everything he'd sacrificed.

"I'll do it. One job, that's it. I'm not joining the SIS again."

Frank stood and extended his hand. Jack grabbed it.

"I need to go to the city before I get started."

"Jack, we really should get to D.C. now."

"Tomorrow. Hell, tonight. Just let me have today."

Frank walked down the three empty rows to the bottom of the bleacher.

"Meet here tomorrow. Noon."

Jack watched Frank walk toward Coppa and Shipley. The three men disappeared behind the trees. Jack hopped to the ground and crossed the football field. He nodded at the two middle aged women as he passed them. He turned right at the street. A short walk later found himself at the corner of 13th Street and 18th Avenue. There was a bus stop on the other side of the intersection. He took a seat at the bus stop and waited. A NJ Transit city bus pulled up. The doors opened. Jack climbed on board.

"What's the best way to get to Manhattan?"

"You start with me, pal."

Jack nodded and took a seat behind the driver.

6

Jack stood outside Clarissa's apartment building. He leaned back against the brick exterior and watched the traffic and pedestrians pass by without acknowledging him. He hoped she'd just appear. It had been over six months since he had last been here. That was the day he had found Mandy on a city sidewalk. That was the day his working relationship with the old man had effectively ended. At once the guilt and shame returned. Clarissa went through a lot in the weeks following that day. Jack took the blame for it all.

Half an hour passed. He decided that he wouldn't wait any longer. He glanced at his watch. Four p.m. He pushed through the front door and took the stairs to her floor. Found her apartment. Knocked on the door. A minute passed with no answer. Maybe she had a new job and was still at work. He knocked again. He turned to head back to the stairs. Stopped when he heard the sound of a lock being turned.

The door opened and Jack felt his heart sink and his stomach knot at the sight of a shirtless man. He stood about six feet tall, had brown hair and was in good shape. Jack knew that it was a possibility Clarissa had moved on. Everyone who knew him believed Jack to be dead. Clarissa would have believed it as well.

"Help you?"

Jack cleared his throat. "I-I, uh."

The man leaned in toward the door. "You alright, pal?"

"I'm here to see Clarissa. She around?"

The man's eyes narrowed a bit and he hiked his shoulders a couple inches in the air. Shook his head. "No one here with that name."

Jack held his hand up, level with his eyes. "About this tall, dark red hair?"

"Sorry, pal. Lived here six months now. No Clarissa in this apartment. Not on this floor. In fact, I've met everyone in this building and there's no one that meets that description. I would have tried to get to know her a little better, if you know what I mean." The man smiled and lifted an eyebrow.

"Yeah, got it. Six months you've been here?"

"Yeah, that's right. Found this place right after I moved to New York from Chicago."

Jack raised a hand. "Thanks. I won't take up anymore of your time."

"Alright. Take it easy, pal."

Jack turned and walked toward the stairs. The door closed with a thud.

Where was she? She had left six months ago. Must have been right after she received news that he had died.

He decided to check the man's story with the building's super. He hurried down the stairs and stopped in front of the door labeled with the number one. A plaque next to the door read "Mr. Whitten."

Jack knocked on the door. A few moments later a heavy set man with curly black hair opened the door.

"What can I do for you? Looking for an apartment?"

"No," Jack said. "Clarissa Abbot. What happened to her?"

The man shrugged. "Who?"

"Tall, red hair, gorgeous."

The man smiled and his eyes widened and his eyebrows lifted into his forehead.

"Oh, yeah. I remember her. What a piece she was."

"What happened to her?"

"Damnedest thing, you know. She just disappeared. No notice or anything. She had rent control on that place, you know. She had it at a steal. Figured she would have sublet it out or something like that. Instead she just disappeared. I remember doing my daily check down the hall, uh, when was that? I guess six months ago now. So, yeah, anyways I did my daily hall check and the door was open. Not a crack or anything like that. I'm talking wide open, you know. So I walk in and the place was empty. Cleared out. Every-thing gone."

Something about the last statement put Jack at ease. If Charles or the old man had put out a hit on her or abducted her, they wouldn't have gone through the trouble of clearing out her apartment. Perhaps she had just left. Got away. Made a break and found a fresh start.

"Got a message you want to leave in case she just shows up again?"

"She's not going to show up again. Thanks for your time."

Jack turned and walked away. Pushed through the door and out into the cool New York air. The sun dipped low in the western sky and the buildings covered the street with shadows. The temperature dropped at least fifteen degrees in the sunless void. He pulled his jacket close together in the front and zipped it. He walked two blocks. Found a drug store and went inside to purchase a pay-as-you-go cell phone. Then, after he exited the store, he dialed one of the only two numbers he knew by heart.

No matter where Bear was, or what phone he had with him, there was one number that Jack could dial that would always go through to the big man. He punched in ten digits and placed the phone to his ear. It rang twice and then clicked over to a recorded message.

"The number you are trying to reach has been disconnected. Please check the number—"

Jack closed the phone, reopened it and dialed again. In his haste he might have pushed a wrong button. Again he placed the phone to his ear. Again the same message played. He cursed under his breath and looked around for a pay phone. He dropped the idea almost as fast as the thought came to him. Bear wouldn't be listed in the white pages or four-one-one. Why was the number disconnected? Something must have happened to Bear. Jack's stomach knotted. Again. Part apprehension. Part guilt.

He started walking toward the apartment they had used as their central base of operations. He pulled the collar of his coat up and kept his head down. If something had happened to Bear, then the apartment, maybe all of their apart-ments, might be under surveillance. He stopped a few blocks away and pulled the cell phone from his coat pocket. He searched his memory and dialed ten digits on the keypad again. A man answered after the second ring.

"Hello?"

"Brandon."

"Who's this?"

"Brandon, is that you?"

"I don't know, man. Who is this?"

"Jack."

"Jack who?"

"Noble."

"No way, man. Jack Noble is dead. I don't know who the frig you are but this ain't funny."

"Brandon, it's really me."

Brandon said nothing. A few seconds passed and then a few more. Jack looked at the small screen on the phone and saw a flashing message indicating that the call had ended. He punched the redial button and held the phone to his ear.

No answer.

He wiped the phone down and tossed it into a trashcan. Then he turned and left the area. Brandon was the kind of guy in the kind of organization that could have a team at any location within ten minutes if they felt the threat was severe enough. Brandon's reaction left Jack feeling less than at ease. Did he just make a huge mistake? Did Brandon know the truth? Or did he figure someone was trying to get to him using Jack's identity? Whatever the reason, Jack didn't want to find out. He decided to get out of the city.

Jack made his way to the 14th Street PATH station. Bought a ticket and got on a train to Newark. The trip took twenty minutes, and they stopped twice along the way. He exited the train at the Newark Penn Station and rented a room at the Penn Station Hilton in between Raymond Blvd and Market Street. He'd stay there for the night and leave for West Side Park late the next morning.

7

Clarissa leaned over the waist high wooden railing. She stared up at a wall of mountains. Snow covered ski trails cut through dark tree croppings like glacial rivers. A large full moon hovered just beyond the mountain's crest. The cold, crisp air stung her cheeks and nose. The smell of wood smoke persisted both day and night throughout the alpine themed ski village known as Vail, Colorado.

When Sinclair offered her the opportunity to take a vacation she had said yes before he finished speaking. She hadn't had a day off in six months. The only condition was that he accompany her. Not in a romantic way, though. Sinclair didn't appear to have those types of feelings for her. He had become a father figure and only sought to protect her. She didn't resist.

The past six months had gone by in a whirlwind. It had been for the best. If she had stayed behind in New York she would have spent her days and nights thinking of one thing and only one thing. Jack. But four-and-a-half months of intense training, physical and mental, kept her occupied eighteen hours a day. An hour a day had been reserved for showers and eating. The five hours that remained were for sleeping. She had been left with no time to think of anything at all. Jack had become a fleeting thought.

Sinclair oversaw her training, although he was not always around. He still had his duties to the team. The men and women who handled her training had been strict and competent. They expanded her already broad knowledge of martial arts. Taught her both Spanish and Russian. And schooled her in the ways of being a special agent.

Immediately upon completion of training she had her first assignment. Infiltrating a strip club in Miami. The place was one of the nation's largest cocaine distribution points. Her background as an exotic dancer made her the perfect under-cover agent. It only took her six weeks to take the operation down. Sinclair had been impressed and that, she figured, was why she had been offered the week-long vacation.

She stared at the top of the mountain range. The moonlight reflected off of the fresh snow. Her thoughts turned to Jack. All she wanted was to spend a month with him. Just the two of them. Her eyes watered at the thought of never seeing or smelling or touching him again. Never hearing his voice again. Never kissing his lips again. She wiped away the tears and brought the wine glass to her lips. The merlot had turned cold and bitter. She drank it anyways.

A knock on the door saved her from delving any deeper into her thoughts.

She opened the sliding glass door and stepped into her suite. Crossed the room and opened the front door. She smiled at Sinclair, who stood there holding a bottle of wine and two white styrofoam to-go boxes. One smaller than the other.

"Missed you at dinner," he said.

Clarissa stepped back and sideways and gestured Sinclair into the room.

"I wasn't hungry."

"No worries," he placed the boxes on the counter and opened them. "I brought you a sandwich and two slices of cheesecake."

"And some wine."

"Well, you are on vacation. Can't ever have too much wine."

"Agreed."

She grabbed the sandwich and a paper towel. Took a seat at the small rectangular glass table that sat off to the side.

Sinclair pulled out the second chair and opened the bottle of wine. He refilled her glass and poured one for himself.

Clarissa unwrapped the sandwich. "A Reuben. My favorite." She took a bite and fluttered her eyelids at the taste of the Russian dressing that flooded her mouth.

Sinclair took a sip from his wine glass and set it down. He stood and walked to the back of the room. Opened the door. Closed it. Walked back to the table.

"What is it?" Clarissa asked, sensing his frustration.

"We have to leave tomorrow."

"Where to?"

"Can't say just yet."

Clarissa sat her Reuben down. Wiped her mouth with a napkin.

"Guess that means the vacation is cut short."

"Afraid so."

"Why can't you tell me?"

"I just can't."

"You told me about Miami a week in advance."

He sat back. Watched her for a minute. "I thought you needed the mental preparation."

"And now?"

"I think you'll be able to prepare on the flight."

"To where?"

"You'll find out tomorrow."

She threw her hands up in defeat and stood up.

"Why'd you even tell me then?"

"To give you time to mentally prepare."

She refilled her glass and crossed to the back of the room. Stepped out on the balcony. The moon had risen considerably higher in the sky during the time she had been inside. It now was small and close to its zenith. Its light was as strong as ever, though, and the packed snow shimmered in the distance.

The door opened and closed behind her. Sinclair's footsteps reverberated below her. She turned and smiled as she leaned back against the wooden railing.

"I'm sorry," she said. "I shouldn't have badgered you."

He looked down at the ground with a smile on his face. The moonlight reflected off of his gray speckled hair.

"Maybe I should have waited until morning. It's just that, well, this is big, Clarissa. Very big. I hesitate to send you."

"You know you can't come out here and say that without cluing me in more."

He set his wine glass down and clasped his hands together.

"There is a Russian terrorist organization that is growing at an exponential rate inside the U.S. Not all the members are Russian, of course, but the primary leaders are. The group has ties to some very powerful people in Russia, as well. There are several cells in several states throughout the country. We believe we have identified the leader. You will need to infiltrate and get close to one of the leaders. He might even be the main leader."

Clarissa straightened her back and crossed her arms.

"You knew, didn't you? All along. That's why I learned Russian."

Sinclair nodded and said nothing.

"What are the stakes?"

"War. Terrorist attacks. Suicide bombings. Dirty bombs. Psychological terrorism. This isn't a case of someone who sticks out like a sore thumb blowing a bomb up on a bus. Mary Jo Smith from Heartland, America could detonate a bomb in the middle of her church."

Clarissa sat her wine glass down on the railing and rubbed her face with both hands. Then she blew into her hands and rubbed them together in an attempt to warm them. Her gloves were inside but she didn't break the conversation to get them.

"I'm the one, then?"

"You are the one. The whole reason I chose you was for this. There was always a chance that the group would slip up and rat themselves out. That hasn't happened. We do have some intelligence to go by, though, and that intelligence tells us that now is the time to move."

"And by get close to one of the leaders, you mean—"

"Yes. We need to make use of every asset you possess, my dear."

"And by any means possible." She shuddered at the thought at first but quickly set it aside. "I'm ready, Sinclair."

8

BEAR AND MANDY WALKED HAND IN HAND DOWN EAST MAIN STREET TOWARD the Knoxville branch of the First Bank of Iowa. The town had started to feel like home to Bear. Certainly more so than when they had moved there six months ago. The air was cold and crisp and the sky was clear and blue. The storms of the previous week had passed and the streets and sidewalks had been cleared. Kids played outside on snow covered lawns. They really could not have asked for a better spring break. Except to be somewhere warmer.

"What do you say we get on a plane and go somewhere for the rest of the week?" Bear said.

"Nah," Mandy said.

"Why not?"

"I've got plans."

Bear straightened up and puffed out his chest.

"Oh, you've got plans, have you?"

He was happy to hear her say that. For the first three months she hadn't talked to anyone but him, and even then she hadn't said much. Mostly "yes" and "no" and "thank you." It turned out their neighbor was a child psychologist. She had started working with Mandy three months ago.

Bear had to tell the woman some things about his life and Mandy's life. He had been hesitant to do so, but the psychologist insisted that anything he said would be kept confidential. He doubted that. But he took a chance and assumed that the bad people in his life were people that she would not know. He told her as much as he could, but had to remain vague on most things, leaving out any details that could incriminate him.

She came over twice a week. The routine was always the same. She spoke with Bear for fifteen to thirty minutes and then she spent an hour or so with Mandy. He noticed a slight improvement the first two weeks and then every session seemed to bring Mandy further and further out of her shell. And now she was a regular social butterfly.

Weekends were packed with friends and movies and sleepovers. School nights resulted in arguments about Mandy needing to hang up the phone or turning off the computer and her instant messenger in order to go to bed. Bear never imagined that he'd be a father and was surprised at how easily he had adapted to the role.

There were still moments where he was concerned. Moments where her face became dark and sullen. But those moments were becoming few and far between.

Mandy smiled and said, "Yes, plans. I'll tell you when we get home so you can mark up your calendar."

Bear laughed.

"What?"

He let go of her hand and wrapped his big hand around her shoulder. Pulled her close. They passed the Marion County courthouse and the frozen water in the fountain at the foot of the front steps.

"What's in there?"

"Lawyers," Bear said. "Bad people," he added with a laugh.

"Lawyers are bad?"

"No, honey, they aren't. Most aren't, at least."

She shook her head and muttered something under her breath.

"Hungry?" he asked as they passed in front of a small diner that served pancakes twenty-four hours a day.

She patted her stomach and looked up at him. "Yes."

They entered the diner and took a booth by the window. He sat with his back against the wall and she sat opposite him. He placed his cell phone on the table and she reached across and grabbed it.

"Don't be calling China," he said.

She giggled and pressed the touch screen. "Just playing a game." The words drawn out and exaggerated.

Bear stood and stretched. He looked down at her.

"Going to the head. Don't move. And don't call China."

She giggled again.

He returned a few minutes later to the little girl with her face buried in his phone. He sat down.

"Did you order me a coffee?"

She shook her head. Didn't lift her eyes.

"Hey," she said. "Why do you call the bathroom a head? That's really weird."

He waved her off. "It's an old military thing."

A young blond haired waitress came to the table. Bear ordered coffee and a tall stack. Mandy ordered orange juice and five silver dollar pancakes.

Mandy continued playing video games on the cell phone while they waited.

Bear studied the street and the people and the cars that passed. Some habits die hard. Some habits shouldn't die at all. He knew that. He also knew that the moment he became comfortable would be the moment that something bad would happen. So he stayed alert. He stayed vigilant.

The waitress brought their food and they ate without talking. Then they left the restaurant and resumed their walk to the bank. Bear checked his phone and saw that the time was quarter till noon. They wouldn't beat the lunch rush. The pancakes were worth it, though.

They reached the bank at five till noon. Bear held the door open for Mandy and ushered the girl through. The line to the tellers snaked through all four roped off rows. They stood at the end of the line. Bear reached inside his jacket for the envelope and then dropped his hands to his side. He felt Mandy's small hand slip inside his. The touch was cold at first, but quickly warmed up.

"Well, look who it is," a voice said from behind them. The voice was old and raspy with a hint of deepness.

Bear and Mandy turned. Bear smiled at the man he knew only as Mr. Jones. The old man was their neighbor on the side opposite the psychologist and he had become as much a fixture in their life as she had.

"How are you, Mr. Jones?" he asked.

"Tired of the cold, and tired of being old. But it could be worse." He winked at Bear and turned his attention Mandy. His hand slipped into his pocket and he pulled out a twenty dollar bill. "Here you go, sweetie. You can add this to your deposit today."

Mandy took the money and giggled. "Thank you, Mr. Jones."

Bear said, "You didn't have to do—"

Mr. Jones waved him off. "What am I going to do with it? Don't have grand-children of my own. Ah, hell, you know that already. I won't bore you with my stories."

"Well, maybe not here in the bank, but how about over dinner tonight? Our place?" It felt natural to invite their elderly neighbor into his home. And Bear found it strange that it felt so natural.

Mr. Jones smiled and nodded. "Thank you, son."

Bear smiled back and squeezed Mandy's hand in his own. He looked around the bank lobby at the customers and the tellers and personal bankers. He realized that he knew half the people in there. He had never known or felt a sense of community before. He took a deep breath and let the calm of the room wash over him. He felt relaxed. He felt at ease. He felt that they had found a place they could call home. A place he could raise Mandy. A place where their pasts could not find them.

Maybe it was the calm. Maybe it was the sense of community. Maybe it was the relaxed feeling. Whatever it was, Bear didn't realize until it was too late that the five men who had just entered the bank were wearing ski masks and were armed and were shouting at everyone to get down on the ground.

And when he and Mr. Jones didn't get down right away, the man in the middle fired a single shot. The single shot hit Mr. Jones in the back. He fell forward into Bear's arms and Bear lowered himself and Mr. Jones to the ground.

9

FENG LAY ON HIS BACK AND STARED UP AT THE CEILING. THE TV PLAYED IN THE background on a twenty-four hour news station. The same thirty minute feed had played for the past two hours. He tuned it out and counted spots and stains and water marks on the ceiling. A knock at the door broke his concentration.

He got up and walked to the door.

"Who is it?"

"Fletcher. Open up."

The old man flipped the lock to the left and pulled back the security latch. He opened the door and nodded at Fletcher.

"Time to go."

Feng turned to gather his things.

"Leave everything. Get it when you come back."

"We'll be returning then?"

Fletcher shrugged.

"Right, then. Well I need to gather the documents your boss needs then, don't I?"

"Grab only the documents. And hurry." Fletcher stepped into the room to prevent the door from shutting.

The old man grabbed his briefcase, sunglasses and his jacket. He pushed past Fletcher and stopped in the hall. Fletcher let the door slam shut and led Feng down the hall to the elevator. They entered the elevator, rode down to the lobby and then crossed the empty entranceway. A black Range Rover waited outside the hotel lobby's front doors.

As they pushed through the front doors, a man got out of the front passenger seat and opened the back door.

"No limo this time?" Feng asked.

Fletcher didn't respond. He held his arm out and gestured for the old man to take a seat.

Feng climbed into the backseat and strapped the seatbelt over his shoulder. He said nothing to the men in the front of the car and they said nothing to him.

Fletcher opened the other back door and climbed in behind the driver's seat. He strapped in and placed a pistol on his lap.

"It should go without saying," Fletcher said. "But don't try anything. I will shoot."

The old man felt his cheeks grow hot and his eyelids narrowed. He bit back the anger. He'd make sure Fletcher would pay for the way he had treated him. But now was not the time and Feng was not a young man. He couldn't take on Fletcher by himself. He had men who would handle it for him. Or maybe even bring Fletcher back to New York so he could show him just how gracious a host *he* could be. Feng's reach and control over so many were what made him powerful. Not brute strength.

They drove west on I-88 and merged onto I-80 heading westbound at the Illinois and Iowa border. They drove for another ninety minutes and exited short of Des Moines on a road that Feng didn't catch the name of. He did see a sign for Newton, Iowa, though the name meant nothing to him. A little while later he saw a white sign with a black border and with the number fourteen painted in black. They crossed a mile long bridge over a lake and then two shorter bridges. After the second bridge, they passed a sign that said "Welcome to Knoxville, Iowa. Dirt Racing Capital of the World."

The driver turned left at a street named Kennedy and drove for a few more miles, passing barren farmland before turning left again onto a long driveway that curved behind a line of trees. Once past the trees, the old man saw a huge house with several cars parked on a paved courtyard. There were high end luxury cars by automakers such as Mercedes, Lexus, Audi and BMW. They parked next to a matching black Range Rover.

The men in the front seat jumped out of the car. One opened Feng's door and stepped to the side. Feng slid out of his seat and onto the pavement. He stretched his back and his legs and took a deep breath. Fletcher rounded the car and stopped in front of him.

"Follow me," Fletcher said.

The old man faked a smile and nodded.

Fletcher walked past the front of the Range Rover and turned right, following a brick walkway to a covered porch. He stopped and held out his hand.

"Wait here."

Fletcher opened the wooden front door with stained glass panels and stepped inside the house. Voices rose and fell. The door closed. Feng looked behind him and saw the men from the front seat standing back fifteen feet. One held a gun in his hand. He held it low by his waist and pointed it at the ground. The other man appeared unarmed, but Feng had no doubt there was a gun inside his jacket.

A moment later, Fletcher returned and gestured for Feng to follow him inside. The old man crossed the porch and stepped through the open doorway.

A tall, bald headed man approached with his hand up, palm out.

"Arms up."

Feng frowned but did as he was told. He extended both arms and stared the big man down as the man ran a metal detecting wand in front of Feng's body. The wand clicked and hissed but did not beep. The big man turned off the device. Nodded. Walked away.

"Come on," Fletcher said as he turned and walked toward a dark hallway.

Feng sighed and then followed. He glanced over his shoulder and took comfort in the fact that no one was following them. Then again, there might be ten men in the next room. They turned twice, once left and once right, and passed several rooms with closed doors. The house was quiet, save for the faint sound of a string quartet playing.

Fletcher stopped at the end of the hall and turned.

"I won't tell you how to handle your negotiations, Mr. Feng. But I will tell you that Boris Melikov does not like to be screwed with. He does not like sarcasm. He does not like it when previously agreed upon terms are changed. He fears no man, not even one as powerful as you. He will not hesitate to take matters into his own hands to complete this deal."

Feng stepped forward. He threw his shoulders back and held his head high. "You listen to me. I might be close to seventy years old, but I am more powerful than your boss in more ways than one. This deal will go down the way I say it will and on my terms. Understand?"

Fletcher shrugged. "It doesn't matter to me, Mr. Feng." He opened the door and nodded at Feng. "Go in."

Feng stepped through the doorway and looked around the room. The walls were covered with built in wooden bookshelves, each stocked with spine out books. There had to be thousands of them. They looked old. The room was at least twenty feet high and there was a sliding ladder on each wall. In the middle of the room near the back wall sat a large mahogany desk. Behind the desk was a tall leather chair facing a floor to ceiling window.

Feng stopped just inside the doorway and cleared his throat. The chair spun around and he nodded at the man sitting behind the desk. The man stood and walked around the desk. Stopped in front of Feng. He was tall. Probably six three or four. He had broad shoulders and short blond hair. His eyes were blue and distant. He appeared to look through the old man rather than at him. He held out his hand and squeezed tight around Feng's.

"Boris," he said. His accent was thick and distinct and Russian. "Let's get started."

Feng stood back as Boris returned to his seat. Then he walked to the desk and sat down. Behind him the door shut closed and locked.

Boris smiled.

Feng frowned.

"It's for both our protection. Last line of defense if you will."

"What about the window?" Feng said with a nod.

Boris shrugged.

Feng studied the man. His face held no expression. His eyes seemed dead. This was a man who had retribution on his mind, no doubt about that. Feng had been that way much of his life and only now eased up as he knew the end was near. This deal was one of the ones he counted on to help push himself into retirement. The Russians were offering a large sum of money for the documents.

"Our talks on the phone," Boris said. "The early negotiations. I don't think that price was quite right."

"You are indeed correct, Mr. Boris. I couldn't possibly let these go for any less than ten million."

Boris smiled. He leaned back in his chair and said nothing.

The old man said nothing in return. They faced off in silence for more than five minutes.

The old man spoke first. "I could go down to eight."

"The agreement was five."

"Times change, my friend. I have had other offers. But I discussed this with you first, so I want you to have the first right of refusal."

"What other offers? Who has made other offers?"

Feng smiled and brought his hands together in front of his face.

"I won't reveal them for fear of retribution against them."

"You might face retribution from me for not disclosing the information."

"If you make a move like that it will be the last move you make. I am old. I am ready to die. You can take nothing from me. Understand? Nothing. I, however, can take everything from you. I know all about you and your operations, Mr. Boris. I know more than you want me to know. Let's cut this out and complete the deal. Five million as originally agreed."

Boris lifted an eyebrow. His cheeks turned red and his nostrils flared a bit. He took a deep breath. Feng guessed it was an effort to hide the anger that his face already betrayed.

"Five million," Boris said.

Feng smiled and leaned back in his chair.

"Why Iowa?"

Boris shrugged. "Why not? Last place they would look for us."

Boris stood and walked to the corner of the room. He slid a section of books, revealing a hidden safe. He punched in a code and opened the safe. He returned to the desk and placed several stacks of cash in front of Feng.

"That's not all of it. My guys are at the bank getting the rest right now."

10

JACK WAITED BY THE ALUMINUM BLEACHERS. THE AIR WAS COOL, BUT NOT COLD. His brown leather jacket was unzipped. The park was full of kids and families playing and walking and enjoying themselves. He couldn't help but feel out of place. He checked his watch. 11:45 a.m. Frank said noon, which meant he would be there within the next five minutes. Jack faced the football field but kept checking in all directions for any signs of Frank or other SIS agents.

Less than five minutes later Frank appeared from the direction of the parking lot. Jack left the bleachers to meet him in the middle. Frank saw him, turned and waved for Jack to follow. Jack double-timed it and caught up with Frank before he reached the parking lot.

"What's the hurry?" Jack asked.

"Like you, I don't like being out in the open like that."

Jack looked around. "Any reason for concern?"

"None other than constant paranoia."

Jack laughed. He related.

"Come on. I want you to meet your new partner."

"You won't be working with me?"

Frank shook his head. "I'm no longer in the field, Jack."

"A pencil pusher. Who would have thought it?"

Frank said nothing. He led Jack to the corner of the parking lot and opened the back passenger side door of the dark sedan.

Jack placed his left foot inside and ducked his head to enter the car. He paused at the sight of the woman in the backseat. Her ringed dark brown hair fell over her shoulders and framed her mocha colored face. She removed her sunglasses, revealing dark brown eyes. Even in her seated position, he guessed she was tall, judging by her long legs.

She extended her arm toward Jack.

"Jasmine Medina."

Jack reached for her hand and responded. "Jack, er, John. Who the hell am I now, Frank?"

"I know who you are," she said.

"Jack," Frank said. "Get in. We need to move."

Jack sat down and closed the door. He didn't take his eyes off of Jasmine. To call the woman beautiful was an understatement. What the hell was she doing working with the SIS? He made a mental note to find out.

Frank twisted in his seat until he faced Jack.

"Jasmine joined us about a year after you left. She's the best agent I've got. I've got no doubt that you two will be able to crack this thing if it goes as deep as I think it does."

Jack cleared his head and let Frank's words settle in.

"What about the CIA? FBI? Homeland Security?"

"Nobody's talking," Jasmine said.

"That's right," Frank said. "Someone knows something and they don't want to give it up."

"What about you guys?" Jack asked. "You giving them anything?"

"No. Nothing. Not even the documents."

"Shouldn't someone know if they are as bad as you made them out to be?"

Frank shrugged and turned in his seat to face forward.

"I give them that, then I have to give them you. None of us wants that, Jack."

Jack stared out the window. Row homes gave way to single family homes. Single family homes gave way to farmland. Farmland gave way to the woods. Trees passed by in a blur. Patches of snow spotted the thin strip of grass between the road and the trees. They reached a clearing and the car pulled into a gas station parking lot.

Frank and the driver didn't move.

Jasmine undid her seat belt and opened her door.

"What's this?" Jack asked.

"This is where you get out," Frank said.

Jasmine stuck her head back in the car.

"Come on, Jack. Let's go."

He opened the door and slid out of the car. Followed Jasmine across the parking lot. She held out her hand and pressed a button on a key fob. Tail lights on a green sedan blinked twice. Jasmine rounded the trunk and went to the driver's door. Jack opened the passenger door and got in.

Jasmine stuck the key in the ignition and started the car.

"Need anything before we go?"

Jack shook his head.

"Where are we going?"

"Cherry Hill."

"What's there?"

"A lead."

He tried to pry more information out of her during the drive to Cherry Hill, New Jersey, but Jasmine remained tight lipped. Jack conceded to her and stayed quiet the last fifteen minutes of the forty minute drive.

They arrived in Cherry Hill and Jasmine pulled into a parking lot. Parked the car in front of a laundromat. Jack opened his door and placed his feet on the ground.

"Stay here," she said.

"What?" Jack held his hands up. "Why?"

"Just do it."

He waved both hands at her and returned to his seat in the car. He watched Jasmine walk into the laundromat. The front of the building consisted of large floor-to-ceiling windows, enabling him to keep an eye on her. She walked to the back corner and began talking with a man. Jack strained to make out the man's features, but the sun glare on the windows prevented him from doing so. He placed his hand on the door handle and thought about getting out. Decided to stay in the car. If Jasmine had been a field agent in the SIS for seven years then she could handle herself.

Jack checked his coat pockets for a cigarette and sighed when he found none. All those months not smoking ruined thanks to the old Greek lady.

Jasmine emerged from the laundromat with the man following behind her. He was middle aged. Thin except for a round bulge protruding from his mid-section. He had a dark beard and a bald head.

Jack opened his door and started to get out. Jasmine waved him back in. She walked past her door and opened the back door. The man got in the backseat without saying anything.

Jasmine got in the car. "Jack, this is Igor. He is going to lead us to a house. Isn't that right, Igor?"

The man nodded with a groan.

Jasmine continued. "If he acts up, reaches for me or tries to leave the car, shoot him. OK? Your piece is in the glove box."

Jack opened the glove box and removed the pistol and holster. He wondered what would have happened if someone had broken into the car while it had been left unattended at the gas station. He inspected the gun, a Glock 17 9mm with a 17 round magazine. Not his weapon of choice, but it would do.

"Works for me," Jack said.

The man in the back seat started giving directions. He had a thick Russian accent.

Jack leaned toward Jasmine. "Where are we going?"

She turned her head to the side and gave him a look that indicated she had no intention of telling him.

"Fine," he said.

Igor spoke up as they passed a white cape cod with green trim. "There."

Jasmine kept the car steady and turned left at the next street and then left again. She pulled up to the curb and parked. She reached under the steering column. Pulled a lever. There was a click and then the trunk popped open.

"Get out, Igor."

The man protested. "Why?"

"Just get out," she said. "Want to help, Jack?"

Jack got out of the car and walked around to the driver's side. He opened the door and grabbed Igor by his arm. Yanked him from the car and then pushed him around back. He gestured to the open trunk.

"Here's your chance, friend. Easy or hard?"

Igor shook his head and spit on the ground.

Jack swung fast and hard and hit the man in the abdomen. The man bowed over and Jack pushed him into the truck and closed the lid. Igor started kicking against the trunk interior a few seconds later.

Jasmine told Jack to stay put and she opened the trunk again. This time Jack stood there with his Glock 17 aimed at the man in the trunk.

"Listen up, Igor," Jasmine said. "If I need to tie you up and gag you, I will. I can't leave you in the back seat. If I did and you decided to run, that would be bad. Or maybe you would decide to run into the house after us—"

"I wouldn't do that," Igor said.

"—and that would just cause a big old mess that would result in you and your friends being shot. Is that what you want?" She didn't wait for him to respond. "No, of course it's not. Trust me, as soon as we are done we are going to return to this spot and let you out of the trunk. OK?"

Igor exhaled and seemed to relax. He lay down and closed his eyes. Said nothing.

Jasmine nodded at the trunk and Jack closed the lid. She ducked into the driver's seat, rolled up the windows, locked the doors and joined Jack on the sidewalk.

"Best we walk from here," she said.

Jack nodded.

"What's the plan?" he asked.

"We knock on the door."

"And then?"

"Depends on what they do after we knock."

"Say they answer."

"I ask them some questions."

"And if they don't answer?"

"The questions or the door?"

"Christ," Jack said. "Are you always this difficult?"

Jasmine smiled and nodded.

"Every second of my life."

They turned right again and then crossed the street. Walked up to the white cape cod with green trim. Jasmine stood in front of the door and Jack stood to the side in between the door and a window. Out of sight. She knocked on the door. Waited a minute and knocked again.

Jack heard muffled sounds from inside.

"They're inside," he said.

She nodded and lifted an eyebrow.

"Ready to kick this door down for me?"

"You hardly strike me as a damsel in distress."

"I'm not. These are expensive shoes, though."

She stepped aside and Jack stood in front of the door. He stepped back a few feet to get his momentum going. He held his pistol in his right hand. He lunged and kicked and smashed the door in. Then he burst through the opening with his gun pointed in front of him.

Four men sitting at a round table looked up at him, horror written across their faces.

"Don't any of you move."

11

BEAR PULLED MANDY CLOSE. THE LITTLE GIRL LOOKED LIKE SHE WAS IN SHOCK. Her eyes glazed over and her mouth hung open. He knelt over Mr. Jones and held his hand against the man's back. He applied pressure to the gunshot wound in an attempt to reduce the amount of blood lost. He looked around the room. Everything happened in slow motion. One teller dropped to the floor. The others worked frantically at their drawers trying to ready themselves for the armed men. The people in line all had different reactions. Some lowered themselves to the ground. One woman stood in place, frozen and crying. A few others backed up to the far wall, distancing themselves from the five men who blocked the only way in and the only way out of the bank.

The bankers who sat at desks all disappeared from sight, hiding behind and underneath their desks. They cowered beneath the false security their desktops offered. They shivered and cried and begged for their lives on the carpeted floor.

Office doors slammed shut. A bad move, Bear thought, and likely to draw the ire of the armed men. Sure enough, one of the men turned and aimed his assault rifle at one of the offices with a closed door.

"Not yet," one of the masked men said.

A man emerged from the last office. He was tall and fit and older. He had a full head of silver hair and wore a gray suit with a blue tie. The bank manager. He approached the front of the bank with his hands held out in front of him. He walked slow and steady. His face held the same expression during the walk. An expression in between shock, terror and defiance.

"Stop there," one of the armed men yelled.

The sound of the man's voice acted as a catalyst to Bear's brain and the events began unfolding at normal speed.

"I just want this to go peacefully," the bank manager said.

Bear turned his head and caught the manager's eye. Bear shook his head and moved his eyes between the manager and the floor.

The manager ignored Bear and continued moving forward. He straightened his outstretched arms.

"I said stop." The voice was deep and thick. The accent eastern European or Russian.

Bear turned his head to the front of the bank.

The masked man lifted his assault rifle and aimed it at the manager.

The manager stopped and held his hands higher. "I just want this—"

"To go peacefully. Yes, you said that already." The masked man started to walk toward the manager. "Turn around and get on your knees."

The manager didn't move.

"Now," the man yelled.

When the manager still refused to move, the masked man rushed him and drove the butt of his gun into the manager's stomach. The manager fell to his knees but kept his shoulders back and his head held high. His face turned bright red and then darkened to a shade of purple as he fought for breath. He never caught his breath, though. The masked man moved behind him and placed the barrel of his rifle against the manager's head.

"Let this be a lesson to all of you," the masked man said.

Bear grabbed Mandy and pulled her to his chest, covering her eyes and ears.

The gunshot echoed through the bank. The room fell silent.

"Anyone else want this to go peacefully? Or, perhaps to go peacefully themselves?"

No one said anything.

The man started barking orders in a foreign language. One of his men guarded the door. Two others went behind the counter and yelled at the tellers and forced them to remove the cash from their drawers and dump it into burlap sacks. If a teller didn't comply, they smacked them across the face and stuck their guns into the teller's back until they did as told.

The fifth man joined the first and they interrogated the bankers under their desks and hidden in their offices until they found one who would lead them to the safe.

Bear turned his attention to the old man bleeding on the floor. Mr. Jones stared beyond Bear. His eyes focused on something not of this world. Bear felt the old man's neck for a pulse. He found it, but it had become thready and uneven and weak. The old man's breaths were shallow and the time between each grew further and further apart. A trickle of blood ran from the side of his mouth and down his cheek toward the floor.

"Mr. Jones," Bear said.

The old man's eyes widened and focused on Bear. He brought his thin hand up in front of his chest. Bear reached out and grabbed the old man's papery white hand. Mr. Jones squeezed tightly. His lips moved and gasps escaped his mouth. Then he became still. His head fell slightly to the left and his unfocused eyes stared at nothing.

The masked man at the door started yelling.

Bear looked up. Rage flooded his body. He stood and started toward the man at the door.

The man aimed his gun at Bear and yelled even louder using words that Bear couldn't decipher.

Bear stopped.

Outside the bank, a cop car pulled up and three more weren't far behind. The man at the door turned. Bear knew that was his opportunity. He dropped a few inches and kicked one foot back. Ready to charge. But before he could take a step, he felt jarring blow to the head. He dropped to one knee. Another blow met his head with a thud. He fell forward.

"Grab the girl," a man said from behind him.

Bear pushed up to his hands and knees. Reached for Mandy. Couldn't get to her in time. One of the masked men scooped her up.

"Bear," she screamed.

Bear forced himself to his feet and stumbled after her and the man carrying her over his shoulder. She reached for Bear. Screamed his name. Her small hand grabbed and clutched at the air.

Bear took three steps.

A masked man jumped in front of him and smashed the butt of his assault rifle into Bear's forehead.

Bear stepped back. Lost his balance. Regained it.

The man hit him in the stomach.

Bear bent over. Then he felt another blow to the back of his head. And then another.

He collapsed to the ground.

Shots rang out. Single shots from the police. Bursts of fire from the bank robbers. Grunts and groans of men being shot and dying filled the air after the firing ended.

Bear lifted his head and saw Mandy's blond hair blowing in the wind as she was pulled inside a waiting car. The door slammed shut and the car drove off. The edges of his vision darkened. He fought against the swelling in his brain. He clawed at the ground. He almost made it to his elbows. Then he went unconscious.

12

"JACK," JASMINE SHOUTED FROM BEHIND HIM. "WATCH OUT."

It took a moment for the four men at the table to realize what had just happened. Between the cards on the table and the music blaring in the background it was easy to see why they didn't answer the door. They never heard Jack knocking. But it didn't take them long to assess Jack as a threat as he stood there next to their unhinged door, aiming a gun at them.

One of the men rose from his chair and pulled out his pistol.

Jack fired off a round. The bullet hit one of the seated men with a thud. Jack didn't see who. He was too busy diving to the right and out of the armed man's line of fire. Jack crawled a few feet and pressed against the wall on the other side of the staircase. He checked through the open doorway and saw that Jasmine had moved out of sight.

The sounds of the men shuffling on the other side of the house died down. Jack hoped that Jasmine secured the rear of the house. Maybe he should have waited to burst in. Maybe she should have given him a bit more information. He had no idea what they would find here or if someone was placed into danger by them knocking on the door.

He looked around the room, making sure there were no mirrors or reflective surfaces he could be seen in. None. Just a couple antique couches facing each other. A closed door sealed the room off from the one behind it. He inched along the angled wall and peeked over the stairs. A mirror hung on the far wall. In it he could see the man with the pistol leaning against the wall on the other side of the stairs. He didn't see any of the others.

Jack moved across the room and opened and slammed the door dividing the two rooms.

The man on the other side of the stairs shouted and began to move, just like Jack expected him to. Jack aimed and fired a single shot over the stairs. The bullet hit the man in the side of the head and a cloud of sweat and blood and gray matter exploded into the air and hung there as the man collapsed to the floor.

Jack rounded the staircase and knelt over the man's body. He checked his neck for a pulse, although judging by the hole in the back of his head, the man was dead. Jack grabbed the dead man's pistol and tucked it in his coat pocket.

"Jack," Jasmine's voice called from the back of the house.

He walked slowly through the dining room toward the kitchen. A door swung open and a man armed with a shotgun jumped out.

Jack fired and hit the man in the chest. The man fell to his knees and Jack fired another round into his forehead. The man's body flinched backward and then fell forward. Jack stepped over the body, not bothering to check for a pulse, and looked into the open doorway. Stairs led down into a dimly lit cellar. It sounded like someone else was down there. Jack placed a foot on the first step.

"Jack," Jasmine called out. Her voice came from the same level of the house, not below.

He closed the cellar door and continued through the kitchen. He held his pistol in the air, close to his face. He stepped through a doorway and into a laundry area. There, he saw Jasmine. She gestured toward the back of the room. He saw a brown haired man with a young woman in front of him. He had one hand wrapped around her waist and in his other hand he held a knife. He pressed the knife against the woman's throat.

"Just stop right there," the man said with a Russian accent.

"Or what?" Jack asked.

The woman's eyes widened and her eyebrows lifted into her forehead. She reached one hand up and grabbed the man's arm, but didn't exert any force.

"I'll cut her," the man said.

Jack laughed.

"What's so funny?"

"That you think I care," Jack said.

"I'm not kidding, I'll slice her neck." He pulled the knife away and then pressed it into the woman's neck. A thin line of blood formed below the blade.

"Then do it," Jack said.

The man cocked his head and his eyes narrowed. His grip on the woman's stomach loosened and the hand holding the knife dropped a few inches.

Jack didn't wait for the man to regain his composure. He squeezed the trigger of the pistol in his outstretched hand. The bullet hit the man in the forehead. The knife fell to the ground and the man fell back against the washing machine. Jasmine rushed forward and wrenched the lady from his grip. The man slid down the front of the washing machine, leaving behind a smeared trail of blood.

"You were going to let him kill me," the woman said frantically.

Jack shook his head. "I was never going to let him kill you."

"You told him to do it."

"Yeah, and he didn't know what to think and loosened his grip and he dropped the knife an inch. It gave me a clear shot and I didn't have to worry about him recoiling and cutting your neck open."

The woman stood there with her mouth open. Her eyes teared over as the gravity of the situation collapsed down on her. She threw her arms around Jack's neck and pulled herself close. Soft sobs escaped her parted lips.

Jack stood rigid at first, his arms out to the side. Finally, he stroked her hair and patted her back.

"Hey, calm down. You're OK. This can't be the first time you've been in danger if you're hanging around with men like this."

She said nothing. The sobs stopped, but she held tight.

"Jasmine, get her hidden. There's a fourth man. I think he's in the cellar. We need to detain him. We need to question him."

Jasmine grabbed the woman and led her to the back door. She came back and said, "OK, Jack. Let's get him out of there."

They walked back into the kitchen and Jasmine pulled the door open while Jack covered the opening.

"Come on up," Jack said into the opening. "Don't make me come down there. Come up with your hands up."

The man in the cellar didn't respond. Shuffling sounds floated up the stairs.

"If I have to come down there, I'll shoot you. I know you heard the gunshots up here. All of those shots killed your partners. They are all dead. Do you want to join them?"

The man in the cellar started talking in a foreign language. Jack didn't understand what he said. He looked back at Jasmine.

She nodded.

"He's cursing in Russian."

Jack shrugged.

"Last chance," he said and then he turned to Jasmine and spoke loud enough that the man in the cellar could still hear him. "Cover me. You see him, you shoot."

Jack took two steps down the stairs.

"I'm coming up. I'm coming up," the man said. "I'm unarmed."

Two hands appeared from behind the wall and the rest of the man followed.

"Take your shirt off and drop your pants," Jack said.

The man did and appeared to be unarmed.

Jack stepped out of the cellar stairway and motioned the man up. He had Jasmine cover him and then he went to the bottom of the stairs and grabbed the man's things. He also cleared the cellar and reported to Jasmine that it was empty. He climbed the stairs and threw the man's clothes at him.

"Get dressed."

"Jack," Jasmine said. "We need to get out of here. Let's get him to the car. You sit in back with him. We'll interrogate him somewhere else."

"Where?"

"Hell, I don't care. The woods. A fast food bathroom. Anywhere but here."

Jack looked around.

"They're all dead. What's the rush?"

"The intel," she said. "The report was that there were five men."

The man smiled and nodded.

Jack swung his free hand and punched the man in the jaw. Then he grabbed him and dragged him out of the house. They crossed the street, made two left turns and got in the car. Jasmine drove and Jack sat in the back seat with the Russian man.

Igor started banging against the trunk and kicking the back seat as soon as the car started moving.

13

BEAR WOKE UP TO THE SOUND OF VOICES ABOVE HIM. THE VOICES WEREN'T directed at him, but he knew they were talking about him. He opened his eyes and scanned the compact room. A yellow tinted fluorescent light illuminated the space. A man and woman sat on opposite sides of him. They were dressed in dark blue pants and wore white button up shirts. They wore light blue latex gloves. ID cards were pinned to their shirt pockets. The room shook and bounced and a siren wailed. A red light reflected off a surface outside and strobed across the ceiling. He tried to sit up but couldn't move. He found himself strapped down.

"What's going on?" he asked in a cracked voice.

"Just relax, Mr. Logan." The woman wrapped a blood pressure cuff around his arm just above the elbow.

Bear processed the situation and searched his memory for clues as to how he ended up here. He was in an ambulance. His head hurt like hell. He suffered head trauma. It might be severe. He was strapped down because they feared a spinal injury. A cold sweat broke out over his arms and chest and forehead. He wiggled his toes and clenched his hands into a fist. Everything worked. He exhaled. Relieved. He thought back to the moment he sustained the injury. He had been hovering over Mr. Jones dead body. A blow to the head. And then... Mandy. Fear flooded every cell in his body and his muscles tightened.

"Where's Mandy?"

They paramedics didn't respond.

"Where's my little girl?" His voice rose to a yell.

The woman's eyes shot up from the blood pressure readout and locked onto her partner. The man opposite her cleared his throat.

"Sir, we didn't find a little girl with you."

Bear shook his head. He had to get out. He fought against his restraints. Thrashed side to side. The thin strips of fabric that restrained him were no match for his size and strength. Not to mention his focus and determination. His right arm broke free. The medics tried to hold him down. He threw the man off of him and into the side of the ambulance.

"Sir," the woman said. "Calm down."

She frantically worked the cap off of a sterile needle and plunged it into a vial of liquid.

Bear worked the restraints, undoing each one in succession down his body.

The man crawled to the front and opened an access door between the cab and the back.

"Stop the ambulance and get on the radio. We need the cops."

Bear reached over his head and grabbed the man by his leg. Pulled him close. Then he felt a pinch in his shoulder. He looked over at the woman. She leaned over his arm. In her mouth was the plastic cap from the sterile needle. She held the needle in her hand. She plunged it to the hilt into Bear's arm.

The panic and rage and fear dissipated. He felt calm. He felt like he was floating. The world slowed down a beat and he sank into the gurney.

The ambulance stopped moving. Stopped shaking. The back doors opened and a police officer stepped in. The man turned blurry as he crossed into the artificial light.

"He's just in shock," the woman told the officer.

Bear felt the woman wrap her hand around his forearm. She squeezed his arm reassuringly. He looked over at her and back at the cop. The officer's face was now clear.

The male paramedic climbed through the access door to sit in the cab with the driver. The cop took his spot in the back.

"There won't be any more trouble, will there?" the cop said to Bear.

Bear shook his head. He tried to speak but his lips wouldn't move. In the end he grunted a few times. Closed his eyes. He felt the ambulance shift into gear and begin moving again. He wanted to fight, to get up and break through the back door and find Mandy. But he couldn't.

BEAR HAD BEEN ALONE in the hospital room for fifteen minutes. The sedative the female paramedic gave him was wearing off. He contemplated getting up and leaving, but wanted to speak with the cops first. He had to find out about Mandy. Maybe they had her and were bringing her in to see him.

A hand poked through the open doorway and knocked against the door. A man stepped forward. He wore khaki pants and a blue sport coat. His shirt was unbuttoned at the top and he had no tie on. He appeared to be mid-forties and had gray hair mixed in with a full head of brown.

"Mr. Logan?"

Bear nodded and sat up.

"I'm Detective Larsen. Hope I'm not disturbing you. We needed to get a statement from you."

"Where's Mandy?"

The detective cocked his head to the side.

"My little girl. Where is she?"

Larsen took three steps forward and stopped at the end of the bed.

"Mr. Logan—"

"Call me Bear."

"OK. Bear, there was a young girl, blond hair, that was abducted."

Bear's mind raced. He thought back. He remembered. They carried her out. Put her in the car. Her hair blew in the wind. He closed his eyes and heard her screams once again.

"I know this is tough, Mr., uh, Bear. We are doing everything we can and are in contact with the FBI."

Bear swung a large leg over the side of the bed and hopped off.

"It won't be enough, Detective."

Larsen threw his hands in the air and backed up toward the doorway.

"You can't do that, sir. They are evaluating you for a concussion. You need to stay in the hospital tonight."

The edges of Bear's vision darkened and he felt his body sway. He gritted his teeth and fought the feelings back.

"No way I'm staying here when they have her."

"Bear, you got no choice."

Bear searched the room for his clothes. Didn't find them. He turned to Larsen and pointed at him.

"You listen to me. You have no idea who I am or what I am capable of. If you want to help me, fine. But if not, stay out of my way."

Larsen said nothing. He stood in the doorway with his hands in front of him. He shook his head slowly.

"You got kids?" Bear asked.

Larsen nodded.

"Then you know what I'm going through."

Larsen continued to nod.

"Tell me everything that you know," Bear demanded.

Larsen pulled the sleeve of his sport coat back and checked his watch. He cleared his throat and took three steps toward Bear, stopping just a few feet away. He lowered his voice and said, "I'm off shift in an hour. I'll get you checked out of here and we'll go someplace to talk."

"Why? Why not now?"

Larsen motioned for Bear to keep it down. "Because the man behind this has half the department in his back pocket, if you know what I mean."

Bear nodded. "OK. One hour. Bring me some clothes."

"What size?"

"Extra frickin large."

14

FIVE MINUTES OUTSIDE THE CITY, JASMINE TURNED ONTO A DIRT ROAD AND continued until they were out of sight from the highway. She threw the car in park, got out and opened the trunk. Jack looked through the back window after the trunk slammed shut. Jasmine ordered Igor to go sit against a tree, then she motioned for Jack to get out.

"Don't move." Jack pulled his pistol from its holster and aimed it at the man in the backseat. He backed out of the car and looked up at Jasmine. "What now?"

"Get him out and bring him back here."

Jack leaned forward and nodded at the Russian.

"You heard the lady."

The man slid across the bench seat and exited through the open door. Jack grabbed him by the elbow and led him behind the car.

"Go stand against that tree." Jasmine motioned toward a dogwood in bloom.

Jack followed the Russian to the tree and then held him there at gunpoint. He glanced over his shoulder to check on Jasmine and Igor.

She placed nylon restraints around Igor's wrists and a black cloth bag over his head.

"Sit," she said.

Igor sat and leaned back against the base of a pine tree.

"We'll be back for you in a minute." Jasmine walked toward Jack and stopped about fifteen feet away. "Jack, come here."

Jack approached her. Kept his gun out to the side and aimed at the Russian. Kept his eyes on Igor.

"We need to get some info on the big picture here, Jack. I don't care what we do with this guy, but I know Frank will want him detained. Fine with me. But we need to get as much info out of him as we can before we call this in."

Jack nodded and didn't say anything.

"I don't know if he'll take me seriously. Most guys don't think a woman is a threat. At least, not until I kick their ass."

Jack smiled.

"How are you with interrogation techniques?" she asked.

"I'm so-so." An understatement. Jack had honed his technique since his days as a Marine on-loan to the CIA, and then as a member of the SIS. He even had an apartment in New York specifically for the purpose of interrogation.

"OK," Jasmine said. "So you can back me up then?"

"Sure."

"You want to start?"

"Yeah, why not." He pointed at Igor. "You sure he's OK there?"

Jasmine nodded. "Hands and legs are bound. He's hooded. Not going anywhere."

Jack walked up to the Russian. The man pressed himself into the tree as if trying to hide inside of it. Jack hit him in the stomach. The Russian leaned forward. Jack grabbed him by the back of his hair and lifted his head. Back-handed him across his face.

"Who do you report to?"

The man said nothing. He couldn't say anything because he couldn't breathe. His face turned red and deepened into a shade of purple.

Jack pulled the man forward so he leaned over, then lifted him back up. Repeated the process three times. The man inhaled with a groan and then took several short breaths.

"Now," Jack said, "tell me who you report to."

"Nobody."

"You like not breathing? Want to stay that way forever?"

The man closed his eyes and shook his head.

Jack leaned in with one hand placed just below the man's neck. "Then tell me what I want to know."

"I know nothing."

Jack whipped his free hand across the Russian's face. The slap of the hand was followed by a grunt from the man.

"Tell me."

The man said nothing. His thick jaw muscles worked as he clenched his mouth tight.

Jack drew his arm back to strike the man in the face with a full force punch. He felt Jasmine's hand on his wrist. He looked back at her.

"Let me handle this, Jack."

Jack held up his hands and stepped back. "You think I did a bad job?"

The Russian shifted his eyes between Jack and Jasmine.

She stepped forward, a smile on her face.

"Look, um, what's your name?"

"I am no one of consequence."

She kept smiling. "Right, well, Mr. Consequence then. I apologize for my partner's technique. Brute force isn't always the best option. Right?"

The Russian returned her smile. "No, it isn't." He glanced at Jack and then back at her. "It does not work with my people. We are strong. Unlike you Americans."

Jasmine's smile broadened. She continued. "Frankly, you look at me and probably don't fear me. Right?" She didn't wait for him to respond. "But you should fear me more. You see, I can't beat you like he can. Which means I have to resort to more drastic actions."

She pulled out her pistol and shot the Russian in the foot.

He screamed and fell over to the side. The bullet went through the top of his foot and out the bottom. He clutched the wounded appendage in both hands. Blood poured from the entrance and exit wounds.

Jack crossed his arms. Smiled. He was impressed.

"Now tell me who you report to," she said.

The Russian had scooted himself back and sat against the tree. He still held his foot in both hands, pressing tightly in an attempt to stop the bleeding. "His name..." He paused to catch his breath. His face twisted and turned upward.

"His name is what?"

The Russian opened his eyes and spoke through gritted teeth. "Lazar."

"Is that a first or last name?"

The Russian said nothing. He leaned his head back against the tree and seemed to be losing consciousness.

"Answer me." Jasmine placed the barrel of her gun against his head.

The Russian pushed his head back against the tree and turned to the side. Tears fell from the far corners of both eyes.

"That's his first name."

Jack watched in amazement at how easily Jasmine had gotten the information. The man didn't fear Jack's strength, but he turned coat at the possibility that Jasmine would kill him one shot at a time.

"What's his last name? And where is he?" Jasmine asked.

The man took two quick breaths and one deep inhalation. He held the air in his lungs for a few seconds and then exhaled. "Chernov. His name is Lazar Chernov. He's in Georgia."

"The country?" Jasmine asked.

"No, the state. Near Atlanta."

Jasmine looked back at Jack and nodded.

He shrugged and held out his hands.

"Call the name in," she said.

"There's lots of us there," the man said.

Jasmine shook her head and gestured for Jack to hold on.

"Wait, what? How many?"

The Russian laughed. Closed his eyes and shook his head. "Screw you lady."

She aimed her gun at him again.

"Jasmine, stop," Jack said. "Come over here for a minute."

She backed up, keeping her eyes and gun focused on the man sitting against the tree.

Jack said, "Let's check out this Chernov guy."

She nodded. Holstered her gun. Reached into her pocket and pulled out her cell phone. She pressed and held down a single button and then hit another button to turn on the speaker when the line began ringing. Frank picked up mid-way through the second ring.

"Jasmine, what do you guys have for me?"

"We got a name. Lazar Chernov. Possibly in the Atlanta, Georgia area."

"OK, give me a minute."

The line went silent. Jasmine leaned in against the side of the car and looked at Jack. He stood a few feet away, around the corner and behind the trunk. They locked eyes for a few seconds while Frank checked on the name.

The Russian yelled something unintelligible.

"Shut up," Jack said.

"What?" Frank said.

"Not you," Jasmine said.

"Oh, OK. Um, yeah, so nothing from our database or the FBI's. Pulling up the CIA's now and running a search on Homeland Security's DB concurrently."

Neither Jack or Jasmine said anything. The Russian groaned. Igor sat still, like he had throughout the interrogation of the Russian.

"Nothing from the CIA. Ah, there it is, Lazar Chernov, aka Lazlo and Lyov Chernov. Current whereabouts are Canton, Georgia. Let's see what else we've got." The line went silent again.

Jack asked, "What do you want to do with him?"

Jasmine shrugged and covered the phone's mouthpiece. "I've got no use for him. He's just going to get blood all over the car."

Jack held up his gun. "Should I—"

"No." Jasmine laughed. "Frank will have our location and he'll send someone out for him. We'll tie him to a tree or something." She motioned toward the trunk. "Look in there."

Jack went to the driver's seat and popped the trunk. Returned to the back of the car and pulled out a length of black rope.

"OK," Frank said. "This is our guy. He's connected with this cell. I can't say for sure that this guy is the top dog, but he's certainly high up there. Makes sense given the location, so close to Atlanta. You two get going now. I'll send a team out there to clean up after you."

Jasmine hung up the phone. Smiled. "See."

"What about Igor?" Jack asked.

"Throw him in the trunk. We'll drop him off in town."

Jack took the rope to the injured Russian and tied his legs and then wrists together. Then he tied his chest to the tree.

"What are you doing?" the man asked.

"Leaving."

"What about me?"

Jack shrugged. Walked over to Igor without looking back at the other man. The Russian yelled in the background.

"Get up."

Igor struggled to get off the ground. Jack reached down and yanked him to his feet. Led him to the car and placed him back in the trunk.

"Not the trunk again," Igor said.

"It's just for a few minutes." He waited for Igor to step in and then slammed the lid shut.

Ten minutes later they dropped him off a few blocks from the laundromat. Less than fifteen minutes later they were on I-95 southbound, crossing the Walt Whitman bridge into Philadelphia.

"We got twelve hours to kill," Jasmine said. "Why don't you tell me what you've been up to since you left SIS."

Jack turned his head to face the window. "I'll pass."

15

"THERE THEY ARE," BORIS SAID.

"Hmm?" The old man lifted his head and looked across the desk at Boris.

Boris held out his hand and pointed at the window.

The old man saw five men walking toward the house. Four of them carried black duffel bags. One of them carried a blond haired girl. Feng narrowed his eyes and leaned forward. The girl looked familiar. As the men passed the window they turned. When the man carrying the child turned, the old man got a close up view. He knew why she looked familiar. She was the little girl he had held at the compound. The little girl that Jack had busted his balls over when he held the documents hostage.

"You've got to be kidding me," he muttered.

"What's that?" Boris said.

"Nothing," Feng said. "I don't want them in the room."

Boris cocked his head and leaned back in his chair.

"I am serious. Deal's off if they enter the room. I don't even want them to see me."

Boris leaned forward and pressed a button on his desk phone.

"Yes, sir," Fletcher said.

"Fletcher, don't escort the men back here. Apparently our guest doesn't like the looks of them." Boris looked up at the old man. "Do you trust Mr. Fletcher?"

Feng nodded.

Boris leaned over the phone. "You bring the money back."

"OK. I'll be there in five."

Boris hung up the phone and sat back in his chair. He had an amused look on his face as he stared at the old man. He interlaced his fingers and wrapped them around the back of his head.

"It's a funny thing, Feng."

"What is?"

"Ah, nothing."

"Need I remind you who I am?"

Boris laughed. "Fine. I was just thinking, here you are. This man with an incredible reputation. Yet, you are afraid of being seen by five of my guys. Five guys I trust enough to bring you your money."

The old man shrugged. He refused to go down this path with Boris. The less Boris knew about Feng's past with the little girl, the better. She was his hassle now. God forbid if Jack was in town. He couldn't figure that part out, though. Every source he had told him that Jack was dead. Then he remembered Jack's partner and figured the girl was there with the large man. That was just as bad as if Jack was alive and around, though. He had no problem letting Boris deal with the fallout that could come.

"What is taking so long?"

Boris held up his hands. Reached for his phone. Before he could press any of the buttons there was a knock at the door.

"Come in," Boris said.

Fletcher entered carrying four black bags.

"Do you need to count it?" Boris asked the old man.

Feng nodded.

Boris motioned toward his desk and Fletcher sat the bags down.

Feng unzipped one bag. Boris unzipped the other. The money was stacked and bundled in wads of ten thousand dollars. It took them several minutes to count it all. When they were done, there was an overage of one hundred thousand dollars.

"Why don't you give that to Mr. Fletcher," Feng said. "He's been so gracious toward me."

Boris motioned toward Fletcher while keeping his eyes on the old man.

"Take it, Mr. Fletcher."

"Is there a way to get outside through your office?" the old man asked.

Boris paused and tapped his fingers against his desk. "Mr. Fletcher, pull your car around. I'll see Feng out."

Fletcher left the room.

Boris stood, grabbed two bags and walked toward the outside facing wall. He looked over his shoulder and told Feng to grab the remaining bags and follow him. Then he slid one of the bookcases to the side and pulled a handle on a hidden door that opened up to the outside.

"PULL THE CAR OVER," the old man said.

"No," Fletcher said.

"Are you not one hundred thousand dollars richer because of me?"

The man in the front passenger seat turned to look at Fletcher. Fletcher looked up in the rear-view mirror at the old man and shook his head. He pulled the car over on the emergency shoulder and put it in park.

"Why did you need me to stop?"

"I need to make a phone call."

Feng opened the door and stepped down into six inches of slush and snow. He cursed under his breath as ice cold water flooded his six hundred dollar shoes. He found a dry spot, pulled out his cell phone and called Charles in Paris.

"Hello?"

"Mr. Charles, how are you?"

"What do you need?"

"Still don't care for formalities, do you?"

"Not particularly."

Feng smiled. "What is your arrangement with the Frenchman?"

"Pierre?"

"Yes, I believe that is his name. Friend of Mr. Jack's, correct?"

"Yeah, that's him. He finally agreed to work for me."

"You mean us."

"Yeah, us. You know what I mean."

The old man paused while three caravanning eighteen-wheelers passed. "Mr. Charles, I want you to contact him. I need a job done here."

"New York?"

"Iowa."

"Iowa? What the hell are you doing in Iowa?"

"Never mind that. I saw something here. Someone. I think Jack Noble's associate is here. I want to close the circle, but I don't want our organization to handle it."

"Gotcha. I'll call him."

The old man hung up and returned to the car. He slid into his seat.

"Take me back to the hotel."

16

Pierre stood in front of the stove cooking breakfast. It was nice to have a working stove again. Kat's apartment was a great place to stay. A bit larger than his. Her appliances were newer, though, and he appreciated that.

"Pierre."

He looked over his shoulder and saw Kat walking toward him. She was wearing nothing more than a white t-shirt with three-quarter length pink sleeves. She held his cell phone in her hand.

"Your phone is ringing."

"Ah." He wiped his hands on a towel and reached for his phone. He recognized the number. "Hello?"

"Hello, Pierre," Charles said.

"One moment," Pierre said into the phone. Then he covered the phone with his hand. "I'll be back in a minute." He kissed Kat on the cheek and left the apartment. Went down two flights of stairs and into the courtyard.

"Sorry about that," he said.

"No problem. Privacy is always a concern."

"Of course. Do you have a job for me?"

Charles chuckled. "I might. First I need to know where your loyalties are, though."

"I'm sorry?"

"Kill the girl."

"Do what?" Pierre looked around the courtyard, paying close attention to corners and shrubs and other potential hiding spots. He scanned the rooftops of the buildings that made up the complex.

Charles laughed. "Just kidding. We don't care about her."

Pierre said nothing. He breathed quickly. He stayed on alert and kept an eye out for anyone suspicious. He wished he was armed.

"I do need to know that once you commit to me, to us, that you are one hundred percent on board. No flipping back to your old job. That Pierre is dead after you sign on. You got it?"

Pierre nodded and then felt stupid when he realized that Charles couldn't see him. "Yes, I can live with that."

"Good. Because if you violate my trust you won't be alive no more."

"I have worked in clandestine operations my entire adult life. I understand secrecy and the need for secrecy. I understand loyalty. Once I agree, you have my pledge that I am bound to your organization for the term of our agreement."

"OK. I'm happy with that."

Pierre didn't say anything. He walked toward Kat's building and stood just inside the landing.

"How much would it cost me to get you to take out a friend?"

"Kidding again?"

"No."

"It would depend on how good of a friend. Who did you have in mind?"

"That's classified."

Pierre laughed. "If you want to work with me then you'll have to—"

"What does two hundred thousand buy me?"

Pierre paused. "Euros or dollars?"

"Euros."

Two hundred thousand Euros could set Pierre up for a while and he knew it. He could take Kat and leave the city and move close to the French Riviera.

"I'll kill anyone you want."

"Pack your bags and grab your passport, my friend. You are going to America. I'll have someone meet you at de Gaulle at six this evening."

Pierre hung up his phone and stuffed it in his pocket. He pulled out a cigarette. Sat down on the stairs in front of the building. He thought about the people he knew in the U.S. Most were operators in various government agencies. He knew a few politicians as well, having worked security on their visits to France. He knew he wouldn't be able to figure it out, so he turned his thoughts to Kat. Things were back on track and now he was leaving. But he was doing it for her. He had convinced himself of that. Could he make her believe it?

He finished his cigarette and flicked it into the grass. He ran up the two flights of stairs and went back into the apartment.

"Is everything OK?" she asked.

He smiled. Walked to her. Took her in his arms and kissed her.

"I have to go to the United States tonight."

She pulled away from him and took two steps back.

"What for?"

He walked to the counter and took a seat on one of the bar stools there. He thought for a second and then responded.

"It's for a job. I can't go into details. I actually don't know all the details yet. But it is going to pay enough that we can leave Paris. We can really set ourselves up nice down south. That'd be nice, yeah?"

She shook her head. Wiped her eyes. Smiled. "Sure, Pierre. It'll be nice."

"Wait for me, OK. I'll be back in just a few days." He hopped off the bar stool and walked over to her. Hugged and kissed her. "Start packing the things you want to bring."

She said nothing. Turned away from him and went back to her bedroom. She closed the door behind her, leaving it open just a crack.

Pierre walked to the door and leaned against the frame. He spoke through the crack.

"I have to leave. I have to go to my place and the bank to get a few things. I'll call you when I get to the States."

Kat didn't say anything.

"Kat?"

"OK, Pierre."

17

CLARISSA BOARDED THE 747. HER TICKET WAS FOR A FIRST CLASS SEAT. SHE found her seat and settled in for the two-and-a-half hour flight. She waited for the cabin to fill before retrieving her laptop from her bag. The seat next to her remained empty and she felt she had enough privacy to review the information on the USB thumb drive Sinclair had given her. He had told her that all the information she needed was on the portable drive, including which gate at Chicago's O'Hare International Airport her next flight would depart from. She had pressed him for more information, but true to his secretive nature, Sinclair would say no more.

Clarissa had a strong feeling that she was traveling to a big city. She would have been OK with Chicago, but that was not to be. She doubted it would be New York City. Not with her history there. Possibly Washington, D.C. She decided not to wait any longer. She pulled down the tray attached to the back of the seat in front of her and placed her laptop on the tray. She got no further than flipping the lid of her laptop open when a flight attendant informed her she would have to wait until they were in the air.

It was approximately ten minutes later when the plane taxied to the runway. Another fifteen before she was able to set up her laptop. This time no one stopped her when she powered her computer on. She pulled the thumb drive from her purse and inserted it into a slot along the side of the notebook. A folder opened up on the LCD display. Inside the folder was a number of documents.

The first document was labeled "Anastasiya Tvardovsky." Clarissa clicked on the file and opened it. The document contained a picture of a woman who bore a strong resemblance to Clarissa, except for Anastasiya's dark eyes and hair. The woman was a Russian citizen. She was supposed to arrive in the U.S. in two days. Apparently, these plans had been set in motion months ago. The NSA had initially intercepted the information, and it made its way through the intelligence community. They had a plan to capture the woman and Clarissa was to take her place.

Clarissa next opened a file labeled "Itinerary." On the first line was her gate assignment, C16. She had a connecting flight to Des Moines, Iowa. Clarissa grimaced at the thought of having to go to Iowa. She had a car reservation in her name at the airport. She also had a hotel reservation for five nights at the Embassy Suites Hotel in downtown Des Moines. The document contained further instructions. While checking in she would have to ask the desk clerk to look for a package in her name. The contents of the package would make it clear to her what do with them.

Clarissa closed the file and moved her mouse pointer over a third file. This one was labeled "Boris Melikov." She lifted her finger above the touchpad and began to strike it when there was a loud explosion.

The plane dropped for what felt like a thousand feet in just a few short seconds. Alarms sounded and lights flickered on and off. The plane leveled off for a second and then began to bank hard to the left. It started to shudder and shake. Oxygen masks dropped from the ceiling. During the drop, Clarissa's computer had flown up and smashed into the ceiling above her. She searched the seat next to her to find it. One hand felt along the seat as the other grabbed for the oxygen mask. She found the computer and placed it on her lap and then used both hands to secure the oxygen mask.

The muffled sounds of screams and cries could be heard. But drowning them out was the incredible sound of the rushing wind. Clarissa secured her computer in her bag. She leaned toward the aisle. At the front of the plane a flight attendant clung to a seat. She was in a fight for her life. Her body was being pulled toward the back of the plane. Her hair and skirt whipped about in front of her.

Clarissa noticed the pressure had built up to painful levels in her ears. She clutched her arm rest tight and turned in her seat so she could see behind her.

The blue cloth drapes that normally separated first class from coach were pulled so tight they clung to the ceiling. Through the opening, she saw a sight that horrified her. Nothing she had ever seen had left her feeling so helpless. A ten foot wide section of the side of the plane was missing, along with the rows of passengers who had been seated in the general area, including the seats at the back of first class.

She felt the plane lurch downward and she found herself looking at the floor. She had to angle her head to see what had once been eye level. She forced herself to face forward again. Grabbed a hold of her bag and searched through zippered pockets. She pulled out two photos and then leaned forward in the crash position she had seen in the plane's pre-take-off literature.

She held the photos just beyond her knees.

One was of her and her father when she was eleven years old. She had just caught a huge largemouth bass during a fishing trip in North Carolina.

The other photo was of her and Jack, taken four years ago during one of their on-again phases. She wished she had fought harder to keep him. Maybe she wouldn't be in this mess right now and maybe Jack wouldn't be dead. Dead because he saved her life.

And then, amid the chaos and carnage of a 747 plummeting to the ground because of a ten foot hole in the fuselage, Clarissa felt a wave of calm and serenity wash over her. She clung to a single thought. When the plane hit the ground she would be reunited with Jack and her father.

PART II

EPISODE 7

18

THE PLANE SHOOK AND PITCHED AND SCREAMED ON A DIRECT PATH TOWARD THE ground. Clarissa clutched the picture of her and her father in one hand. The picture of her and Jack in the other. Even though they were out of sight with her head between her knees, the photos comforted her. She recalled the in-flight literature showing the need to place her hands over the back of her head. She figured that anything that might land on her would be heavy enough that it wouldn't matter.

She remembered a documentary on plane crashes she watched on TV a few years prior. The show revealed that most passengers don't die upon impact. Bodies drove downward and seats drove upward upon impact. Femur bone snap like twigs, hobbling those who survived the initial impact. Heads bang and roll and passengers are left unconscious. Most victims found themselves unable to escape their seats, and they died slowly of asphyxiation from the smoke, or painfully as they burned to death in the fire.

Clarissa's calm faded. Although she had resolved herself to dying, she didn't want to suffer in the process. How long until they hit the ground? A flicker of hope remained that they would land safely. That hope faded a bit each time the plane pitched or dropped or made a sound like it had ripped open further.

She fought the pressure against her body and lifted her torso a few feet. She turned in her seat to take a look at the carnage behind her. More seats had been torn from the bolts. Bolts that had secured them to the floor.

First class had not been spared.

Finally, equality.

The jagged opening in the fuselage revealed a glowing orange sky. Daylight? Fire?

She turned her torso and her attention to the front of first class seating. The flight attendant who had so recently hung on for dear life was nowhere to be seen. Lost her battle with the negative pressure. Sucked out of the plane like a cockroach flushed down a toilet.

How long had the woman lived? Perhaps she hit her head on the way out and had been knocked unconscious, or even more mercifully, had her neck broken. Or had she escaped cleanly through the hole, untouched and unscathed, enjoying the ultimate free fall from thirty or twenty or however many thousands of feet they were in the air?

Clarissa spotted a small child sitting alone diagonally and in front of her. She didn't need to see the child's face to realize the little girl was terrified. Everyone on board who managed to stay conscious thus far had to be scared beyond their wits.

Clarissa strapped her bag across her chest. Unlatched her seat belt. Stuck one leg into the aisle. The pull and the pressure nearly ripped her from the seat. She realized that she had to get into a position that spread the pull over the width of her body. That is where the flight attendant had been at a disadvantage. She had been standing straight up and facing the front of the plane when the explosion, or whatever it was, occurred. The woman had been instantly knocked off her feet.

Clarissa slid out of her seat. She kept her body low and spread out. Half in the aisle. Half in front of the seat. She reached out, forward and diagonally, and clutched the armrest of the little girl's seat. Clarissa resisted the urge to pull herself up or try to enter from the row behind the little girl. The wrong move now would leave her high and exposed. Ripe for the hole and the sky to swallow her alive.

Her right hand gripped the girl's armrest. Her left hand reached around the seat in front of her. Her plan was to explode across, with her body low and flat. In a fluid motion, she pulled herself from the protection of her seat.

Forced her body across the aisle, forward and diagonally. She flung her left hand across her body and grabbed the armrest on the other side of the girl. A moment later she crouched in front of the child. Spun and sat down. Buckled herself in. Wrapped an arm around the little girl. She placed her head next to the child's.

"It's going to be OK."

The little girl turned her head. Long brown hair whipped in front of her brown eyes. Her tear stained cheeks were flushed red. She grabbed Clarissa's hand.

The plane pitched forward and the noise that followed terrified Clarissa to the core. She stifled a yell in her throat.

Don't scare the girl.

Clarissa felt the urge to look behind her and see if any further damage accompanied the sound she'd just heard. But to do so she'd have to stand and that was not a safe option. Had the gaping hole grown? Had the plane finally torn in half?

A faint voice tried to communicate from above. The pilot or the co-pilot or another member of the flight crew was speaking. They were going to land. They had found a spot and that was why the plane took a nose dive. Of course, Clarissa didn't know if that was what they were saying at all. In fact, the voices from above might be made up. Or that of her father or Jack. She wasn't sure, and there was no way to tell.

A moment later the plane leveled out. The pull remained, but the downward pressure and subsequent tearing at her stomach dissipated. She heard the sound of gravel from above again. The words "emergency" and "landing" stood out to her.

She hugged the little girl tighter, pulling her into her chest. She leaned over and across the little girl's head and neck.

The last moments of the flight were filled only with the roar of the wind. No creaks. No groans. No screams. No cries. Just the wind. Louder than she had ever heard it in her life.

The plane hit the ground and the wind stopped and the sound of metal grating against metal began. Things that weren't meant to twist and bend were twisting and bending. They snapped and tore. The screams and cries returned.

Clarissa felt her body being jarred left and right and up and down. Something smacked her head. Or had she smacked her head into something? It didn't matter. She fell unconscious.

THE FIRST FEELING Clarissa had was dread. *The real danger in a crash was smoke and fire and broken limbs.* She felt the heat of the fire. She swam in the black smoke. She wiggled her toes, then rolled her ankles, then bent her knees. Nothing felt broken.

A hand ran through her hair. She turned her head and saw the little girl kneeling in her seat.

"Are you OK?" the girl asked.

Clarissa sat up, rising further into the cloud of smoke.

"Yes. We need to get out of here."

The girl nodded.

"I want you to get out of the seat and crouch down low," Clarissa said. "Stay close to me."

The little girl got out of her seat and dropped to her knees in the aisle. She made herself low and kept her eyes on Clarissa's.

Clarissa slid out of her seat. She knelt down as low as she could while still allowing herself to move. It took a moment to remember which side of the plane she was on. Once she had her bearings straight, she began to move toward the back of the plane. She looked to her right, at the seat she had previously occupied. The seat had been crushed. If she had remained there, she'd be dead.

She continued on. Felt the heat of the fire, but couldn't see its glow. Where was the fire? Would the smoke block it out completely?

Clarissa's plan was simple. Find the tear in the side of the plane and get the hell out.

She inched her way to the back of the plane with the little girl close behind. The heavy smoke skewed any view of her surroundings. Clarissa had no idea what lay ahead. The plane could be split at any point. They could fall into a crack and get stuck. She operated on blind faith.

A few feet later Clarissa made out the shape of the hole in the fuselage. It appeared to be huge. At least thirty feet in width.

The smoke started to thin, rushing up to the ceiling and out through the hole. Clarissa abandoned her crouching position and stood with her back hunched over. She motioned for the little girl to rise.

A fire raged inside the plane beyond the hole. The desperate cries of the survivors in the back of the plane carried through the blaze and rode along with the smoke. Clarissa wanted to run to them. Help them. Save them. Impossible, though. She knew it. Her heart ached and tears flooded her eyes. How many survivors would perish?

The real danger in a crash was smoke and fire and broken limbs.

Her skin felt like it was going to melt against the heat of the fire. Her throat ached from the smoke stained air. She walked a fine line between life and death, and that is why, despite the panic and desperation, she fought her way to the hole in the side of the plane.

They reached the opening. Her heart pounded harder in her chest. So close to freedom. Still so close to death. Clarissa grabbed the little girl. Picked her up and held her tight to her chest. The plane was tilted on its side and the drop from the hole to the ground was only a few feet. She carefully positioned herself on the edge and jumped. She navigated through the wreckage, picking up speed the further they got from the plane.

Emergency vehicles approached with their high beams flashing and strobe lights turning. Sirens filled the air. For a moment Clarissa was happy to hear a sound other than the crackling of fire, and the burning of flesh, and the desperate screams of those trapped in the plane.

She kept moving away from the plane, trying to get far enough away to escape injury should there be an explosion. She set the little girl down and waved her arms in the air.

As the vehicles neared, their headlights lit the scene. The plane had crashed in the middle of a field. Mangled and twisted and split into three sections. The cockpit was upside down and forty feet or so ahead of the body of the plane. The tail had also split off and sat at the edge of the artificial lighting, barely visible. She saw the outlines of bodies on the ground. Likely ejected through the hole during the crash. The lucky ones, she thought, who didn't have to suffer in the fire.

One thing struck her as odd, though. She did not see any other survivors walking about. That didn't mean there weren't any, of course. But so far she had not seen another living soul aside from her and the child.

A squad car stopped nearby, while the fire trucks and ambulances formed a semi-perimeter around the wreckage.

A young dark-haired officer stepped out of the cruiser. He panned his flashlight across the ground as he made his way toward Clarissa and the girl.

"Ma'am, are you and your daughter alright?"

"Yes." Clarissa paused for a moment. "She's not my daughter. She was alone on the plane. I moved to sit next to her after the explosion."

The officer nodded. He opened the trunk of the police car and pulled out a blanket. He walked over to Clarissa and the little girl and wrapped the blanket around them.

"Can you walk?"

Clarissa nodded. So did the little girl.

The officer said, "Follow me."

Clarissa reached for the girl's hand and they followed the officer. They walked for thirty yards or so, away from the wreckage. He turned and pointed toward an ambulance.

"Go there and get checked out. Someone will be along to take a statement."

They continued walking, and the young officer returned to his car. Clarissa looked down at the little girl and noticed her crying.

"Are you OK?"

The girl shook her head. She lifted her leg and pointed at her foot, which was positioned at an odd angle.

19

BEAR SAT IN THE FRONT PASSENGER SEAT OF DETECTIVE LARSEN'S UNMARKED police cruiser. The detective had said he'd only be a few minutes. That was ten minutes ago. They were wasting time as far as Bear was concerned. Every minute they weren't looking for Mandy, she could be another mile further away. Larsen still hadn't told him anything. Said that he needed to make a stop first.

Bear looked over the small one story house. He opened his door and placed a foot on the ground. Tired of waiting, he was going to walk in. He started across the lawn and then Larsen stepped out of the house. He waved, gesturing for Bear to come inside.

Bear walked up the cracked concrete walkway that split the brown excuse for a front lawn. He stopped on the porch, in front of Larsen.

Bear said, "What's this? What's going on? You need to tell me something."

Larsen lit a cigarette. Offered one to Bear. He declined.

"OK, the guy that lives here, he saw your little girl today. Described her exactly."

"Where is she?"

"I'm getting to that. I want to brief you on some things first."

Bear opened his mouth to speak. Changed his mind.

"The man that lives here is one of my informants. He works for a man named Boris Melikov. That name ring any bells?"

Bear searched his memory. Came up with nothing. He shook his head.

"He's a Russian terrorist."

"That a fact?"

"Opinion. At the very least he's a thug. He's the one I mentioned in the hospital. Has half my department on his payroll. I suspected him from the get go. There's no way that anyone gets away with what they pulled off at the bank. They were in there far too long. Hell, we're only a two minute drive to the bank from the precinct."

Bear nodded and said nothing while gesturing for Larsen to continue.

"So anyways, this guy, he confirmed it. Saw the men return to the house with dark duffel bags." Larsen stopped and wiped his brow. "And a little blond-haired girl."

"Let me talk to him."

Larsen held up his hands, extending his index fingers into the air. He said, "I'll let you talk, but don't screw with this guy. OK? He's one of my best sources. The best source I have for anything related to Melikov. Nobody, and I mean nobody, knows I've got this guy talking. I'm close to bringing Boris down. You got that?"

"Yeah," Bear said. "I got it. Now, let me talk to him."

Larsen nodded. He pushed the brown front door open and walked into the house.

Bear stepped through the doorway. The warm air coated his face and a thin layer of sweat formed. The residual smell of a burnt dinner invaded his nose. Two antique lamps lit the room, giving it a yellowish glow.

The man sat on the couch. His right leg crossed over his left. His left leg bouncing up and down. He had light brown hair and a slender pale face. Pale except for the red spot on his cheek where Larsen must have punched him.

"This is my associate," Larsen said. "His name is Logan."

The man nodded at Bear. Crossed his arms. Said nothing.

"Tell me what you saw," Bear said.

The man sat up. He leaned forward and dropped his arms over his bent knee. He spoke in a deep voice, deeper than Bear expected from a man so small in stature.

"Like I told the detective, I was working at Melikov's place today—"

"You work for him?" Bear asked.

"Yes."

"Part of his organization?"

"No," the man said. "It's not like that. I don't go out and commit crimes or any of that stuff. I work in the house. Cooking and stuff."

"A servant."

The man pursed his lips and dropped his head an inch.

"Go on," Bear said.

"There really isn't much to tell, I'm afraid. The door opened and five men stepped through. Four carried duffel bags, from the bank robbery, I guess. One carried a little girl."

"Describe the men," Bear said.

"They were a blur. I tuned them out. Probably because I had seen them in the house before. The girl stood out, though."

"Describe her to me."

"Blond hair. Looked to be about ten. She had on a red t-shirt and jeans. I started toward them and one of Boris's men told me to go to the kitchen. I really don't know what happened after that. I went off shift an hour later and didn't see the girl or the men again."

Bear studied the man for a few minutes. Locked eyes with him. The guy didn't waver. Didn't look away. Didn't blink but once or twice. Bear believed him.

"I think he's legit," Larsen said. "He's provided me with solid intel before."

Bear walked around to the back of the sofa where the man sat. Each step he took was slow and deliberate. He asked, "What's your name?"

The man started to speak but Larsen cut him off.

"That's unnecessary, Bear. You don't need his name."

Bear stopped and glanced at Larsen. He felt his cheeks burn hot. He took a deep breath decided to concede the name. For now.

"OK, no names then. This is what you are going to do. Tomorrow, you are going to find out wherever they are hiding her, and you are going to tell her not to worry because Bear is coming for her soon."

"I—I can't do that. They could kill me."

"I can kill you," Bear said. "And I can make it a hell of a lot more painful than anything they will do."

"Bear," Larsen said. "C'mon, he's not in a position to be able to do that."

"You think I friggin' care?" Bear said. "As far as I'm concerned he's a notch below those bastards. He saw them bring in a child and did nothing to stop it."

"What do you think I could have done? These men are killers."

Bear paused. He circled the couch and stopped in front of the man. Knelt down so that he was eye level.

"This is my little girl. You got that? I will stop at nothing to rescue her. Don't care how many people I have to kill to rescue her. I don't care if I have to die for her to be free. You mean nothing to me. Boris means nothing to me. Larsen means nothing to me. Only her. You understand?"

The man bobbed his head up and down in a short, jerky motion.

"OK. There's one more thing. Either you do as I ask, or the first person I kill is you."

"Bear," Larsen said. "That is uncalled—"

"And the next person will be you, Detective. I'm not screwing around here."

Bear stood and turned to face Larsen. He took a breath in an effort to compose himself.

Larsen's face was bright red. His thick jaw muscles worked overtime. His eyes were narrow and dark and burned with anger.

The informant stood. He reached out his hand toward Bear.

"I'll do it, Mr., uh, Bear."

Bear grabbed the man's hand.

"On one condition," the man said.

"What's that?"

"You do me a favor when this is all over with."

Larsen said, "Wait a minute. I don't know that this—"

"What's the favor?" Bear asked.

"I'll tell you after you've rescued the girl."

Bear said, "I'll do anything." And he meant it.

20

ALL CLARISSA WANTED TO DO WAS WALK AWAY FROM THE WRECKAGE. SLIP INTO the darkness and disappear. No one had to know that she survived the crash. Not Sinclair, not anyone.

She held the little girl in her arms. The child's adrenaline had worn off and the pain of her broken ankle had hit her full force. Tears streamed down her face. She clenched her eyes. Soft whimpers had given way to sobs. She cried for her mother.

"Over here," a voice called from near the ambulance.

Clarissa picked up her pace. She was careful not to go too fast, for fear of dropping the child. She still didn't know the girl's name and didn't think this was the appropriate time to ask, although she was sure the medic would want to know.

"Is she unconscious?"

"No," Clarissa said. "She did good. Walked out of the plane and all the way over here. But, it's her ankle. Looks broken."

The medic motioned toward a spot on the ground and Clarissa set the girl down. She took a few steps back and watched the medic go to work. He examined the little girl from head to toe. It seemed he spent an exorbitant amount of time checking her head and neck. Clarissa figured that was standard and probably an extra concern considering they appeared to be the sole survivors of a major crash. The only survivors she had seen so far.

The medic stood and turned to face Clarissa.

"Your little girl is going to be OK," he said. Before Clarissa could correct him, he continued. "She has a broken ankle. I'm betting her tibia is broken as well. Lots of sensitivity to touch. We'll get her to a hospital soon. Need to assess the rest of the injured and see how many walking wounded we have, and how many serious injuries there are. Once we know that, we can get her moved. She's in no danger of further injury."

Clarissa nodded. She decided not to tell him that she wasn't the girl's mother. A free ride away from the crash site sounded nice.

He asked, "Did you see many survivors?"

She shook her head.

"Only us. There were..." her voice trailed off and she paused a few moments. "There were voices from the back of the plane. But the fire, it was too big. There were flames everywhere and I couldn't get to them." Her eyes watered over.

The medic reached out and grabbed her arm. Squeezed it reassuringly. "There's nothing you could do. That's why we're here. If anyone on that plane survived, we'll get them out alive."

Clarissa smiled despite the pain associated with the loss of the lives of people she never knew. The lives of the survivors she could not save.

The medic put a splint on the girl's leg to stabilize it, and then left them alone by the ambulance to check on the rescue operations.

"Hey," Clarissa said. "What's your name?"

"Sarah," the girl said.

"I'm Clarissa." She knelt down and took a seat next to the girl on the ground. "Is it OK if I ride with you to the hospital?"

Sarah nodded.

Clarissa felt around her bag and found her cell phone. She pulled the phone out. Turned it on.

"Do you want to call your parents?"

Sarah reached for the phone and dialed her parents' number. Clarissa heard the sound of a frantic mother on the other end of the line. Panic turned to sobs and tears of joy when the little girl said, "Hi, Mommy," and then everything, at least in one person's world, was OK.

Twenty minutes passed and the medic returned. The glimmer of hope his eyes once held was gone. In its place were sorrow and emptiness.

He grimly said, "We're going to transport you to the hospital now."

CLARISSA TRIED to leave when they reached the hospital, but an army of nurses and medics and doctors escorted her along with Sarah to an empty bay in the emergency room.

It wasn't until the doctor started asking about Sarah's medical history that Clarissa spoke up.

"I'm not her mother."

"What?" a thin, dark nurse said.

"I saw her sitting alone and moved seats while the plane was going down. Didn't want her to be alone."

"Courageous of you," the doctor said. "Now, do you know a way of reaching her mother?"

Clarissa reached into her bag and pulled out her phone. She held it out to the doctor, who redirected Clarissa to the nurse.

"Yes," Clarissa said. "She called her from my phone."

They dialed the last number and got the mother on the line. She provided the staff with the information they needed.

Clarissa moved to the head of the bed and leaned in toward Sarah. She whispered in her ear.

"I'm going to leave now, OK. Your mommy will be here before you know it. Everything is going to be OK." Clarissa paused and thought back to the wreckage. She recalled that the seat she had been sitting in had been crushed, the back folded over the front, mashed to the floor. If she had remained there, she'd be dead. "Thank you for saving me."

The girl smiled at Clarissa. She turned her head and kissed Clarissa's cheek.

Clarissa put her hands to her face and walked out of the room.

"Miss," a nurse called from behind. "Where are you going? You need to be checked out, too. You could have a concussion or an internal injury."

Clarissa ignored the nurse's warning. She followed in reverse the path they took when they arrived. Turned toward the emergency room waiting area instead of continuing down the hall to the door the medics used as an entrance and an exit. She passed through the waiting room. All eyes darted to her. She tried not to pay attention to them. The fact that everyone stared at her took her aback a bit, though. When she reached the glass double doors she saw why. The dark sky behind the doors turned them into an eight by eight mirror. Her clothes were torn and singed and colored dark from ash. Soot covered her face. How had anyone been able to take her seriously up to this point?

She looked over her shoulder. Located the bathroom. Made her way in and washed up. She couldn't do much about her clothes, but at least she was able to make her face a little more presentable.

People continued to stare after she exited the bathroom. She didn't care. She stepped in front of the glass doors and waited for them to open. The cold night air stung her face and arms like thousands of tiny pin pricks. She had no coat. It had been lost during the crash. She crossed her arms and hugged herself tight.

Where to go? She scanned the parking lot for a taxi or a shuttle. Saw neither.

The question lingered. Where to go? More importantly, what to do? The thought she'd had after the crash crept up again. She could be free. She could disappear. No one would ever know. She hadn't given her name to anyone except the little girl. For all anyone knew, Clarissa Abbot had died in the plane crash.

Maybe she could find Bear and Mandy. Start a new life. With her training and new skills she could go into business with Bear.

She felt torn. A decision about what to do once she'd disappeared didn't have to be made at that moment. But she did have to make a decision on whether or not to leave. She had a job to do for Sinclair. Should she reach out to him? Or should she let him, and the rest of the world, believe that she was dead. What about her remains? Her belongings? She traveled light, and had no checked-in baggage. Only carry-on. And she had it all with her. There would be no body, no computer, no clothes. And no phone.

She looked down at her hand and the buzzing cell phone. She turned the phone over in her palm to see who was calling her. Sinclair. She didn't answer.

Clarissa stuffed the phone into her pocket. She looked across the parking lot at a sea of empty cars and vans and SUVs. She stepped off the curb and began crossing the road. Her first steps toward freedom. A freedom that was a city bus stop and Greyhound station away.

She heard the sound of a car. A car that traveled far too fast for a hospital parking lot. Clarissa turned her head to the left and saw a pair of headlights racing toward her. Close. Too close. She leapt out of the way, landing on a narrow strip of soft grass.

Brakes squealed. A door opened and closed. Footsteps approached.

She rolled over on her back and propped herself up on her elbows. Recognition filled her mind at the sight of the approaching man. He was on the team. Clarissa knew little of him, though. They had never worked together. She had asked Sinclair about him one time and he told her that Randy was there to clean up the messes they made.

One of his arms dangled further than the other. A weapon. A gun. And it was equipped with a canister at the end. She knew the canister was a suppressor.

"Randy," she said. "Don't shoot."

Randy said, "Get up."

She took her time getting to her feet, making sure to keep him in her line of sight. She was unarmed. Had to be to get on the plane.

"What's with the gun?"

Randy raised his arm and looked sideways at the weapon. "In case you decide not to come."

"What makes you think I wouldn't come?"

"You didn't answer Sinclair's call."

Clarissa said nothing. She squeezed her cell phone. So many split second decisions had to be made to get off the plane alive. The thought of leaving her phone behind had never crossed her mind. Of course, the phone. They kept track of all of them via their cell phones.

"I mean, we thought it was odd that your phone traveled thirty miles from the site of the crash, all the way to this hospital, and you never bothered to call. Then when your phone rings, you just look at it and stuff it in your pants." His eyes traveled down her body and stopped on her midsection.

Clarissa asked, "What are you doing in Omaha? Why were you here to begin with?"

"I wasn't. I was in Des Moines, Iowa."

Clarissa narrowed her eyes and recalled any and all knowledge she had of Des Moines and Iowa, which turned out to be not much at all.

"That's where you were going to end up," he said.

Randy was there to clean up the messes they made.

"I—I, but..."

He smiled and took a step forward. He reached up and brushed strands of blowing hair behind her ear.

Her body wanted to convulse at his touch. She fought the urge.

"Don't worry, Clarissa," he said. "As long as you are on board, I'm not going to do anything to you. Unless the boss instructs me otherwise."

"Then what were you doing in Des Moines if that's where I was going?"

Randy was there to clean up the messes they made.

"I've been taking care of something in Minneapolis related to what you're getting into. Sinclair asked me to come down and brief you. After that I was gonna bail."

She watched his dark eyes as they darted left to right. His heavy brow and face appeared relaxed.

Randy took a step back. Tucked his gun away. Said, "So what's it going to be, kid?"

Clarissa looked around. Nowhere to run. Nowhere to hide. At least, nowhere Randy wouldn't find her. And if she ran, and he found her, then he would have a mess to clean up. It seemed that her tough decision had been made for her.

She said, "Let's go to Iowa."

21

THE RISING SUN SILHOUETTED THE KING AND QUEEN BUILDINGS. THE TWO buildings, along with several others, dotted Atlanta's perimeter. They had traveled on I-85 through the night and were now on I-285, skirting along the outer edges of the gateway to the South.

Jack turned his attention forward and weaved the car through the thickening traffic. Poor saps, he thought. Dressed up and driving to a job they hate. Most of them probably on the road this early so they could skip out one of Atlanta's least-popular attractions, the traffic.

A mile later red brake lights lit the highway like a festival dragon, winding and rising along the asphalt.

"Christ," Jack muttered.

"One of the worst traffic cities in the country," Jasmine said. "People here spend, on average, over a full week sitting in traffic each year."

Jack nodded. Said nothing.

"It should ease up soon. Then we'll get on I-75 and it'll be smooth sailing heading north."

"You should get a job with a radio station. Traffic girl. It'd suit you."

"You think?"

"TV voice, radio face." He looked over and smiled.

Jasmine rolled her eyes and turned toward the passenger window. She said, "Why don't you talk much?"

"Thought I was talking."

"You know what I mean."

Jack cleared his throat. "Got nothing to say."

"With everything you've been through, you have nothing to say?"

Jack shrugged. He inched the car forward and then pressed the brakes again, slowing the car to a stop. Then he said, "What do you want to know?"

"The answer to the question I asked you yesterday. What have you been doing since you left the agency?"

"Not going to tell you."

Jasmine shifted in her seat and turned to face him. "Why not?"

"Too much to tell. Too much I shouldn't tell."

Jasmine waved him off and shifted in her seat again.

He wasn't trying to piss her off. He didn't know the woman and a lot things he had done over the years weren't exactly legal. Why give her information she could use against him?

"Why don't you tell me why you joined the SIS?" Jack said.

"Where to begin?" she said. "Well, blew out my knee in college. Ruined my chances to compete in the Olympics. Went to law school. Finished fourth in my class. Had no desire to become a lawyer. Applied to the FBI and the CIA. Tested for the latter. Got a phone call from Frank inviting me to interview for a special position. Pretty standard."

Jack nodded. Noticed a sign for I-75 north and started maneuvering the car across six lanes of bumper-to-bumper traffic.

"Why don't you tell me why you joined the SIS?" she asked.

"I guess I can tell you that." Jack's eyes darted from his rear view mirror to the passenger side mirror. He crossed one lane at a time. He pulled into the exit lane and continued, "I was a Marine. Actually, I was loaned out to the CIA. Did a lot of domestic stuff. Worked in Europe, South America. Was in North Korea once, but no one knows about that."

Jasmine nodded. "OK. Then what?"

"9/11 is what. Everything changed."

"That's why I went to law school. I never wanted to be a lawyer. I wanted to hunt terrorists."

Jack glanced over at her and noticed her fists were clenched tight. She stared beyond the dash, the traffic, and the mess of intertwined highway crossings ahead.

"Yeah, well, it changed things for a lot of people." He looked at her again and saw her nodding, slowly. "So, my group went from domestic and friendlies to Iraq."

"In 2003?"

"2001."

"What?" She no longer stared ahead. Her head spun and she stared at Jack, her mouth hanging open an inch.

"Eighty or ninety percent of the teams went to Afghanistan. Not us, though."

"What were you looking for in Iraq?"

"Beats me. Everything changed. We were on the outside. Provided security for the agency guys."

"What do you mean?"

Jack shook his head. "Long story. Anyways, there was a big mess. People started dying. Someone tried to frame me. It went," he paused a beat while thinking over how much he should tell her. "It went pretty high up the government food chain."

"The President?"

"No, not quite that high, and I won't say who or what or when, either."

She nodded. Didn't say anything.

"So, this whole mess, never really got resolved back then. Cleaned it up later, though."

"When you were in the SIS?"

"No. That's beside the point. How and why did I join the SIS? OK." Jack paused and checked over his left shoulder before merging onto I-75 northbound. "I got my discharge and had three months leave banked. I got paid for those three months while doing nothing. I had planned to travel. Ended up stopping in Key West a week after my journey started. Didn't leave. Not for three months. I was waiting, well, yeah, waiting on something. Someone. Frank showed up instead. Made me a job offer. Two weeks later I was in D.C., learning the ways of the SIS."

"I've read some of your case files," Jasmine said.

Jack looked across at her and lifted an eyebrow above the frame of his sunglasses.

"The kids," Jasmine said.

"What about them?"

"The thing with the kids. I... I don't know. That was something else, is all. How you and Frank took the abductors down, and then, well, you know."

Jack nodded. He dropped one hand onto his thigh and the other hand shifted to the top of the steering wheel.

"Yeah, I know. I still think about that."

"Did you ever find him?"

Jack glanced between her and the road a few times. "You don't know?"

Jasmine shook her head in reply.

"If it's not in the files," Jack said, "then I can't tell you."

"Jack," she said.

"Another time. Let's get through this and then we'll see."

They drove the next ten miles in silence. Took an exit that put them on I-575. Passed through Woodstock and got off the highway in Canton.

"Not a lot of options for a place to stay here," Jack said.

"No, there aren't. Maybe we should head back toward Atlanta?"

Jack pointed toward a Hilton. "That should do."

He pulled the car into the parking lot and found a place to park.

"I'm going to get us a couple rooms," Jasmine said.

Jack nodded and stretched. He waited until Jasmine was inside the hotel lobby and then he took a walk on the sidewalk, between the hotel parking lot and the road.

Cars backed up at a stop light. Jack turned away from them and cut across the parking lot. He still wasn't too keen on being seen. Any car in any town could be driven by a member of law enforcement. Someone who might have at one time or another seen Jack's face. Of course, no photo of him ever taken resembled the way he looked now. He relaxed a bit. Slowed his pace. He was met at the door by Jasmine.

"Got us two rooms, but check-in time isn't for another seven hours."

Jack looked at his watch. Seven-thirty a.m. He looked past the parking lot and spotted a Waffle House. If Atlanta was the gateway to the South, Waffle House was the staple restaurant.

He said, "Let's figure it out over breakfast."

They left the car in the parking lot and crossed the street on foot. The yellow roofed square building welcomed them with the smell of coffee and hash browns and pancakes.

"Pick a seat. Be right with you." The waitress had brown curly hair that was mostly tucked under a red ball cap sporting a blue "A" for the Atlanta Braves. She looked a few years on the wrong side of fifty, and a few pounds on the wrong side of thin. Jack and Jasmine found a seat and the waitress spoke to them from the other side of the counter. "What'll you have?"

"Coffee, two eggs, and three pancakes," Jack said.

The waitress nodded and looked at Jasmine. "What about you sweetheart?"

"Oh, I'll have the same," Jasmine said.

"How do you want those eggs?" the waitress said.

"Surprise me," Jack said.

"Scrambled," Jasmine said.

The waitress dropped off their coffee and went back to the grill to help the cook.

"Want to do a drive by of the house?" Jasmine asked.

"You know where it is?"

"Yeah, pretty sure we do. Got a call from Frank while I was in the lobby. He's sending details by email." She pulled her phone out and tapped at the screen. "Yeah, there it is. We aren't that far away. Maybe fifteen or twenty minutes."

"We got the time. Makes sense. Maybe we'll luck out and find our guy walking his dog."

Jasmine laughed. "You know it won't be that easy."

"He send you any details on the guy?"

She twisted her lips to the side and shook her head. "So far only the house. They're still working on the rest."

The waitress handed them their plates from the other side of the counter. They quickly ate without talking. Jack paid the bill and grabbed two coffees to go. He left the restaurant and met Jasmine in the car. She had taken the driver's seat. Jack didn't protest.

"Ready to check out this house?" Jasmine asked.

"Ready as I'll ever be after driving non-stop for twelve hours and then filling up on grease and coffee and carbs."

22

Boris sat alone in his study. The room screamed of masculinity with its oversized desk, dark wood tones, and aged books. He had wanted it that way. Anyone who entered should feel threatened and intimidated. People usually did when near him, whether they were in this room or not. Even complete strangers took extra care to get out of his way on the sidewalk or in the supermarket, among other places.

He rose to his feet at the sound of a knock at the door. Crossed the room and opened the door.

"Fletcher," Boris said. "Glad you could make it."

Fletcher nodded and waited for Boris to gesture him in.

"Have a seat over there." Boris pointed toward his desk.

The men sat down opposite each other. Boris in his large patent leather chair. Fletcher in a smaller, stiff chair with wooden arms and a padded seat and back.

"The reason I wanted you here," said Boris, "was to begin to review these documents. We need to identify our initial targets."

"What exactly are these documents?"

Boris smiled without lifting his head. "A lot of effort went into obtaining these." He picked up a manila folder and dropped it onto the desk. "What I am told is someone inside the government has turned."

"The U.S. government?"

Boris leaned back and drummed the edge of the desk with his fingertips. He said, "Yes, that is correct."

"For who? Us?"

"No, not us. My understanding is that these documents were on their way to someone or some place that is in direct opposition of the U.S."

"Iraq?"

"Don't think so. Iran or North Korea, if it was a nation."

"You think it might have been another organization?"

"It's possible. Frankly, it doesn't matter."

"How did Feng know about these?"

"I would assume someone tipped the old man off. But I don't think he realized what he was getting when he hired the man to steal the documents. And I don't think he realized what he had when he sold them to me. He could have received a lot more money for them than what I paid. Hell, I would have paid a lot more to procure them."

Boris gave Fletcher a few minutes to let it sink in. The man squinted and nodded as he worked through the information.

Boris opened the folder and leafed through paper after paper. "Over one hundred vulnerable places for us to target. Each place being critical infrastructure or psychologically important to the weak people of this country."

"We could figure out targets, Boris."

Boris lifted his head and nodded. "Yes, this is true. But what we don't know are the weaknesses, the vulnerabilities of each target, my friend. This information has it all."

Fletcher reached out and grabbed a piece of paper. "Bridges." He looked from the paper to Boris. "I could tell you how to take out a bridge."

Boris smiled. Waved his hand.

"Read on."

Fletcher mumbled through the document, stopping occasionally to nod and soak up the information. As he neared the end, his eyebrows remained arched an inch into his forehead. He finished reading and sat the paper on the desk, exhaling loudly.

"Yes," Boris said. "We could figure out how to take down a bridge. But that document right there lists the top ten bridges, plus the why and the how. And that's not the end of it. Look at what we have here."

He dropped stack of paper after stack of paper onto the desk. It was all there: airports, tunnels and bridges, nuclear power plants, national monuments, environmental targets, and places where thousands of people would be gathered and the times they would be there. Detailed instructions on bypassing or overcoming security measures were included for each target.

"What's the plan?" Fletcher asked.

Boris smiled. He placed his palms on the desktop and stood. Walked around the desk and stopped behind Fletcher. He placed his hands on the man's shoulders and squeezed. Said, "We are going to hit as many of those targets at one time as is possible. Six months from now. On the day of rest when these poor saps gather for sporting events. I foresee over one million dead and injured. I foresee national monuments crumbling. I foresee an environmental catastrophe unparalleled by anything in history."

"Greater than..." Fletcher brought his hand to his face and rubbed his cheeks.

"Yes," Boris said. "Even greater than Chernobyl."

Boris let go of Fletcher and the man rose from his chair. He paced the room and stopped at the far wall. Leaned against the bookcase.

Fletcher said, "How do we know the old man won't turn on us?"

Boris laughed and waved his hand dismissively at his associate. "Of all people, he would be the last person to call attention to himself. If he turned us in, then the matter of how he came to be in possession of such documents would be called into question."

"Good point. What about the mole in the government?"

Boris returned to his chair. "Wish I knew who he was."

"Bring him on board?"

"Kill him."

"Why?"

"As I see it, he is the only one who can disrupt our plan. His conscience might get in the way. Some of these documents have recommended dates for attacks. Dignitaries scheduled to be in attendance. Look at this one." Boris held up a paper for Fletcher to see. "There will be a Queen in attendance. And that isn't the only event where someone of notoriety from another country will be present. Can you imagine, Fletcher? Not only will the citizens of the U.S. be terrified, but other nations will turn on this country, and its government, for failing to protect their famous citizens."

Fletcher's smile broadened. "Brilliant."

Boris leaned back. Crossed his legs. He opened a drawer and pulled out two cigars. He pointed one in Fletcher's direction.

"Yes, please," Fletcher said.

Boris clipped the ends and handed one to Fletcher. Pulled out two wooden matches and lit them.

"Have you spoken with him yet?" Fletcher asked.

"Ivanov?" Boris nodded. "I let him know we had something special in our possession."

"Are you going to go see him? Or will he be coming here?"

"God, I hope not," Boris said. "Old bastard gives me the creeps."

Both men laughed.

"I've never met him," Fletcher said after the laughter had trailed off.

"You're lucky. He's a, what do they say here in the U.S., a heartless bastard. But he's in charge now. Has been since Dorofeyev and his men were murdered off the southern coast of France."

"What ever happened with that? They caught the assassin, yes?"

"Yes. Black Dolphin is what happened."

Fletcher lifted his shoulders and shuddered.

"Didn't take long for him to die there," Boris said.

Silence fell over the room. The men smoked and stared at the papers spread across the desk.

"Jack something or other," Boris said.

"What's that?"

"The assassin. His name was Jack."

"Wish I would have been there. He would not have gotten away with it."

Boris rested his cigar along the edge of a large glass ashtray. "Likewise, my friend. Likewise."

23

Pierre slid across the backseat of the stopped cab, and opened the door, and stepped out onto the curb. The driver didn't get out. Only popped the trunk. Pierre walked around the back of the taxi and grabbed his two gray duffel bags. He closed the trunk lid and the cab sped off.

Pierre moved to the curb and scanned the crowded sidewalk and street. He didn't know who or what he was looking for. Charles had told him that he needed to be at the corner of Madison and Market in Manhattan by ten-thirty a.m.

Pierre looked at his watch. Nine-thirty a.m. He ignored the crowds and looked for a place to grab a cup of coffee. Spotted a cafe a block and a half away on the other side of the street. He adjusted the handle straps in his hands and started down the sidewalk. A break in the traffic gave him the chance to cross the street. After another half block he walked into the small cafe named *Cuppa*.

An attractive early twenty-something woman with short blond hair streaked with pink smiled at him from behind the counter.

"What can I get you? Cappuccino? Maybe an iced coffee? You look like an iced coffee kinda guy."

"Espresso. Double."

"You Dutch?"

Pierre laughed. The woman's smile broadened and she winked.

"I'm French," he said.

"Well I'm Marcy." She turned her back to him and started on his order. "How long have you been in New York?"

"Two hours, give or take."

"Fresh off the boat, eh?"

"Excuse me?"

She turned and placed his drink on the counter. "Just an expression, hun. So what brings you to New York? Business or pleasure?"

He took a moment before answering. Sniffed the black liquid in the small cup in his hand. The smell matched the drink, dark and bold.

"Business. Definitely not pleasure."

She leaned across the counter. Her unbuttoned blouse revealed her small, bare breasts. She said, "I can add the pleasure if you are going to be in town for a few days."

Pierre lifted his gaze from her breasts to her eyes. He smiled. Shook his head. "Thank you for the coffee."

"Espresso."

"Right, double."

He took a seat in the corner. Got up and grabbed a copy of the *Times* from the table next to him and buried his face in the paper for the next fifteen minutes. He felt her staring at him, but did not look over at the counter. He might be thousands of miles from Kat, but that didn't mean he could indulge in guilty pleasures. It didn't take long for the other side of his conscience to create a somewhat convincing argument.

Kat hadn't seemed happy when he told her he had to go to the U.S. for a job. She looked sad, in fact. It didn't matter that with the job came the promise of enough money for them to semi-retire for a few years. Enough time for Pierre to sort himself out mentally. And it wasn't like he couldn't do a job or two on the side from the French Riviera. Many people who deserved to die passed through Monte Carlo on a daily basis. He just had to get his name out there.

He didn't know for sure that Kat would be waiting for him when he got back. He had a feeling that she would take off. Leave her job and apartment and even her cat behind if necessary in an effort to give Pierre the slip.

He finished his espresso. Dropped the newspaper on the table. Got up and went to the door. He heard a sigh from behind him. He opened the door an inch or two and stopped. Turned around.

Pierre said, "Do you have a phone number?"

Marcy smiled and handed him a slip of torn notepad paper. He took it from her hand and stuck it in his pocket without reading it. If he read it, the number would be committed to memory. He still hadn't decided whether or not he would call her. Better to not have the number stored where he could easily access it until he made a decision he couldn't back out of. Besides, he didn't know that he would still be in New York come nightfall.

Pierre merged onto the sidewalk and walked to the corner. There, he joined a throng of people waiting to cross the street. A man made of light bulbs changed from orange to white and the group moved like an amoeba across the asphalt.

He walked until he reached the corner of Madison and Market. Looked at his watch. Ten a.m. He spotted a row of bistro tables outside a restaurant and took a seat.

A waiter walked out. "What can I get you to drink?"

"I'm waiting for someone."

"Better go wait somewhere else then, pal."

Pierre felt the rage build inside of him. The muscles in his chest and upper arms constricted. He knew that the man would last no longer than ten seconds if Pierre decided to take him out. He smiled.

"I'll have a coffee then."

The waiter disappeared into the restaurant.

"I'm back," Pierre whispered under his breath. He felt more like himself than he had in a long time. He wondered if being on the job would bring him full circle. Back to the man he was. The man he wanted to be again.

He lit a cigarette while waiting for the waiter to return with his coffee. He already felt amped from the double espresso, but figured a little more caffeine wouldn't hurt. He spotted a white Mercedes as it pulled up to the curb. The tinted rear passenger window rolled down. Pierre instinctively reached for his gun. Came up empty handed.

A thin older Asian man peered over his sunglasses at Pierre.

"Mr. Pierre?"

Pierre pulled five dollars from his pocket and dropped it on the table. Picked up his bags. Walked over to the Mercedes.

He said, "You Charles's boss?"

The old man nodded then called to the driver. "Help Mr. Pierre with his bags."

A large, burly man got out of the car and rounded the back. Opened the trunk. Placed Pierre's bags inside. He motioned for Pierre to follow him. They waited at the back corner of the car for a break in the traffic. They didn't have to wait long. The man opened the rear driver's side door and waved Pierre inside.

Pierre took a seat next to the old man. "Where will I be staying?" He hoped the old man would tell him that he'd be staying at one of those posh hotels that overlooked Central Park.

"With me. For tonight, at least. Tomorrow you'll be on a plane."

Pierre felt the paper in his pocket with Marcy's number written on it. He crumpled it in his hand.

"A plane to where?"

The old man smiled without looking at Pierre. His yellow stained teeth blended with his aged skin. "I promise to tell you tomorrow, Mr. Pierre."

"You don't have to go to the trouble of putting me up for the night. I can get a hotel by the Park."

"Nonsense," the old man said. "You will stay with me. It's no trouble. Besides, I can't risk having you get into any trouble and revealing your reasons for being in the States."

Great. Stuck with this old bastard all night.

Pierre shrugged and stared out the window. The car sped up and then stopped. The process played out several more times. People on the sidewalk went from blurs to still images and back to blurs again. He thought about Marcy from the cafe. Her imaged blurred, too, into that of Kat. He reached inside his jacket for his phone. Thought better of it. He'd wait until he was at the old man's house. He'd have privacy there. Besides, the old bastard might confiscate his phone and replace it with one that could track Pierre.

"Driver, stop." The old man shifted in his seat and removed his glasses. He stared at Pierre for a moment. "Are you sure you can do this?"

"I've been doing this since I was twenty," Pierre said without hesitation.

"I understand that. I've killed for a long time, too. Still, it might give me pause to take out someone I've known and fought alongside of."

Pierre's eyes flitted between those of the old man. Deep lines etched themselves into the sides of the old man's face and ran down his cheeks.

Pierre said, "It's business. That's all. I accepted the job. I can do whatever you need me to do."

"Driver, continue." The old man didn't change his position in his seat. "Jack Noble, a friend of yours, correct?"

"Was," Pierre said. "He's dead."

"Yes, so I've heard. But he has, or had I suppose, an associate. A large man."

"Bear."

"Yes, Logan I believe is his last name."

Pierre didn't need to ask anything else to confirm what he knew. But he did anyway.

"What about him?"

"He is your target. There is a little girl that travels with him—"

"Clarissa? The redhead?"

The old man clenched his jaw and made a fist. "If you happen to see her, kill her as well. But, no, I am referring to a child."

Pierre stuck out his hands, palms up. He'd do just about anything for the amount of money the old man was offering. But there was a line and that line was close to being crossed.

"No children. I won't kill a child."

"Heavens no, Mr. Pierre. I do want her returned to me, though. She is the daughter of a woman who I employed. The woman met an unfortunate ending, and I feel obligated to make sure the girl is taken care of."

The smile on the old man's face sent shivers down Pierre's spine. He had met many men he classified as evil during his twenty years with the agency. But none as evil as the old man. He thought he might be in the presence of the devil himself.

The old man continued. "She might not be with Mr. Logan, though. If she's not, you let me know and I'll give you her location."

"Why not give it to me now?"

"I'll give it to you when you need it. Anyway, if you have to travel to that location to find her, then there will be a bonus job available. It'll pay you handsomely."

"How handsomely?"

"Twice what this job pays."

Pierre ran his fingers along his jawline, feeling the prickliness of his stubble.

"Why don't I start there then?"

"I appreciate your enthusiasm. I'll consider it."

"Sir," the driver said. "We're here."

24

"DOESN'T THE TRAFFIC EVER END?" JACK SAID.

The drive had already taken ten minutes longer than the expected twenty. And they still had a few miles to go.

"Nope," Jasmine said. "You can be driving through the city at eight o'clock at night and get stuck in a backup."

"At least in New York you can walk everywhere or take the subway or a bus."

"Yeah, they really didn't plan that well down here. It just kind of exploded on them, I guess."

Jasmine slowed the car down as they approached the entrance to the neighborhood. She turned right and pulled to the curb twenty yards later.

"OK, Jack. No heroics. Got it? If we are seen, we just keep driving. If we are made, then we call it in and wait for another team."

Jack broke his gaze from a yellow lab sitting behind a chain link fence and turned to face Jasmine. He didn't know what he was going to do. A plan had not yet formed in his mind. He felt so far away from this aspect of his life that he was sure that anything he decided would result in a catastrophe for anyone and everyone in the immediate vicinity.

"You're on point, Jazz. Not me. I'll follow your lead."

"OK. And don't call me Jazz."

Jack smiled and held up his hands. "You got it, ma'am."

She shot him a look and dropped the shifter into drive. Pulled away from the curb and drove two blocks before making a right turn. She nodded as they approached a two story colonial with white siding and red trim. "That's it. Number two-two-four."

Jack placed his elbow on the window sill and covered the lower half of his face with his palm. He turned his head slightly to take in as much of the house and the surrounding yard as he could. Four windows downstairs with a red front door in the middle. Three windows upstairs. A six foot wooden privacy fence on either side of the house. Two cars parked in the driveway. One of them was a beater. Looked like an old Toyota pick-up truck. The other was a late model Lexus. The lawn was neatly manicured with rock-ringed trees, and hedges in front of the house.

"Can we make another pass?"

Jasmine nodded. She pointed at the dead-end cul-de-sac ahead of them. "We'll turn around there and go by again."

"Anything look out of place to you, Jazz?"

"No. And stop calling me Jazz."

She kept the car at a steady fifteen miles per hour. They passed the house on the passenger side of the car and Jack had the best vantage point. He made a mental note of the license plates so that they could call them in from the hotel. He also zeroed in on the front door. Above the doorknob were three security locks. He assumed that there were at least two more on the inside that could not be unlocked from the outside. A chain and a bolt, he figured.

He noticed a black and orange sign posted on the fence. It said "Beware of Attack Dog" and had a picture of a Doberman Pinscher below the lettering. While he didn't have a plan yet, he knew that he didn't want to enter the house through the back yard. Killing a dog was not something he wanted to include.

"Did you see it?" he asked.

"Wait a minute." Jasmine kept her eyes straight ahead. She said, "Jack, look."

Jack spun his head forward and scanned the street. A man dressed in a silver and blue track suit walked on the sidewalk, toward them. He held a leash in his right hand. A Doberman was attached to the end of the leash. Flanking the man were two bodyguards, dressed similarly. They stayed back ten yards or so. All three men had the distinctive bulge of a weapon protruding from each man's right hip.

Jack said, "That's our guy."

Jasmine gripped the steering wheel with both hands and maintained a steady speed. She kept her head forward, but Jack could see that her eyes had shifted to the left to watch the man.

She said, "I think you're right."

"I know I'm right," Jack said. "That's the dog from the fence."

"What?"

"Attack dog. Warning sign on the fence."

Jasmine did not reply.

The man looked at them as they passed. Jack felt his stomach tighten and his hand instinctively reached for his gun.

The man nodded and gave a waist high half-wave.

Jack relaxed and sunk in his seat.

"He must think we live in the neighborhood."

"That might work in our favor, Jack. A man like that, probably remembers everything. He sees us again, walking down the street, whatever. He'll recognize us and not associate us with a threat."

"We need to get a dog."

"What?"

"A dog to walk."

"Ah. I gotcha, Jack."

A plan started to form. It was just the bones, but before he could flesh out anything, it helped to have a proper structure in place. "Look for a park. Or a dog park. Something like that nearby."

"Google it."

"What?" Jack said.

"Use your phone," Jasmine said.

Any concessions that Jack had made toward technology had evaporated during his six months in Greece. He'd have been driving all over this neighborhood and the next looking for a dog park if he were alone.

He pulled out his phone and tapped at the touch screen. He found an icon labeled "GPS" and pressed it. A few moments later a map pulled up with their location centered.

"There it is." Jack pointed at his phone. "Turn left out of the neighborhood and drive one more block down the main road. Big park with a dog park."

"And that's where the dog comes in, right?"

"You got it."

Perhaps they wouldn't have to use force with this man. They might be able to strike up a conversation with him. After all, that's the way these cells operated. Assimilate into the local community and attack when the time came. The man might be more open than he normally would be if he assumed they were a couple from the area. Maybe they could get Frank to find a house they could use. Jack realized that wouldn't work. The lead time required would be too great to pick up a rental home. They did have the option of forcing a family out of their home, but that could have consequences.

Jack didn't want to forget the details of the house so he shifted the conversation back in that direction. "So did you notice anything out of ordinary at the house?"

"Um, not sure, Jack. What are you angling toward here?"

"Think, Jasmine. It was right there in plain view."

He saw her eyebrows lift into her forehead and sink back down. They did this four or five times. She had both hands on the wheel. Her index fingers raised up and danced side to side as she processed the scene in her mind.

She said, "The blue truck?"

"Right."

"It was totally out of place. Didn't belong in the neighborhood. Shouldn't have been parked next to a Lexus."

"You got it."

"So what's it doing there?"

What was it doing there? Jack hadn't placed it just yet. He only had a hunch. "It's gotta belong to someone in the group, but not so close that they would live at the house or high ranking enough to be given a top notch car."

"Someone recruited then. Right?"

"Yeah, most likely. Brought in after. Not trusted. Not from Russia."

"You don't know that for sure. They could be Russian."

"OK," Jack said. "I'll concede that. But if they are from Russia, they didn't come over with Chernov."

Jasmine nodded in short quick movements. It made sense to Jack and he felt like he had convinced her as well.

"I got the plate numbers," he said. "Let's call those in."

Jasmine pulled the car into the park's main lot. They stopped under a blooming Dogwood tree. She pulled out her cell phone and pushed a few buttons. Held the phone to her ear.

"Hey Frank," she paused. "Yeah, we got something for you." She lowered the phone and looked at Jack. "What are those license plate numbers, Jack?"

He closed his eyes and read off the first tag and then the second. Jasmine repeated them into the phone and then covered the receiver.

"He's looking them up now."

Jack felt certain that the Lexus would come back to Chernov or an alias. He wondered if the beat up truck belonged to one of the men who had been walking with Chernov, or if the man had been inside the house. And if so, what was he doing in there?

"You have a name for the Lexus? OK, what is it?"

Jack looked at Jasmine. In his hands were a pen and pad of paper. He waited for her to repeat the name.

"Evan Lowery. OK, you close on the truck yet?" She paused. "OK, Frank."

Jack wrote the name down and gestured toward Jasmine to get her attention.

She covered the mouthpiece on the phone again. "Yeah?"

"Get him to run an alias check on that name. I'm betting it comes back to our man."

She nodded and spoke into the phone. "Hey Frank, check Chernov's file for any aliases. See if that Lowery name shows up. If not, do a cross check on both names and see what matches."

She gave Jack a wink. Said, "Good thinking."

Jack waited for the second name. He realized that the job was coming back to him. Bits and pieces. Slowly but surely. It had been eight years since he last associated himself with the SIS. He felt as though he had refined his skills in those eight years working for himself. Maybe this was the job for him. Of all the agencies, the SIS had the least to do with government bureaucracy.

"The owner on the truck," she paused. "Kenneth Quioness." She turned and looked at Jack. "OK. Jack, you got that?"

"Spell the last name," Jack said.

"Frank, how do you spell that last name?" She repeated the spelling out loud. "Got it, Jack?"

Jack scribbled the name down. He said, "Yeah, I got it. What else do we know about him?"

Jasmine asked Frank. A moment later they had his date of birth, place of employment and his home address.

"Alright," Jack said. "I think we should visit Kenny this afternoon."

25

BEAR AND DETECTIVE LARSEN SAT IN A PARKED CAR ON A STRETCH OF HIGHWAY between two small bridges. They waited for the man who Larsen had finally identified to Bear as Curtis Hale.

They had arranged a plan with Curtis. He was to report to work this morning. He'd find a way to check on Mandy. After he confirmed the girl was alive and OK, he would inform his supervisor that he needed to go to the store for some basic household items. Instead of driving south into town, he would go north on highway 14 and meet Bear and Larsen to deliver the update.

"You think he's gonna show?" Bear asked.

Larsen shrugged. "Your guess is as good as mine. Can you blame him if he doesn't?"

"Nah. The way I see it, he knows he's a dead man. He gets caught, they'll kill him. He doesn't do what we want, I'll kill him."

Larsen shook his head. "Don't tell me things like that. I took an oath, you know."

Bear laughed. He couldn't imagine Larsen trying to haul him into the police station. Especially not with how entrenched the detective had become in the outcome of this situation. Besides, he had already said half the department was on the take. Suspicion raised in Bear's mind. Maybe Larsen himself was in that half that supported the Russian. He decided he'd have to find a way to test his new associate.

"I think that's him," Larsen said as he pointed toward an oncoming car.

Bear got out of the car and stood at the rear of the vehicle.

The car slowed down, and pulled over, and parked in front of them. Grill to grill.

Bear waited for Larsen to initiate contact with the man and then he stepped forward. He said, "How is she?"

Curtis Hale looked between Bear and the detective. Then he looked down at the ground.

"I—I couldn't get in to see her."

"What do you mean?" Bear did his best to reign in his temper.

"They have a guard near her door. I tried. You know, I brought her a snack but..."

Bear placed his hands on his hips. Turned toward Larsen.

"Why would they have a guard at her door?"

Larsen thought about it for a moment and then hiked his shoulders in the air. "Not sure."

"I saw her though," Curtis said.

"How'd she look?" Bear asked.

"Fine. Scared. She smiled at me when I made eye contact with her, though. So, she must not be too scared, I guess."

"She's been through this before," Bear said.

Curtis shook his head and held out his hands.

"I'm not asking. I'm telling you. She's been through this before."

Larsen spoke next. "We have the supplies in the trunk." He led Curtis to the rear of the car to grab two paper shopping bags full of items.

Bear remained at the front of the car. He didn't get the exact information he wanted. He was happy to know that Mandy was alive, though. He had to find a way to reach her. The thought of her being inside that house with a terrorist ate at him. He reached into his pocket and pulled out a camera. He stopped Curtis on his way back to his vehicle.

"This is what you are going to do," Bear said. "You take this camera and you get me photos of the outside of the house. The street, the driveway, the front and back of the house. You get me pictures of the inside. When you step inside. The path you take to Mandy's room. The kitchen, the garage, even the bathrooms. I want it all on this camera. We'll come to you tonight."

Larsen lifted his hand and opened his mouth to speak. Bear shot him a look and Larsen backed down. Nothing was going to stop the big man from getting his girl back.

"Do you understand?" Bear said.

"Yeah," Curtis said as he took the camera from Bear's outstretched hand. "I got it. I'll get that for you. As much as I can."

"All of it," Bear said.

Curtis nodded and got inside his car. He started the engine and backed up twenty feet and then made a U-turn onto the road.

After the car disappeared from sight, Larsen turned to Bear and said, "It's good to know she's alive."

Bear said nothing. He stared into the woods that blocked the view of the lake.

"We'll get her back, Bear."

"We can't wait much longer."

"I," Larsen paused a beat. "I'll do everything I can to help you."

"Why?" Bear asked. "Why are you risking your neck like this?"

"It's personal."

Bear thought for a minute on how to respond to this. After all, Larsen had interjected himself into one of the most personal situations in Bear's life. What could be so bad that he would hold out now? That he didn't want Bear to know about?"

"What is it?" Bear asked.

Larsen turned around and headed back to the car without responding.

Bear rejoined him in the car. He didn't press the issue. The detective would talk when he felt like talking.

"I want to see the house," Bear said.

Larsen shook his head. He pulled onto the road. Did twenty over the speed limit all the way to town. He stopped a block from City Hall. Said to Bear, "Get out here."

Bear opened his door and dropped his size fifteen onto the street.

"Come by around six. OK, Larsen?"

The detective nodded and pulled away. Bear looked around for something to do. Found nothing. He walked home and took a nap.

26

"WHAT THE HELL ARE YOU DOING IN THERE?" RANDY CALLED FROM THE ROOM.

Clarissa rolled her eyes and didn't respond. She returned her attention to the mirror and the dye in her hair. Another ten minutes, then she could rinse it out. She had already placed the contact lenses in her eyes. The lenses turned her eyes from blue to dark brown. Quite a change in and of itself. She was curious to see what she would look like when she rinsed the dye out of her hair and eyebrows. Her dark red hair would be dark brown.

Randy pounded on the door and yelled something unintelligible.

"What?" she said. "I'll be done when I'm done. Go away."

She had picked out fifteen items lying around the room and bathroom that she could kill him with. If he were any other man she might have done it by now. But she knew that she'd have to get one hell of a drop on Randy to take him out. He was ruthless. A psychopath, in fact. He was the only member of Sinclair's team that routinely worked alone. And it was easy to see why.

He knocked on the door and yelled again.

Clarissa didn't respond. She heard him walk away and flop on the bed. What the hell was the rush? Was something predetermined? Had it all been a lie and he was taking her somewhere else?

She pushed the questions from her mind and turned on the water. Leaned over the sink and started to rinse a section of her hair. She wanted to double check and make sure it had changed colors before stepping into the shower to rinse out the remaining dye.

She grabbed a towel and blotted the section of hair. Satisfied with the transformation, she turned on the shower and slipped out of her robe. Before stepping into the stand-up shower stall, she made sure that the bathroom door was locked. She wasn't afraid of Randy doing something to her, but she wouldn't put it past him to try and sneak-a-peek at her.

She finished her shower and dried off. She searched through drawers under the sink until she found a hair dryer. Working from memory, she styled her hair like the woman in the picture. The transformation was complete. The transformation was amazing. Clarissa stared at herself in the mirror, but it was as if she stared at someone else entirely.

She dressed and put on minimal make-up. Walked out of the bathroom and over to the round table at the far end of the room. There, she took a seat and opened the documents Sinclair had given her.

Randy sat up and said, "Well, look at what we got here. You look halfway decent now."

Clarissa ignored him and said nothing.

"I think I'd consider hitting that," Randy said.

Clarissa looked up and laughed. "Even if I…" She waved him off and returned to the documents.

"Yeah, whatever," Randy said. He stood and pulled his greasy hair back into a pony tail. "Finish up. It's about time to get you on your way."

"Where are we going?"

"The airport."

"What's the plan?"

"You're gonna walk in, and then you're gonna walk out a bit later."

Clarissa placed her palms on the table and pushed herself up. She pulled back the blinds and scanned the parking lot. Habit more than anything else.

"What if they are watching the airport? Won't it look odd if I walk in and walk back out?"

Randy walked over to the closet and grabbed a bag. Tossed it on the bed.

"Put those on. Pull your hair up under the ball cap."

Clarissa rolled across her bed and stood in the small aisle between the two queen beds. She picked up the bag and dropped its contents onto the blue comforter. She sorted through the clothes. A pair of jeans with torn knees. A gray t-shirt with the American flag on it. A pair of Chuck's that looked fifteen years old. And a plain dark blue baseball cap.

She said, "You shouldn't have."

"Least I could do. Only cost me eight bucks at Goodwill. Don't worry about paying me back unless, you know, you want to do it sexually."

She rolled her eyes and lifted the left side of her mouth in a smile that said "Go screw yourself, Jackwagon." She grabbed the clothes and returned to the bathroom. She shook the clothes out. Nothing fell out, but that didn't ease her mind about their condition.

She stepped out of the bathroom looking like a scarecrow. She belonged in a cornfield, not a hotel room. She tucked her hair under the hat and walked over to the table. Her files were missing.

She asked, "Where'd everything go?"

"Sinclair's orders. You won't need that stuff. In fact, if you had documents on this Enya chick you're supposed to be —"

"Anastasiya."

Randy threw his hands up in the air and said, "Whatever, like I care. Anyways, you roll in there with those docs, you're dead. Now, it makes no difference to me. But Sinclair seems to think that you're our best option for this operation. You succeed and everything's cool, right. You fail and, well, that's when I get some action."

Clarissa said nothing. She put her clothes into the empty bag and left the room. Randy followed her out and met her at the elevator lobby.

"What about luggage?" she said.

Randy shrugged.

"I should have luggage, shouldn't I? They'd be expecting that."

"For Christ's sake, Clarissa. Yeah, we got your luggage in the car. Don't worry. Sinclair arranged everything."

A ding sounded and the elevator doors opened. They stepped in. Randy continued complaining. "I can't wait to get back to friggin' Minnesota. Away from you."

Clarissa tuned him out. She started to step through the next few hours in her mind. They'd get to the airport and she'd get away from Randy. Hopefully it would be the last she'd see of him, unless she was ordered to put a bullet in his head. How fun that would be. She smiled.

Randy noticed. "What?"

She shook her head and shrugged. They reached the lobby, and she left the elevator and crossed the room. She waited outside for at least thirty seconds before Randy made his way out of the hotel.

"There," he said, pointing toward a silver SUV. It wasn't the same vehicle they used the previous night.

It took twenty minutes to reach the airport. They didn't talk during the drive. They didn't talk when Randy stopped at the curb and let Clarissa out. She hoped she'd never have to talk to him again.

She hopped out and opened the rear passenger door and grabbed the bag with her clothes and her luggage. Then she closed the door and didn't look back as Randy and the SUV pulled away.

The airport was like any other medium-sized International airport. People milled about on the walkway. Some smoking, some talking, others waiting for their ride. A few cars idled along the curb. One of them might be full of Russians, and with that thought, Clarissa entered the airport. She saw a sign for restrooms. Made her way to the lady's room.

Five minutes later she stood in front of a mirror in fresh clothes. At her feet was her new luggage. The ragged clothes she wore into the airport were now in the trashcan. Her hair was a disheveled mess after being tucked up under a ball cap for close to an hour. She pulled a brush out of her bag and worked through the tangles. After dealing with her hair, Clarissa applied more make up than she would normally wear. Just in case she had been spotted on the way in.

She took a step back and looked at herself.

If only Jack could see me now.

Clarissa checked her watch. It was time. She smiled at her reflection and grabbed her luggage and left the bathroom.

The short walk from the restroom to the exit took no more than thirty seconds. The warm air that had been beaten back by her jeans now felt cool as it slipped between her bare legs and under her dress. She stopped just outside the door. Closed her eyes and breathed in deeply. The air smelled like gasoline fumes and burned out cigarette butts. She didn't care.

"Anastasiya."

She opened her eyes. A stocky balding man made his way toward her. She smiled and nodded. She remembered him from the file. Said, "Akim. So good to see you."

He spoke in Russian. "We were getting worried. You should have been out here twenty minutes ago."

She replied in Russian, "I was hungry."

Akim smiled and gave her a pat on the back. He reached out and took her luggage.

She wished she had inspected the bags further.

He led her to a red two-door Nissan and opened the passenger door. He pulled the seat forward and then tossed her luggage in the back seat. After returning the seat back to its normal position, he gestured her inside the car.

Clarissa slipped inside and buckled up.

"How was your flight?" Akim asked as he closed his door and put the car into first gear.

"Eh, a flight is a flight."

Akim nodded. They merged onto the highway and headed east. After a few minutes he spoke.

"Boris is excited for you to be here. We have the plans and are setting things in motion. Exciting times, Anastasiya."

"Indeed."

27

"THAT'S THE PLACE."

Jasmine pointed at a small brick house with a brown door and matching window shutters. She drove another block and parked the car.

"What a dump," Jack said.

"East Marietta."

Jack looked around at the desolate area. The houses were small and poorly constructed. The lawns were brown. Not uncommon for that time of year. But he could tell that many of them were not cared for during any season.

He said, "I never spent much time down here, so that means little to me."

Jasmine smiled, her eyes focused on nothing in particular. "I was raised near here."

Jack decided to change the subject. "There's an Air Force base nearby, isn't there?"

"Yeah. Dobbins. Not too far away." She grabbed her door handle and pulled on it. "You ever stationed there?"

"I was in the Marines."

"That means no?"

Jack didn't respond. He got out of the car and started walking toward Kenneth Quioness's house. The house was small. Jack estimated it at less than one thousand square feet.

"Driveway's empty."

"No garage."

"No one home."

"We should knock first, Jack."

Jack shrugged. He crossed the dead lawn and knocked on the battered door. Chips of brown paint hung from the door and vibrated as his knuckles pounded against the wood. They waited a minute and no one answered. Jack placed his ear to the door and listened. All quiet. He nodded toward a window.

He said, "Take a look in there."

Jasmine scanned the area and then peeked through the window. "It's a mess. But it looks empty. Like nobody's home"

Jack grabbed the door handle. To his surprise it was unlocked. He turned the knob and pushed the door open. He let Jasmine walk through first and then followed. He held his Glock in his hand and kept it aimed in front of him.

"I'm gonna check the back," Jack said. "You stay in here."

She nodded.

"Stay alert," Jack added.

He walked down a dark hall. There were three doors. Two on either side and one at the end. He figured the one at the end was to a bathroom. Opened that door first, slowly and cautiously. It was a bathroom, and it was empty. He pulled back the shower curtain just to make sure. He left the room and closed the door. Next he opened the door to his right. The room was bare. Just some trash on the floor in one corner. The room had a lingering smell that Jack associated with marijuana.

He checked the closet and found it to be empty. He wondered if Kenneth might have grown pot in the room at one time.

He returned to the hall and closed the door behind him. He stopped before opening the next door. Closed his eyes and listened. Nothing going on in the front of the house. Not a sound coming from the back.

He took his time opening the door. He stuck the barrel of his gun through the small crack and then pushed the door open the rest of the way. A bed was pushed against the far wall. A stack of clothes five feet wide and four feet high leaned against another wall. The clothes were not folded and were just strewn about. This room had a distinct smell as well. It smelled like rotten eggs.

Jack checked the closet, using his gun to move hanging clothes side to side.

Then he checked under the bed covers and finally under the bed itself. He left the room, closing the door behind him.

He reached the end of the hall and saw Jasmine standing by the window, staring out at the street.

"Any movement?" he asked.

"No. Anything back there?"

"A bathroom, an empty room that smells like pot, and a messy bedroom."

"Think he lives alone?"

"I'd bet on it. House is missing that feminine touch."

He joined Jasmine by the window and stared at the empty street.

"When I was a girl, we used to visit my grandparents every week. They lived one block over." Jasmine nodded toward a side street. "Back then, kids were everywhere. Outside playing. Riding bikes. It was fun to come visit."

Jack said nothing. He watched Jasmine's face as she spoke. Her smile slowly faded and her eyes darkened.

"Then things changed. The neighborhood went south. More kids with no respect for their parents or the elders of the community or any kind of authority." She paused and cleared her throat. Crossed her arms. "My grandparents were murdered in their house."

"Jesus."

Jack placed a hand on her shoulder. She lowered her shoulder and turned.

"It happened ten years ago. A year before that my father, who was in New York training for his new job, died."

"How?"

"He was in the North Tower."

Jack nodded and said nothing. He had a feeling Jasmine wasn't through. He also realized that was the reason behind her decision to not become a lawyer.

"Then two years later, a year after my grandparents were murdered, my mother killed herself on the second anniversary of my father's death." She crossed the room and leaned against the back wall. "I had already left by then. Was in my last year of law school. I don't know that I ever really grieved over any of it, Jack. I didn't have the time. I couldn't spare the time. And I can't help thinking that if I had come back home, been there for her, that at least she'd be alive."

Jack walked up to her and reached for her shoulders. "You couldn't have known. Even if you were here she still might have done it."

"I know. I know you're right. Still—"

"What was that?"

They both rushed to the window and saw the man they believed to be Kenneth Quioness getting out of his beat up blue pick-up truck. He was tall and wide with a full head of bushy, curly brown hair. He moved with a hint of athleticism. Jack realized taking the man down might be a challenge.

"Let's go to the kitchen," Jack said.

They crossed the room and ducked into the kitchen. The front door opened. Kenneth's heavy steps reverberated throughout the cheap flooring. He came toward the kitchen. Toward them.

Jack gestured for Jasmine to duck behind the island. He stood still, his gun aimed at the narrow opening between the living room and kitchen.

Kenneth walked in with his head down. It took a full three seconds before he noticed Jack standing there.

"Don't move," Jack said.

"Who the hell are you?"

Jack failed to place the man's accent. He said, "I'll be asking the questions. Have a seat." Jack gestured with his gun toward the table butted up against the wall.

Kenneth stood there for a moment. Was he going to sit? Or did he have something else in mind? Finally he reached across and pulled out a chair and sat down.

"What were you doing at Lazar Chernov's house this morning?" Jack said.

"That's between me and Mr. Chernov," Kenneth said.

"No, that's between all of us. What were you doing there?"

"I'm not going to tell you that."

Jack smiled. He stepped out from behind the island and walked toward the table. He reached out, grabbed a chair and pulled it away from the table. He sat down. The whole time he kept his gun aimed at the large man.

Jack said, "Mr. Chernov is believed to be a terrorist. You spent time with him today. I believe you might be a terrorist. Do you know what we do to terrorists?"

"Blow them?"

Jack cocked a fake half-smile. Then he rushed to his feet. Yanked the table away from the wall and threw it behind him. He kicked Kenneth's chair out from under the man. Kenneth crashed to the floor.

"What the hell?" Kenneth said as he used the wall to get to his feet. He leaned over and rubbed his right hip and knee. "I could take you out right here man."

Jack placed his gun on the counter. Kenneth's eyes locked on the Glock. Jack knew to get anything out of this man he would have to beat him. At this point he knew that Kenneth had no respect for him.

Jack said, "Go for it, man. See if you can get it."

Kenneth lunged forward. He took two lumbering steps toward the island in the middle of the kitchen.

Jack twisted his body and leapt in the air. He whipped around and drove his elbow into the bridge of the man's nose. Kenneth grunted and fell to the side, hitting his head on the fridge. He didn't hit the ground, though. Instead he used the fridge for balance and pulled himself up. He reached over the top of the appliance and turned around. In his hand he held a half a bottle of Jack Daniels. Took a step forward and swung wildly at Jack.

Jack dodged the swing. He leaned in and waited for the big man to try again. He didn't have to wait long. This time Jack ducked the blow. He popped back up, delivering an uppercut that sent his large foe reeling.

Kenneth fell backward. He dropped the bottle on the way down. His back missed the fridge and he hit the ground hard. His head crashed into the floor with a thump.

Jack grabbed his gun off the counter and stuck it in its holster. He grabbed Kenneth by his feet and pulled him back to the middle of the kitchen.

"Get some rope, Jasmine."

Jack lifted the unconscious man off the floor and onto a chair. Jasmine returned with rope and they bound Kenneth's hands and feet. They secured his torso and legs to the chair.

After a few minutes Kenneth came to. He said, "Jesus, man. What the hell is all this?"

"I told you," Jack said. "All I wanted to know was what you were doing at Chernov's house this morning."

Kenneth looked at Jack and then at Jasmine. "Who's the piece?"

Jasmine stepped forward and smiled. Then she kicked Kenneth in the chest. His head snapped back and then fell forward. His face twisted in a painful howl, but no noise escaped his mouth. He fought for breath. His cheeks turned bright red. Finally, he filled his lungs and let out a loud groan.

"To hell with you people," he said.

"Is it worth dying for?" Jack asked.

Jasmine pulled her gun and walked around to the back of Kenneth. She placed the barrel against the man's head.

He shook his head in quick bursts. "OK, OK. I'll tell you. Get her away from me first."

Jack nodded and Jasmine backed away. She circled the island and stood next to Jack.

"I had access to something he wanted," said Kenneth.

"Be more specific," Jack said.

"Materials. I was able to get my hands on them and some other things that Chernov wanted. I never had any real dealings with him prior. Well, just some sales, but that's it."

"What kind of sales?" Jasmine asked.

"Weed," Jack said.

Kenneth nodded. "Yeah, weed. But we got to talking and it turned out I could help him and he offered to pay me a lot of money. Enough money I could get out of here, you know. So I did it."

"What the hell did you get him and what was he going to do with it?" Jack said.

Kenneth said nothing. His breaths quickened and it looked like was going to pass out.

Jack pulled his gun. He jammed it into the side of Kenneth's face, under his cheekbone.

"What the hell did you sell him?"

"He wants to make a bomb, OK?"

Jack eased off the man. Looked up at Jasmine. Their eyes locked and both shared the same look of concern mixed with adrenaline.

"Who else we got down here?" Jack asked.

"I'll call Frank," Jasmine said.

28

Akim navigated the vehicle down the gravel driveway. The car dipped and bounced as it rolled through the narrow opening between the line of trees that wrapped around the property. They pulled into a clearing. An expanse of lush green lawn enveloped a sprawling house.

"Home," Akim said.

Clarissa smiled and said nothing. She figured her time outside would be limited and she began taking a mental inventory of the property. She noted the best place to hide. The best route to take to escape.

Akim pulled into the square courtyard that served as a parking lot. He parked between two luxury sedans and cut the vehicle's engine.

Clarissa reached for her door handle. She stopped when she felt Akim's hand on her left thigh.

"Wait," he said.

She kept her shoulders facing the door. Turned her head. Said, "What are you doing?"

He smiled at her, revealing a pair of chipped and yellow stained front teeth.

"I thought you and I could establish some ground rules now. When we get in there, Boris might—"

"I'll give you a ground rule. Remove your hand from my leg or I'll chop it off while you sleep."

Akim straightened up and pulled back. His smile remained. He held out his hands and said, "I like a tough woman."

Clarissa shifted in her seat. Blinked slowly. Smiled. She struck fast and hard, driving her right palm into Akim's diaphragm.

He bowed forward, striking the steering wheel with his forehead. A guttural exhale escaped his mouth. He clutched at his seat and the dashboard while trying to refill his lungs. His mouth opened and closed and his eyes bugged out. He looked like a fish who just found himself inside an SUV.

"That tough enough?" Clarissa opened her door and stepped out of the car. "Don't forget my things."

Three guards approached and met her in the middle of the courtyard. One of them held out his hand and yelled in Russian for her to stop. She took note of his appearance as the group approached. He stood out from the other two. His hair was gray, thin, and cut close to his head. He wore silver rimmed mirrored sunglasses that were too small for his broad face. He had on sweatpants and a hooded sweatshirt, quite a contrast compared to the youth of the other two men and the tailored suits they wore.

"We've been expecting you Anastasiya," he said.

She smiled and dropped her hands to her side.

"What's Akim doing?" he asked.

Clarissa looked back over her shoulder. Akim still appeared to be hunched over in the front seat.

"He said he needed a moment to catch his breath. He'll be out in a minute. Said he'd get my bags."

"Right. Let's go inside. Boris is looking forward to meeting you."

Clarissa nodded in acknowledgment and followed the older man through the courtyard. The other two guards waited for her to pass. She knew they were following her by the echo of their footsteps.

She scanned the front of the house. Windows lined the exterior. There was barely a stretch of more than eight feet without one. She knew that if it came down to an assault on the house, she would want to be far away from the exterior walls. Bullets would tear through at every angle. Her gaze lifted toward the roof line. She spotted three guards. One positioned at either end of the house, and one in the middle. She assumed there were at least three more taking similar positions at the rear, if the rear was the same shape as the front. She made a mental note to investigate that.

They took the sidewalk to the entrance, passing by hedges and carefully manicured flower beds. Two more guards dressed in dark suits and wielding semi-automatic weapons greeted them with slight head nods when the group rounded the corner and stepped through an opening and onto the front patio. A heavy cast iron gate had been opened in advance of their arrival.

"Stop here," the older man said. He looked past Clarissa and continued. "Go see what is taking Akim so long. We'll wait for you here."

"Quite a place," Clarissa said.

The man nodded and said nothing.

She asked, "What's your name?"

He lowered his sunglasses and stared at her for a moment before responding. "That is not of consequence."

She shrugged and then turned around at the sound of the two guards returning with Akim, who narrowed his eyes and glared at Clarissa.

"Take her bags," the older man said to one of his men. "Let's go in."

One of the men positioned next to the door opened it and gestured the group through.

Clarissa crossed the threshold into the foyer. She quickly dismissed most items she saw as ornamental. She did however take note of the complicated alarm panel. She figured that somewhere else in the house was a matching panel, or one that was even more complicated.

The older man pointed at Clarissa and his men. "Wait here." He took three steps and looked back at the group. "Akim, you come with me."

Akim dropped Clarissa's bags on the floor. He drove his shoulder into her upper back as he passed. The impact knocked her forward a few steps. She refrained from retaliating. Something she was better at these days.

"That's enough of that, Akim," the older man said. "Apologize to Anastasiya."

Akim turned his head enough so that one eye made contact with Clarissa. "Sorry."

Akim and the older man turned down a hallway and disappeared from sight.

Clarissa started to take a step. A hand on her shoulder instructed her to remain in the foyer. She heard a child's voice and caught site of the back of a young girl. Blond hair passed by in a blur. Boris's daughter, she figured.

Although the voice sounded somewhat familiar. Clarissa dismissed it and soaked in every inch of the house available to her.

Footsteps approached and a man appeared. She identified him as Boris based on the pictures she had seen on the flight.

He smiled and held his arms out wide. "Anastasiya, it is so nice to meet you."

Clarissa smiled and stepped forward. She leaned into his embrace and turned her face side to side so he could kiss her cheeks.

"Likewise, Boris."

"Can I get you anything? A drink, some food?"

"Not at the moment. I'd like to see my room."

"Of course." Boris snapped his fingers at one of the men and instructed him to take Clarissa to her room, then bring her to his office. "I'll see you in a few minutes."

Clarissa followed the guard down an unlit hallway and into her room. She dropped her bags on the bed and then stepped into the attached bathroom and washed her hands and face.

A few minutes later she was escorted into Boris's office.

"Please, sit," he said as he waved her escort out of the room.

She sat opposite him at his desk.

"I can't tell you how good it is to have you here," he said.

"Yes, I imagine looking at all these men all the time gets old," she said.

Boris laughed and leaned back in his chair. He clapped his hands together. His smile lingered as he spoke. "I've heard that about you. Very funny."

She lifted her shoulders and held out her hands. *If he only knew.*

"There's a lot I would like to ask you, about things back home," he said. "But I think it's best we get into what we are doing here."

"I agree."

He nodded. "Good." He opened a desk drawer and leaned over it.

Clarissa took it as an opportunity to look over the room. Nothing out of the ordinary. Row upon row of books. At least a thousand of them, maybe more. She wanted to get a better look out the window and the view it provided. She found it odd that there was no way out of the room except for the way she entered.

Boris straightened up and placed a set of files on the desktop. "Wait till you see what we've got here."

Boris rifled through the papers, placing them on the desk in organized stacks. He explained the targets and the opportunities and the best dates to strike. Clarissa nodded and smiled and asked simple questions.

"Now," he said, "for your role in all this."

"Please, do tell."

"I'll oversee the overall operation. But I need people, strong people, to be leaders in certain strategic areas. Three to be exact. One in the east. One in the west. And one in the middle. My three captains, so to speak."

"I've read Machiavelli," she said. "The best way to instill fear in an organization is to lop off the head of one of your captains. Is that in your plans?"

Boris cocked his head and leaned back. His smile returned. His eyes, however, narrowed. Clarissa had the feeling he was wondering if he had misjudged her.

"Only if said captain gives me a reason to lop off his, or her, head," he said.

"Then this captain will make certain that she does everything in her power to make you happy with her work."

Boris nodded and didn't say anything. He didn't take his eyes off of her. Didn't even blink.

"Where do you want to place me?" she said.

Boris stood and stepped away from the desk. He paced the room for a few moments and stopped in front of the window. Clarissa thought to join him, to get a look outside. Decided against it.

He turned his head and made eye contact. "In seven days you will travel to the west coast."

"California?"

"I'll tell you where in seven days."

"Why must it be a secret?"

He turned to face the window again. "Return to your room and get ready for dinner."

Clarissa remained seated for a minute and then got up and walked to the door. She stopped before grabbing the handle. Looked over her shoulder. Boris remained at the window, staring out at nothing as if in a trance. She opened the door and stepped into the hall. No one waited for her.

She walked down the hall, retracing her steps back to her room. A young girl's humming floated down the corridor. The melodic sound became louder as

Clarissa approached an open door. She stopped outside the room. Stepped toward the wall, placing her palms against it. She shifted to the right and peered inside.

Clarissa had never seen a ghost, not that she was aware of at least. But the feeling in her stomach at that moment was what she imagined seeing the spirit of a dead person would feel like.

"Mandy," she said in a voice slightly louder than a whisper.

The little girl turned from her desk. Her eyes grew big and her mouth dropped open.

Clarissa brought a single finger to her lips. She stepped into the room and closed the door. They met halfway and embraced. Mandy buried her face into Clarissa's chest. Clarissa held the girl's head close in an attempt to muffle her sobs. She checked the room for a security camera. Didn't see one.

Mandy stopped crying and pulled her head back. Her blue eyes had become bloodshot and her pale cheeks were stained with tears.

"What are you doing here?" Mandy asked.

"It's hard to explain, sweetie. I'm on a mission. The question is what are you doing here?"

"They stole me at the bank. They hurt Bear and took me."

"Bear is here?"

"We live here now."

"Give me the address, Mandy."

The little girl told Clarissa the address.

"I'm going to get you out of here. You have to trust me."

"OK."

"But I need you to pretend that you don't know me."

"OK."

"They can't know who I am. They think I'm from Russia."

"I won't say anything."

29

BEAR RECLINED ON HIS COUCH, WATCHING THE CLOCK. ONE LEG STRETCHED OUT on the couch. The other on the coffee table. His doorbell rang at six o'clock on the dot. He crossed the room and opened the door without first checking to see who was there. Two uniformed officers stood on his porch. Bear said nothing.

"Riley Logan?"

Bear nodded.

"We need you to ask you a few questions, Mr. Logan."

Bear stepped back and held the door open. "C'mon in."

The police officers stepped inside. One pointed at the couch and nodded at Bear.

Bear took a seat and said, "What can I do for you?"

One of the officers paid no attention to Bear. He walked around the living room, checking behind chairs and tables and books.

The other officer stood in front of Bear. "Where were you around two p.m. this afternoon?"

Bear shrugged. He thought the officers were there to discuss Mandy and the question of his whereabouts threw him off. He had been with Detective Larsen at two p.m. But Larsen had made a point to tell Bear that half the department was being paid off. Could these men be in that half?

"Here. Haven't done much, you know, waiting to hear word about my little girl."

"We have a witness who says they saw you with Detective Larsen, outside of town, around two p.m. today."

Curtis Hale?

Bear said, "Yeah, I guess that sounds about right."

"What were you doing with him?"

Bear lied. "I was showing him the different places we used to go. We went to the lake and I showed him where we went fishing a few weeks ago."

"In this weather?"

"Yeah, in this weather." He knew it sounded bad, but he had to give some reason for being out there.

"What do you do, Mr. Logan?" the other officer said from behind him.

"Huh?"

"For a living. What do you do?"

"I'm independently wealthy. I just raise my little girl. Read. Watch TV."

The officer behind him walked behind the couch. Bear didn't look back.

"Sounds like the life of a slacker."

"I worked for it."

"Why don't you tell us what you were doing with Detective Larsen?"

"I just did."

The cops said nothing. The one behind him rounded the couch and walked to the open front door. He closed the door. Turned the deadbolt to the right, locking it.

Bear started to get a sense that these two officers were in the corrupt half of the department.

Bear asked, "Did something happen to Detective Larsen?"

"Why would you think that?"

Bear placed his hands on his knees and started to stand. Both officers raised their hands and gestured him back down.

"Well," Bear said, "I've been around cops with an agenda. And I'd be hog tied if you two weren't cops with an agenda."

They looked at each other.

"Just tell us what you were doing, Mr. Logan."

Bear felt his cheeks redden and his neck grew hot.

"I told you. He's helping me find my little girl, which is more than you two bastards are doing right now. So I'd appreciate it if you'd get the frig out of my house."

"Detective Larsen is not a good man. Did he tell you what happened?"

Bear had been wondering what Larsen had referred to earlier that day. When Bear pressed, the detective refused to answer.

"You know he lost his own daughter not too long ago?"

Bear shook his head.

"His fault. Recklessness. But he blamed it on someone else and now he has an agenda against that person. We are concerned that he's using you to fulfill his own agenda."

"Don't know what you are talking about," Bear said. "We just went around to places that me and Mandy frequented. There was no talk of an agenda."

One of the officers unlocked the door, opened it and stepped onto the porch. Bear saw him reach into his pocket and pull out a cigarette. He found himself wanting a smoke.

"Mr. Logan, I did some digging around on you. There's not much information out there."

Bear hiked his shoulders up to his ears and held out his hands.

"Why don't you tell me about where you and Mandy were before you came to our city?"

"We were in New York."

"And?"

Bear said nothing.

The cop waited a minute or two before speaking again. "We're watching you, Logan. You best believe we are watching you. One step outta line and we'll put you behind bars for forty-eight hours minimum. If I catch you jaywalking, you'll be arrested. Got it?"

Bear opened his mouth to speak. Paused a moment. The cop stood only a few feet away. The man's posture indicated that he greatly underestimated Bear, and Bear calculated the attack in his mind. He wasn't sure that he could secure the cop's weapon before the other officer could fire a shot.

"Yeah," Bear said. "I got it. Now get the hell off my property."

LARSEN ARRIVED AN HOUR LATER.

"Nice of you to show up," Bear said as he opened the door.

"I was here," Larsen said from the edge of the porch. "I saw the patrol car, though."

Bear stepped outside.

"Who were those jackwagons?"

"Miller and Stevenson."

"Are they on your side?"

Larsen shook his head. He pushed past Bear and walked around the room. He checked in all the same places the cop had earlier.

"What're you looking for?" Bear asked.

Larsen walked over to Bear and spoke in a low voice. "I'm checking for a bug."

"Maybe we should go back outside then. I got questions for you."

Larsen took one last quick glance around the room and then walked outside. Bear followed.

"Tell me about your little girl," Bear said.

Larsen leaned against a support post and reached inside his coat. He pulled out a pack of cigarettes. He lit one and inhaled deeply. After he blew the smoke out, he spoke.

"She died. Four months ago. Hit by a car."

Bear waited for Larsen to continue. When the man didn't say anything else, Bear prompted him for more information. "What happened to the driver?"

"It was a hit and run."

"Were you there?"

Larsen nodded.

"Was it your fault she was in the street?"

Larsen shook his head.

"Did she just take off into the road?"

Larsen rubbed his jaw and thought for a moment.

"She was on the sidewalk. I was in the yard, raking leaves. I heard tires squeal. I turned and saw the car coming down the street. He was on the wrong side of the street. I dropped my shovel. Yelled at my daughter. She was sitting on the sidewalk with a bunch of, uh, sidewalk chalk I guess they call it. Drawing flowers or stars or something. She heard me and turned. Hopped to her feet. The car got closer. I took off in a sprint, but didn't reach her in time. The car hopped the curb and hit her. Her little body..."

Bear knew the rest.

"Jesus, Larsen, I..."

Larsen looked up. His eyes had watered over. They were dark and angry.

"The cops that were here, they said you had an agenda. They also said your daughter's death was your own fault."

Larsen flicked his cigarette onto the lawn. It landed in a small patch of left over snow. He lit another.

"In a way, I guess so."

"How's that?"

"I got too close to Melikov. Brought too much heat. Refused his offer when confronted."

"So you do have an agenda."

Larsen nodded. "He's a bad man. I'd want him taken out no matter what. The fact that he had my little girl killed only resolves me to pull the trigger myself."

"So why haven't you?"

Larsen crossed the porch and placed his hands on the wooden railing. "I've asked that question of myself so many times. I guess, I don't know. I think it's the badge, man. I need to catch him in the act to justify it. If I see the man who drove the car, I'd pull the trigger no matter what. But with Boris, I need something else."

"You got a good enough look at him?"

"Yeah, I saw him. Haven't seen him since, though."

Bear said nothing. He felt and understood the man's pain. They'd both been wronged by the same man and Bear decided that he would do whatever it took to avenge Larsen's daughter and rescue Mandy.

"Our guy's working tomorrow night. Some event, a gala, Boris is having. I think it's our best chance."

"You think we can just walk in there? Surely someone will notice you. Someone will remember me from the bank."

"The event isn't at his place. It's in town."

30

JACK AND JASMINE BROUGHT KENNETH BACK TO THE HOTEL WITH THEM. A GUN in the middle of his back was enough to keep him compliant. They handcuffed him to a chair. They had to wait for Frank to get a team to Atlanta to take over the interrogation. That would free Jack and Jasmine to pursue Chernov. The problem was that Frank couldn't get anyone down till early the next morning. That meant another night of less than adequate amounts of sleep.

They took turns watching over the man. Two hours on, two off. Kenneth didn't seem to mind being watched or the fact that he was handcuffed to an uncomfortable hotel room chair. He fell asleep shortly after ten p.m. and was still asleep at five a.m. when there was a knock at the door.

Jack stood and grabbed his pistol off the bureau. He crossed the room. He checked through the peephole and saw two men dressed in dark suits. He realized that he should have woken Jasmine and have her answer the door since she would recognize anyone that Frank sent.

Jack unlocked the door and opened it. He held his gun behind his back.

"Yeah?" he said.

"You Jack Noble?" one of the men asked.

Jack nodded. Two more people knew that he was alive.

"I'm Fegan, this is Reed."

Fegan stood close to six feet tall and had dark well-groomed hair. He had an athletic build. Looked the part of a government agent. Reed, on the other hand, was shorter than average and about fifty pounds overweight. His thinning hair was wild and unbrushed and his face was covered in stubble. He held a cardboard tray with four cups of what Jack assumed was coffee.

"Come on in, guys," Jack said.

He turned to lead them and saw that Jasmine had got up and was sitting in the chair he had occupied moments ago. He was a bit taken aback that he hadn't noticed her moving in the background. Would he ever regain his edge?

"Morning Jasmine," Fegan said.

She smiled and nodded.

Reed placed the cardboard tray on the table. "Help yourselves." Then he looked at Kenneth and added, "Not you." Reed laughed at his joke. No one else did.

Jack grabbed two cups. Handed one to Jasmine and kept the other for himself.

"So what'll you do with him?" Jack asked.

"We've got a place to take him nearby," Fegan said. "We'll start with the info he gave you and then we'll dig in. I see us becoming great friends over the course of the day. Ain't that right?"

Jack watched as Fegan smiled at Kenneth. It was a cold smile that held a hint of evil. He recognized it and imagined he had held a smile like that a time or two himself.

Jasmine said, "Make sure you give us updates throughout the day. Anything he tells you, I want to know. He knows more than he let on, I'm sure of that." She stared at Kenneth for a moment. "I don't need much, guys. So no matter how trivial you think it is, you tell us."

Fegan shifted his eyes from Kenneth to Jasmine. "You got it. Go ahead and uncuff him from the chair."

Jack reached into his pocket and pulled out a set of keys. He unlocked the handcuffs and removed them from Kenneth's wrists. The man instinctively began to rub his wrists to stimulate feeling and blood flow. Reed pushed in front of Jack and placed a new set of handcuffs on the man.

"Come on, pretty boy," Reed said as he grabbed Kenneth's elbow and pulled him up from the chair.

Kenneth straightened his legs and arched his back. He looked at Jack and gave him a wink and a smile. "Nice working with you, Noble."

Christ, three more people.

JACK AND JASMINE remained in the room. They were waiting for Fegan to get back to them. Jack took it as an opportunity to catch up on his sleep.

He woke and looked toward the window. A thin beam of sunlight squeezed through a sliver of an opening between the heavy drapes and hit him in the eyes. He flinched and covered his face and sat up. Jasmine spoke on the phone, out of sight.

Jack stood up and walked over to the narrow hallway between the main portion of the room and the front door. Jasmine stood in the bathroom with her cell phone to her ear. She smiled at Jack and held a finger in the air.

"OK, Frank. Sounds good. I think we got what we need. Enough to make a move, that's for sure."

She covered the mouthpiece and spoke to Jack. "He cracked. Fast. Gave up everything. We got enough to go in. Fegan and—" She uncovered the mouthpiece and spoke to Frank. "Yeah, that sounds good. We'll wait for them and then plan our next move." She hung up the phone.

"What gives?" Jack said.

"Turns out our boy Kenneth was way more involved that we thought."

"How so?"

"He's Chernov's second in command. This is deep, Jack. Real deep."

"How deep?"

"We don't have a name yet, but Chernov reports to someone else here in the U.S. They have something in the works. From what Kenneth told our guys, they are planning a series of attacks and Chernov is responsible for coordinating everything on the East coast."

"How much is everything?"

"From Boston to Miami."

"We think this guy is credible?"

"Frank's working on that. With the info Ken gave, Frank can do some checking with friends and see if there's any intelligence to corroborate what Ken's telling us."

Jack walked back into the room. He pulled the drapes back and took a seat at the table. The sunlight felt warm on his skin, though he doubted it was as warm outside.

Jasmine grabbed the seat against the wall and dragged it over to the table. She sat down and said, "What's on your mind, Jack?"

"It's too easy."

"How so?"

"It's barely four hours and this guy gives everything up?"

She shrugged. "It's not the first time, Jack. Reed and Fegan are good at what they do." Jasmine's phone rang and she answered it. "Reed, yeah, we're ready to roll." She stood and started toward the door.

Jack got up, grabbed his gun and his jacket. He followed Jasmine through the door and into the hall. She had a ten foot lead on him and he struggled to keep up with the conversation she was having. They reached the car and he got in on the driver's side. Started the engine and waited for Jasmine to join him.

She pulled the door open and finished her conversation and then stepped in.

"Where to?" Jack asked.

Jasmine pulled up directions on the GPS. "We're going to the interrogation house. It's about fifteen miles from here. Shouldn't change our overall distance from Chernov by much."

Jack pulled the car out of the parking lot and followed the directions on the GPS. Jasmine caught him up on the conversation she just had with Fegan.

"They got it all, Jack. The power structure, locations of other cells, even some of the targets they are planning on hitting."

"Why would he do that?"

"They made a few deals with him."

"They wouldn't make the kind of deals that would return that kind of information so soon."

Jasmine said nothing.

"So did he give you the information?"

"No, they have it written down there. We'll review it when we get there. Then we'll get a chance with Ken and you can judge for yourself if he's leading us on. Maybe he is feeling guilty over what he's done now that things are getting close to being real."

"That's another thing. How does this guy go from being on the outside looking in, to being second in command, or whatever he claims to be?"

"I'm guessing he was feeding us a line, Jack."

Jack gave it some thought while the GPS instructed him to turn left and then right. Kenneth had lied to someone at some point in the last twenty-four hours. Who though? Had he lied at the house or had he lied to Fegan and Reed?

The GPS told them to turn right one more time and then said that their destination would be on the left. Jack counted ahead and picked out the house. Noticed the open front door.

"Did you text them and tell them we're close?" Jack asked.

"No," Jasmine said. "You want me to?"

Jack shook his head. Slowed the car down as they passed the house. He was not able to see much through the open doorway.

"What's going on?" Jasmine said.

"Not sure." Jack made a U-turn at the end of the street and drove by the house again. He stopped the car a few houses down and parked next to the curb.

They got out and crossed the lawn. They made their way to the house, staying close to the front of the neighboring houses to shield themselves from view. It was quiet outside. The neighborhood seemed empty. Typical for a weekday in a suburban area.

They reached the house and approached the open doorway. Jack went inside first and Jasmine followed.

"Fegan? Reed?" she called out.

Jack stopped to listen. There was a slight whirring sound in the background. Nothing else. He took the hall and Jasmine went toward the kitchen.

"Jack," she yelled from the kitchen.

He backed out of the hall and crossed the living room. Stepped into the kitchen. Jasmine stood at the front of an island, next to the refrigerator. At her feet was a pool of crimson liquid. Jack walked around the island to the opposite end. He looked down at the floor. There, piled one on top of the other, were the bodies of Fegan and Reed, the heavier Reed on top of Fegan.

Jack knelt down by their heads. Both men had been shot at close range with a small caliber weapon. Two entrance wounds on each of them. Front of the head for Reed. Back of the head for Fegan. No exit wounds.

He looked up at Jasmine, who already had her cell phone out and was dialing.

"Wait," Jack said.

"What?"

"Just wait."

He looked around the kitchen. He hadn't paid attention to the whirring sound until now. He saw that the microwave mounted over the stove top was on and counting down. He stood up and looked inside. A single gray square with pins and wires sticking out of it turned in a circle on the microwave's tray. He looked at the timer. It read twenty-seven seconds.

"Jasmine," he said in as calm a tone as he could muster. "We have to get out of here right now."

She turned her head and gave him a puzzled look.

"Now. Run."

They made it through the door and crossed the neighbor's lawn before the explosive detonated with a thunderous roar. He lunged to the side and brought Jasmine to the ground with him in between two houses. They scooted back to the wall to protect themselves from the debris that fell around them.

"What just happened?" she said.

"What just happened? We were set up. That's what just happened."

He stood and looked around the corner. Debris had stopped falling. He helped Jasmine from the ground and led her to the car.

"Get in. We need to get out of here now."

He glanced around the neighborhood. Several people now stood outside their homes. Most of them held phones to the side of their heads. A few looked in his direction. He distinctly saw one person with a video camera pointed at them. Jack spun around and got inside the car. He started the engine and sped off.

Jasmine stared out the window with a blank expression on her face.

Jack thought to console her. Changed his mind. "You should call Frank."

31

"WHERE ARE YOU GOING?" THE GUARD AT THE FRONT DOOR ASKED.

Clarissa said, "Just into town to get a few things."

"Has this been cleared with Boris?"

"I'm not a prisoner here. I can come and go as I please."

The guard didn't move.

"Yes, he knows I am going out. Now get out of my way."

The guard stood his ground for a moment and then stepped aside. Clarissa pushed past him and found the car that matched the keys Boris had given her. She pressed the lock button on the key fob a few times and saw the taillights of a black Lexus coupe light up.

She slid into the driver's seat and started the engine. Then she fumbled with the GPS. It required a lot of panning and zooming in for her to see individual street names. She couldn't enter the address Mandy had given her. It would be saved in the settings and that would alert Boris that she had been up to something. There was no doubt in her mind that he would check behind her. It was in his nature.

She finally found the street and panned back out. Close to Bear's house was a shopping center. She configured the GPS to navigate to the shopping center and then drove off.

Twenty minutes later she pulled into the shopping center parking lot. She parked toward the back of the lot, in front of a discount clothing store. She took a moment to get her bearings while looking at the GPS. A mental map formed in her head. She got out of the car and started walking.

A quaint little town, but not as quiet as she expected. Plenty of kids playing outside. It hit her that it must be Spring Break.

She didn't think there was any way she could live in a place like this. Not enough going on for her taste. Plus, it was just too nice, if there actually was such a thing.

She made one last turn and passed in front of four houses. Stopped at the fifth. Without drawing attention to herself, she scouted the street. Empty. A good sign. No cars waiting. No people watching. She crossed the concrete walkway and then up the stairs and then across the porch. Knocked on the plain front door.

She felt slight vibrations under her feet as someone crossed a room toward the door. Someone large. The door cracked open. Though the figure was little more than a shadow, it had the indistinguishable shape of the man she had come to see.

"Hi, Bear."

"Jesus, you gotta be kidding me." He flung the door open and wrapped his thick arms around Clarissa, lifting her off the ground and squeezing her so hard she couldn't breathe while in his grasp. He pulled her inside and set her down. Closed the door.

"What are you doing here, girl?"

"It's a long story."

"I got a few hours to kill."

"Got a beer?"

"Sure do. C'mon."

He led her into the kitchen. She took a seat at the vintage chrome edged fifties-style table. He opened the fridge and pulled out two beers. Popped the caps and dropped them on the counter. He placed a beer in front of her and then sat down across from her.

Bear said, "I can't believe you're here. It's been, what, six months now?"

She nodded. Took a pull from the bottle.

"What have you been doing?" he asked. "And how did you even find me here? And what the hell are you doing here?"

Clarissa felt her cheeks flush as she thought about how to break it to him that she'd seen Mandy. She'd only known that she had to come see the big man. There were no plans made beyond that.

"It's Mandy."

Bear lowered his head and sunk back in his chair. He set his bottle down on the table. Crossed his arms.

"I'm going to get her back," he said.

"I know where she is."

"So do I. And I'm going to get her."

"No, Bear, listen. You don't understand. Look, I can't say too much, but basically I'm undercover. I'm staying in the house, down the hall from her."

"You need to get her out of there then."

"It's not that simple."

"Like hell it isn't. Get her out of there, Clarissa."

She took a long pull on the bottle and thought for a moment before speaking.

"That place, it's a compound, Bear. The guy has professional security everywhere. Guards inside the house. Outside. Probably positioned in the woods surrounding the house. There is no way I can get out with her."

Bear uncrossed his arms and let his hands fall in his lap. "Did you talk to her?"

"Yes. She has her own room. Seems to have free reign in the house. She's being treated well."

"Then why're they holding her?"

"I don't know Boris well enough to find out, yet."

"Tonight, there's an event. Will you be there?"

Clarissa shrugged. "I'm not sure what you're talking about. If there is something going on, they haven't told me yet."

"We were just going to go to crash it and get some more information out of someone. But, Clarissa, you need to go. Bring Mandy."

"Who is 'we'? And how am I supposed to get her out of the house?"

Bear thought it over for a few moments. "You're right. Suppose you can't get him to allow her to go. But, what if, well won't security at the house be reduced while they're at the event?"

"How should I know? Besides, there will still be some security. Not to mention the alarm system they have in place."

"Dammit."

Clarissa reached her hand across the table. Bear's hand met her's.

"I'm inside," she said. "I'll make sure she stays safe and get her out. When the time is right, though. OK?"

Bear nodded. He picked up the beer bottle and lifted it to his lips. Set it back down. "You got your own phone? A safe phone?"

"I do."

He gave her his number. "You text me and let me know what happens tonight. OK? If you can bring her, then this is going down tonight."

She hesitated a moment and said, "I'll help as much as I can. But Bear you have to realize, I can't compromise my position yet. I have to get something solid on this group. That can't happen if I reveal myself."

"Understood." Bear paused. "You hear gunshots, get out of the way."

32

PIERRE OPENED THE BRIEFCASE THAT HAD BEEN HANDED TO HIM AFTER HE EXITED the Des Moines International Airport. The briefcase contained two Glock 17 9mm handguns, three fully loaded magazines per gun, and a suppressor for each weapon. There was also a tactical knife with an ankle sheath.

He placed the knife and magazines on the table. Inspected each Glock carefully, running his finger down the weapons as he did so.

He placed a series of photographs on the table as well. The pictures were of the man he knew as Bear. He had never worked directly with Bear, though. Pierre only knew him through his association with Jack Noble. The job turned out not to be as bad as he thought when Charles presented it to him. He wasn't close to Bear and therefore didn't think that taking his life would pose a moral problem. Especially not for what they were paying him for the job.

A wave of doubt passed through Pierre just then. What if the old man and Charles were simply using him? He knew that Bear was a loose end. Pierre thought about his own involvement in the Jack and Clarissa situation. His actions then might have caused him to be a loose end as well.

The dilemma played on his mind as he prepared to go out for his first look at Bear's property and the potential location for the hit. Should he take Bear out now? He could take his chances with the old man and be prepared to do battle when back in New York or Paris. Maybe he should make contact with Bear, anonymously, before taking any action on him. Perhaps there was something he didn't know. Some rift in the organization the he should be made aware of.

He decided not to dwell on it. He'd let the scenario when he arrived at Bear's house determine his course of action.

Pierre dressed and put on an overcoat two sizes too large. He holstered his weapons inside the coat and placed the extra magazines in his pockets. Finally, he strapped the knife around his lower leg. He doubted that the knife would help much should he find himself in a position to use it against Bear.

He found his Ford rental car in the hotel parking lot. Drove toward the small town the old man had told him Bear lived in. The drive was long and flat and boring. Fortunately, the town was small and it didn't take long for Pierre to find Bear's street. He parked next to the curb a block away. Pulled out a pair of binoculars and focused on the house. The view wasn't as good as he had hoped, so he drove another hundred feet and stopped again. He was only a few houses away now. He climbed across the car to the passenger seat and hunkered back so that he was as far out of sight as possible.

Pierre had been watching the house for twenty minutes when the door opened. A big man stepped out and Pierre recognized the man as Bear. Bear held the screen door open and Pierre figured the little girl would step out next. He would not do the hit here and now, not with the child around.

But the girl didn't step out, a woman did. Pierre squinted behind the binoculars. She looked familiar, but he couldn't place her. The face resembled the woman that Jack had been with in Paris. Clarissa, he thought. But the hair was too dark. Her hair had been red, dark red, but red nonetheless. This woman had dark brown hair. The facial resemblance was uncanny and he thought that he might mention it to the old man when he called him later that night. If he called him.

Bear stood on the porch. The woman crossed the yard and turned down the sidewalk, walking toward Pierre. He lowered his seat even further in an attempt to stay out of view. While he wanted to verify if she was the woman from Paris, to be spotted now would throw a major kink into the way he planned to do the job.

He stayed motionless for ten minutes in case the woman decided to stop and take a phone call or smoke a cigarette. The thought made Pierre crave a smoke of his own and he fumbled around in his jacket until he found an unopened pack. He tore the cellophane wrapper off the top and placed a cigarette in his mouth. Lit it and closed his eyes and inhaled. He was just about to sit up and return to the driver's seat when the passenger side door opened.

Pierre dropped his cigarette and reached inside his jacket. He froze when he felt the cold barrel of a gun against the top of his head.

"Don't bother," a man said. "Put your hands where I can see them."

Pierre slowly pulled his hands from his coat and placed them in the air in front of him.

"Sit up."

Pierre did as instructed.

"What the hell are you doing watching my house? Wait a minute. Don't I know you?"

Pierre turned his head and smiled at Bear. "Yes, you do."

BEAR WATCHED the Frenchman shift uncomfortably on the couch. Any other time he'd tie him up and make Pierre sweat it out. But time was a commodity.

"Go over this again," Bear said. "And tell me why you were sitting outside my house."

Pierre cleared his throat and massaged his temples with his thumbs.

"Let me start off by saying that since, you know, since Jack and Russia and him losing his life, I've been a depressed mess."

Bear nodded. Said nothing. He kept his eyes on Pierre, his hand on his gun and his gun aimed at the Frenchman.

"I got a job offer from Charles," Pierre said.

"So, from the old man then?"

"Yeah, in a roundabout way, I guess you could say that. But I believe that Charles has taken on an increased role in their organization. He runs things in Europe now."

"OK."

"They asked me to do a job and told me it would pay well."

"How well?"

"Two fifty."

"American?"

"Euros."

Bear shook his free hand in front of him. "Not bad."

Pierre shrugged.

"So the job was to take me out?"

"Yes, but I did not find that out until I was over here."

"And you were willing to do it?"

"Yes. Maybe. I don't know. I don't know if I could have gone through with it."

Bear stood up and his gun's aim dropped down toward the floor. He paced the front of the room. He tried to understand why the old man would want him taken out. What had he done? It was always Jack that dealt with the old man. Bear assisted, but he stayed out of everything else.

"Pierre, why?"

Pierre shrugged again. "Do you ask why when you take a job?"

Bear shook his head. That was a good point. Start asking questions and things quickly take a turn for the worse.

"OK, then, how did they know I was here?"

Pierre sat back in his chair and let his head fall against the upper cushion. His eyes darted side to side as he scanned the ceiling.

"The old man never told me how he knew. He just gave me the address."

"Did he say anything that came off as unusual to you?"

"Yes," Pierre said as he leaned forward. He crossed his right leg over his left and placed an elbow on his knee. "Come to think of it he did say something quite odd."

Bear stopped pacing. His mind raced and he felt his heart rate speed up.

"The little girl," Pierre said. "He mentioned the little girl. He said if she was with you, I was to take her."

"Kill her?"

"No, take her. Bring her back to him."

"And if she wasn't here?"

"Call him and he'd give me her location. Said he'd also have another job available."

"What kind of job?" Bear asked.

Pierre shook his head while lifting his shoulders.

A knock at the door startled both men. Bear lifted a finger and an eyebrow and pointed at Pierre. "Don't move." He crossed the room and opened the door. "Detective." He stepped aside, pulling the door open and letting Larsen in.

"Who the hell is this?" Larsen asked.

"He was sent to kill me," Bear said. "But now he's going to help us. Right?"

Pierre nodded. "I'm at your service."

"What kind of experience does he have?" Larsen asked Bear, ignoring the Frenchman.

"Plenty. Worked for the French government. Did some freelance stuff. Worked with my old partner a few times."

"You trust him?" Larsen asked.

Bear paused. His eyes shifted from the detective to the Frenchman. He studied Pierre for a few moments and said, "Yeah. He's gonna make this right."

"Good," Larsen said. "Nobody here knows him. He's our in for tonight."

"How's that?" Bear said.

"He's going to work the event as a waiter. I've got communication equipment so he can give us a real-time view of what's going on inside. We've got a few hours to make our plans."

33

JACK PASSED THE ENTRANCE TO CHERNOV'S NEIGHBORHOOD AND SLOWED THE CAR down. Jasmine didn't speak during the ride over. He thought he knew what was playing on her mind. He decided to ask.

"What is it?"

She shook her head slowly, then stopped and looked at him. She said, "Could've been us, Jack."

"That's nothing new. It's the risk that goes with the job."

"I know, I know. And we've lost men before. But, they weren't even cold yet. Their bodies were still warm. It had just happened. And then we were what, thirty seconds from needing to be reassembled by some forensics team?"

Jack nodded. The same thoughts had crossed his mind. He compartmentalized them, though. They had a job to do and he wanted to get the bastards before they took off.

"Jasmine, we gotta put this behind us and take care of business. They knew someone else was coming. That's why they placed the bomb."

"You don't think that was just to destroy the crime scene?"

"It's possible. But I think the reality is someone was there when we got there. They placed the explosive and bailed."

"You think they waited around long enough to see if they were successful?"

Jack took his time responding. The escape played over and over in his mind.

Full speed, half speed, slow motion. He tried to pick out anything that had been out of the ordinary. A car that didn't belong or had been driving by at the time. Anyone who had been lingering around outside, or sitting on their porch before the explosion. And where would the person who placed the bomb have gone when Jack and Jasmine entered the house? They couldn't go through the front, so the back was their only route for escape. Jack recalled that he hadn't been able to search the house. Jasmine called him to the kitchen when she found the dead bodies and he had only made it halfway down the hallway.

"I'm thinking they had a car on the next street over. Ran out the back, hopped over a fence and then got the hell out."

Jack pulled the car into an empty parking lot where a Waffle House had once stood. He stopped and got out and reached into his pocket. Pulled out a pack of cigarettes and lit one.

Jasmine stepped out of the car and walked around it. She stood next to him.

"That'll kill you, you know."

Jack laughed. It wasn't that he found the joke funny. The stress had built up to the point where he had no other outlet. Yet.

"Do you miss this?" Jasmine asked.

Jack paused. Reflected back on the six months in Greece. The relaxed feeling. And despite the calm state his mind had entered there, there was no place he'd rather be right now than in the middle of things.

"Yeah, I miss this."

"Think you'll stick with us after this is over?"

Jack wasn't so sure. "I don't know about that. But I'll stay involved in something."

"Going back to your old business?"

"I don't know. There's lots of options. Lots of things I can do with my talents."

He finished his cigarette, dropped it on the ground and crushed it out with the heel of his shoe. They got back in the car and drove into Chernov's neighborhood. They passed his house and saw the driveway was empty. Jack turned around and drove by a second time. He made a right turn onto the next street and parked. The sun was setting and the sky above was already a dark shade of blue.

"Front or back?" Jasmine asked.

"Let's both go in from the back."

"We won't know what's happening in front then."

"I'm aware of that, Jasmine. But I don't want either of us alone in case someone is waiting in there."

The houses of two parallel streets butted up to one another. There was no alley or access lane behind them. They all shared the same back fence.

"We've got two yards to go through," Jack said. "Let's be quick."

Jack hopped the first fence and Jasmine followed. They sprinted the width of the yard and hit the next fence, hopping over in a fluid motion. They sprinted through the next yard and stopped at the fence separating the yard from Chernov's.

"Wait a sec," Jack said.

Jasmine nodded. She leaned back against the fence and pulled her weapon, holding it in front of her and angled toward the ground.

Jack stretched and peered over the top of the fence. Scanned the yard. He said, "No dogs. Lights are out. Let's go."

He went over first and Jasmine followed. They stayed close to the side fence that separated the two yards. Moved forward, toward the house. Then they hugged the exterior wall of the house, stopping at each window and looking inside.

"Place looks empty," Jasmine said.

"Yeah, seems like they were ready to move."

"Where to? Christ, I should call Frank." She pulled her phone out and tapped on the screen a few times. Placed the phone up to her ear. "Frank, look we got problems here." There was a short pause and Jasmine nodded a few times. "We're outside Chernov's and the place is deserted. Yeah. Yeah. What?" She covered the phone with her hand. "He doesn't want us to go in, Jack."

"Screw him."

Jasmine uncovered the phone and spoke. "How long is that going to take, Frank. I mean, seriously, we've got two men down and an empty house. Someone tried to blow us up. Almost succeeded. These guys could be moving to set up for the next phase. Where the hell is that?" Another long pause. This time Jasmine shook her head and looked at Jack with confusion spread across her face. "What's in Iowa?"

Jack mouthed "Iowa" back to her in the form of a question.

She shrugged. "OK, Frank. Keep us posted and let us know more about Iowa when you get a chance." She hung up the phone and looked at Jack. "What do you want to do?"

"We're going in. I don't care what Frank says. I'm not waiting twelve hours to check out this house. Someone could come by and clean it and we'll have nothing. These guys left in a hurry. I'm betting they made a mistake and left something behind."

Jasmine stood and paced a few steps back and forth. She stopped. Nodded at Jack.

"Let's do it."

They walked to the back door. Jack tugged on the handle and it gave way.

"Unlocked."

He slid the door open and entered with his gun drawn and aimed in front of him. He stopped. Listened. The house was quiet and still and cold.

"Jesus," Jasmine said. "It's colder in here than outside."

Jack looked around the room. In front of them was a large couch with a smaller couch next to it. The two seats formed an L-shape. A flat panel TV hung from the wall. There was a square wood coffee table in the middle of the room. To their right was a kitchen full of stainless steel appliances. An island separated the two areas.

They passed through the room toward the front of the house.

"Let's clear the downstairs then move upstairs," Jack said.

They went room by room and found each to be empty, both downstairs and up. Furniture had been left behind, but dressers and shelves and desks had been cleaned out.

"C'mon," Jack said. "There's got to be something here."

"Maybe we should double check the microwave," Jasmine said.

Jack chuckled and shook his head. Then it occurred to him that they hadn't checked the kitchen. He gestured for Jasmine to follow him. They went downstairs and moved slowly and quietly toward the kitchen. Had anyone been hiding behind the island they would know that the two were in the house. Jack picked up his pace.

He stopped in the hall just before reaching the great room. He closed his eyes and listened for any movement. There was none.

"Wait here," he said.

Jasmine backed up a few feet and Jack stepped into the room. He kept both hands on his weapon and pointed it in front of him, ready to fire. He pressed back against the wall, keeping a few feet between him and the island. When he was directly across from the end of the island, he leaned over. The area between the island and the rest of the kitchen was empty. Jack let out a loud exhale and moved toward the pantry. He placed his hand on the doorknob.

"Jack, you gotta see this," Jasmine called from another room.

He met her in the room that appeared to have been used as an office. She looked over at him as he entered and he said, "What is it?"

"I don't know how we missed this, Jack." She unfolded a map of the United States. There were several areas circled in red.

"I wonder what those areas are. Targets? Cells?"

"Not sure. I'm gonna get a picture of this and send it to Frank, though."

Jack pointed at the center of the map and the biggest red circle. "Look. Iowa."

Jasmine smiled and nodded. Her eyes met Jack's.

He returned her smile. Then he noticed Jasmine's eyes grow wide and her pupils dilated.

"Jack, look out." She dropped the map and reached for her gun.

Jack brought his gun up and started to spin. Then he felt the weight of something heavy strike down on his head with force. He fell to the ground. His head ached and warm blood streamed over his forehead and down the side of his face. His vision darkened. He felt another blow across his head and passed out.

When Jack came to, the house was still again. It had the same empty feeling as when they entered. He didn't trust that feeling this time. He felt around the floor and found his gun. Then he pushed himself up. Pain spread from the top of his head through his face. His stomach turned and he felt like he was going to vomit. A few moments later the nausea subsided. He brought one leg up and then the other. Used the edge of the desk to help him get to his feet.

The map was on the desk. It had fallen face down when Jasmine dropped it.

Jasmine.

Where was she?

"Jasmine?" Jack called out.

There was no response. He looked around the room. Saw her gun and her phone on the ground. He reached over to grab both items. The room spun and so did his stomach. Jack fell forward. He threw his forearm out in front of his head to break his fall. A few moments later he steadied himself and got up, retrieving the phone and gun on the way up.

He returned to the desk and flipped the map over. Studied the areas circled. Cherry Hill, New Jersey. Atlanta, Georgia. San Diego, California. Austin, Texas. And a little town outside of Des Moines, Iowa.

The last location stood out. There were three arrows pointing toward the circle. It meant something. And it was all Jack had to work with. He grabbed the map and left the house through the front door. Walked half a block and turned right on the first street. A short distance later he stood next to the car. He got in, put the key in the ignition and sped out of the neighborhood.

Questions flooded his mind. In some ways he was back to himself. But in others, he was making rookie mistakes. How had he missed whoever it was inside the house? Had they come in after he left the kitchen? The pantry, why had he not checked the pantry? And, the question that played over and over, why was he still alive?

The best answer he could come up with was that whoever was in the house, was not one of the major players. They must have panicked, struck quickly, and took who they assumed was the weaker of the two. Perhaps they looked down at Jack and figured the blow had done enough damage. That he'd bleed out on the floor, or was already dead.

Twenty minutes later he was southbound on I-75 heading toward the Atlanta airport. He pulled Jasmine's phone out and called the last number she had dialed.

"Jasmine," Frank answered. "What's going on?"

"It's Jack."

"Jack? Is everything OK?"

"No, Frank. It's not. They got her."

"What do you mean they got her?"

"They ambushed us. Blindsided me. Took her."

"Jack where are you? I'll get a team there a.s.a.p."

Jack hung up the phone and tossed it onto the empty passenger seat.

"I'll do this alone."

PART III

EPISODE 8

34

JACK ROLLED DOWN HIS WINDOW AND TOOK A DEEP BREATH. THE CAR IDLED quietly. He sat behind four vehicles, waiting to grab a ticket for long-term parking. Long-term in this case being forever.

The woman at the front of the line had stopped too far away from the automated ticket dispenser. She opened her door and stepped out of her car. Half in, half out. One leg on the ground. The other in the car. She grabbed onto the top of the door frame with one hand. Reached out to the ticket machine with the other.

He looked through the passenger side window. There stood the North Terminal of Hartsfield-Jackson Atlanta International Airport. He scanned the artificially lit six lane one-way road that separated the parking garage from the terminal. The crowd crossing the road was thick. The farthest lane was packed with idling cars. Friends and co-workers and loved ones. Travelers coming or going. Happy or sad or indifferent. A full spectrum of people and emotions and situations.

A car door slammed shut. Jack turned his head. A red and white striped gate lifted into the air and the woman at the front of the line pulled her small hybrid vehicle past the ticketing machine. The blue car disappeared into the orange wash of the parking garage.

Three, then two, then one. Cars pulled up, arms stuck out, tickets were dispensed, and the gate went up.

A minute later Jack had his parking ticket. He tossed it onto the dash despite the printed warning not to do so. It didn't matter. He had no intentions of ever retrieving the vehicle.

He stayed in the pass-through lane until he reached the final row in the garage. Turned right. Drove to the end. Found an empty spot and parked the car in the furthest corner of the garage. He opened the glove compartment box and tossed the keys inside. Opened the trunk and placed his pistol under the spare tire. He did a once over of the front, back and trunk of the car to make sure he'd left nothing behind.

Inside the North Terminal he located the Delta counter at the far end, near Terminal T. He joined a line that snaked through several man made rows, all separated by a blue velvet rope. A man in a Delta uniform approached him. The uniform made him look far more important that he actually was.

The man gave a nod and a clap of his hands and said, "Any bags to check, sir?"

"No," Jack said.

"You can step over here and use our automated check in then."

"I need a ticket."

The man looked around, first at the line and then at the five employees busy at work behind computers, checking people in and taking their baggage. He looked over his shoulder at a group of computer kiosks. In between two rows of computers was another employee.

"Come with me," the man said.

Jack looked over his shoulder. The line he stood in had doubled in size. He ducked under the blue velvet rope and followed the Delta employee.

The man said, "Gracie, can you help this gentleman? He needs a ticket to," he looked over his shoulder at Jack. "Where you going, sir?"

"Des Moines."

"Des Moines, Gracie."

Gracie smiled at the man and then at Jack. She said, "Sure thing, darling. Step on up."

Jack nodded his thanks to the man and then walked to the makeshift ticketing counter. Although there were two computers, no one else would be able to work behind the counter with Gracie standing there. She was an older woman. Large and dark with short gray-streaked hair and an infectious smile.

She said, "Des Moines, huh?" 'Des' came out like 'day', long and drawn out.

"Yes ma'am," Jack said.

Gracie punished her keyboard with thick fingertips. Her eyes moved side to side. Left to right and right to left. "What's going on out there in, uh, Iowa?"

Jack shrugged.

"Just a spur of the moment thing then, huh?" she asked.

Jack laughed and said, "Yeah, I'm sure a lot of people head to Iowa on the spur of the moment."

"It's a woman isn't it?"

Jack sighed. Nodded. "Yeah, I'm going out there for a woman."

"Betchou met on the line, didn't ya? What they call that, uh, computerized dating. Right?"

Jack responded with a smile.

Gracie said, "OK, here's what I got. There's a flight leaving in thirty minutes, non-stop to Des Moines, Iowa."

"Great. How much?"

"Three-thirty, sir."

Jack retrieved his wallet from his back pocket. Slid the ID card that said he was John J. Martin out from under its protective shield. Pulled out a credit card with the same name on it. He had an urge to look over his shoulder as he handed the driver's license and credit card to Gracie. He hadn't used either at any point. He didn't know if they were stolen, or if they had been fabricated for his use only. Perhaps Frank had set him up. Or maybe, after Jasmine's capture, Frank was done with Jack and had flagged the ID and credit card.

Three police officers gathered nearby. One was old. One was young. And one looked to be Jack's age. The cops mirrored each other in posture and stance. Their hands on their utility belts. Thumbs tucked inside the belt, palms and fingers resting on the outside. Their right hands inches from the handle of their guns. Their faces, expressionless. Not a one looked at the others. Their trained eyes scanned the terminal, resting on no single person, taking in the entire scene. A boring job, for the most part. But if something went down, they'd be first in line for the action.

The cop that looked to be Jack's age was looking in Jack's direction. His eyes inched along. He turned his body slightly. He reached the ticketing counter and those ever moving eyes stopped. He looked at Jack, but beyond him at the same time. He lingered longer than normal, though, and that gave Jack cause for worry.

Jack held his breath. Five seconds felt like thirty. He wondered if his picture hung in a room below or above. A room that few people ever saw. Only cops had the privilege, and suspected criminals the displeasure, of setting foot in there.

Finally, the officer moved on. Looked elsewhere. Jack exhaled and turned to face Gracie again.

"Here's your credit card, Mr. Martin." Gracie slid the card across the narrow counter. "I'll be done with your license in a sec." A few minutes later she placed the fake driver's license on the counter. "Any bags, Mr. Martin?"

"No bags. Just me."

Gracie handed Jack his ticket and said, "Now you only got about thirty minutes. When you pass through that little hallway over there," she reached out and pointed over his shoulder, "turn to the left. Go to the North security check-point, not the main checkpoint. Got it? You'll wait three times as long at the main checkpoint. Use the expert traveler lane, since you don't have any carry-ons. Then follow the signs to the train and get off at Concourse C. Then it's just a short walk to your gate."

Jack took the ticket and smiled. "Thanks, ma'am."

35

TWO DAYS PAST FULL, THE MOON LIT UP THE SIDEWALK AND THE STREET AND buildings. Bear looked over the heads of Larsen and Pierre, over the rooftops. He focused on the moon and thought about Mandy. There'd been plenty of time for guilt since the abduction. Bear had managed to push the thoughts aside, though. But at that moment, so close to the time when they'd be reunited, he fought with his feelings. He struggled with the thought that he had let her down. He hoped it wouldn't show on his face, and at the same time, he hoped that it would.

Bear stood a few feet from the other two men. He listened as Larsen went over the plan for the third time.

Pierre was to pose as a waiter at Boris's event. They assumed that the staff would be searched, so Pierre's weapon would be hidden outside the building. Taped to the inside of the dumpster. During an early smoke break he'd retrieve the weapon. Before he did that, though, he had to locate Mandy and Clarissa. Bear held out hope that both would be in attendance. It would make the job easier.

Larsen popped the trunk of his car and ducked under the lid. He pulled out a red garment bag. Pierre stuck his cigarette between his lips and reached out for the bag.

Larsen said, "That's your uniform."

Pierre unzipped the bag and made a face at the outfit. Said, "It's what the others will be wearing?"

Larsen nodded. "Yeah, I got a friend in the catering company. Try it on."

Pierre changed next to the car, not bothering to hide himself from view.

"Skin and bones," Bear said. "How'd you manage to last twenty years in the field?"

Pierre laughed and said nothing in response. He slipped the white collared button-up shirt over his undershirt. Then he slowly buttoned the shirt to the neck. Afterward, he tucked the shirt into the waistband of his black pants.

"How do I look?"

"Like a French waiter," Bear said.

Larsen smiled and said, "You look the part. Can you speak with an American accent?"

"Ya'll want I should talk like this?" Pierre said, mocking the question.

"Not quite like that," Larsen said. "Just normal, even tone."

Pierre nodded. "I've done it before," he said in as neutral an American accent he could muster. He took one last drag from his cigarette and dropped it on the street. A cloud of red ash burst into the air, fading out instantly.

Bear walked over and crushed the cigarette out with his heel. "What's the next step?"

Larsen said, "OK, we're a few blocks away from the hall where this thing is taking place. It's an art gallery."

"Russian owned?" Bear asked.

Larsen shook his head. "That section of town, all the buildings are two stories high with tall first floors. They all have basements. Wouldn't expect too much going on down there. Likely used for storage. We'll encounter security teams on the rooftops." Larsen looked up at the buildings surrounding them. "Expect security on top of the gallery, the buildings in front and behind, and probably a block away in each direction. Bear," Larsen pointed in Bear's direction, "You and I will scout that."

Bear nodded. Said nothing.

Larsen continued, "It's imperative that you let us know before you are ready to leave with the girl. Got that Pierre? We need to create a distraction."

"What'd you have in mind?" Bear asked.

Larsen lifted a finger and shook his head. "You'll see. I don't want to reveal that just yet."

Bear's curiosity got the better of him and he tried to imagine what Larsen would consider a distraction. He didn't come up with anything interesting.

"Bear?" Larsen said. "You got that?"

Bear shook his head. "Sorry?"

"You'll need to be ready for the transfer, Bear. I'll be about a mile away. Pierre will do a little recon to see if he's been missed at the event, then we'll all meet back at the house."

"Got it," Bear said.

Larsen leaned into the trunk again and pulled out a bag. He retrieved two radios and an earpiece. He handed Bear a radio and the earpiece to Pierre. Kept the other radio for himself. "These are all tuned to a specific frequency so we can communicate. Pierre, this will be invisible in your ear. It works both ways all the time. Talk when you want to talk. You'll hear us when we talk."

Pierre grabbed the device and slid it inside his ear canal. "I'm familiar with how they work."

"Bear," Larsen said. "You got the car. I'm on foot and will walk Pierre to the event."

Bear shook hands with both men and wished them luck. He held Pierre's hand a few extra seconds and stared him in the eye. "Do it right, Pierre."

Pierre nodded, and then he and Larsen turned and walked away.

Bear leaned against the car and watched them round a corner and disappear from sight. It was cold and he hadn't brought a jacket. He thought about going back to the house to get one, but knew that would be foolish. Instead, he sat inside the car. Turned on the heat. Dropped the shifter into drive and drove around. He stuck to right turns only, following a four block perimeter.

He resisted the temptation to deviate from his path and drive by the art gallery. It wasn't worth the risk of being spotted by someone who might know him, or by the security team who might take note of him.

His radio clicked and hissed and Pierre's voice came through the speaker. "I'm inside. Made it through with no problems. There is security inside. They patted me down, but found nothing. I don't know that I'll be able to get to the dumpster without being seen. At least not now. Maybe when the party picks up. It's pretty empty in here at the moment."

Larsen spoke next. "Great, Pierre. Stay out of trouble and let us know when you see the girl."

Bear said nothing. He gripped the steering wheel tightly and breathed in and out. Slow and steady. It felt good to be back in action.

36

Boris scanned the crowd inside art gallery. Young and old. Black and white. Rich and poor. He didn't recognize eighty percent of the people in the room. Freeloaders, he thought. They'd come to eat the food and drink the alcohol that *he* had paid for. The remaining people in the room, the ones he did know, were a mix of cops, local politicians and his own men. In short, people who were there because of money. They were on his side because they were on his payroll. Or afraid of him. Or both. Either was enough to buy a little loyalty. For now.

He hated hosting these events. But such was the way things were done. Boris understood that running a criminal organization in the U.S. required extra effort. He knew that parties and charitable events would help endear him within the community.

He invited those cops who he knew went out of their way to look the other way when his name came up.

He let the politicians in and made sure that when they left, their pockets were fatter. That way, when he needed a favor, they'd be ready to step up to bat for him.

As for the bad stuff, it was all rumors. Low level crime. A few break-ins. His guys had roughed up a few people. The farm-folk, as he liked to call them, had no idea what he really had planned.

"Mr. Melikov, I've been looking all over for you."

Boris turned and found himself face to face with Michael Hiller, the Mayor of Knoxville.

"Mayor Hiller," Boris said. "How are you?"

Instead of saying fine or okay and making small talk, Mayor Hiller launched into a campaign speech. He spoke of his upcoming election race and the need for funding and the challenge his competitor posed. Not just for him, but for the entire city of Knoxville. Boris did his best to appear to be paying attention. He nodded his head. He smiled when he thought it appropriate. But in the end, his thoughts drifted elsewhere.

Soon he'd send Anastasiya to Portland, Oregon. Everyone would be in place. They could begin planning and preparing and practicing for the attack. The thought of the chaos and destruction that he was going to be responsible for set a shiver down his spine. It was a good feeling. He reveled in it.

"Now, will I be able to count on you, Mr. Melikov?"

Boris lifted his eyebrows and searched for the last thing he heard Hiller say. "Of course you can, sir. Anything you need."

Hiller laughed and clapped his hands together. He rubbed them and said, "Well, I'll take a donation check right now then!"

Boris smiled and said, "Of course. I'll see to that..." He felt his phone buzz and reached inside his jacket. He looked at the caller ID and held out his hand to the Mayor. "Sir, if you'll excuse me, this is an emergency line. I have to take this."

"Sure thing, Mr. Melikov."

Boris said, "Hang on," when he answered the phone. He pushed his way through the crowd, smiling and nodding at everyone he passed. He had been standing closer to the front than the back, so he left through the gallery's entrance. He stepped into the cool night air, which provided a welcome respite from the warmth and stuffiness inside. Streetlights cast pools of pale light on the wide sidewalk. He found a dark spot close to the building and stopped.

"Lazar," Boris said. "What is going on?"

"We're in Iowa," Lazar Chernov said.

"Say again?"

Chernov didn't respond.

"Did you say you are in Iowa?"

"Yes, sir."

"Why?"

"We were compromised."

"How so?"

"My man here, Kenneth, somehow the feds got to him."

"Do they have him now?"

Chernov hesitated. "No, he's with me now. The feds had him and were questioning him. We rescued him. Killed two of the agents."

"Did they get any information from him?"

"Yes, but we cleaned the scene."

"How?"

"Blew up the house."

Boris hesitated a moment, then said, "Who were they? CIA? FBI?"

"I don't know. What I can tell you is that there were at least two more. We took one of them out and have the other with us."

"Who is he?"

"She, sir. And we don't know yet. She won't talk."

Boris scanned the area around him and across the street. He lowered his voice. "Here is what you are going to do. You take her to my place. You will wait in the main living area. The woman and your man Kenneth will be taken downstairs. You will all wait for me to return. I'm going to talk to you first and then to the other two. Now, is there anyone else with you I should know about?"

Chernov cleared his throat. Boris pictured him looking around, scared and nervous. "No, I sent my other men away."

Boris felt that Chernov was lying, but decided not to push him on it. "Very well. You three head to the compound and I'll notify security that you are on the way." He hung up the phone and stuffed it in his pocket. Anger built up and he kicked the wall with the sole of his shoe. Atlanta had been compromised. Now he had to determine a new location and recruit new men.

How much information had Kenneth given the feds? How much did the man know? The entire operation could be shot. They blew up a house. Big deal. If Kenneth had talked, they could have relayed the information digitally.

Chernov had been handpicked and had earned the trust of Boris. That trust is why Boris allowed the man to recruit his own team. If Kenneth had betrayed Boris, then it would not only be his head on the line, but Chernov's as well.

The best way to instill fear is to lop off the head of one of your captains.

Sound advice.

Advice Boris might act upon.

37

"I want to leave," Mandy whispered.

Clarissa placed a reassuring hand on the little girl's shoulder and squeezed. "I know, sweetie."

"I just want to run for the door and disappear."

The words were so close to her own thoughts after the plane crash.

Clarissa glanced left and right and behind her. She didn't recognize anyone nearby. "Come with me." She led Mandy out of the exhibit area and into a small hall. They pressed against the wall as a line of waiters passed by with trays of champagne and finger foods. She gave Pierre an imperceptible nod as he passed. The hall fell silent after the waiters vacated the area. They continued on and she cringed at the echo created by her heels against the tile floor. She backed into the door to the lady's room and pulled Mandy inside.

"What's going on?" Mandy asked.

"We are getting you out of here."

"How? Who's we?"

"There is a man here, he's a friend of Bear's. Was a good friend of Mr. Jack's, too."

Mandy stared at her with huge eyes and didn't say anything.

"He's going to sneak you out shortly. What I need you to do is to hang back, out of sight of Boris for a while, so that I can talk to the man who is going to get you out. Can you do that?"

"What's his name?"

"I can't tell you yet."

"Will I see you again?"

"Of course you'll see me again."

"I mean tonight. Here."

"After I talk to him, I'm going to come and find you and get you in position. This has to be done just right." She tapped the end of the girl's nose with her index finger.

Mandy stared at Clarissa. Her face twisted, scared and flushed.

"Trust me, Mandy," Clarissa said.

Mandy nodded. Grabbed Clarissa's hand and pulled her to the door. "Let's go."

Clarissa walked Mandy to the back of the gallery, where tables with food were set up.

She scanned the room. Found Pierre. Took a direct line to him and upon passing him said, "Meet me out back." She continued toward the front of the gallery and then turned around. The place was full. Old people, young people, short people, bald people. She assessed every potential threat in the room, and there were plenty. She figured that fifteen percent of those in attendance could pose a problem. Not a good sign. Then again, only a few of them would have the same training and skills as her and Pierre.

She stepped into the same hall she had escorted Mandy through a few minutes earlier. This time she passed by the restrooms and pushed through a swinging door that led into the kitchen. The staff largely ignored her. Cooks continued to cook. The wait staff continued to tray food and alcohol. She saw a man open a screen door leading outside and followed him.

She took two steps and stopped on the concrete patio. An orange bulb cast a dim pool of light on the area. Pierre turned as the wood framed screen door slammed shut behind her. He held a lit cigarette in one hand. Lifted it to his lips. Took a deep drag. He held a gun in his other hand. The gun pointed toward the ground.

Clarissa looked left. Looked right. Over Pierre's head. She took a step back and reached behind her back, feeling for the door handle.

"Relax," Pierre said. "It's for you."

"That's what I'm afraid of."

"Not the bullet. The gun."

Clarissa dropped her hands to her side. Took two steps and stopped at the edge of the concrete patio. She stepped down onto the first of six wooden steps that were anchored to the concrete. She took her time, stepping slowly and cautiously. The entire time, she scanned the back lot and adjacent lots and buildings. She knew that a man like Boris would have security everywhere. Where were they?

"There's security all around," Pierre said. "On some of the buildings. A roving unit, too."

She glanced up. Saw nothing. Said nothing.

"He's on the other side right now."

Clarissa held her hand out. Pierre spun the gun on his palm and handed it to her, handle facing her, barrel facing him. She hiked up her blouse and tucked the gun inside her waistband.

"Do you have a specific use for that tonight?"

She shook her head. "I still have a mission to fulfill. Taking him out negates that and puts us back at square one. Or close to it at least."

"You should kill him."

She ignored his suggestion. Said, "What happened, Pierre? In Russia?"

Pierre pulled an unlit cigarette from the pack and placed it in his mouth. He lit it with the smoke in his other hand and then discarded the old one by flicking it into the dumpster. He wiped his mouth with the back of his hand. His face hardened. He looked in her direction, but his eyes focused elsewhere.

"Please, Pierre. I need to know."

"They kept us in a dungeon. I never treated..." His voice trailed off. He continued a few seconds later. "Let's just say it breaks every rule of ethics that we are to abide by. They kept us chained in a hole. Couldn't even stand. They beat us. They tried to break us. They succeeded with me, although I never admitted it. But Jack, he stayed strong."

Clarissa could do nothing but nod along.

"So," Pierre continued, "when it came time, we were tried by a military man. Ivanov's his name."

Clarissa's face lit up with recognition. "I know that name."

Pierre nodded. Said, "He's a bad man. He's into a lot of things. I spent some time gathering information on him after I returned to France. Definitely not on the right side of good." He took a drag and leaned his head back. He blew smoke toward the sky. It drifted up and created a halo around the light bulb that was fixed to the side of the building. "We were guilty before we ever stepped foot into the courtroom as far as Ivanov was concerned. Jack took the fall. I was prepared to go down with him. Jack wouldn't have it. He took all the blame, and that granted me my freedom. After I came back, I tried to continue with the agency. Pointless, really. The depression, it enveloped me. Normally, an agent would be terminated, either figuratively or literally, for such behavior. They worked with me. I lasted three months, and then I left. After that, I tried to drink myself to death. Couldn't. Stuck the barrel of my gun in my mouth a few times. Too chicken to pull the trigger."

"And now you feel guilty."

"Of course I feel guilty. Wouldn't you? I'd have rather died next to him than live out my life as a coward."

"You're not a coward."

He locked eyes with her and slowly shook his head. "It's not for you to decide."

"If you had died or been locked up you wouldn't be here to help rescue Mandy."

Pierre shrugged.

"It's redemption, Pierre. Jack risked his life for that little girl. Now it's your turn. Do right by her and you do right by Jack."

A thin smile crossed Pierre's lips. "Thank you."

She wasn't sure if he meant it.

"I'm going back in," Clarissa said. "Wait five minutes then come through the kitchen. She'll be walking toward the bathrooms. She'll nod once and wink twice. You do the same. She'll follow you into the kitchen and outside."

He nodded.

"Sinclair could use a guy like you. Do right by Jack tonight and I'll put in a word for you."

She left Pierre outside and slipped through the kitchen, back to the exhibit area of the gallery. She stopped inside the hall and scanned the room, starting at the far corner and working her way toward the refreshment table. Boris was still occupied with a group of older gentlemen that Clarissa thought looked like politicians or lawyers. Blood suckers.

She found Mandy. Checked her watch. A minute had passed since she had left Pierre. She said, "Mandy, listen to me. Here is what is going to happen." She gave the girl the simple instructions and emphasized that she was to nod once and blink twice.

"Which eye?"

Clarissa laughed. "I guess it doesn't matter. I don't think too many ten year olds at this party are going to be standing in the hall in four minutes winking and nodding."

Mandy averted her eyes and smiled shyly.

"Three minutes. I need to leave you now. I'll be watching, though. OK?"

Mandy nodded and set her glass of punch on the table. She looked down at her watch and said, "Got it."

38

Jasmine gazed at her surroundings through the oval shaped window. The darkness prohibited her from seeing too much. The private jet landed on a small runway near a small airport. There were trees on all sides. No signs. At least none that she could see through the dark or that meant anything to her. She had no idea where they were. The men who abducted her hadn't spoken to her. Not a single word since they left the house in Georgia. If she spoke, they jammed a gun into her neck or her cheek or her chest.

She followed Chernov off the plane. Behind her came Kenneth Quioness. There were two other men that she did not recognize. They stood next to the plane. The men formed a circle around her.

She figured she'd try her luck again and said, "Where are you taking me?"

"Shut up," Chernov said.

A car pulled up. They forced her into the back seat. Chernov sat to her right. Kenneth on her left. The car pulled away from the jet. They passed by the hangar. She looked to the left and saw a parking lot that led to a highway. They drove by.

Why weren't they leaving the airport?

When the car stopped, she looked forward and saw why.

Chernov got out of the car and grabbed her by the arm. He pulled and she slid across the seat. He was a strong man, and she worried that if she hesitated, he'd yank her shoulder out of its socket. He nodded at her, then at the helicopter. He said, "Don't try anything."

Kenneth joined them a few seconds later. Both men wrapped their arms through hers and escorted her to the helicopter. Kenneth boarded first, then Jasmine, and finally Chernov.

The helicopter lifted into the air. Again, the men sat to her right and to her left. Prevented her from being able to get a good look at the terrain below. Not that it would have mattered. She still had no idea where they were. When she saw the helicopter, she had hoped that she'd overhear something, anything that would give her an indication. No such luck. Chernov handed her headgear, but it wasn't connected to the rest. It only helped to reduce the constant noise and *thump, thump, thump* of the contraption they flew in.

She sat still, between the men, a row behind the pilot, and weighed her options. It boiled down to two. Sit and do nothing, or strike Chernov, and strike Kenneth, and strike the pilot. Then they'd crash. They'd all die. She wouldn't win, but she sure as hell wouldn't lose. Neither option appealed to her all that much. In the end, it didn't matter. After a few minutes, she saw the pilot pointing past the front windshield. She craned her neck in an effort to get a better view. She saw a landing pad lit up in an x formation. It stood out against the darkening sky.

Jasmine sat back. Crossed her arms. She'd wait it out and see what opportunities were afforded to her at the next destination.

Less than five minutes later the helicopter touched down. She looked left and right through the windows and saw an expansive lawn ringed by the dark outlines of trees. The lawn and the trees surrounded the house they had landed on top of.

What kind of house has a helicopter landing pad on it, and who would live there?

"Get out," Chernov shouted, although it barely sounded like a whisper amid the noise created by the helicopter's rotors.

She slid to her left and dropped to the ground through the open door. There were four men on the roof. There was nothing distinguishable about them. Homogeneous, she thought. They all were armed with automatic weapons. She couldn't make out the exact weapons in the dark, with the wind from the rotors blowing her hair across her face.

Jasmine felt a hand at each elbow. They pulled her toward a corner of the roof. At first she dug in her heels, but then quickly realized that would be the quick way to a fast ending. She allowed the hands at her elbows to guide her. At the edge of the roof was a staircase that clung to the house diagonally and led to the ground.

Kenneth let go of her arm and started down the stairs. Chernov urged her to go down, and then he followed.

She heard the helicopter lift off. Glanced over her shoulder. It rose into the air and then banked to the east and disappeared into the night.

At the bottom of the stairs were two more men. They were as uninteresting to her as the four at the top. Except for their weapons. They were both armed with HK MP7 submachine guns. Their weapons had suppressors and extended magazines, which told her they had forty rounds at their disposal. Each. An ideal weapon for close quarters combat. Popular with a highly covert special operations team in the U.S. While the men didn't impress her, their weapons certainly did.

The man to her left reached over and opened the door. He snapped back into position, keeping his eyes on Jasmine. She looked from him to his weapon and then back to him.

She felt Chernov's hand at her back and she stepped through the open doorway. They stood in a dark hall. She noticed two doors on each side and one at the end. All the doors were closed.

"Forward," Chernov said.

She followed Kenneth.

"Stop," Chernov said after they passed the second door.

Jasmine stopped and turned around. She saw Chernov at the door. He punched in a code and waited. She heard a series of beeps and then a click. He reached down and turned the doorknob. Pushed the door open. He said, "Go in."

She stepped inside. The two men followed. She felt the vibrations of their steps on the stairs.

"I can't see anything," Jasmine said.

There was a click and then a beam of light traveled over her head and lit up the area in front of her. She gasped. She would've preferred to be in the dark after all.

"Continue," Chernov said.

She did. Reached the bottom of the stairs. Took three more steps and stopped at the wall. Turned around and waited for the men to reach the bottom. If there was ever a time to act, it was now. Jasmine leaned back against the wall to steady herself and took a deep breath. She envisioned her first move and then struck. Kenneth was closest to her and he received the brunt of the attack. She launched herself at him, using the wall as a springboard. The force it helped her create was enough to drop Kenneth with two successive blows. One to his throat, the other to his solar plexus. He dropped to the ground and lay there like a pile of laundry. A huddled mass, struggling to breathe or talk or move.

She let her momentum carry her through and forward. She would attempt a similar attack on Chernov. Both hands, at the same time, throat and solar plexus. Unfortunately, Chernov had started to react the moment she launched herself at Kenneth. She saw it and she knew it and she still wasn't prepared for him. The heavy metal flashlight came down across the side of her head. Her own momentum worked against her. Her lower body continued forward, her upper body didn't. She flipped backward, but only halfway. The back of her head hit the floor with a thud. The room around her was dark. Was she unconscious? Or had Chernov turned off the light during the fight?

Jasmine placed her palms on the floor, under her shoulders, and pushed up. She wasn't unconscious. She brought her knees up under her. Bad move. A boot connected with her side, near her stomach. The impact of the kick was enough to lift her off the ground and flip her over. She landed hard on her back. The air escaped her lungs. An attempt to roll over was quickly thwarted by a hand on her head. She was lifted into a seated position. Pulled up by her hair.

"You stupid bitch," Chernov said as he continued to lift her.

Jasmine struggled to breathe. The effort reduced any chance she had at landing another blow. She glanced around. The flashlight provided minimal illumination behind her. Her eyes widened at the things she saw. She had to catch her breath. She had to continue to fight.

"Kenneth," Chernov said. "Are you up?"

The man grunted and staggered to his feet, using the stairs to prop his body off the ground.

"Dammit, Kenneth, at least take the flashlight."

Kenneth came around using the stairs and then the wall to support himself.

He took the flashlight from Chernov's outstretched hand and shined it on Jasmine.

She flinched when the light hit her eyes. At once, her lungs expanded and damp air rushed in through her mouth. She brought her arm close to her chest and drove her elbow into the side of Chernov's face. He let go of her and she attempted to sweep his feet out from under him. Another bad move. As she lowered herself to deliver the kick, he brought his fist down, catching her on her cheek. She had been in an awkward position and, while the blow was not particularly hard, it was enough to knock her off balance. She fell back.

Chernov jumped on her and used his weight against her. He said, "Get the restraints." He pressed her flat to the ground and held her arms out and above her head.

Jasmine felt the cold metal touch her wrists and then envelop them. First her left, then her right. She could do nothing to stop it. She tried, but her thrashing and kicking and biting and head butting did nothing to free her from Chernov's grip.

She heard one click, then another. Then Chernov exhaled and rolled off of her. The sound of metal grating against metal filled the room and she felt her arms stretch taught as they were yanked into the air. Her body followed. A moment later she hung in the air, toes barely touching the ground.

"Lower her a bit." Chernov passed by her and grabbed the flashlight while Kenneth dropped the chains a few inches.

Her feet hit the ground and her arms dropped a little. It wasn't much, but it was enough.

Chernov directed the flashlight to the corner of the room. He walked over and opened a box mounted on the wall. Flipped a large rectangular framed switch and three lights turned on. One at the base of the stairs and two above Jasmine. They cast yellow light across the room.

It became clear to Jasmine that she was in a dungeon.

39

PIERRE STOOD BEHIND THE ART GALLERY. HE REPLAYED THE CONVERSATION HE'D had with Clarissa over and over in his head. He tried to shake the guilt, but couldn't. Hadn't been able to for six months. Why would he be able to now? It made no sense to him. He was trained to have no conscience. How could someone with a conscience do the things he had done during his twenty years in the agency?

We were on the side of right.

A teenage boy dressed in jeans, a t-shirt and an apron burst through the screen door. He carried two bags of trash, one in each hand. Pierre stepped aside and let the young man pass, glad that he had already retrieved his weapon from inside the dumpster. The boy took the six steps again, two at a time, yanked the door open and disappeared inside the kitchen area.

Pierre had decisions to make. The first, whether or not to take the girl, was already decided. But what to do once he had taken her? That was the question that played on his mind. The honorable thing to do would be to uphold his end of the deal with Bear and return the girl to him. It's what he promised. Sure, there was the certainty that Bear would kill him if he refused to comply. He was, after all, there to kill Bear.

Pierre found the lure of the money to be strong, though. And to top it off,

Clarissa was inside. He could lure her out and terminate her, too. Surely, the old man would be doubly happy if he did so. If Bear was worth two-fifty, and the old man offered to more than double the payment in exchange for the little girl, imagine what he would pay if Clarissa had been disposed of as well. Seven-fifty? A million? The money tempted Pierre like a twenty dollar whore after six weeks stuck in a ten by ten room with four male agents.

The door burst open again and the same young man stepped through carrying a third bag of trash. He asked, "Can I get a smoke?"

Pierre nodded and pulled out two cigarettes. Lit both. Handed one to the teenager.

"Nice night," the guy said.

Pierre nodded.

"Was supposed to go out with this girl tonight. Total babe. A buddy of mine was supposed to work this gig. Called in sick, though. So they asked me to come in."

"And you did?"

The guy shrugged. "They offered an extra two dollars an hour. Plus, if I didn't, my buddy would have been fired."

"So you ditched the girl to save your friend's job."

"Yeah."

"Dumbass."

The guy laughed and said, "Thanks for the smoke." He flicked the lit cigarette into the dumpster and hopped up the stairs and back into the kitchen.

Pierre looked over at the dumpster and noticed a stream of smoke lifting above it. The cigarette had started a small fire. Pierre smiled. He pulled out his lighter and set more trash on fire. Then he checked his watch and realized he had just a few seconds before he was supposed to meet Mandy.

The only people in the kitchen were the cooks and the teenage boy. Pierre nodded at him and the guy smiled in return. Pierre walked to the swinging door and looked through a round window cut in the center. He saw the little girl in the hall. She had only taken a few steps on her way to the restrooms. He pushed through and stopped.

The little girl looked at him, nodded once and winked, once with each eye. Close enough. Pierre nodded back, winked. They both walked toward each other and Pierre turned and ushered her in front of him. They crossed through the kitchen, empty except for the cooks and the teenage boy. He didn't acknowledge Pierre this time. The guy's head was down and his hands worked a metal tray with a sponge.

Pierre opened the screen door and waited for Mandy to step out.

"Quickly," he said. "Down the stairs and turn right."

She took the stairs one at a time, stopped at the bottom and turned to the right.

"Go. Walk ahead of me for a minute. I'll catch up to you."

Pierre stood at the stairs. He scanned the rooftops of the buildings nearby. Saw no one. He knew that didn't mean they were clear, though. Someone could be hunched over, or blended into an area where Pierre would not be able to distinguish them from the building and the sky. He pulled the gun from his pants and held it tight. Started walking in the same direction as Mandy. Caught up with her a few seconds later.

"Where are we going?" she asked.

He didn't respond. He placed one hand on her shoulder and held the gun in the other. His eyes scanned the buildings. Red brick during the day. Masses of black at night. His heart raced. Something wasn't right. He stopped. Closed his eyes. He centered the girl in front of him. Wrapped an arm across her face, covering her eyes and ears and mouth. He lifted the gun over her shoulder.

Mandy wriggled against his grasp. Every movement she made resulted in her becoming pulled closer and tighter.

Pierre brought the gun up a few inches, turned it inward. He opened his eyes. Looked down at the top of her blond head. He held the gun tight and placed his finger on the trigger. It felt ice cold against the tip of his index finger.

He heard a click, like the sound of a small twig snapping. He looked up, to the left. Saw a glint of light. Saw a man standing there. Saw him raising a gun and aiming it at them.

Pierre lifted his arm and quickly aimed in the direction of the man. He pulled the trigger three times. At least one bullet hit the man and he fell back and hit the ground.

Pierre scooped Mandy in his arms and ducked behind the first alley he could find. He ran as fast and as hard as he could. He crossed the road without looking left or looking right. Continued on and into the next alley, between two buildings. He stopped. Set the girl down and then bent over, catching his breath. The little girl cried. Pierre pulled her close and hugged her.

"I'm sorry, darling," he said. "I had to or he would have shot us."

She continued to cry.

He looked up at the sky and said, "Jack, I did right by you and trust that you'll do right by me."

40

BEAR STOOD IN FRONT OF A BRICK WALL, IN BETWEEN TWO POOLS OF LIGHT CAST down from street lights that sat atop chipped wooden utility poles. The air was still. The block wide buildings on either side of the alley shielded him from the breeze. The narrow alley was empty. Cars passed by on the city roads at each end. None stopped. None turned. The view above offered no signs of life. No light filtered through sheer curtains. No noise slipped through cracked windows. The alley, much like the town itself, had the appearance of being, for lack of a better word, dead. Of course, Bear now realized that Knoxville was nothing like it appeared.

He tried to remain as inconspicuous as a man of his size could. He checked his watch and saw that Pierre was ten minutes late. Bear forgot about trying to stay out of sight.

He pulled out his radio and said, "Pierre? Larsen? Anyone out there?"

He lifted his finger off the transmit button and received static in response. Had he been double crossed? He looked left, then right. Still alone. He started to form a plan should things take a turn for the worse.

Finally a voice came over through the speaker on the radio. "Bear, it's Pierre. I have Mandy. We are a few blocks away."

Bear leaned over and placed his hands on his knees. He took a deep breath and exhaled. Lifted the radio to his face and said, "Which way? I'll start making my way over."

"No," Pierre said. "Stick to the plan. Too many moving parts complicates things."

Bear nodded to no one and then said, "OK."

The radio returned to silence. Bear paced a ten foot span of the alley. He stopped, facing north, and noticed several cars passing on the street. Eight cars in total. Four close together, then a slight break, then four more. They didn't stop, and that was all that Bear cared about. He continued pacing. By this point he had retrieved his pistol and held it in his hand, letting it hang down to the side.

Footsteps echoed through the corridor and he stopped. The sounds came from behind him. He slowly turned his head to his right and looked over his shoulder. He saw two silhouettes. One held a gun. The other stood four feet six inches tall. He spun and started walking toward them.

"Bear," the familiar voice called out.

Bear knelt down and waited for Mandy. She ran into him and hit him with the force of a small car. Threw her small arms around his neck. He wrapped her up and lifted her into the air.

Pierre continued to approach, slowly.

Bear watched with caution. The man had been sent to kill him, after all. Perhaps he was still intent on doing so.

Bear nodded.

Pierre stopped and nodded back.

"Clarissa will meet us at the house tonight," Pierre said.

"We should head back then."

"We should split up."

"Not safe."

"Neither is traveling in a group."

"Pierre..."

"Take her, go to the car, and get to the house. I'll walk. I think I'll set up across the street from the house."

"Why?"

"To watch for bad guys."

"They don't know nothing about me, Pierre. Come to the house. Come in. We'll wait for Clarissa and hammer out our plan."

Pierre said nothing. He saluted Bear and turned and ran through the alley. He turned the corner. The echo of his footsteps faded.

Bear set Mandy down and looked her over. "Are you OK?"

She nodded and wiped tears from her cheeks and eyes.

"You sure? Did they harm you? Do anything to you?"

She shook her head. "No, they were nice to me. I had my own room. It was OK."

A weight lifted off Bear's chest. He grabbed Mandy's hand. "Let's go. I think we might skip the car and just go to the house."

"What if we need to leave later?"

"It's Larsen's car, not ours."

"Who's Larsen?"

"You'll meet him soon."

They walked hand in hand to the south end of the alley. Turned left at the corner. Streetlights turned night into day on the main road. The stores were all closed, their lights were off. Bear looked at their reflections in the dark windows. Traffic from Main Street, two blocks away, hummed in the background. The noise blocked out the sound of footsteps behind them until it was too late. Bear spun around and saw two men, armed, standing ten feet from them.

The guy on Bear's right spoke with a Russian accent. He said, "Where do you think you are going with our girl?"

Bear felt Mandy squeeze in next to him on his left side. He placed his hand on her shoulder. Just inside his jacket was his gun. But he dared not reach for it for fear of the men unloading on them. He had to get the men closer. Draw them in. That would be a fight he could win. But until that happened, he knew he was screwed.

41

JACK LANDED IN DES MOINES AFTER NINE P.M. HE GRABBED A RENTAL CAR. Reached out to Frank. They had narrowed down his search zone to a nearby city called Knoxville. Best guess, Frank had said. Jack shook his head. Might as well have reached into a hat and pulled the name out. He took solace in one thing. Frank's best guesses were better than the facts most others provided.

He left the airport and drove southeast on Highway 5. Twenty minutes later he found himself in Knoxville.

The town was small and quiet and didn't offer much in the way of answers to finding Jasmine. He drove through the grid-like city streets east to west and north to south. Turning left then right, at random. Something pushed him. Told him to keep going. He'd find her if he kept on. And that was what he would do. He wouldn't stop until he found her, and he'd kill anyone that got in his way.

He found himself on Main Street again. He had already driven the length of it west and was now making a pass going east. He reached the edge of the downtown district. Turned right on 5th Street, and right again on Robinson. He drove another block and pulled up to the curb. Cut his headlights. Leaned forward and narrowed his eyes as he scanned the sidewalk ahead.

Jack saw four people. Two men standing side-by-side, their backs to Jack. Ten feet or so in front of them stood a man and a little girl. The man looked huge. The shape all too familiar to Jack.

It couldn't be.

He looked at the two men, backs to him, side-by-side. Studied them. They stood with similar posture. Slightly hunched over. Left arms dangling. Right arms cocked at the elbow. In front of their bodies they aimed weapons at the man and the child. Jack couldn't see it, but he'd seen the posture enough to know.

Jack placed his left hand on the door handle. His right hand traveled inside his jacket instinctively, reaching for his gun. He didn't have one. He had to ditch it at the airport.

"Christ," he muttered under his breath.

One of the men stepped forward. The man's arm straightened and Jack saw the gun. A car turned a corner about the same time and its headlights washed over the scene. There was no denying it.

Bear and Mandy.

Jack's spine and hands and feet tingled. The hair on the back of his neck stood up. The excitement he felt over seeing his old friend quickly dissipated as the gravity of the situation they were in became clear. Panic started to set in. All Jack's training and experience kicked into gear and he channeled his emotions into action.

The man closed in on Bear. Jack knew his friend needed a hand. Something that Jack could provide. The element of surprise. He dropped the car into drive and peeled off. Tires screeched against asphalt. Rubber burned as it tore against the jagged road. He placed his hand on the horn and didn't let up.

Bear reacted as Jack guessed he would. With his left hand he pushed Mandy behind him. With his right, he disarmed the guy who had turned his head, looking back at Jack. Then Bear placed him into a choke hold. The second man watched as Jack's rental car approached. Jack hit the brakes and the tires squealed. Jack hit the sidewalk and yanked the wheel to the right, sending the car into a fishtail. It stopped sideways. Back tires on the street. Front tires on sidewalk. Only a car door and ten feet of concrete separating Jack from the man.

Jack flung the door open and charged the stunned man. The guy lifted his arm and squeezed the trigger, firing wildly into the air. The bullet missed Jack by several feet. The man didn't recover quickly enough and Jack knocked the gun out of the guy's grip with his left hand. Drove his right hand into the bridge of the man's nose.

"Jack?" Bear said.

Jack had leaned over and delivered four more blows to the man's head. Then he looked up and smiled at his old friend, who had already disposed of his attacker.

"Is that really you?" The big man threw his hands behind his head and stared at Jack in disbelief. He opened his mouth repeatedly, but the only sounds to escape were unintelligible grunts.

"I'd love to stay here and catch up, maybe grab a cup of coffee, but I've got business to take care of." He cast his eyes toward at the men on the ground. "Looks like you do too. Care to team up?"

Bear nodded.

"Get in the car, get Mandy in the car."

The trio jumped in the rental vehicle and Jack pulled into the street and headed out of town.

After a minute or two, Bear said, "What the hell is up with that beard? And the hair? And..." he paused, his face a mixture of confusion and excitement and adrenaline. "You're dead. What the hell are you doing here?"

Jack grinned. "I'm not dead."

"Mr. Jack?"

Jack looked over his shoulder at Mandy. "Yeah, sweetie?"

Mandy leaned forward and stuck her head in between the front seats. "I'm glad you're not dead."

Jack laughed. "Me too."

"I was scared for you."

"Me? You don't have to be scared for me. Just like I don't have to be scared for you. Not when Bear is around to protect you."

The little girl smiled and leaned her head against Bear's shoulder.

Jack looked at Bear. "Where're we going?"

Bear gave him directions to the house and Jack told him everything that had happened. He told him about *Black Dolphin*. About the escape and the paralytic agent. Bear had questions about that and Jack had to shrug. He hadn't had time to broach the subject with Frank. Jack moved on to Greece and the six months he spent there. How he tried to call Bear, but the number had been disconnected. Bear only nodded and offered up no excuses as to why. Jack told him how he ended up back in the States and the commitment he made to Frank.

And then he told him about Jasmine and the Russians and the plot for a massive terrorist strike.

"Jesus, Jack," Bear said. "That's one hell of a story."

"Couldn't make it up, big man." Jack looked out the window at a line of dark houses with box shaped yards. Was Jasmine inside one of these homes? "Now I just need to find where they are keeping her."

"We can help with that."

"Yeah?" Jack said. "We?"

Bear smiled. "Yeah, we." He pointed across the dash. "That's the house. Turn on the next street. We should park a few houses away."

42

THE CROWD INSIDE THE GALLERY HAD THINNED OVER THE PAST HALF HOUR.
Clarissa noted that if she was going to leave undetected, now would be the time.
A large group gathered by the front door. They were talking and hugging and
saying their goodbyes. She joined them. Placed herself in the middle of the group
as they moved in unison through the doors.

She cast a glance over her shoulder. No one had watched her leave. A clean
escape.

She hung with the group, drifting toward the back, as they left the gallery
and turned right. One man, close to the front said, "Let's go to Ted's Bar for a
drink."

The others in the group voiced their approval.

Clarissa figured she should join them and look for an opportunity to leave
from within the bar.

They walked the block or so to Ted's and the man in the front who
suggested the bar held the door open. He was tall with a full head of gray and
black hair. He wore steel rimmed circular shaped glasses. Had a broad smile
spread across his face. He spouted off each person's nickname, or real name, or
perhaps a name he invented on the spot. When everyone had passed through
the open doorway and only Clarissa remained, he lowered his gaze and said,
"Well, I have no name for you, now do I?"

"Janice," she quickly said.

"Well, hello, Janice. I'm Gary. Care to have a drink?"

She smiled and passed by and sought the anonymity that only a dark and crowded bar could provide. The group huddled around the bartender and she passed by, choosing an empty table toward the back of the establishment. She sat with her back to wall. She had a view of the room, the bar and the door. If anyone entered, she'd notice. At least, she would when Gary got out of her way.

"Help you?" she said.

"How about that drink?" he said.

"I'll pass."

"Waiting for someone?"

She looked at him, then at the door, then back at him. "Yes."

He lifted his hands and stepped back. "I'll be up at the bar if he doesn't show."

She wished she hadn't followed the group inside. Gary was making it hard for her to go unnoticed. His lingering by her table had cast several unwanted eyes in her direction. A waitress came by and Clarissa ordered a beer. A few moments later the waitress returned with the beer and set it on the table. Clarissa took a long pull from the frozen glass mug. She savored the taste. The bar remained in a state of equilibrium for several minutes. No one entered. No one left. People chose tables and a few remained on barstools.

Would the balance change soon? Would some of Boris's men leave the party and take refuge at Ted's?

Clarissa finished her beer, dropped a five dollar bill on the table and placed the mug on top of the money. She followed a corridor behind her to the lady's room. She stepped into the restroom and noticed a window on the opposite wall. She went to inspect it. There was enough space for her to slip through. What was on the other side? She flipped the latch in the middle and lifted the glass pane. Pulled herself up and stuck her head out. The space between that building and the next was over five feet wide. Plenty of room. She turned her head left then right. The alley connected to both Main and Marion Street.

She reached behind and pulled out her gun. Having her gun drop in the bathroom as she passed through the open window would not be ideal.

With her gun in hand, Clarissa pulled herself up and out through the open window. She switched to a seated position on the window sill and swung her left leg over. Then the right. She hopped down onto the asphalt coated alleyway and walked toward Main Street.

The most treacherous part of her journey would be walking through downtown, a five block radius full of too many streetlights and, on this particular night, too many Russians. She slipped out of her heels and picked them up. Ran down the alley. She slowed her pace in an attempt to blend in once she hit Main Street. She headed east and turned right on 4th Street, then left on Robinson. One block to go until she entered the residential part of town.

Footsteps echoed off of the buildings that surrounded her. They came from behind. They indicated whoever was behind her was moving quickly, possibly running.

She squeezed the handle of her gun and lifted it to her chest. Her left hand wrapped around her right, keeping it steady.

The steps closed in on her quickly. She waited until they were within twenty feet and spun around. Arms stretched out, gun aimed at the first person she saw.

A man and woman, dressed in dark tracksuits with reflective strips, froze in place. She looked them up and down. They wore running shoes that matched the tracksuits. The man reached his arm out in front of the woman and ushered her behind him. He spoke between deep breaths, "We don't have any money on us."

Clarissa shook her head. "I'm sorry. Someone's after me."

The woman peered over the man's shoulder. "We can call the cops for you."

"No good. Just forget you saw me. Please."

Clarissa spun on her heel and took off in a sprint and didn't let up until she'd run at least a half mile. She slightly decreased her pace and ran another half mile in less than three minutes.

She saw Bear's house. One car in the driveway. Porch light on. Light on inside the front window. Light on around the side, where she remembered the kitchen being located. She hunkered down next to a car parked on the curb and watched the house while she caught her breath. Finally, satisfied that the area was clear, she crossed the street and Bear's front lawn. She stood in front of the door. Straightened out her clothes. Dropped her heels to the ground and held her gun behind her back. Then she knocked on the door.

43

"WHO THE HELL ARE YOU?" THE GUY SAID.

Jasmine lifted her head and stared at the Russian who had identified himself as Boris. They were the only two in the basement room used as a dungeon of sorts. She said nothing to him.

"I'm going to ask you again, and I expect a response. Who are you?"

"Or what?" she said. "What're you gonna do? Beat me?"

Boris smiled, let out a soft chuckle and leaned in. He placed a hand on her waist and slid it up her side, stopping just past her ribs. He brushed the hair caked with blood and dirt to the side of her head, out of the way. Said softly, "I'm not going to beat you. I'm just going to shoot you. And eventually kill you."

Jasmine turned her head away and stared at the wall, the wall that might be the last thing she ever saw. She took a deep breath and composed herself.

Boris said, "Well?"

"Screw you."

"I'll be back." Boris turned and walked away from her. He walked up the stairs, one at a time, one heavy step after the other.

She placed her upper back against the wall, letting her arms relax. Blood flow returned to her wrists. The pain remained. She looked around, checking the wall and the floor for anything she could use against Boris when he returned. Found nothing. Even if she had, she wouldn't be able to reach it. Not when chained to a wall.

Her best chance was to get her legs around him and climb. Squeeze and work her legs upward and wrap them around his neck. That only solved one problem, though. She'd still be stuck down here, and someone would come down and see her chained up and Boris dead on the ground. They'd likely fire a bullet into her head before they asked what happened.

She brushed the thought aside and tried to come to grips with the fact that she'd be dead before sunrise. Not that she'd know the exact time. Not while stuck in the windowless basement.

Should she just give in? Give him her name? Tell him who she works for and what she was doing?

It violated everything she had ever worked for and every ounce of her training. Besides, Boris wouldn't stop at just her name, and she knew it. He also seemed to be the kind of man who could gather a lot of information based on her name. So even if she refused to talk any further, he'd be able to use his resources to get the answer, making her useless to him. And when dealing with men like him, useless was not ideal.

In the end she decided that the best thing to do would be to hold out as long as possible. They'd gone through the trouble of bringing her here, wherever here was, all the way from Atlanta. They wanted something from her and wouldn't dispose of her until they had it.

Fight, resist, stay strong.

The door opened and the far corner of the room by the stairs lit up. She heard Boris start down the stairs. Then she heard two more sets of footsteps descending behind him. He had brought reinforcements.

Pussy.

He rounded the corner and she tensed. He had a black bag in his hands. The men that came down with him were two that she did not recognize. Boris stopped in front of her. The men moved to the side of her, out of range of her legs.

"We had a party tonight," Boris said. "Couple hundred people there, I guess. Mostly people I don't know. Leeches who just show up for the free booze and free food. Do you know why we do this?"

Jasmine stared at the floor and said nothing.

"So that they will tolerate me and my men. The police, most of them don't mind. I've got two in my house right now."

Jasmine looked to her left and to her right at the men standing beside her. They didn't look like cops.

Boris smiled. "No, not them. They are mine, from back home. Anyway, where was I?"

"Shut up and get on with this," Jasmine said. "I don't care about your social life."

"Didn't I tell you she looked feisty?"

Jasmine fought back a smile. "You got no idea. Let me out of these chains and I'll show you."

Boris stepped to the left, turned and stepped to the right. "Oh, you'll be out of those chains soon enough. But you won't be in a position to do anything to me, or these men, or the corrupt policemen upstairs."

"Threatening my life is a waste of your time. I'm ready to die. It's an everyday reality with my job."

"And who is that job with?"

Jasmine didn't respond.

"Just tell me your name and who you work for and I'll see about letting you go."

She still didn't respond.

Boris sighed and dropped his head. "Fair enough." He unzipped the bag and pulled it open wide. He reached in and took out a vial and a clear plastic wrapper containing a syringe.

"I hope that's sanitary," she said.

Boris laughed. He ripped the plastic away and pulled the cap from the needle. He plunged it into the vial and filled the syringe. He said, "Do you know what this is?"

Jasmine shook her head.

"Well, in Russian we call it..." he paused a beat and smiled. "You don't care about Russian, do you?"

She shook her head again.

"Let's just call it truth serum. I'm going to inject it into you. After a few minutes you are going to be lightheaded and happy and loose-lipped." He paused for a moment. Smiled. "At the same time, it might hurt a bit."

Jasmine let her head drop. She focused on Boris's feet as he approached. She saw the men closing in on her in her peripheral vision. Now was the time. She pushed back into the wall and then exploded forward, driving her left leg back into the wall and her right leg forward. She caught Boris in the stomach or the groin, she couldn't tell and just assumed it was probably a bit of both. He dropped the vial and the needle and fell to the ground.

She brought her right leg down and pushed it back against the wall. The man to her left was closest, so she pulled her left knee into to her chest and then drove her leg down and out to the side. Her foot connected with the guy's kneecap. His leg bent unnaturally backward. She thought she heard a snapping sound or two. The man let out a grunt and a scream. He fell to the ground, clutching his deformed leg.

Jasmine felt her arms jerk upward, followed by her body being stretched. She was pulled off the ground. She turned her head to the right and saw that the third man had grabbed the chains and began pulling down. The chain threaded through a pulley mounted on the ceiling. The chain connected to her wrists and each time he pulled, she jerked upward.

The man on her left remained on the ground. His hands wrapped around his knee.

Boris got to one knee and rested for a minute, catching his breath she presumed.

Finally, he stood and said, "Hold her still."

The man on her right closed the distance and wrapped his arms around her legs. Pulled her forward, away from the wall. She was stretched out diagonally, arms near the wall, feet toward the middle of the room.

She kicked and twisted and turned. It turned out to be wasted energy. She felt a pinch in her side and looked down. Boris had jammed the needle into her abdomen. Not the ideal location but it would work its magic soon enough. Now the only decision she had to make was to pretend like it went to work before it actually had.

She knew what the drug felt like. They had applied it during her training. She mimicked the effect. Her charade only lasted two minutes. The drug kicked in. Her world slowed down to half speed, maybe less. She went limp and felt her body hit the ground.

44

When Jack and Bear had entered the house, Pierre went white as a ghost and fell to his knees. He hugged Jack. Thanked him for saving his life. Then the Frenchman apologized profusely for betraying Jack and agreeing to work for Charles and the old man. He told Jack that he hoped his actions and effort to rescue Mandy would allow for Jack to forgive him. He said he'd do anything Jack wanted to make up for his transgressions.

Pierre then joined Larsen and Mandy in the kitchen.

Jack and Bear sat across from each other, catching up on the events of the past six months.

The house fell silent after a quick and decisive knock on the door.

Bear said, "Jack, why don't you get that for me?"

"Why me?"

"I'm fixing to start dinner."

"When did you become so domesticated?"

"Bite me, Jack."

Jack laughed. Got off the couch and crossed the room. He stood in front of the door. Grabbed the knob and turned it to the right. Pulled the door open. The face that greeted him was one that he knew too well. A face that he thought of every single day. More than once a day. And for the better part of the last ten years.

"Clarissa."

Clarissa's eyes widened. Her mouth dropped open as she tried to speak. Said nothing. She flung her arms around Jack and pulled him close and kissed his cheek.

He did the same. Lifted her up and carried her over the threshold. He kicked the door shut and sat her down. "What are you doing here?" He ran his hands through her hair and added, "What did you do to your hair?"

"I—I should ask the same." She ran her hands through his hair and tugged lightly on his beard. "You're alive?"

Jack felt his chest and head and said, "Yeah, I think so."

"How did this... Where have you been?" She looked across the room at Bear, who leaned back against the wall, arms crossed, a big grin on his face. "Did you know about this?"

Bear said, "Just found out tonight. Had no idea."

The room had a warm vibe. Friends reunited. The smile on their faces told a story that any stranger could read.

"I wanted to tell you," Jack said. "But they said I needed to stay invisible. I'm a ghost. Everyone thinks I'm dead. I couldn't compromise that, even though I tried a time or two."

"Where were you?" she demanded. Her fists curled into balls and she slammed them into Jack's chest.

He wrapped his hands around her wrists, holding them close together. The tension between them started to slip away. He leaned forward. Let go of her arms. Wrapped his around her back. Their lips crossed the void and met in the middle.

He pulled back a minute later and continued, "When I got back to the States a few days ago the first thing I did was go to your apartment."

"That could have been risky."

Jack hiked his shoulders and inch. "Maybe. The super said you left six months ago. Where did you go?"

"I," she paused and bit her bottom lip. "I joined Sinclair's team."

"You're here for the same reason I am then? To take down the Russians?"

"I'm impersonating one. She was going to take over their main west coast cell."

"Why are you standing here right now?"

Clarissa looked past Jack and smiled at Mandy. "I helped her escape tonight."

"You blew your cover?"

"Maybe." The room fell silent for half a minute and then Clarissa said, "What do you have to do with the Russians?"

"Frank's the one that got me out of that Russian hell hole of a prison. He's also the one that—"

"Skinner?" Clarissa asked.

Jack nodded. "Yeah, Frank Skinner."

"You're working for him again?"

"For now. Got a debt to repay. He saved my life."

Clarissa nodded and gestured for Jack to continue.

"He doesn't work in the field anymore, so he partnered me up with one of his best agents. We were in Atlanta. They took her."

"Who?"

"The Russians. She's here. All the intelligence and evidence points to here."

Clarissa stood and walked past Jack. She paced the room, stopping to squeeze Bear's arm. She nodded at Larsen and smiled at Pierre and hugged Mandy. "If I haven't blown my cover then I can get you in there. He trusts me. They all trust me. They won't stop us from entering."

"You have a car here?" Jack asked.

"Not far," Clarissa replied.

Jack looked at Bear and then the clock on the wall. Almost midnight. It would be easy to remain content after being reunited with the people he considered his family. Everyone was relaxed and happy. But there was a dark undertone to the feeling in the room. "I'd love for this reunion to be on more pleasant terms, but it looks like we got a job to do. Let's get this planned."

The five of them sat around the kitchen table. Clarissa told them the layout of the house and the property. She explained where the guards were positioned.

"We can do this," Jack said.

"I want to join you," Pierre said.

Bear and Jack turned toward the Frenchman.

"You can trust me," Pierre said. "Allow me to make it up to you."

"OK," Jack said. "Double cross me, and I'll kill you first."

Pierre nodded without hesitation.

"I want in," Larsen said.

Bear shook his head. "Detective, I need you to stay with Mandy. Bring her some place safe."

"Dammit, I want my revenge."

"I know you do, but you aren't trained for this kind of thing. We are."

Larsen clenched his jaw and grabbed the edges of the table. The veins in his neck stood out and his cheeks trembled with anger.

"You can help us," Jack said. "We need weapons. Two sniper rifles and whatever tactical weapons you can get your hands on."

Larsen looked at Bear. "What about the informant?"

"Screw him," Bear said. "He didn't get us anything and I don't want to repay him for nothing."

Larsen took a series of deep breaths and his anger appeared to drop a notch. He said, "I can get you weapons. I'll go now. Take me half an hour." He rose from the table and left the house without another word.

Jack waited until the front door closed and said, "Can we trust him?"

Bear nodded. "He wants them dead as much as we do."

Jack turned to Clarissa. "Where would they keep Jasmine?"

She shrugged. "They kept Mandy in a room down the hall from me. But I doubt that's where they would keep an agent."

"Me too. Did you ever see any kind of holding cells or a cellar or anything like that?"

"No."

"Wherever she is, she'll be guarded and locked up. No way they take a chance on letting her out."

Bear nodded and so did Clarissa.

Jack said, "What else do we need to do while we're there?"

"The documents," Clarissa said. "He has information on several targets. Weaknesses and the best time frame for a joint attack. Landmarks, infrastructure, more. It's bad."

Jack nodded and said nothing. The documents were his second highest priority and he had no intention of leaving the house without them.

"We should get those," Clarissa said. "And take out everyone in that house. Most importantly, take out Boris."

"Frank might want him alive," Jack said.

"I don't know that he'd go alive. Not after the file I read on him."

"Frank'll want to know who the boss is back in Russia."

"I can get close to him. He trusts me," Clarissa paused and smiled. "He trusts Anastasiya. I'll tell him that someone roughed me up outside the gallery. That'll set him on edge a bit. Then you guys start the attack inside. I'll knock him unconscious."

"Everyone else?" Pierre asked.

Jack looked past the group. Nodded at the little girl at the kitchen table.

"Mandy," Bear said. "Go to your room and pack a bag with some clothes and stuff."

Jack waited until the girl was out of earshot. "Kill them all."

"We need a plan," Bear said.

Jack leaned over the table and spread his arms. "Here's what I'm thinking."

45

"HOW ARE YOU FEELING?" BORIS SAID TO THE WOMAN LYING ON THE FLOOR. HER eyelids fluttered and then remained half open. She slowly looked from him to the ceiling to the stairs. Her eyes stopped at the stairs. He said, "There's no point. You'll never make it. Besides, you can't even stand. Try it."

He watched the woman move her hand in slow motion. It took a minute for her fingers to travel three inches. Tears formed in her eyes and slipped off her cheek and onto the floor, forming a small puddle. Boris grabbed her by the shirt and pulled her up. Propped her against the wall. He grabbed her by the cheeks and forced her to face him.

"Can you talk? Why don't you say something for me?"

"Something," she said.

Boris smiled. "It's a shame I didn't get to know you under different circumstances. You and I could have been something together. You know that?"

The woman said, "Something." Her head swayed to the side and her eyes closed.

"Right," Boris said. "Why don't you start by telling me your name?"

"Jas," she paused. "Jasmine."

Boris nodded to the man next to him who then scribbled her name onto a pad. "Jasmine what?"

"Medina."

"Jasmine Medina. That's lovely. What's your background? No, better yet, who do you work for Ms. Medina? It is Miss, right?"

"Yes."

"And who do you work for, Ms. Medina?"

"Nobody."

"Now, I don't believe that."

"We're ghosts."

"Ghosts?"

"We don't exist."

"Well, obviously you exist. You are sitting in front of me right now."

Jasmine shook her head. Smiled.

"What is the name of the organization? Who is your boss?"

"Ess," she said.

"As in the letter 's'?"

She half-nodded, her head collapsing to her chest after each upswing.

"OK, S what?"

"S.I.S."

"And what is that?"

She lifted her head and locked eyes with him. Held his gaze for half a minute and said, "A group for ghosts."

Boris sighed and turned to his man. "Take note of SIS and we'll get someone back home to check on that." He turned back to her. "Ms. Medina, who is your boss in the SIS?"

"There are no bosses."

"Surely someone has to direct and decide what your assignments are."

"Frank."

"Frank what?"

She shrugged. "I never asked."

Boris nodded at his man and looked back at Jasmine. "It's come to my attention that when my men apprehended you in our house in Georgia, you had a partner with you that they left behind. What's his name?"

"John," she said.

"John what?"

"John Martin." She smiled and winked.

"Is that his real name?"

"It's a fake name because he really is a ghost."

"You said you were a ghost. Is Jasmine Medina a fake name?"

She shrugged.

Boris slapped her across the face, not hard, not lightly.

"It's my real name."

"What's John Martin's real name?"

"Jack Noble."

Boris stood and walked to the other end of the room. "Jack Noble? That name, so familiar." He returned to his position in front of Jasmine and said, "Why do I recognize that name?"

"He's probably the reason your teeth are so crooked."

Boris ignored the last statement. "What were you two doing in my house in Georgia?"

"Closing in on you." She paused, tilted her head back and forced a smile. "We're going to bring you down." She closed her eyes. Her head bobbed down, then back up. "There's nothing you can do to stop us." She licked her lips. Smiled. "Kill me. Kill Jack. Kill Frank. It won't matter." Her body twitched and she coughed. She took a deep breath and steadied herself. "We've got you and we are going to take you down one cell, one man, one life at a time."

Boris stood. Brushed himself off. "That's enough for now. Chain her wrists but leave her seated. Let her sleep it off. We'll review the details with her in the morning. See if she comes around at all. Maybe after that I'll contact Ivanov."

46

Jack lay in the dark next to Pierre. He tried to remain motionless while holding the cord that kept the trunk lid closed, but not latched. The car slowed down. Muffled voices slipped through the sliver of a crack that split the rear seat. The car dipped low on the passenger side and then sprung up. Bear had just stepped out, Jack figured. That meant they were close.

Detective Larsen had returned with a cache of weapons. He wouldn't admit it, but Jack guessed that the Detective had raided the SWAT team's stock. For Bear, he brought two Heckler & Koch MSG90 semi-automatic sniper rifles. A good choice and popular with the police and military. He'd also brought each of them a Glock 17. And each received an H&K MP5 equipped with a 30-round magazine and a spare magazine, giving them sixty rounds, or twenty shots when setting the gun to its three-shot burst firing mode. Finally, he had handed them each a pair of ATN night vision goggles.

They had the fire power. They had Clarissa to get them next to the house. They would have the darkness of night and the element of surprise.

"You ready?" Jack said.

"Yes," Pierre said. "And Jack, I never got the chance to thank you for saving my life in Russia."

"Don't mention it."

"I have to. That would have been it for me. It lifts my spirit that you are alive. I'm going to—"

"Pierre," Jack interrupted. "Stop. We have a job to do. Help me complete this and then we are even. I don't care about the agreement with the old man and Charles or anything else that happened in Russia. We're here now, and we have a job to do."

"OK."

The car began moving again. Slowly. Made a sharp turn. The ride became bumpy. Gravel crushed under the weight of the car. The tires kicked up small stones, some of them hitting the car's undercarriage. The noise would certainly be noticed by the guards Clarissa told them would be positioned in the courtyard.

A minute later the car stopped, then kicked in reverse. She was backing the car up, like they had planned. That would allow Pierre and Jack to slip out of the trunk undetected. The car rolled to a stop and jerked a tad when Clarissa threw it into park.

He heard boots on the pavement. More than one pair. Clarissa's door opened, her feet hit the ground, took a few steps and then the door closed. The boots stopped. Clarissa walked away from the car and said something to the guards. The sound of their steps faded.

Jack slipped his night vision goggles over his head and switched them on. He lifted his head and saw Pierre do the same. Jack then gave Pierre a signal that they would go in thirty seconds. Based on the layout of the property that Clarissa had provided, it should take Bear less than a minute to cross the wooded area between the compound and the road. It would take less than thirty seconds for Clarissa to cross the parking lot and make her way into the compound. Once inside, she was to find Boris and convince him that she needed to speak with him in private.

An internal clock counted down the seconds. The countdown was interrupted by the sound of music. An old song. Jack couldn't place it. Sounded French.

"Shit," Pierre said.

Jack heard the Frenchman fumbling around and then the music stopped. He had forgotten to silence his cell phone. Jack shook his head and said nothing.

Tension filled the trunk. They waited, but heard nothing to indicate that any of the guards had heard the cell phone's ring tone.

"Let's get out," Jack said. He inched the trunk lid up and checked behind them. Another inch and he checked to the side. "Clear over here."

"Here too," Pierre said.

They lifted the trunk as high as necessary for them to slip out. They got flat on the ground. Crawled twenty yards to the left and found a clearing. Time to wait for the three guards positioned on the roof to cluster together. Then the attack would begin.

47

"I GOT IT," CLARISSA SAID, SHAKING HER ARM FREE FROM THE MAN'S GRASP. SHE looked around the foyer and caught another man's eye. "Where is Boris?"

"Where have you been?" the man asked.

"That is not for you to know. Where is Boris?"

The man twitched his head to the right, toward the hallway.

Clarissa walked through the foyer and down the hall. Stopped at the door to Boris's office. She took a deep breath and ran her hands through her hair in an effort make herself look disheveled. She tugged and pulled on her dress to give the effect that it had been torn. Finally, she knocked on the door.

The door opened and Boris stood in front of her. His eyes were dark with anger. He only glanced at her before spinning around and walking back to his desk. He held up a hand and gestured for her to follow.

"Boris—"

"Silence."

She said nothing. Crossed the room and took a seat in front of his desk.

"Where were you?"

"That's why I came in here. I was attacked."

"You? Attacked?"

"Yes." She cast her eyes down toward the floor and folded her hands in her lap.

"Where?"

"Outside the gallery. I went out to get some fresh air. Decided to get a drink at the bar next door."

"You did what?"

"I know I shouldn't have. I just had to get out of that gallery for a while. I didn't feel comfortable around those people."

Boris shrugged. He seemed to be buying the story. "Then what happened?"

"I was in the bar. Took a seat near the back and ordered a drink. I went to the lady's room and this man followed me."

"What did he look like?"

"I never really got a good look at him."

Boris narrowed his eyes and watched her as she spoke.

"I was looking in the mirror and he burst in, the door blocked my view. Then he came up behind me and tried to attack me. Had my by the hair and tried to pull my dress off."

"And you just let him?"

"Of course not. I attacked him. Left him a bloody mess in the bathroom. And then I fled."

"So why didn't you come back here?"

"I wanted to. But there was only one way out of the bar and that was through the front. I ran through the place, but everyone saw me and they must have heard what had happened in the back."

"No one went back there?"

"They had started to, I guess, but I finished him off too fast. I might have finished him off too well. I don't know if he lived. They all saw me. Everyone in the bar saw me. I took off down the street and hid for a while, but I could still see the bar. The cops came, and I waited and then they left."

Boris held up a finger. "Wait a minute, I can place a call and get this taken care of with the police." He reached for the phone. Clarissa leaned forward and placed her hand on his. He stopped and looked up at her. "What?"

"Not tonight, Boris," she said. "Wait till morning. After all, I was able to get to the car and drive back here. If the cops show up you can deal with them in person, right?"

"That's true. Probably better that way. You'll go nowhere for a few days. Got it?" He leaned back in his chair. Opened a drawer and pulled out a cigar.

Offered it to Clarissa, who declined. He struck a wooden match and lit the cigar.

The smell of the cigar quickly filled the room. Reminded her of her father. She studied Boris for a few minutes and wondered if he planned to send a few of his men in the middle of the night to question her further.

She decided to try to feel him out with conversation. "How did the gala go tonight?"

Boris shrugged. "It's always a waste of my time. I hate kissing up to those fools. I hate Iowa. Hate the U.S."

There was a knock at the door and Boris placed his cigar down on the edge of the glass ashtray on the corner of his desk. "Excuse me for a moment." He stood and stepped out from behind the desk. Walked across the room and opened the door.

Clarissa remained seated and listened to the conversation.

"Sir, the girl is missing."

"The agent? She's locked up downstairs. How is she—"

"Not the agent, sir. The little girl."

"She was at the party. Anastasiya was supposed to be watching her."

Clarissa felt the heat of his stare through the back of her chair.

"Leave me," Boris said.

The door closed shut and then she heard the distinctive click of the lock. He took his time turning around. She watched his reflection in the window. He reached inside his jacket. Was he going for a gun? She felt like a fool for coming in unarmed. Jack had argued that she needed a weapon on her, but she feared being searched on her way to see Boris or after she came in. Walking in armed would have been a death sentence if he had checked.

He dropped his hand to his side and she didn't see a weapon. He walked slowly across the room. Stopped behind her. Placed his hands on her shoulders.

Clarissa glanced at her watch. Enough time had passed and the attack would start soon.

"Anastasiya, my most promising assistant, where the hell were you tonight, and where is the little girl?"

She said nothing. Felt his hands closing in around her neck. She stared at the window, at him and then beyond him. She saw the muzzle flash across the parking lot, from the woods. The attack had started. Now was the time to strike.

She twisted in her seat and slammed her elbow into his crotch and he let go of her neck. She leapt from the chair. Grabbed the heavy glass ashtray off the desk. She cradled it against her forearm and twisted her body to the right, then spun to the left. Her right arm stretched out behind her and whipped around with great force. The heavy glass ashtray connected with Boris on the left side of his forehead. He immediately collapsed to the ground. She held the ashtray above her head and slammed it down one more time, ensuring that he was unconscious.

Clarissa turned Boris over on his back. Blood poured from a deep gash on his forehead. She ignored it and pulled his jacket opened. Grabbed the pistol he had holstered there. She moved behind the desk and opened the drawers and rifled through the files and papers. She found another pistol. Continued to search for something to restrain Boris with. She found a roll of duct tape and decided that was her best option. She wrapped his ankles together, then his knees, then his hands behind his back. Then she connected the three shackles together. She dragged him behind the desk and walked to the door.

The plan called for her to wait for Jack or Pierre or Bear to arrive.

48

Jack watched Bear's position in the woods. Pierre kept an eye on the courtyard, making sure no one approached them.

"It's almost time," Jack said.

"OK."

Three quick muffled shots were each followed by a quick burst of muzzle flash. Jack turned his head and saw the three guards on top of the roof drop dead. Two more appeared. Two more shots were fired from the woods. The men fell. That left one more guard on the roof. Chances are he wouldn't make himself visible, which meant that the units on the ground would soon be aware of the attack.

"Now," Jack said. He looked over his shoulder and saw Bear approaching. Bear had ditched one of the MSG90s and aimed the other at the roof. He signaled to Jack that he was going to skirt the perimeter to the west. Jack hoped that the big man would get a shot on the last remaining roof guard.

Pierre moved first, staying low to the ground and behind a car for cover. He rose up and fired four three-round bursts into the dark. Jack looked over, saw three men drop. He spotted a team approaching from the area near the front door. Jack fired once and took out the man in the middle. The other two stopped. He fired several more times, and hit the man on his right. The guy on the left turned and started to run. Jack fired again, hitting him in the back near the base of his neck. Each shot hit an inch above the previous one. The final bullet penetrated the man's skull, and as he fell a cloud of blood hovered in the air.

Jack and Pierre started to move toward the house. They crossed the courtyard quickly. Pressed back against the wall. Headed west. Based on Clarissa's description, that was where the alternate entrances were located, as well as rooftop access.

Jack looked into the field and saw Bear hunched over. Bear gave him a signal to let him know that the area around Jack was all-clear. He and Pierre walked under a set of stairs leading to the roof.

"I'm going up there," Pierre said.

Jack signaled to Bear and then said, "Go. Bear's got you covered."

Pierre slipped out of sight and made his way to the roof. Jack heard a burst of fire and the thud of a body hitting the rooftop. Pierre had found the sixth guard.

A door opened. Jack pressed into the wall. Heard multiple footsteps, soft and slow. Saw a gun barrel appear and a man followed. He heard a gunshot and the lead man dropped. Jack looked across the field and saw Bear stand, ditch his rifle and start approaching. Jack spun to his right and took out the next man. Bear fired and the third dropped.

Jack waited for Bear. By this time, the men inside knew that they were under attack. They'd taken out fifteen men during the initial attack. Clarissa estimated twenty-two at the house, plus Boris. Jack knew that there might also be men from Atlanta. He counted on running into them. Hoped to run into them. He had a little unfinished business to take care of with them.

Pierre came back down the stairs. "Rooftop is clear. I checked the other side of the house and there is no one out there. Same for behind the house, although we should probably watch it. I can take that."

Jack didn't want them to split up, but having someone behind the house to catch anyone who fled was a good idea. He found himself wishing they could have brought the detective along rather than leaving him to take care of Mandy. They could have rented a hotel room and stashed her there.

"OK," Jack said. "Once you see one of us inside, you come in."

Pierre nodded and disappeared around the corner of the house.

Jack pulled open the door and stuck the barrel of his MP5 through the opening. Didn't see anyone. He heard voices, though. Panicked and desperate voices.

They stepped into the long narrow hallway. There was a door on each side. Another further down the hall. Bear kicked in the one on the right. Empty. Then he kicked in the one on the left. Also empty. They moved to the third door. Before they attempted to open it, two men appeared at the end of the hallway. One fired. Bear let out grunt and then opened fire, sending three separate three-round bursts down the hall, striking one man with three bullets and the second with six. Both men collapsed.

"Are you injured?" Jack said.

Bear took a moment to respond. "Just a knick."

"Can you continue?"

"Yeah."

They continued down the hall. Reached the end. Jack lifted his night vision goggles. The house seemed empty. It should after taking out seventeen of it's inhabitants.

Jack crouched low and scanned the open area of the middle of the house. The front door was open. He heard cars starting and pulling out.

"Dammit," Jack said. "Let's find Clarissa now."

"What about that last room?"

"Go check it. I'll cover you from the end of the hall."

They both returned to the dark hallway. Jack waited at the end and kept an eye on the open living room and dining room. He heard the back door open. Aimed his gun. Pierre stepped in. They signaled to each other and Pierre moved to the corner of the room where he could see Jack and keep an eye on the front door and the second hallway that was out of Jack's view.

"Jack," Bear said. "It's a basement."

"OK. Check it out."

"There's someone down there."

"Kill them."

"They are calling for help."

Jasmine.

"Go clear the house with Pierre," Jack said.

He passed Bear in the hall and ran down the stairs. Spun around and saw Jasmine laying there. He moved toward her. Knelt down by her side to check for a pulse. She was alive and barely conscious.

"Hello, Jack," a voice said from behind him in a thick Russian accent. "Had a feeling that was you. Or, well she did. She said that Jack was here and that he was going to kill us all."

Jack said nothing. He slowly stood up and looked over his shoulder. He recognized the man he had seen a day before walking his dog. It was Chernov.

"So of course," Chernov continued, "I knocked her out. No way some has-been agent is taking us down."

"Seventeen dead, so far."

Chernov laughed. "Going to be eighteen soon then. Overall, that is. Now turn around slowly, weapon out. Hold it by the barrel."

Jack did as told and turned to face Chernov.

"Toss it," Chernov said, gesturing toward the MP5.

Jack knelt down and set the weapon on the floor and then pushed it toward Chernov.

"Stupid American." Chernov kept his gun aimed at Jack. Pulled out a cigarette and lit it. "Let me ask you something, Jack Noble. When you killed my brother, did you give him an honorable death, or did you sneak up behind him like the pussy that you are?"

Jack shrugged. "Who the hell are you talking about?"

"His name was Aleksander Chernov. He was Dorofeyev's bodyguard."

Jack nodded. "I didn't kill him. He fell off a boat. Screamed like a child, though."

Chernov took a step forward and stopped in front of Jack's gun. Picked it up and aimed it at Jack's head. Said, "Tell me, before I kill you, how will it feel to be taken out by your own weapon?"

Jack smiled.

Chernov smiled back. He knelt down, letting the barrel of the gun in his hand rest on the floor while he reached for Jack's. He took his eyes off of Jack. It wasn't long, barely a second or two. But that was long enough.

Jack reached behind him and retrieved his Glock from his waistband. He whipped his arm around.

Chernov looked up, at first bewildered, and then recognition flashed across his face when he saw the gun in Jack's hand. He lifted the MP5 from the floor and jerked it up. Pulled the trigger. Nothing happened.

"I set the safety," Jack said. He fired a single shot. It hit Chernov dead center in his forehead. His body twitched back and then fell forward. Jack reached over and pulled the MP5 from the dead Russian's grasp.

"What's happening? What's going on?" Jasmine said.

Jack looked over his shoulder and then spun around on his knees. "Jack's here, Jazz. It's OK now."

"I told you," she paused and took a deep breath and pushed herself off the floor, "Don't call me Jazz." She smiled at him and held out her arms.

Jack freed her from her shackles and helped her off the floor. He said, "I don't know how safe it is up there yet. You feel strong enough to hold a weapon?"

She nodded. "Think so." Then she wiped the sweat and blood from her brow and her face and took the Glock from Jack's outstretched hand.

"Follow me."

49

Clarissa tensed at the first knock on the office door. Was it Jack or Bear or Pierre? She looked around the office. One way in. One way out. She pulled her gun to her chest and stood behind the door. "Who is it?"

"Bear."

She grabbed the handle and turned it slowly. She pulled it open a crack and peered through. Saw Bear's massive figure looming in the hallway. Pierre stood next to him.

She pulled the door open and ushered the two men into the room. After they passed, she stuck her head through the doorway and checked the hallway. Empty. She shut the door and flipped the lock.

"Where's Jack?" she asked.

"We found a basement," Bear said. "He went to clear it. Betting that's where his partner was being kept. He should be here in a minute."

"You left him alone? What if there was someone down there or getting ready to check?"

"He told me to clear the house with Pierre."

"Did you?"

"Yeah."

"How many people did you take out?"

"'Bout a dozen-and-a-half."

"There's more than that."

"Well they ain't in the house."

Clarissa shook her head and reached back with one hand, grabbing a fistful of hair. She looked over at Pierre and lifted an eyebrow, looking for any input he might have.

Pierre said nothing.

She double checked the door. Made sure it was locked. She paced the space between the desk and the door. She wanted to leave the room. Find Jack. That would be a mistake and she knew it. Don't deviate from the plan unless something catastrophic happens. So far, nothing had.

"That him?" Bear asked as he pointed to the man bound on the floor behind the desk.

"Yeah," Clarissa said. "Boris Melikov."

The Russian moaned and rolled slightly, side to side. He looked up and his eyes widened when he saw Bear reach down and grab him by his shirt.

Bear hoisted Boris into the air and yelled at him. "You like kidnapping little girls?"

Boris shook his head.

Bear slapped the man across the face, open handed, then back handed.

Boris's head snapped to the right and then to the left. He shut his eyes tight and then opened them. He lazily stared at Bear before his head fell to the side. Eyelids fluttered and then remained shut.

"What did you do to him?" Bear said. He dropped Boris to the ground.

Clarissa shrugged. "He'll be alright." She paused. "In time."

"Bastard's lucky he's out of it right now."

"What now?" Pierre asked.

"We wait for Jack," Bear said.

Pierre moved to the corner of the room and stared out the window. He lightly tapped the barrel of his MP5 against the glass. His trained eyes scanned the parking lot. Left to right, right to left. Front to back, back to front.

Bear took a seat behind the desk and opened each desk drawer, inspecting the contents.

"What are you looking for?" Clarissa asked.

"Jack needs those documents. Figured I'd get them ready for him so we can get out of here a.s.a.p."

Clarissa pointed to a stack of papers on the desk. "They're right there."

"OK. I'm going to double check whatever else Boris has in here. Maybe we'll luck out and find something one of you spooks can use."

Boris moaned on the floor. He rolled to the side again, eventually making it to his back.

Clarissa stood over him. She almost felt bad for the man. He had a rough road ahead. Several agencies were going to want to talk to him. Once they used him up and got every bit of intel they could from him, they'd shove him in a cell three hundred feet underground.

The room fell silent. Clarissa watched Boris. Bear read through papers at the desk. Pierre watched a motionless parking lot. All three reacted to the door crashing in. Their reactions were too late, though.

"Freeze, police," a man barked. He stepped into the room carrying a semi-automatic weapon similar to the one's wielded by Bear and Pierre. He had dark pants and a dark shirt on. He wore a Kevlar helmet on his head. A bullet proof vest covered his chest and back.

Clarissa looked back at the man in disbelief. He aimed his gun directly at her. "Officer, we're—"

"Shut up," the cop said. "Everyone drop your weapons. Try anything and the woman dies."

Bear sat with his hands on the desk. He pushed back in his chair and stood up slowly. He held his hands up in the air and stepped out from behind the desk. Pierre placed his Glock and MP5 on the desk and stepped a few feet away. Clarissa dropped her pistol on the ground and lifted her hands in the air.

"Move to the corner." He gestured with his head while keeping his weapon trained on Clarissa. Once the three were huddled together in the corner of the room, the cop said, "Come on in."

A single Russian man with shoulder length blond hair entered the room. He wore black pants and a black jacket. He pulled out a knife and cut the duct tape from Boris's wrists, knees and ankles. "Let me help you, Boris."

Boris took his time getting to his hands and knees and then used his desk to lift himself from the ground. He wiped blood away from his eyes and face with his palms. He stepped forward and stood in front of Bear. "Tell him to move."

"You heard him," the cop said.

Bear stood still.

"Move." The cop fired a round into the ceiling above the group. A cloud of plaster descended on the room.

Bear still didn't move.

The cop pulled a blackjack from his utility belt. He stepped forward and slammed the thick rubber club into Bear's midsection. The large man bent over. Not much, but enough for Boris to lean in and grab Clarissa.

"Leave her," Pierre said.

The cop swung his blackjack at Pierre, catching the Frenchman on the side.

Pierre groaned and stumbled back a few feet. He wrapped his arms around his midsection.

Boris forced Clarissa to sit on the edge of the desk. He paced in front of her. He said, "You betrayed me, Anastasiya? Why? How much did these men pay you?"

Clarissa smiled and didn't answer.

Boris said, "I will not ask again."

She still didn't answer.

Boris turned his head, looked at the cop and then at Bear. Smiled at the big man. Then he backhanded Clarissa across the face.

"Bastard," Bear said through gritted teeth.

The impact of the blow snapped Clarissa's head to the side and turned her body a few inches. She took a few moments to compose herself. "I'm not Anastasiya. She's in a cell in Langley, Virginia. Giving up all your secrets."

Boris backed up. "What? Who are you?"

Clarissa straightened up and said, "Screw you."

Boris pushed his man to the side and grabbed her pistol off the floor. He stood back a few feet and aimed it at Clarissa. He said, "Tell me what the hell is going on here."

50

JACK REACHED THE TOP OF THE STAIRS AND STEPPED INTO THE HALLWAY. JASMINE was close behind. He saw Kenneth Quioness only half a second before the man drove his large fist into Jack's stomach. There was no time to prepare for the blow. Jack's momentum carried his head and chest forward. The force of Kenneth's blow drove Jack's midsection backward. Jack found himself crumpled over and forced his hands to his face to soften the blow he knew would come from Kenneth's knee.

Kenneth stepped forward. Grabbed the back of Jack's head. He drove his knee upward. The blow could have been severe and enough to put Jack on the ground for a minute or two. However, his hands and wrists absorbed the impact and the knee only served to drive the back of Jack's wrists into his forehead. He fell over anyway, and lay on the ground like a helpless invalid.

Kenneth stood to Jack's right, looking down and laughing at him. He said, "Where's that partner of yours? I want her to see me stomp your brains onto the floor." The man lifted his right foot into the air and placed it over Jack's face.

Jack reached up with both arms and wrapped them around Kenneth's ankle. He rolled to his left, pulling the big man into a standing splits. Jack continued his roll until he butted up against the wall. He reassessed Kenneth's location. The man was on the floor, sitting up with one leg draped over Jack.

Jack sat up and drove his fist into Kenneth's solar plexus. The blow landed with a thud and forced the air from Kenneth's lungs. The man fell forward over his outstretched leg.

Jack got to his feet. Grabbed Kenneth by the back of the head. He pulled the man's head toward him. At the same time, he drove his right knee up and toward the man's head. Knee and face met with a sickening crack. Jack let go of Kenneth's head and the man fell onto his back, his nose split open at the bridge and bent to the right.

"Jasmine," Jack said. "Find my gun."

Jasmine stepped through the open doorway and knelt down. She picked up Jack's gun and held it out for him.

"You want to do the honors?" he asked.

She shook her head.

Jack dropped his right hand to his side, fingers stretched open, palm facing out. He felt her press the Glock into his hand. He clenched the weapon tight. He brought his arm around in front of him. Aimed the gun at Kenneth's head.

Kenneth rolled his head left to right. "Don't," he managed to say.

"Give me one reason why I shouldn't."

Kenneth didn't answer.

Jack pulled the trigger. The bullet smashed into Kenneth's forehead and the man ceased to exist. Just a shell. Lifeless eyes staring up at Jack.

Jack turned to face Jasmine and asked, "You alright?"

She nodded and reached up for his outstretched hand. He pulled her up and said, "Let's go get the others and get the hell out of here."

They walked to the end of the hallway. Jack stopped and scanned the great room. Still empty. He took his time walking the fifteen feet to the next hallway. The front door was open. He looked through the open doorway into the darkness. Saw nothing. Didn't expect to. The front entrance was pretty well shielded from outside view. It worked in reverse as well. They stepped through the hallway, taking their time. He counted the doors, turned where Clarissa had said to, and stopped a few feet from the door to the room where they were to wait for him.

"What's your gut tell you?" he said.

"I don't think my senses can be trusted right now," Jasmine said.

"Mine either." Jack took two quick steps. "Door's cracked open." He looked through the opening and then stepped back.

"What is it?"

"Someone got the drop on them." He looked at Jasmine and noticed she had the H&K MP5 strapped around her chest. He held out the pistol and said, "Switch weapons with me."

She lifted the strap over her head and held out the MP5 for him and then snatched the pistol from his hand.

Jack said, "Three men in there. Two Russians and a bad cop. Bad cop has on body armor. I'm going to fire on him twice. You come in behind me and take out the Russian with blond hair. He's wearing a black suit."

Jasmine nodded.

"You sure you're up for this?"

She nodded again.

"OK. On my count. Three, two, one…"

Jack lifted his gun to his chest and supported the barrel with his left hand. He kicked the door open. He scanned the room in a fraction of a second, quicker than the men in there could respond. The blond Russian stood to the left of the desk. He appeared to be unarmed. Looks could be deceiving, though. Jack knew that if he had a weapon on him, it would be at least three seconds before he fired. Jasmine should be able to neutralize him before those three seconds were up.

The man he assumed was Boris stood in front of the desk. He looked to be armed. Behind Boris, sitting on the desk, was Clarissa. He had to be careful if he fired in Boris's direction so as not to hit her with an errant bullet.

To the right of the desk he saw Bear and Pierre. They were facing him. Both were unarmed. The cop stood a few feet in front of them, holding them at bay with his firearm. The cop's back faced Jack. At least it did when Jack kicked open the door.

The cop spun. Jack aimed and squeezed the trigger. Three bullets slammed into the cop, one above the other. All three hit him in the vest. The cop fired wildly, his bullets spraying the room, crashing into the wall. The cop's momentum, combined with the impact of the first three shots, kept him turning around. Jack squeezed the trigger again. The first bullet hit the cop in his shoulder. The next in his neck. And the third slammed into his helmet. The corrupt officer fell to the ground.

The blond Russian had his weapon out and was starting to swing it toward Jack.

Jack dropped to his knee. He saw Jasmine's arm stretch out over his shoulder. She fired three shots. The first hit the Russian in the chest. The next two hit him in the face.

Boris had also begun turning around. Clarissa tried to jump him, but he managed to evade her and then wrap his free arm around her neck. He pressed the barrel of his pistol to her head.

"You," Boris said. "Drop your weapon. Who the hell are you?"

Jack lowered his weapon and dropped it on the floor. He looked at each person standing in the room. His eyes went from Pierre to Bear to Clarissa. Then he locked eyes with Boris. Said, "Jack Noble."

Boris smiled and a hint of recognition flashed across his face. "My boss can't wait to see you again."

"Who's your boss?"

"General Ivanov."

"You two will have something to talk about in Hell then."

"You'll have been there years before us, Noble."

Jack stuck his hand behind his back. He wrapped his hand around his pistol as Jasmine placed it in his palm.

Jack said, "Would you like me to give him a message for you?"

"That won't be necessary, Jack. I'll be seeing him in a few days." Boris motioned with his head. "You two, move against the wall, near the door."

Jack took his eyes off Boris for a second and saw Bear and Pierre move to the wall next to him. What was Boris's plan? Did he have more men en route? Was he planning on killing everyone in the room except for Clarissa? He replayed the last minute in his head. He had to stall Boris, if only for a few more moments.

"When are you going?" Jack asked. "Or is he coming here?"

"Not for you to worry about."

"How are you going to get all of us there?"

Boris smiled. He slid the hand wrapped around Clarissa's neck down a few inches. He motioned with the gun as he spoke. "There will only be two of us, Jack. The rest of you are staying in Iowa. Your place of rest, so to speak."

"Only person resting here is gonna be you, Boris," Jack said.

Boris laughed. His eyes scrunched up as he did so. His left hand fell a bit more, down and away. The gun moved away from Clarissa's head and pointed toward an area of the room that had nothing but books.

Jack whipped his left hand around, and brought the gun up, and stretched his arm out. He quickly aimed and squeezed the trigger. Being right-handed, aiming and firing in the span of less than a second with his left hand was not ideal. The bullet missed and smashed into the window behind the desk instead of into Boris's head.

Boris froze for a second. His smile still etched into his face. Fear in his eyes. He brought his left hand around and grabbed at the fabric surrounding Clarissa's chest. She pulled to the left, twisting and turning and forcing herself away from Boris. Away from being his human shield.

Boris brought his other hand forward and pointed the gun in Jack's direction. He didn't take time to aim, just fired. The bullet traveled over Jack's head and slammed into the wall behind him and Jasmine. He felt small chunks of drywall pelt the back of his head.

Jack brought his right hand up, steadied his left, and fired two more shots. Both connected with Boris. One in the chest, the other right between the eyes.

The gun fell from Boris's hand and hit the floor. Clarissa wrenched herself from his grip and ran to Jack.

Jack hugged her. Took a moment to clear his head and then said, "The documents? Where are they?"

Bear said, "The desk."

Jack went to the desk and grabbed a stack of papers. Now wasn't the time to review them. They had to get out.

"That's them," Bear said.

Jack looked over his shoulder and nodded. He looked around for something to place the papers in. Saw a briefcase behind the desk, against the wall. Grabbed it and dropped the papers inside.

"We need to get out of here," Bear said. "Might have more cops coming."

"OK," Jack said.

They grouped up, armed themselves and left the office. Down the hall, into the foyer and through the front door. They located a passenger van in the courtyard. Easy to find as it stood out against the luxury vehicles. Pierre hotwired the van and Bear drove. They sped through the lot and down the gravel driveway. Turned right on Kennedy Street and left on Highway 14.

"We need to get Mandy," Bear said.

Jack nodded. Said nothing. One more stop. Hopefully one with no gunfire.

Bear pulled out his cell phone and called Larsen. Larsen told Bear he'd be waiting in the hotel lobby with Mandy.

They pulled up to the hotel ten minutes later. Larsen came out with the girl. Jack and Bear got out of the car.

Bear rushed over to Mandy. Picked her up off the ground and squeezed her to his chest.

"I trust everything went well?" Larsen said.

"Yeah," Jack said. "Most of them are dead."

"You should come with us, Larsen," Bear said. "At least for tonight. It's not be safe for you here."

Larsen agreed to join them.

They drove east on I-80 for four hours, crossing into Illinois. Found a hotel forty miles from Chicago. They rented three rooms for the night. Jasmine contacted Frank, and he arranged for a private jet to fly them to D.C. in the morning.

51

Clarissa walked across the hotel parking lot. The night air was cool and damp and carried the sweet fragrance of dogwoods in bloom. A hazy ring surrounded the moon and streams of thin clouds floated across the dark sky.

She continued thirty yards and then pulled out her cell phone. Placed a call to Sinclair. He answered midway through the fourth ring.

"Sinclair, it's Clarissa."

"What happened?"

"Things got out of control. We weren't the only ones in town."

Sinclair remained silent for a moment. "Did you get your assignment from Melikov?"

"Melikov won't be giving anymore assignments."

"Who was there?"

"I can't really say."

"Why not?"

"He'd prefer I didn't."

"I can find out, Clarissa. You don't want me to find out on my own."

"It's Jack."

"Noble?"

"Yes."

"I thought he was dead."

"So did I."

"Who is he working for?"

"I think the S.I.S. again."

Sinclair said nothing.

"And I think we should team up with them to bring down the man Melikov worked for."

"Do we know who that is?"

"Boris said a name. Jack knew who it was."

"Did you get it?"

"There was so much going on."

Sinclair paused and it sounded like he scratched at the stubble on his face. "Will Jack agree to work with us?"

"I'm sure he will."

"You haven't asked? He hasn't offered?"

"Correct."

"If you can sell it to him, I'm in."

"Thanks, Sinclair."

"Call me tomorrow with an update."

The line went silent and she stuffed her phone in her coat pocket. She pulled the zippered edges of her jacket close together and turned around. Saw Jack standing ten feet away. She froze.

"How long have you been there?" Clarissa said.

"Long enough."

She bit her lip and let go of her coat, letting her hands fall to her side. "Can we work together?"

"Sure, but that's not why I'm standing here."

She stood motionless while Jack approached her. He stopped six inches away and reached for her. His hands felt cool to the touch, warm to her soul, and electric to her heart. He drew her close and leaned forward. Her heart rate doubled. Their lips met. He grabbed her by the waist. She brought a hand up and slipped it behind his head, running her hands through his hair.

Jack pulled away and said, "I thought about you every day. In that dungeon cell waiting for my bogus trial. In Black Dolphin. Your face is the last thing I remember thinking about before I took my last breath when they gave me that paralytic agent to fake my death. Every day in Greece, when I watched the sun rise and set, I thought of you. I saw you in everything."

Clarissa melted at the words she had longed to hear from Jack for so long. She said, "Same here."

Jack smiled, and leaned in, and kissed her again.

"Let's go to your room," she said.

"OK," he said. Then he added, "Wait. I'm sharing with Bear."

She stepped back. "I'm sharing with Jasmine."

Jack looked around as if the answer was waiting for him on a billboard.

Clarissa said, "We could get another room."

Jack nodded. Grabbed her hand and led her inside the hotel lobby. They approached an older man who stood behind the counter. He had thinning gray hair, a full mustache and brown eyes.

"Help you folks?"

"One room," Jack said.

"Sorry, no vacancy."

"No vacancy?" Jack repeated.

"Yup."

"How is that possible? We're forty miles from Chicago."

"Guess it's that convention," the man said.

"What convention?" Jack said.

"Oh, some sci-fi slash fantasy convention they're having right now."

Jack turned to Clarissa and said, "Guess that explains the elves I saw earlier."

Her disappointment momentarily lifted and she burst out laughing.

Jack looked back at the old man and said, "Thanks anyway, pal."

Clarissa grabbed his hand and led him through the lobby. They went back outside and found a bench near the building where they sat and talked and kissed and relaxed.

After some time, Jack looked at his watch. "Four a.m. We really should get some sleep. Tomorrow's gonna be a long day."

She nodded and stood. Grabbed his hand and pulled him up. They walked hand-in-hand through the lobby, to the elevator. They split up, Jack going right and Clarissa going left, when they stepped onto their floor.

52

"Jack, Jasmine," Frank said. "How was the flight?"

Jack nodded and Jasmine said, "Good."

Jack looked around the gray painted room. Over his shoulder at the city street. The building was inconspicuous. Had to be since it was in the middle of D.C.

Frank walked past the empty receptionist desk and stopped in front of the group.

"Think you know most of them," Jack said.

Frank nodded. "Logan, how are you?"

Bear smiled. Said nothing.

"Clarissa, I understand you're going to be helping us with this, uh, operation." Frank's eyes stopped on Mandy and he smiled and winked. Then he looked at Larsen and said, "Don't believe we've met."

"Detective Larsen, Knoxville, Iowa, P.D. Was, at least."

"He stepped up for us, Frank," Jack said. "That department's corrupt. Larsen needs our help now."

"I'll see what I can do. Shouldn't be tough. I'll put him and the girl up in a safe place until this is over and then we'll talk." Frank then looked at Pierre and smiled. "Been a long time, Pierre."

Pierre stood and reached his hand out. Frank grabbed it. There was a knowing look shared between the men.

Frank said, "Glad you're back on our side, Pierre."

Pierre looked at Jack, who shrugged.

"We know everything, Pierre," Frank said. "You made the right choice. I want to talk to you and Bear about doing a job for us. We want to tie up all the loose ends that exist regarding this situation." Frank paused and nodded toward the briefcase that Jack held. "A certain old man was responsible for delivering some highly classified material into the wrong hands."

"Not to mention the bastard wanted me dead," Bear said.

Frank nodded. Then he pointed at Jack and Jasmine and said, "You two come with me."

Jack stood and waited for Jasmine to do the same. He smiled at Clarissa. Squeezed her shoulder. Then he followed Frank past the empty receptionist desk to a well-lit hallway. The passage contained no doors except for a single one at the end.

Frank stopped, swiped a card through a card reader and then opened the door, which led to an elevator lobby. There were three elevators. One on the right, on the left, and straight ahead. Frank continued forward, swiped his card again and pressed the down arrow next to the elevator in the middle. A moment passed and the elevator opened. Frank stuck his arm in the opening and gestured Jack and Jasmine through with the other.

Jasmine entered, then Jack. There were five buttons on the right side of the doors. Two were for opening and closing the doors. A third had an alarm symbol on it. The fourth was labeled with an "L" and the fifth with a "B." Jack watched as Frank pressed the "B" button.

The elevator dropped and the lights dimmed. They descended for approximately thirty seconds. Jack worked it out in his head that they had traveled close to two hundred feet when the elevator stopped and the doors opened.

"New headquarters?" Jack asked.

Frank lifted a single eyebrow into his forehead and nodded. He then led them through two security doors and finally into his office. He took a seat behind his desk. The surface area held nothing more than a keyboard, widescreen monitor and a pad of yellow legal paper. On top of the pad was a black ball point pen.

"The documents, Jack." Frank held out his hand.

Jack lifted the briefcase and sat it on top of the desk.

Frank placed the briefcase on his lap. Pulled the documents out and sat them down in front of him. He went through them one by one. He nodded. He shook his head. He grunted. He groaned.

Jasmine leaned forward and followed along.

Frank looked at Jack and said, "You had no idea?"

Jack shook his head. "Never would have done it if I had."

"That business you're in—"

"I'm done with it," Jack interrupted. "No more."

"You'll come back to work for me?"

"Not saying that." He looked at Jasmine who appeared to watch the conversation with great interest. Jack added, "At least, not yet."

"So what do you think?" Frank asked.

"Let's finish this."

"Ivanov?"

"Yeah."

"How do we get to him?"

"Clarissa," Jack said. "She impersonated some Russian agent. Well enough to fool Ivanov's number one guy over here."

"So you think she can get to Ivanov then? Maybe lead him somewhere where you two can get to him?"

"That's right."

"OK." Frank leaned over and Jack heard a drawer being opened. Frank reappeared a moment later with two blue passport folders. He tossed them on the desk. "Your identities for this trip. Fly to Athens. Go down and check on Alik and see if you think he can be of any use to us on this. He knows the layout, right?"

"He knew Black Dolphin."

"We got him in there for you."

"You ever gonna tell exactly how you pulled that off?"

"No."

Jack shook his head. Said nothing.

"Once you meet up with Alik, I'll arrange transport into Russia."

Jack grabbed his passport without looking inside.

"Does Clarissa need our help getting over there?" Frank said.

"No, I'm sure her team can arrange it," Jack said.

"She's squared away then?"

"Yeah."

"Who's she working for?"

"Sinclair."

"Christ," Frank said.

"You gotta let it go, Frank. We need their help on this."

Jasmine said, "What's this about?"

"Nothing," Jack and Frank said at the same time.

"Before your time," Frank added.

Jasmine held up her hands in a "back off" gesture and stood. "We should get going. Need to get to the airport."

"I'll arrange your flights while you head over."

He led them out of the office. Through two security doors. He swiped his card next to the elevator and the doors opened. They returned to the lobby. Mandy and Detective Larsen were gone.

"Where'd they go?" Jack asked.

"They're safe, Jack," Frank said.

Jack looked at Bear, who nodded while his lips thinned.

"Gotta trust me, Jack," Frank said. He pointed at Bear and Pierre. "Come with me for a minute."

He walked them to a corner and they spoke in hushed tones. Three minutes later they returned.

Everyone stood.

Frank said, "Clarissa, get on the next flight to Russia. Coordinate it with Sinclair." He handed her a card. "Memorize that number. No matter what phone I'm near, you can reach me at that number. Call me when you get settled in and we'll figure out where Ivanov is and the best way to get to him."

"OK," Clarissa said.

"You two." Frank pointed at Bear and Pierre. "Book the first flight to New York." He handed Bear a card. "Call me as soon as you land. I have a safe place you can stay."

"OK," Bear said.

"Jack," Frank said.

"Frank," Jack said.

"Take care of my girl."

"He's the one that got clubbed in that house," Jasmine said.

Frank smiled for a moment and then looked through the glass door and to the street. He pointed a stretch limousine. "Your ride's out there."

The group of five filed through the double glass doors and onto the sidewalk. They got inside the limo and headed to Dulles Airport.

53

"WHAT IS THE DAMAGE?" IVANOV SAID.

Julij looked up from the report in his lap. He wiped a thin layer of sweat from his brow. "All the players are dead, except for Anastasiya."

"Where is she?"

"Missing."

Ivanov drummed the edge of his desk with his fingers. He stared at Julij. His young ward averted his eyes and focused at a blank spot on the desk. Ivanov followed his stare. How had this happened? They had everything in place. Then New Jersey fell apart. Atlanta ran into the feds. And now Iowa and, more importantly, Boris and Chernov had been incapacitated. Everything had been ruined. He lifted his hands and balled them into a fist. Drove his fists down onto the desk.

Julij flinched and looked up at Ivanov.

"How did this happen?"

Julij hesitated and then said, "Sir, I, uh, we don't know."

Ivanov stood and turned his back on the younger man. He stared out the window. The setting sun cast an orange glow over the normally brown and dreary courtyard behind his office. How would they recover? Who did he have, in Russia, that he could send and pick up where the others had left off? Where the others had failed.

"Any more bad news?" Ivanov asked.

"Yes," Julij said.

Ivanov looked over his shoulder. "What?"

"The documents, sir. They're gone."

Ivanov clenched his jaw. "Who do we think has them now?"

"CIA maybe. Possibly Homeland Security. Whoever it is, there's no getting them back. Our guy in the government probably doesn't have the resources."

Ivanov dropped his chin to his chest. Shook his head. "It's over then?"

"Nothing is ever over, sir. But, it might take a while for us to recover. We've had so many losses these past six months."

"Who is behind this?"

"We don't know."

"Who is behind this?"

"We're not sure."

Ivanov turned. Placed his hands on his desk and leaned forward. He narrowed his eyes and said, "Who is behind this?"

"There's a chance that it's... That it's Jack Noble."

Ivanov backed up until he reached the wall. He felt the color drain from his face and his stomach knot up. "Jack Noble," he paused a beat, "is dead."

"That's what we thought. But a man at the house in Iowa, he, well, he hid and he heard the name. He saw him. We sent a photo and it was close enough. Noble has a beard now, and his hair is a bit longer. But he said it was him."

"Impossible. He died in Black Dolphin."

"No, sir. He's alive. He killed our men. He took the documents. And we have reason to believe he knows it's us behind it all."

Ivanov didn't respond. He stared at his desk in disbelief.

"Sir?"

Ivanov slowly looked up. Met Julij's stare and held it for a moment. Then he exploded in a fit of rage. He started in the center of his desk and with his right hand, knocked everything off of it and then did the same to the left. Papers, pens, keyboard, mouse and monitor. All fell and crashed to the floor. Afterward, he stood in front of his desk, breathing heavily. He spoke slowly and said, "See if we can get a location on Noble. And see about getting a security team here."

Julij nodded. Said nothing.

"God help us if Jack Noble arrives here first."

PART IV

EPISODE 9

54

Bear and Pierre sat side by side on a bench, facing Rat Rock in Central Park. The sun hid behind thick clouds that held the promise of a spring storm. The large rock cropping in front of them was as gray as the clouds, and if not for the budding trees and skyscrapers in the background, it would have blended into the sky behind it.

The rock shielded the men from the cold wind. The area was quiet and calm. The climbers who typically scaled the rock were absent today. Too cold and too early. The playground behind them was empty, as all the kids were back in school.

Walkers and joggers and bikers passed at sporadic intervals. Thin white cords dangled from their ears. Sunglasses shielded their eyes. They largely ignored the two men who appeared to be enjoying the morning sun on a brisk thirty-five degree New York City morning.

"You were inside the old man's compound, right?" Bear asked.

"I remember the layout pretty well," Pierre replied.

Bear nodded. Although he'd never been inside the old man's house, he'd seen it from the outside. Heard stories about the inside. Mandy had been in there. So had Clarissa, but she'd be hard pressed to remember the layout. Didn't matter. She wasn't around to help.

"If we can get inside, pretty sure I can locate his office," Pierre said.

Bear thought for a moment. "No way we get inside. That place is guarded like the White House. Roving security teams on the outside. Always a team on all four sides. A team at the front entrance and one at the back. Besides that, everything is electronic access controlled."

Pierre nodded. "It is."

Neither man spoke for a few minutes. All Frank had told them was to take out the old man. Didn't provide any further instruction or offer any additional help. Kill him. Plain and simple. Bear didn't hesitate to accept. The old man took out a contract on his life. Now he would pay.

"Any ideas?" Pierre said.

"We need to stalk him. Figure out his routine." Bear paused while two women jogged past. "That day you spent with him, did anything seem habitual? Breakfast at a specific place? Coffee at a certain cafe?"

Pierre leaned back and took a sip from a disposable coffee cup. Steam escaped through the narrow slit in the lid. "Not that I saw. He picked me up around 10 a.m. and we drove to his place. We waited there until I left. If he has any routines, he didn't make me privy to them."

"OK. That's the first thing we need to establish."

"We'll have to tail him for a while then. Can we get close to the compound in order to do so?"

Bear shook his head. "It'll be a stretch. This is going to be a pain. We can't rely on luck, though, so we have to figure out a way."

"Should we call Frank?"

"No," Bear said. "I've got someone who might be able to help us."

"Who?"

Bear glanced sideways at Pierre. He still wasn't sure how much he could trust the Frenchman. Better to keep the name close to the vest. "I'll let you know when you need to know."

Pierre nodded. "I understand."

A group of small children approached from the west. Bear estimated there were twenty kids. They followed a woman dressed in khaki pants and a blue sweater covered by a black vest. He figured she was their teacher. They filed past Bear and Pierre, following the wrap around walkway to the park behind the bench.

"You think Frank will honor his end of the deal?" Pierre asked.

"What, give you a job?"

"Yeah."

"You really want a job in the SIS?"

Pierre hiked his shoulders an inch and held out his hands.

"Do this job and get on his good side," Bear said. "But you don't want to be a part of that group. Trust me."

"Did you work for them as well?"

"No, but Jack did. For two years. Maybe things have changed since, but based on what he told me, I'd never work with there."

Pierre didn't speak. He stared out over the rock formation in front of them.

"Working for yourself is where it's at," Bear continued. "Hell, you saw that. How much they offer you to take me out?"

"Two-fifty," Pierre paused to take a drag from his cigarette. "Euros," he added.

A few minutes passed and Bear got up and started walking. Pierre followed. They walked north to 67th and then headed west until they reached Columbus. They turned north again and walked five more blocks to 72nd, where the apartment Frank provided them was located. They stopped outside the door.

"Let's do a drive by of the old man's place," Bear said.

They turned and headed east. Walked two blocks. Frank had a car for them. Kept it garaged on 72nd, next to the park. Ten minutes later they were on the road.

Bear drove from memory. It had been over six months since he stood outside the old man's compound. They drove past the sprawling house, then turned around a block away. Bear pulled the car over to the side of the road once they had a view of the compound. They faced the rear entrance, where the cars were parked. There was little chance of Feng leaving through the front door. If he were to step out, it would be through the back.

"That's the car," Pierre said. "The white Mercedes. That's the car he picked me up in."

Bear nodded. Leaned back. He looked at Pierre and said, "Get low."

"Where's the security teams?"

"Wondering that myself. Maybe they don't rove during the day. Just at night."

"Guys on the roof probably see everything during the day." Pierre pointed above the house, at the armed man standing at the corner nearest them.

"We should probably back up," Bear said.

He placed his hand on the shifter. Stopped. The rear door of the house opened and the old man stepped out. A large man followed him out, then walked past him toward the white Mercedes.

"That's the driver," Pierre said.

"We need to turn the car around. He knows both our faces. The driver knows yours. Might know mine."

Bear dropped the car into reverse and backed up twenty feet, then whipped the wheel around and drove another block away. He stared into the rear-view mirror, waiting for the Mercedes to get on the road. He didn't have to wait long. The Mercedes pulled out of the lot and drove toward them.

"Get down," Bear said as he ducked into his seat.

Pierre did the same.

They waited until the car passed, then sat up. Bear put the car in drive and followed the white Mercedes.

They drove into Queens. The vehicle in front of them turned onto 73rd. Pulled to the curb in front of a diner.

Bear passed and stopped at the end of the street. Watched from the rear-view mirror.

The driver stepped out of the Mercedes and walked around the back of the vehicle. He opened Feng's door. The old man stepped out. They headed toward the diner.

A horn blared and Bear shifted his gaze. A line of cars had formed behind him. He dropped his eyes an inch and saw that the traffic light had turned green. He said, "Tomorrow we come here for lunch."

55

THE LONG FLIGHT ACROSS THE ATLANTIC AND EUROPE PASSED BY QUICKLY FOR
Jack. He had forty-eight hours of non-stop action and seven shots of whiskey to
thank for the sleep he found on the plane.

Jack and Jasmine landed in Athens just after noon. Grabbed a connecting
flight to the island of Crete. Rented a small car and drove to the town of Palaiochora. He found it hard to believe that he'd only been gone a week. His life had
changed drastically in the span of seven days. The six months of relaxation that
had seemingly reprogrammed him were nothing but a distant thought now, like
candles set adrift on the open sea.

He slowed the car down as he approached the cafe. Stopped next to the curb.

"This is the place?" Jasmine said.

"Yeah," Jack said. "Lived here for six months."

Jasmine got out of the car and looked around. "It's beautiful. Must have been
boring, though."

"At first. Then it became relaxing. I can't explain it. A feeling I only ever had
once before in my life."

"When was that?"

"Three months in Key West."

She said nothing.

Jack walked into the cafe and an old man stepped out from behind the counter. "Jack, my friend, how are you?"

Jack met the man halfway and shook his hand. "I'm OK. Need to get a few things from the apartment and then we'll be on our way."

"Sure, sure. Let me get the key for you." The old man slipped behind the counter and ducked out of sight.

Jack looked around. Old men nodded in his direction as they sipped on their coffee and ate their pastries. Jack said, "Has anyone been here since I left? Looking for me or Alik?"

The old man poked his head up and shook it. "No, it's been quiet. We had a few men here all week. Americans. They wouldn't tell us who they were. Only said they were here to protect us for the week."

Jack looked over his shoulder at Jasmine. She lifted an eyebrow and nodded. It was a clear enough of a gesture to tell Jack that Frank had sent multiple teams to Crete.

"Here it is," the man said as he stood. He walked out from behind the counter. Tossed the key in Jack's direction.

Jack reached up and snatched the key out of the air, then walked past the man toward the stairs. He motioned for Jasmine to follow him. They climbed the stairs. He took his time and stayed alert. He had no reason to distrust the old man. But someone else might have shown up in the past week and threatened him. That same person could be waiting, or have a team waiting, in Jack's apartment.

They reached the top floor. Jack held up a finger directed at Jasmine and then pressed his ear against the door. Didn't hear a sound. His hand grasped the doorknob and he turned it. Unlocked. The key had been unnecessary. Someone had been there, whether the old Greek knew it or not. The door pushed open and Jack waited. Nothing and no one stirred inside. He stepped in and gestured for Jasmine to follow him.

Nothing seemed out of place. It looked the same as best he could remember. He had reached a point where he didn't mentally inventory a room before he left. The apartment was a six month blur in his mind. If the couch had been moved, he would have noticed. But if a knife were missing from a drawer, that would go undetected.

"Looking for anything in particular?" Jasmine asked.

"I've got a few guns here. Stashed in a safe in the back. If it weren't for them we wouldn't have come here."

"You really think that old guy downstairs sold you out?"

"No."

"Why are you being so cautious then?"

Jack didn't reply. He stepped into the kitchen and grabbed a butcher's knife from a wooden block. He stepped into the hall. Heard Jasmine grab a knife as well.

He pushed the door to his old room open. The mess that greeted him was confirmation that someone had been here, inside the apartment. Clothes were strewn across the floor. The bed was stripped down and the mattresses flipped and laying half off the bed. The only question was whether it was the Russians or the Greeks who had been inside.

"Didn't realize you're such a slob, Jack."

He looked at Jasmine and shook his head. "Nothing in there anyway. Whoever it was wasted their time."

He turned around and returned to the hall. Walked past the closed door to Alik's room. Opened a closet door. Got down on his knees and tossed blankets and towels over his shoulder. He pulled out a metal safe. Punched a code in and opened the door. Pulled out a 9mm Beretta and handed it to Jasmine. Pulled out a second weapon and tucked it in his waistband. He grabbed the extra magazines and some cash and then closed the safe.

Jasmine inspected the weapon and sighed. "I feel safe again, Jack."

He nodded. "Me, too. Mostly." He looked at Alik's door. "Let's check his room as well." He walked past Jasmine. Grabbed his Beretta and stuck the barrel next to the edge of the door. He tried to open it a crack. It barely moved. "What the hell?"

"What is it?"

"Door won't move." He banged against the door. It opened an inch at a time. "Anyone in there?"

No response.

He kept pushing and kicking at the door, eventually breaking through the middle. He saw several items on the floor piled up like a barricade. His eyes shifted to the back of the room where he noticed a series of wires. He traced the wires back and saw that were connected to the door. The wires split the middle of the room. One ran to the side and connected to a device on the dresser. The device had a green LED display. The display had two numbers, big and bold. A three and a zero. A timer. Frozen. It wasn't counting down.

"Christ."

"What is it?"

"A bomb."

"What?"

"Someone was expecting us."

They backed out of the apartment. Closed the door. Reached the bottom of the stairs and approached the counter where the old man was standing. He was smiling at them.

"You need to get everyone out of here," Jack said.

Confusion spread across the man's face. His smile faded. "What are you talking about, Jack?"

"There is a bomb in one of the rooms upstairs. The room Alik used. Someone was in there. They ransacked my room. Put a bomb in his."

"A bomb?" the old man said loudly.

Forks dropped against plates. Coffee mugs hit the floor and shattered. The patrons of the cafe stood and raced toward the door. What a week it had been for them. A shooting and now this.

"Yeah, a bomb," Jack said. "Get out. Call the cops. Don't tell them I was here. Just say that you were getting around to cleaning the place up and found it in one of the bedrooms."

"It's not going to explode?"

"No. Not yet. Don't go up there and mess around. You might set it off."

The old man nodded. Dropped his apron on the floor and walked past Jack and Jasmine, through the front door. He stopped outside and waited for them to follow him out. Then he locked the door and took off down the street.

"Poor guy," Jasmine said.

Jack nodded and said nothing. Walked back to the car and got in behind the steering wheel. He waited for Jasmine, and then pulled away from the curb and left the town behind.

"Where are we going now?"

"To check on Alik. Only problem is, I don't remember the exact route."

Jack had watched the drive to the old Greek lady's house in reverse. When he had left with Frank's men, they had driven from the house to the small airport, which was on the opposite end of the island. He knew they had traveled north when they left the cafe a week ago. He tried to recall any landmarks that might have been hidden deep in his memory. There weren't many, and the ones he did recall weren't near a turn.

"We should call Frank," Jasmine said.

"Not yet. I want to see Alik first. Besides, it's early in D.C."

"Maybe he can help us get to the house."

Jack shook his head. "I have an idea. I know the way from the house to the airport. If we head toward there, I'll know the intersecting road and can work backward."

Ten minutes later he saw the road. Turned right and navigated to the house. He turned onto a dirt driveway, past a line of trees and pulled in behind the pickup truck he had ridden in back of the week before.

"Be alert," he said.

"OK," Jasmine said.

"The guys were old. The woman was older. But who knows who might have come by in the past week."

"OK."

He cut the engine and got out. Approached the house slowly and cautiously. The air was still and mild. Nothing seemed out of place. Curtains hung in the windows, blocking any view of the inside of the house. He heard Jasmine's footsteps behind him. Other than that, not a sound. Then the door flung open and Jack stopped. He aimed his gun at the open doorway and waited.

56

THE OLD GREEK WOMAN STEPPED OUTSIDE, A LIT CIGARETTE IN HER HAND. SHE lifted her hand to her mouth and took a long, deep drag.

Jack tucked his gun away and nodded at the woman.

She nodded back and said, "Your friend is gone."

"What do you mean?"

"He left."

"Dead?"

"No."

"Where did he go?"

"Wherever they took him."

"Who took him?"

"Some men."

"How many men?"

"Several."

"Did you know them?"

"No."

"Were they American?"

"Not with those accents."

"What were they then?"

"Not sure."

"What did the accents sound like?"

"Like his."

"Russian?"

"Yes."

Jack glanced over his shoulder at Jasmine. She still had her gun in her hand and aimed it at the front door. He didn't try to encourage her to put it away. He looked at the old woman again and said, "Is your son around?"

"He's working."

"Where?"

She shrugged.

"Did he see the men?"

"No."

"Was he here when they came?"

She shook her head.

"Did they threaten you?"

She didn't answer. She lifted her head and stared up at the trees.

"Did they say they would come back to hurt you?"

"Who cares what they said."

"When did this happen?"

"Yesterday."

A day after they had taken out Melikov and Chernov.

Sorry, Alik.

"We had men here. Men that were supposed to watch over Alik. Protect him."

She nodded.

"What happened to them?"

"They're dead."

"Thank you for your time."

Jack turned and walked toward the small rental car. He stopped in front of Jasmine.

"Those were our guys," Jasmine said. "They were well trained. It would've taken several men to take them out—"

"I know who it was," Jack said.

"Who?"

"The same guys who captured me in Italy."

Jasmine stepped back, out of his way. Said nothing.

"Call Frank." He slid in behind the steering wheel and started the car. Pulled away before Jasmine managed to close her door.

"Jesus, Jack." She slapped the dashboard. "Calm down."

"He saved my life. Got me out of that hell hole. All I've done is let him get shot and now abducted. They've probably killed him by now. Christ, considering the torture they are putting him through, I hope they've killed him by now."

"Don't talk like that. You don't know what's happening. He's OK and we are going to find him and we are going to rescue him."

Jack said nothing. He concentrated on the road as he pushed the small car to its upper limits.

"I'm calling Frank." She pulled her cell phone out and placed the call. "Frank, yeah it's Jasmine. Yeah, lots going on here." She paused. "We went to town, gathered a few things from Jack's apartment." A pause. "What? It was his call. Just shut up for a minute, Frank. There was a bomb in the apartment. It hadn't been set off, but it was there. The place had been trashed, too. They were looking for something and planned to blow up whoever went in after them. Then we drove out to see Alik. He wasn't there, Frank. Someone took him and killed our guys."

"Make sure you tell him it was Russians. Probably the same guys who caught me."

"Frank, listen, Jack thinks it was the guys who managed to capture him in Italy." She covered the mouthpiece and looked at Jack.

He noticed a glint of hope in her eyes.

"He thinks he has a lead on them. Private contractors with ties to Ivanov."

Jack nodded. He had already figured that out.

They left the wooded area behind and drove north to the Chania Airport. Frank had a contact there that could get them on a private plane.

"Where did he say they were taking us?" Jack asked.

"Ukraine. Place called Kharkiv. Frank's got another contact there that can get us across the border into Russia. From there it's about a four hundred mile trip to Moscow."

"Moscow?" Jack's eyes traveled between her and the road. "I don't know exactly where I was, but I know it wasn't near Moscow."

"You're right. Black Dolphin is near Orenburg. That's close to the Kazakhstan border. And the place they held you and Pierre, that was Volgograd. You probably remember it from your history books as—"

"Stalingrad," Jack interrupted. "I remember."

Jasmine nodded.

"So why aren't we heading there?"

"Frank believes that Ivanov's in Moscow right now."

"I hope he's right if we're gonna be stuck traveling by car. That's a hike between Moscow and Stalingrad."

"Volgograd."

"Whatever."

Jasmine waved him off. "Frank's not the only one gathering intel. He's got others involved. Other agencies."

"Who?"

"Not sure. He wouldn't tell me."

Jack shrugged.

"Why would he?" Jasmine said. "Anyway, once we get to Moscow we're going to rendezvous with Clarissa. She'll be on the ground. Might have been able to arrange a meeting with Ivanov already."

Jack tensed. The thought of Clarissa being in the same room with the overbearing General made him uneasy. If Ivanov had a single doubt about her identity, he'd kill first and ask questions later.

"She'll be all right, Jack. Don't worry."

Jack looked at her and lifted one shoulder. Clarissa was a tough woman and well trained. She could handle it. He knew that.

"You can't hide it," Jasmine said. "I saw you two together."

"It's nothing."

"Yeah, nothing." Jasmine laughed.

"We go back a long time, her and I."

"You don't have to explain yourself to me, Jack."

He didn't say anything.

She pointed to the right. "There it is."

Jack slowed the car down, turned right. Drove around the airport to the northwest corner of the parking lot, as Frank had instructed them to do. He backed the car into a parking spot that bordered on grass, then cut the engine.

"Did he give you a specific time?" Jack asked.

"No. He just said the man would be here."

"Did he give you a description?"

"Yeah." Jasmine turned her head and smiled. "A man."

"That's him." Jack gestured with his head.

The guy who approached was mid-sixties, bald, wore glasses. He had on grease stained blue overalls. He stopped twenty feet away, smiled and waved.

Jack scanned the parking lot for any sign of danger. Saw none.

"Look clear to you?" Jack said.

"Yeah."

"Feel safe?"

She pulled the Beretta out from under her jacket with her right hand. Traced the length of the barrel with her left index finger. A slight smile formed on her lips.

"Yeah," she said. "Very safe."

Jack got out, grabbed their duffel bags and set them on the ground. Reached inside the car and placed the keys in the glove compartment box. Pressed the lock button and closed the door.

The man stopped five feet in front of the car. "Got a plane waiting for you folks." He turned around and added, "Let's go."

Jasmine looked at Jack. He shrugged and said, "Guess we should follow."

The man led them to a golf cart. He sat in front. Jack and Jasmine in the back. He drove them across the parking lot, past the runways and past a terminal where half a dozen planes waited for passengers to board. They drove another five minutes, then pulled up next to a small commuter jet.

"That's your plane," the old man said.

Jack stepped out of the golf cart. Grabbed their bags. The old man drove off without another word. They walked toward the white plane adorned with swooping blue stripes. A door on the side, behind the cockpit, swung open and a man greeted them.

"Jack and Jasmine?"

Jack nodded.

The man dropped a set of stairs and said, "Get on board. We don't want to miss our window."

Jack climbed up first and stopped in front of the man.

"I'm the pilot and I'm a friend of Frank's. That should be good enough, right?"

Jack nodded. The pilot had his first name and that was all he needed.

Jasmine pushed past Jack and he followed her onto the plane. They seated themselves. Twenty minutes later they were in the air, on their way to the Ukraine.

57

THE HOTEL ROOM SINCLAIR HAD ARRANGED FOR CLARISSA WAS SMALL AND PLAIN and centrally located in Moscow. The size of the room didn't bother her. She didn't plan to spend much time in Russia. Besides, the view from her window of St. Basil's Cathedral was breathtaking. She stared out the window at the beautiful building. It looked like a bonfire rising into the sky. Her thoughts turned to Jack, as they so often had the past few days. Their time together was short but powerful. She felt the pull of him in her heart. She worried that it might start to affect her decision making.

She looked past St. Basil's, toward the east end of the Arbat District where Anastasiya's apartment was located. Sinclair had told her to expect a package with keys to the building and the apartment. Clarissa planned to do a walk by in the late afternoon. There could be any number of spies or government officials waiting for Anastasiya to return. She wanted to be prepared if that were the case.

She heard a knock at the door and crossed the room. Stopped at the door. Checked through the peephole. Didn't recognize the man standing on the other side.

"Who is it?" she said.

"Marco."

She slid the security lock and opened the door. The guy that stood in the hallway was her height, but probably fifty pounds heavier. He had brown hair.

Sideburns stretched down to his jaw and he kept a trimmed patch of hair under his bottom lip. She stepped aside and let him in.

He walked past her. Carried a duffel bag in his right hand. He looked around the apartment. Said nothing.

"What did Sinclair tell you?"

Marco shrugged without looking back. He placed the bag on the table. Turned around to face Clarissa. "Nice place." His accent was European. Spanish.

She said nothing. Watched him from across the room.

Marco remained stationary. He fished a rolled cigarette from his inside coat pocket. Pulled out a lighter and lit the end of the smoke. He took a deep drag, blew it toward the ceiling. Glanced around again and then settled on Clarissa. Smiled at her.

"Is there anything else?" she said.

"Thinking maybe I should stay around for a bit. Show you how to use the weapons. Take you out to dinner."

Clarissa stood with her back to the door, holding it open. "I don't eat and I already know how to use them. I think you should leave."

He approached her, cigarette dangling from his mouth. "Leaving is no fun."

"I guess they didn't tell you about me."

"They didn't need too. I can tell right now you got everything I like." He stopped a foot and a half away from her. Reached out and placed his right hand on her left arm. Kept eye contact. Leaned in.

Clarissa smiled for a second or two. She brought her left hand up, under and then around Marco's outstretched right arm. She pulled and twisted. Brought her right hand up and caught the man under his chin. She flipped him backward, into the hall. He landed on his head and crumbled into a ball and then stretched out on his stomach.

He slowly got to his hands and knees. "What the hell, lady?"

"I told you to leave. You didn't listen."

He grabbed a hold of the wooden banister and pulled himself to his feet. Took a step toward Clarissa and stopped. Waved his hands at her. "You're not worth it." He turned and stepped onto the stairs. Looked back over his shoulder and spat.

Her first reaction was to step into the hall. A single kick to the middle of the back would send him reeling down the stairs. He'd hit his head, most likely multiple times. He might break his neck.

Instead, she backed up and closed and locked the door. Whoever Marco was, he worked for a friend of Sinclair's. It was better to bite her tongue than the hand that fed her.

She waited by the door with her ear pressed against it. She heard the echo of Marco's footsteps diminish and eventually fade away to nothing. Satisfied he had left, she walked over to the table where he sat the duffel bag down. She leaned over the table and unzipped the bag. Marveled at the collection of weapons that had brought her. There were two Russian made Marakov PMM 9mm pistols with 12-round magazines. There was also a PP-19 Bizon 9mm submachine gun. The nine inch long weapon was equipped with a 64-round magazine and could easily be concealed under her coat. There were two additional 64-round magazines in the bag. The PMM pistols and the PP-19 both used 9x18mm Marakov cartridges. She also found two tactical knives with ankle sheaths, as well as holsters for the pistols.

Clarissa laid the weapons out on the table. Picked them up one at a time and inspected them. She was well equipped and ready to take on anyone who got in her way.

She strapped one of the knives around her lower right leg, between her calf and ankle. She looked at the holsters. One was intended to be strapped around her thigh. Not ideal for what she was about to do. The other holster was a pair of compression shorts. The shorts had two pockets in the back, just above waist line that would allow her to conceal both pistols behind her back.

She undressed and put the shorts on. Pulled her jeans on over the shorts. Secured the pistols behind her back. She looked at the Bizon submachine gun. The weapon was short enough that she could conceal it underneath her jacket. But if someone were to stop her, whether it be a cop or an agent, they'd quickly find it and possibly put an end to her mission.

Clarissa looked around her apartment and decided to stash the submachine gun in a dresser drawer, underneath her clothes. She grabbed a sweater to hide the slight bulges near her lower back, a good idea in case she ended up inside and had to take her jacket off. Finally, she put on her heavy brown leather jacket and left the apartment.

After four flights of stairs and a short walk through a narrow lobby, she was outside. It was cold and gray and misty. The sun hid low in the sky behind a wall of dark clouds. Snow piled two to three feet high on the side of the roads, once white, now black from the exhaust of cars.

She headed east toward Anastasiya's apartment building. Her phone's GPS application guided her. She passed through the Red Square and St. Basil's, which looked even more impressive from the ground. She turned and admired the fortified building she knew as the Kremlin.

The trek took longer than a one mile walk should have. She blamed the crowds and the weather and perhaps her own curiosity. She'd never been to Russia, and she found the center of Moscow quite fascinating.

Historic buildings and crowds of tourists faded into apartment buildings and shops and restaurants. The crowd was just as thick, but consisted mostly of locals.

Clarissa's sense of awareness became heightened. Every face was a potential threat. Every car that passed might contain someone ready to take her out. She stayed close to people and next to the buildings, away from the street. She wore a hat and tucked her dark hair underneath. But the sunglasses she brought served no purpose and drew more attention than she wanted, so she stuffed them in her pocket.

She located Anastasiya's building. It took up half the block. Alleys ran down either side of the building. She snapped three quick photos with her phone and then placed the device inside a coat pocket.

The building had a doorman. He stood outside wearing a heavy black jacket and hat. He'd likely recognize Anastasiya if he saw her, so Clarissa decided against getting any closer. She had no key and that would likely raise some suspicions.

She wanted to get a look at the block behind the apartment, so she turned right onto a parallel street and then made a left. Walked two blocks and turned left again. She was now on the street behind the building. The block turned out to be one block-wide building. No alleys. No way to escape the apartment building from behind. The alleys either dead ended or connected behind it. They did not reach the street she stood on.

The sky continued to darken. The harbinger of an impending storm. There were fewer locals on the street. She realized it wasn't a good idea to stay out any longer. No point getting caught in a spring storm a mile or so away from her hotel.

She backtracked toward her hotel. Stopped two blocks away from Anastasiya's apartment building and took a few more pictures, zooming in on the doorman. Maybe Sinclair could get her a name.

"Anastasiya?"

Her heart stopped and her stomach sunk. Muscles clenched in reflex. The voice came from in front of her. She dropped her head and turned around. Walked away at a brisk pace.

The voice called again in Russian. "Hey, Anastasiya. Come back here."

Her eyes scanned the street. Left to right. Right to left. She looked for something that would block the man's view of her, and allow her to slip away at the same time.

"Where are you going?"

She cast a quick glance over her shoulder and saw the man that had called for her. He was tall and athletic looking and wore a dark trench coat, the kind that made hiding a weapon easy. He moved toward her, weaving in and out of pedestrian traffic. He was a block away. Far enough for her to give him the slip. Close enough that he could take her out with a single shot, if he had the right weapon under his coat.

Her feet moved quickly through the packed snow. She had to make decisions even quicker. Duck into a store or an alley? She'd be cornered. Run to the hotel? She'd give up her position.

A crowd gathered a hundred feet in front of her at a stopped bus. Old and young. Men and women. They boarded one at a time. She reached the bus after the last person had boarded. She jumped on the bottom step as the driver was closing the door.

"Please," she said. "I don't have fare, but I need to get on board."

"Sorry," the driver said. "You have to pay."

She stuck her head out and looked behind the bus. The man was running toward her. He held a pistol in his right hand.

"That man is coming after me. He has a gun. He's going to kill me."

The driver turned his head, then squinted, then straightened up. Said, "Get on now."

Clarissa climbed two more steps and stopped next to the driver. The door behind her closed. "Can you go off route?"

"I can take you wherever you need to go."

"Just lose him and I'll get off and you can take these people where they need to go."

The driver nodded. Grabbed the mic off the dashboard. "We are going to pass the next few stops. Everyone sit tight. I'll double back in a few minutes."

The groans of the passengers behind gave way to the groan of the big diesel engine as the bus pulled away.

Clarissa placed her hand on the driver's shoulder. She squeezed and said, "Thank you."

58

Kharkiv, Ukraine was probably a nice place in the summer. Green trees mixed with the tan and khaki colored buildings that spiraled outward in a circular pattern from the center of the city. In late March, when temperatures hovered just above freezing while the sun spread its rays from above, dead trees littered the ground around those same buildings, and the scene looked desolate.

The plane continued northeast past the city and landed at what looked to be an abandoned runway.

Jasmine turned on her phone and pulled up a map that centered on their location. She held it in front of Jack and said, "Halfway between the city and the border."

The pilot came out and opened the door. Dropped the stairs and disappeared again.

"Guess that's our cue," Jack said.

Jasmine nodded and stood.

Jack stepped into the aisle, grabbed their bags and headed toward the front of the plane. He stopped at the door and poked his head out. A car pulled up, a large late model sedan. Black. Two men got out. The man on the driver's side stood next to the car. The man on the passenger's side walked toward the plane.

Jack dropped the bags and reached behind his back. Grabbed his Beretta and held it out of sight.

The man stopped five feet from the base of the stairs. He lifted his arms to the side, stretched his fingers wide. He spoke with an American accent. "I'm unarmed. You can put your weapon away, Jack."

"What about him?" Jack nodded toward the driver.

"He's unarmed. We're on your side."

Jasmine placed her hand on Jack's shoulder and leaned past him to look outside. She smiled at the man on the ground. "Jack, that's Harris. He's one of us." She squeezed past Jack and went down the stairs.

Jack tucked his gun away and picked up the bags. As he stood up, he noticed Harris reach into his coat. Jack dropped the bags again. Reached behind his back. His hand wrapped around the handle of the gun. Then he saw Harris's hand emerge with two dark blue passport folders. Jack let go of the gun. Took a deep breath, then grabbed the bags and walked down the stairs.

Jasmine was already on her way to the car. The driver walked around the back, met her and opened the rear passenger door for her.

Harris stepped up and reached for one of the bags, then he handed Jack his passport. "I don't think we'll have trouble getting across. These passports are legit."

"What about the passports Frank gave us?"

"We've taken extra precautions with these."

"What kind of precautions?"

"Monetary."

"Paid someone off at the border?"

"Paid to have someone in particular at the border." Harris turned and walked toward the car. The trunk popped open. He lifted it with one hand and tossed the duffel bag in with the other.

The men passed each other, Harris to the passenger's side, Jack to the driver's. He opened the rear door and slid in next to Jasmine.

"Are we going straight to the border?" Jasmine said.

"Yes," Harris said. "After that we'll take you to your car."

They spoke little during the thirty minute drive. Jack said nothing at all. He stared out his window, catching glimpses of barren farmland between thick clusters of trees that formed a ten foot wide barrier between the highway and open land. He wondered why they hadn't planned to let them out close to the border. They could cross by foot somewhere off the beaten path. Then they could arrange to meet further down the road. The scenario played out in his mind. He found a major hitch. The area would be patrolled. Hell, there might even be a physical barrier. It was probably safer to take their chances crossing where they could pay someone off than to risk being picked up by the Russian Army in a field crossing an arbitrary line.

The vehicle slowed and eventually stopped behind a line of cars. They were ten deep. It would take a few minutes to pass.

Harris turned in his seat and said, "Just stay cool. They'll want to look at your passports. They won't ask any questions. Don't speak. Don't make eye contact. Simple instructions. Follow them and we'll make it across with no problems."

Jack nodded. Looked past Harris. The scene ahead looked like something out of the 1970s. An old wood framed building stood next to the road. The windows were darkened. A high fence topped with barbed wire wrapped around the building on three sides and cut across the landscape as far as he could see. Two armed guards stood in front of the building. He figured there were a few more inside. Four more armed men positioned themselves around the car at the front of the line. One man stood next to the driver's window and spoke. Two more stood in front of the car, and the last man at the rear.

The process repeated itself as each new car pulled up. At the sixth car, they pulled the driver and passenger out. Inspected them, then the car. Normal operations resumed after that.

Finally, it was their turn. The driver pulled the car up and stopped when one of the armed men held his hands out.

All four windows rolled down. Cold air rushed in and swirled around the car and enveloped them. Jack resisted the urge to pull his jacket tight. The move might alert the guards.

The guard approached the driver's window. He said, "Passport," and waited for the driver to hand his over.

The driver obliged.

"Why are you visiting Russia today?" the guard asked.

Jack shifted his line of sight from the two armed men in front of the car to Harris. Harris's head turned to the side. The look on his face matched the feeling in Jack's gut. Harris had said they'd ask no questions.

The guard straightened up and appeared to gesture toward the front of the car. One of the men left his position and went to the passenger side of the vehicle. He asked Harris for his passport and followed it up with a question. "What do you do for a living?"

"Contractor," Harris said. "We're all contractors. U.S. based and heading into Russia to make an estimate."

That was all Jack caught before the guard on his side of the car stuck his hand through the open window. Jack lifted his hand, the passport held lightly between his thumb and forefinger. The guard snatched it and took two steps back. It felt like the process was taking longer than it should have. Out of his peripheral vision, Jack saw the guard approach again. The man's hand hit the side of the car and the door next to Jack opened.

"Get out," the guard said.

Jack cast a glance toward Harris, then stepped out. He felt Jasmine staring in his direction. Didn't look back.

"State your name."

Despite Harris's proclamation that there would be no questions asked, Jack had studied the passport and created a back story. He hoped Jasmine had done the same.

"Milton," Jack said. "First name, Mark."

"What are your plans in Russia?"

"Like the man already said, we're contractors and are on our way to estimate a job."

"Don't move."

The guard backpedaled toward the front of the car. He handed the passport to another guy. Each guard took a turn looking at the picture on the passport, then at Jack, then back to the passport.

The open fields and possible physical barrier and roving teams of guards along the open border seemed like a better idea as far as Jack was concerned at that moment. He glanced over his shoulder and saw that the guard on the other side of the car. He now stood with his weapon aimed at Jack's head.

Jack slowly turned his head forward. Stared out across the empty field in front of him. No place for cover. Nowhere to run. No place to hide. He felt the heft of his gun against his back and wished he had hid it under the seat.

Just stay cool.

Easy to do with the air temperature. Tough to do under the circumstances.

But Jack was trained for this. If it came down to it, he'd go out in a hail of gunfire rather than allow himself to be taken back to that hell hole prison.

The voices from the front of the car stopped. He heard the footsteps of the guard approaching. He didn't turn to look.

The sound of the guard's hard-soled boots hitting the pavement rose above the wind and idling engines. The man kept his rifle aimed in Jack's direction.

His mind raced, thinking five steps ahead. He let his right arm drift toward his back. Toward his gun.

59

THE MAN STOPPED A FEW FEET AWAY FROM JACK. THE GUY'S EYES WERE NARROW and dark. His cheeks red and chapped. A few seconds stretched into twenty. What was the delay? Either they knew who he was or they didn't. Finally, the man lowered his weapon and stepped forward. Lifted his other hand and said, "Here is your passport, Mr. Milton. Get back in the car."

The guard lifted his rifle halfway, pointed in Jack's general direction. Aimed at nothing. He stood there like a statue.

Jack reached behind his back and opened the door. He kept his eyes on the guard and had decided that any sudden movements he deemed as a threat would be met with equal force. The guard didn't move until Jack sat down.

"What the hell?" Jasmine said.

Jack closed the door. "Roll the windows up." He waited for the driver to oblige, then continued, "Someone recognized my face. They couldn't place it, though. They all looked at my passport picture. The face wasn't quite what they recalled. The name didn't match."

"The assassination," Harris said. "The politician last year."

"Yeah," Jack said. "They sent me to Black Dolphin over that."

"I thought no one gets out of Black Dolphin alive?" Harris said.

"I wasn't alive when I left."

Jack waited for Harris to ask the inevitable follow up question. He didn't.

Instead he leaned back in his seat and stared out his window. The driver put the car in gear and slowly started forward. They rolled past the guards, who lined up two to a side. Knees locked. Shoulders pinned back. Weapons aimed down.

The driver accelerated quickly past the old wood framed building on the side of the road and the guards positioned inside and out. Tall trees lined the road again, blocking the views of barren farmland. No one spoke. No one moved. Thirty minutes dragged on and felt like three hours. Jack was relieved when Harris finally spoke.

"We're here."

"Where's here?" Jack asked.

"Outside Belgorod," Harris replied.

The location meant nothing to Jack.

The driver pulled the car into a residential neighborhood. Turned onto a street that dead ended into a cul-de-sac.

Harris pointed toward a two door, white car parked in front of a dirt lot and wood framed skeleton of a house. Said, "That's your ride. All the papers are inside."

"Did you put them there?" Jasmine asked.

"No," Harris replied. "I had a friend do it."

"Like your friend at the border crossing?" Jack said.

Harris twisted in his seat and turned toward Jack. "I apologize for that, Jack. He wasn't there. I'm going to make sure that never happens again."

"Do what you want. Don't leave until we know everything we need is in that car." Jack stepped out and walked around the back of the vehicle. Met Jasmine on the other side. They grabbed their bags from the trunk then walked toward their new ride.

"Think it's rigged?" Jasmine said.

"Wouldn't doubt with the luck we've had with explosives lately," Jack said.

She laughed. "Seeing as how I've got nobody waiting for me, I'll open the door." She reached out and grabbed the white handle, pulled up and opened the driver's side door.

Jack looked back at Harris, who sat in the car and had his feet on the street. "Keys?"

"In the glove box."

Jack crossed the front of the car to the passenger side and got inside the vehicle. He opened the glove box and pulled out its contents. There were two keys and a plastic bag containing paperwork. He pulled the papers out. They were in Russian. "These do me no good."

"Give 'em here," Jasmine said. "I can read Russian." She looked over each paper, top to bottom, front and back. "We're legit."

Jack stepped out of the car. Looked over the top and nodded at Harris.

Tires squealed and the engine roared. A minute later Harris and the unnamed driver were gone.

"They left in a hurry," Jack said.

"If I weren't tied to you, I'd be gone too."

Jack laughed. Slipped into the passenger seat.

Jasmine waited for Jack to close his door. Then she put the car in drive. She had already programmed the GPS in the dash to take them to Moscow. "We got about six or so hours to kill. Ready to tell me what you did after you left the S.I.S., Jack?"

"No."

60

"I HATE BEING IN MOSCOW," IVANOV SAID.

"Why's that?" Julij said.

"Feel like I'm under a microscope. These people always around. Can't operate like I want to."

"It's only temporary."

Ivanov stood and stepped out from behind his desk. He crossed the room. Opened the door and poked his head into the gray industrial colored hallway. Satisfied it was empty, he closed the door and returned to his desk. "So what is the latest on the woman?"

"We know that she's not in Iowa anymore. At least, not at the compound."

"She'd be a fool to stay there after what happened."

Julij nodded. "Her body wasn't found. I think the logical next step would be for her to return home."

"Agreed. Where is home?"

"Here, sir. Arbat district."

"Do we know the address?"

"Yes."

"We should get a man there."

"Already did, sir."

"Any luck?"

"Sort of."

"How do you sort of have luck, Julij?"

"He believes he saw her," Julij paused. He brought his hands together and rested his bottom lip on the tips of his index fingers. He continued, "He saw a woman that resembled her. Her hair was up. According to our man, he called her name and she fled. Ended up on a bus and he says that he lost her."

"Why would she run?"

"Perhaps she was afraid it was someone out to get her. If we're her friends, that means she has some powerful enemies here."

Ivanov nodded slowly as he stared at the younger man through narrowed eyes. "So how many men do we have watching over her place now?"

"Four."

"Make it eight."

"Sir?"

"You heard me. Eight men."

"And then?"

"What do you mean, 'and then'?"

"Do you want them to kill her?"

"I don't trust her, but I don't want her dead. Not yet. Bring her to me."

"Here?"

"Do you think this is the kind of place I can question her?"

"No."

"No, it's not, Julij. Have her brought to my place."

"What will you question her about?"

Ivanov felt his cheeks grow hot. He took a deep breath and placed his hands flat on his desk. "I'm getting tired of you questioning me, Julij."

Julij said nothing.

"I don't trust her. I want to find out why she is the only high ranking person who made it out of Iowa alive. Why didn't she go down with the others defending the plan?"

"I see."

"Yes, Julij, you see. In fact, you can see yourself out of my office."

Ivanov waited until Julij left the office. After the door closed shut, he pulled out his cell phone. Placed a call. Midway through the third ring a man answered.

"Yes, sir."

"Any news?"

"On?"

"You know what. Noble. Do you have news on Noble?"

"Yes, I can confirm that he is now in Russia and is headed toward Moscow."

"Excellent. Do we have a fix on him yet?"

"No, sir. We're still working on that."

"Call me when you do. I want to know the exact moment Noble arrives in Moscow." Ivanov ended the call and placed his phone on the desk. It wouldn't be long, he thought, until Jack Noble was back in his custody. He would not make the same mistake this time. He would not leave Noble's death to someone else. He'd pull the trigger on his own and cut the man's heart from his chest.

61

Clarissa had the bus driver drop her off near St. Basil's Cathedral. She crossed the artificially lit walkway in front of the huge building. The sky was white due to the impending storm. The wind whipped her face. The cold air stung her cheeks and nose.

She moved quickly, partly in an effort to keep warm, but mostly to get to the safety of the hotel. She stepped into the lobby and the man behind the counter looked up from his computer, nodded and then looked away. Fine with her. The less attention she drew, the better. She walked past the elevator and took the stairs. The hallway outside her room was empty. She stuck her key in the door and opened it. The room appeared undisturbed.

She sat on the edge of the bed. Noticed the light flashing on the phone. Picked it up and was directed to the front desk.

"Ma'am, we have a package addressed to your room. I'll have somebody run it up now."

"That's OK. I'll come down and get it."

Five minutes later she was back in her room with the package. There was no return label, which she viewed as both good and bad. Sinclair would not use a return label. Neither would someone who had sent her a bomb.

She placed the package on the table. Grabbed the unsheathed knife and cut the thick brown packaging tape. She stuck her fingers in the slit and pulled the flaps of the box apart like a heart surgeon spreading his patient's ribs apart.

Inside the box she found a manila folder that contained a dozen or so papers. There was a key chain with four labeled keys. She looked at each individually. *Front. Mail. Room. Bank.* Were the keys labeled like this when Sinclair got his hands on them? Or had he coerced Anastasiya into giving him the information? She flinched at the thought and quickly buried it. She didn't know. She would never know. And she was fine with that.

She set the keys aside and grabbed the folder. It seemed Sinclair had been busy with the woman. Each page had new information on Anastasiya. Most of it was about her background, and not exactly classified intelligence. Clarissa learned that the woman had attended boarding school in New England for three years. She was the daughter of a Russian government official. Their family bred horses. She had been an athlete, but not good enough to make the cut. At the age of twenty she joined the Federal Security Service of the Russian Federation, formerly known as the KGB. She specialized in counter-intelligence, and then counter-terrorism.

Finally, there was a note from Sinclair that indicated Anastasiya might be on the same side as them and was planted into Boris's group to take them down. He also advised her to treat every person she met with caution. People who appeared as friends might be foes, and vice versa.

Was the man outside the apartment building a friend? Or was he a foe? He had obviously been waiting for Anastasiya. It might be a good idea to find and question him.

Pain stabbed at her stomach. She looked at her watch and realized that she hadn't eaten in nearly twelve hours. She called down to the lobby and ordered a steak. While she waited for her dinner, she reviewed the information again. She wanted to make sure she hadn't overlooked a single detail of Anastasiya's life. The thought crossed her mind that maybe the woman had deliberately lied to Sinclair in an effort to throw the operation off. Clarissa knew that's what she would do if in a similar situation. If the woman really was on the up and up, and intended to take down Boris, she would fully comply in order to regain her freedom as soon as possible.

A young man arrived with dinner. Clarissa signed for the meal and gave him a tip. She placed the food on the table and put the papers back in the folder and tossed the folder on the couch. Mid-way through her meal, the phone rang.

"Hello?"

"It's Jack."

"Where are you?"

"Close. Almost to Moscow. How're things there?"

She thought about the man who called out for Anastasiya and subsequently ran after her. "Not sure yet. Just got the key to the woman's apartment."

"You heading over there tonight?"

She walked to the back of the room and pulled the curtain back. Fat snowflakes flew straight at her, hitting the window. The flakes melted and slid down, leaving a slushy trail in their wake. She said, "Weather's kinda bad tonight. I need to get over, but I want to be able to see what I'm walking into. There was a man near her apartment today. He seemed to recognize me, well, her."

"Don't take any unnecessary risks, Clarissa. Wait until we get there. We'll meet and put a plan together."

"OK."

"We're going to stay nearby. Apparently Frank felt it wasn't a good idea for us to be in the same hotel."

"Since when did you start taking orders?"

"I know, I know. He had a good point, though. If one of us were followed back to the hotel, we could all end up compromised or dead."

She wasn't dead, but had she been compromised? "OK, Jack. Call me when you guys get settled in."

She placed her phone on the table and finished eating. The phone didn't ring. She grabbed a bottle of Vodka from the freezer and filled an eight ounce glass halfway. Took a drink. The phone still didn't ring. She finished the glass and poured another. The phone rang.

"Jack?"

No one replied.

"Who is this?" she said.

No one replied.

"Who is this?" she said again.

The line was silent.

She ended the call and tossed the phone on the table. She walked to the window, pulled back the curtains. Couldn't see anything through the wall of white that pelted the glass. The flakes stuck to one another and started to form a coating on the window.

She paced the room, front to back, over and over. The phone began vibrating on the table. She picked it up and looked at the display. Unknown caller. Every call said that. She tapped the screen and lifted the phone to her ear. Said, "Who is this?"

"It's Jack."

"Are you in Moscow?"

"Yeah, we're about half a mile away. Other side of the Red Square, across the river. Place called the *Hotel Baltschug Kempinski.*"

"I saw a sign for that."

"Where are you?"

"A hotel called Metropol."

"We're coming over."

"No, stay. I'll come to you. I need to get out for a bit."

62

Clarissa left the warmth of the hotel and stepped out into the heavy snow and the blustery cold. She trudged down an alley along the side of the hotel. Past the rear parking lot. The well lit street provided enough visibility to stay clear of objects in her way. Surprisingly, there were other people out, couples and singles, likely on their way back to a hotel after dinner.

She passed a set of buildings and turned left, toward the Red Square. The outline of St. Basil's stood out amid the sheet of white in the sky.

As she approached the square, she noticed a man in a dark jacket leaning against a tree. He stared her down as she approached. Straightened up as she walked by. Fifty feet later she looked back and noticed that he was following her.

She picked up her pace, not an easy thing to do when trudging through five or six inches of fresh powdery snow. The crowds had dispersed before the storm hit and the snow was not packed. Each step required extra effort.

She glanced over her shoulder and noticed the man had closed the gap between them. That pinned him as a local, or at least a Russian that was used to the weather. She reached inside her jacket, around her back. Grabbed one of her pistols and stuck it in her coat pocket.

The area in front of her began to narrow, leading to a four lane bridge. Tall light posts lined each side of the bridge. A car crossed, coming toward her. Its headlights lit up the wall of snow and made it impossible to see more than ten feet ahead. If she couldn't see, neither could the man behind her. She took the opportunity to break to her right toward the Kremlin. Several trees stood between a tall red brick wall that separated the Kremlin from the road.

The effort required to sprint when her feet were buried under snow left her slightly winded. She took cover behind a thick tree. Back to bark. Steadied herself. Listened to the sound of the wind. Watched shadows dance on the bright white ground. Branches swayed rhythmically. Snow swirled and passed her in every direction. Left to right and back again. Up and down, then settled on the ground.

A sound penetrated the relative calm of the swirling wind. The unmistakable sound of snow crunching under heavy steps filled the void behind her.

She reached into her pocket and pulled out the Marakov pistol. Removed the glove from her right hand. Bare skin met the icy handle. The tip of her index finger lightly touched the steel trigger. One drop of snow and finger and trigger would freeze into one.

The steps grew louder, slower, closer. Were they to the left or to the right? She honed in. Another step. Impossible to tell. She pressed back against the tree, becoming part of it. Perhaps he would walk right by.

The bridge was less than one hundred feet away. She could try to sprint again. Flag down a vehicle, if she saw one. The bridge was well lit and might provide some safety from the man.

A gloved hand wrapped around her face. Pulled her head back against the tree. The rough bark scratched her scalp and neck. The glove stifled her scream.

The hand came from the right. The man was to the right of her. She decided to roll toward him. Fire a shot.

Before she could, the man spoke in Russian. "What are you doing over here, Anastasiya? Why are you hiding out in a hotel?" He slid his hand off of her mouth.

"Who are you?"

"Listen to my voice. You know who I am."

Clarissa searched her mind, going over all the points she thought were important on the papers that Sinclair had sent to her. Nothing about a man came to mind. Who was this guy? Her partner in the field? Her partner in bed?

"I can't tell," she said. "Let me go and come over here."

"Tell me what you are doing out here first."

"I'm working."

"I would know if you were working."

Partner in the field.

"No, you wouldn't. This is special and only involves me."

The wind increased and so did his voice. "Why are you lying to me?"

She heard a clunking sound against the tree, to her left. He was armed. And possibly left handed. Again, no recollection of a fact like that from the documents.

He let go of her. She looked at the ground, at his shadow. It moved to the right. His left hand was blocked by the tree. She couldn't tell if he held it up or down or out.

She rolled to the right to face him, keeping her right arm behind her. The snow on the ground and the snow in the sky and the snow in between created a false daylight effect. She could see the man clearly and he could see her. The recognition she expected him to have wasn't there. She recognized him, though. It was the man from earlier. The man from outside Anastasiya's apartment. She hadn't lost him after all.

His eyes traveled back and forth between hers. He leaned back. Said, "Who are you?"

"It's me."

"No, it's not. Tell me who you are." He stepped to the side. The tree no longer shielded his left arm. It hung down, the gun aimed at the ground. He started to lift it into the air.

"It's Anastasiya."

"Then who am I?" The man continued to lift the gun.

Clarissa reached for his face with her left hand. She faked a confused and hurt look. She leaned forward and to the left, as if going in for a kiss. It had the effect she desired. His left hand started to drop. She brought her right hand out from behind. Fired a single shot. She didn't want him dead. She wanted answers. She had aimed low and sent the bullet into the side of his leg, above the knee, away from the femoral artery.

He dropped his gun. Fell to the ground. Clutched his leg. The wind whipped his cries around her in all directions.

She kneeled down. Grabbed his gun. Placed hers to his head.

"Who are you?" she said.

"Ivashov."

"Who do you work for?"

He looked up at her. "Same people you do." He shook his head. "Same people Anastasiya does."

Clarissa stared at him, waiting for him to name the organization. She pulled the gun away from his face.

Instead, he said, "Where is she?"

"Who's side are you on?"

"What?"

"It's a simple question. Who's side are you on?"

"Where is Anastasiya? Tell me."

"United States. Detained."

He shook his head. Brought his hands to his face. Yelled into his gloves.

"Do you work for Ivanov?" Clarissa said.

"No. I'm against Ivanov."

"Why did you corner me like this?"

"I thought..." He let his hands drop to side and he lifted his head an inch or two out of the snow. "I thought that maybe they had turned her. Why else would she have run from me this afternoon? Now I see it wasn't her. It was you. And you are telling me they have her detained."

She aimed the gun at his head again. "Who's side is she on?"

"She's the same as me. The people we work for want Ivanov taken out."

"That's what I'm here for."

He fell back into the snow. The ground around his knee had turned dark red.

Clarissa pulled up her pant leg and grabbed the hidden knife. She opened her jacket and lifted her sweater. Cut a large strip from her undershirt. She used the fabric to bandage the wound.

She stood and took a few steps back.

"Are you just going to leave me here?" he said. "I'll freeze to death."

"Do you think you can make it a thousand feet?"

"Why?"

"I'm going to meet someone. We are going to discuss our plans to take down Ivanov. I can take you there and we can see about getting you help."

He stuck out his right hand. Clarissa reached out and grabbed it. She leaned back. Helped him to his feet.

Instead of standing straight up, he bull rushed her. He had at least seventy pounds on her. Tall and athletic. She was no match for his large frame and the momentum he had built up. She fell to the ground. The gun she held in her hand was no longer there. Only snow that melted against her touch.

He rose up above her and swung a fist toward her face.

She dodged her head to the left. The fist still connected, but at far less force and in a far less damaging place than if he had been on target. She gave the impression that the blow had been successful. She closed her eyes and relaxed into the snow. She felt him lift off of her. He hobbled through the snow. She looked back and saw him heading for the gun that had been in her hand. He reached down to pick it up.

Think fast. Act faster.

She had tossed his gun behind them. She still had one of her pistols holstered behind her back, but there was no way she could get to it in time. She lifted her left knee and brought her ankle to her waist. Reached under her pant leg and grabbed the second tactical knife. She cradled the handle in her palm, and let the blade slip inside the arm of her coat.

He trudged over to her, dragging his left leg. He stopped beside her. Looked down at her. A maniacal look spread across his face. He said, "I lied."

Clarissa spoke softly. "I need to tell you something."

He shook his head slightly. Leaned forward. "What?"

"I need to tell you something."

His lips thinned. He hovered over her.

"It's about Anastasiya," she said.

"What about her?"

"This," she said. The motion was quick and fluid and decisive. She flipped the blade in her hand. Her right arm traveled straight up. The point of the blade entered the lower left portion of his neck. It sunk in three or four inches. Clarissa whipped her body to her right. The motion caused the blade to rip the man's neck open. Blood gushed and sprayed over her and the virgin snow.

He dropped the gun. Grabbed his neck. His eyes rolled back in his head and he fell forward, face first into the snow. Crimson fluid spread along the pits and peaks their violent dance had created in the snow like a Hawaiian lava flow.

Clarissa felt his wrists for a pulse. Found none. She hunted around and grabbed all the weapons in sight. And then she ran as fast as she could through the ever deepening snow. She crossed the bridge and made her way to Jack's hotel.

63

THE BANGING ON THE DOOR WAS LOUD AND HARD AND FRANTIC.

Jack rushed across the room and opened it without first looking through the peep hole. The sight before him doubled his heart rate.

"Clarissa," he said. "What the hell happened to you?"

The woman stood before him covered in blood. Her skin, her clothes, her shoes. Nothing was spared.

"Are you OK?" he asked. "Are you hurt?"

"It's not mine," she said.

Jack pulled her into the room.

"I was followed," she said. "Same guy from this afternoon. He followed me over here. We were in the Red Square. He was closing in on me. I had an opportunity and I ducked behind a tree. He found me. He was looking for Anastasiya and knew her well enough to know that I wasn't her."

Jasmine handed Clarissa three wet towels and took her coat off of her.

Clarissa continued. "I shot him in the knee. He said he was against Ivanov. I was going to bring him here and let you question him. Then he attacked. I managed to get him with a knife."

"Where is he?" Jack said while trying to process the information Clarissa had thrown at him. "Did he follow you over?"

"He's dead."

"Where?"

"Red Square."

Jack looked at Jasmine. "Should we clean this up?"

"Did anyone see you, Clarissa?" Jasmine said.

"No, not that I know of."

"I can reach out to Frank and see what he wants to do," Jasmine said.

"No," Jack said. "Not yet. Let's wait for her to calm down and go over this again."

Jasmine helped Clarissa to the bathroom and then brought her fresh clothes.

"She's going to get washed up," Jasmine said.

Jack nodded. "Someone knew Anastasiya was coming home."

"I'm sure they figured she would, Jack. After what happened in Iowa, why would she stay in the States?"

"What if someone is waiting for that guy?"

"Maybe he was acting on his own. Wait for her to get out of the shower. She'll have calmed down and can tell us what happened."

Jack started a pot of coffee and grabbed boxes with leftovers from the mini fridge. He heated the food in the microwave when he heard the shower cut off.

Clarissa stepped out of the bathroom wearing a pair of blue sweatpants and a matching sweatshirt. She took a seat at the table.

Jack placed a cup of coffee and a plate of food in front of her.

She pushed the food away and took a sip of coffee.

"Go over this again, Clarissa," he said. "Starting from earlier today when the man saw you outside her apartment building."

Clarissa recounted the entire day. The weapons delivery. The excursion through the center of Moscow. Being spotted by the man. The extra documents she received on the woman she was impersonating. She went over every step she took after she left the hotel. Where she saw the man. When she noticed him following her. What he said when he grabbed her. The look on his face when she stuck his neck with the knife.

"What's your gut say?" Jasmine said. "Did he act alone or did someone know he was out there?"

"He knew that woman as more than a partner in the field. I sense that she betrayed him or his beliefs. He said he was going to kill her at her apartment. He was going to kill her after she left the hotel." She paused. "After I left the hotel."

"He acted alone," Jack said. "Ivanov doesn't work this way. He'd want to see Anastasiya first. Put fear into her. Then kill her."

"Why? Why not just kill her?" Jasmine asked.

"Why didn't he just kill me? He dragged it out. Court. Prison. Sticking me in a cell with a psycho who tried to kill me. It's all a game to him."

Jasmine shrugged. "It's possible, but I still think he might have had something to do with it."

"Well if he doesn't know about this we can use it to our advantage."

"How's that?" Jasmine said.

"It's her in. Her way to get to him." He looked at Clarissa. "Did you get the man's name?"

"Yeah. Ivashov."

Jack gestured to Jasmine. "Get Frank to check that name against all known agents in the Russian Federal Security Service." He looked back to Clarissa. "How old was he?"

"Probably around your age."

"OK, this is what we are going to do. You are going to make contact with Ivanov through the phone. You are going to tell him that Ivashov attacked you and he said that the attack was on Ivanov's orders."

"OK."

"And then you are going to tell him you want a meeting with him. You have some information for him, and you want information from him. It has to be a public place. No matter how much he protests that he didn't order a hit on you, it has to be public. We can't take a chance on that."

"Are we going to take him out at the meeting?" Clarissa asked.

"That depends. It depends on where and when he agrees to meet you. Once we know that I can plan the hit."

Jasmine came back into the room. "Catch me up."

"What did Frank say?"

"He's looking into it. Will have a full report for us by daylight."

"We're going to get a public meeting with Ivanov arranged."

Jasmine said, "Will he go for that?"

"We can only hope."

64

Bear scanned 74th street. He was just north of Broadway and the traffic was one way, heading north. Cross under Roosevelt and to the other side of Broadway, and it was one way, heading south. The view from the shoe store was good enough. He saw every car that passed by the diner. In fifteen minutes he counted six Mercedes. None white. None stopped.

Bear had eaten at the diner before. All you can eat Mediterranean cuisine. Whether or not the old man showed up, Bear was going to get lunch there.

"Why do they call this area Queens?" Pierre asked.

Bear didn't answer. Didn't turn to look at the Frenchman.

"Think he'll show?"

Bear shrugged. "If he doesn't, we start over."

"And if he does?"

"We observe."

"Do we strike?"

"Maybe."

"Maybe?"

Bear cast a quick glance toward Pierre. He exhaled heavily, then said, "It has to be done right. We can't just walk up and take him out. Too many people know him. Chances are if he shows up today and eats at that restaurant, then he eats there a lot. That means he probably sends a lot of people there. Knows the people that work there. They probably like him. If we go in there and shoot him, they'll definitely give the cops our description. Hell, someone in there probably knows me. The other thing is, you don't know who is in there. Who's working and who's eating? There could be someone armed in there. They see us, maybe we get a shot off, maybe we don't. But if we don't see someone, and they are armed, and they see us, then we're as good as dead."

"I see your point."

"We don't have anyone to clean this up for us, Pierre. Yeah, we're doing Frank a favor, but we don't work for him. He's only going to offer us as much help as he wants to give. And based on my past history with him, that ain't all that much."

Pierre didn't reply.

"If the old man shows today, then that means he'll probably show tomorrow. And after he leaves today, we can go in. Scout the place. Get a read on the people in there. We can look at these buildings. Maybe tonight you'll head out here and climb on top one of those buildings and sleep under the stars with a rifle next to you. That apartment building next door might make a good spot. Five stories high. Get on top, you got a great shot."

"That was my specialty."

"I've heard."

A store employee approached them. She was short and thin and unnoticeable. She leaned around Bear and said, "You guys need any help?"

"Piss off," Bear said.

She walked away without saying another word.

"There," Pierre said as he pointed to the south end of the street. "That's the car."

The white luxury car stopped in the lane and the rear door opened. Feng stepped out. He was dressed in his usual attire. He stepped between two parked cars and crossed the sidewalk. Waited under the green and white awning that covered the cafe's front door. Like a man who had spent his life on the streets, the old man's eyes were constantly moving.

Bear could relate. He judged people within a second of seeing them. He could easily tell who had the potential to ruin his day, and he was sure Feng could, too.

"Should we move?" Pierre asked.

"No," Bear said. "He'll notice that. Just stay still. The glass reflects on the outside."

The driver walked toward the diner from the north. Bear looked past him and saw the Mercedes parked on the road near the end of the block. He said, "Give anything for a way to track that car right now."

The old man disappeared behind the glass door. Thirty minutes later, he reemerged. He walked next to his driver on the sidewalk. Stopped at the car. Got in the backseat. The car drove off.

Pierre had recorded the time they arrived and when they exited the restaurant. They waited ten more minutes, then left the shoe store and went inside the diner.

A middle aged woman with her hair dyed dark welcomed them. "Take any seat. Be by in a sec to get your drink order. Buffet's in the back."

Bear headed straight to the back and started piling Tandoori Chicken and Seekh Kabab on his plate. He returned to the dining room and found Pierre sitting in a booth against the wall. "Not going to eat?"

Pierre shook his head. "Not hungry. Breakfast was enough."

Bear looked at his watch. "That was two hours ago."

Conversation was light while Bear ate. Pierre checked out the restroom, faking an accidental entrance into the kitchen. He noted the rear door and when he came back to the table, mentioned it to Bear. "We should check behind the building."

Bear nodded. Scooped one last bite of chicken into his mouth and drank the remainder of his water. "Let's go."

They left the diner and turned left. Walked less than one hundred feet and made another left on 37th Road. Halfway between 74th and 75th, they ducked into an alley that ran between the streets and behind the buildings.

Bear counted doors along the way, trying to match them to the establishments that faced outward on 74th. They saw the diner. Unmistakable due to the grease traps next to the back door. It looked like the diner shared a dumpster with the Indian joint one door north. Beyond the grease traps and the dumpster, the alley widened and opened up into a parking lot.

"I think that's where I'll be," Bear said. "In case they park in the back or try to escape through the rear of the restaurant."

The back door to the diner opened up and an older man stepped out. He froze when he saw Bear. "What are you doing back here?"

Bear quickly placed the man. They had a history. It had been a few years, though. "Just passing through."

"Bear?"

He tried to hide his disappointment at being recognized. "Do I know you?"

"It's Ahmet. You helped me out a few times in the past."

Bear nodded. Reached out and shook the man's outstretched hand. "I did some work for free, too. You remember that, right?"

"Of course."

"Then do me a favor," Bear said.

"Anything. Name it."

"Forget you saw me here."

65

PIERRE SAID GOODNIGHT TO BEAR AND CHECKED HIS WATCH. EIGHT P.M. TOO
early to go to bed. He doubted he'd sleep much at all. If things went well, he'd kill
tomorrow. It had been too long since the last time.

He fiddled with his cell phone for ten minutes. Twice he'd tried to dial the
number. Twice he'd hit the home button to abort the call. Finally, he pressed all
ten numbers and then stuck the phone next to his ear.

"Hello?"

"Is this Marcy?"

"Yes."

"This is Pierre."

"Who?"

"From the cafe. The Frenchman."

"Oh, Pierre. Why didn't you call sooner?"

"I had to leave the city unexpectedly."

"Are you back?"

"Yes."

"Do you want to go out?"

"Yes."

"Do you know how to get to Park and 73rd?"

"Yes." He lied.

"See you there in half an hour?"

"OK."

Pierre slipped on his black leather jacket, feeling the silk-like material that lined the interior as he slid his hands through the jacket's arms. He quietly stepped down the stairs. Stopped at the bottom and ran his hands through his dark hair. He stepped out into the cool dark night and walked to Columbus. He hailed a taxi, got in and told the driver where to take him.

He paid no attention to his surroundings during the drive. Only stared at his phone. He had his contact list opened. This thumb slid up and down on the screen, centering Kat's name, then pushing it off the screen. She had not called since he left. Not once. Perhaps she had already moved on.

The taxi pulled over and came to an abrupt stop. Pierre handed the man a twenty dollar bill. Said, "Keep the change."

The driver nodded and waited for Pierre to step out of the car, then he pulled off, leaving Pierre standing alone on the corner of 73rd and Park.

He crossed the sidewalk and leaned up against a building. Traffic passed at regular intervals. People passed him on the sidewalk without a word or hint of acknowledgment. He had no problem with this.

"Pierre," her voice called from his right.

He turned and saw Marcy approaching. She had on jeans and a sweater. Nothing fancy. Not what he expected, either.

"Been waiting long?" she asked.

"Just a few minutes," he said.

She grabbed his hand and pulled him. "Come on."

"Where are we going?" he asked.

"Just around the corner. A theater. Friends of mine are in a show there."

They walked south on Park and turned right on 72nd.

"It's right there," she said.

"Why didn't you have me meet you there?"

"Thought you might run if you saw I was taking you to a play."

"You were right," he said while checking around for another idea to offer up. "I still might," he added.

She squeezed his hand and leaned into him, shoulder to shoulder.

He wondered why this woman felt so comfortable with him. Would she, like all the others, panic and freak out if he told her what he did and who he was?

She led him inside the theater. They sat near the front of the stage. The play consisted of one-act comedies and dramas. Five of them, each lasting ten minutes apiece. Pierre found it odd, but Marcy seemed to enjoy it, so he acted like he was into it, too. She introduced him to her friends. He and Marcy were asked to come out for drinks, but Pierre declined. Told them he had to be up early.

They walked hand in hand to her apartment building. Stopped out front.

"Want to come up?"

"Yes," Pierre said.

She turned and pulled at his hand. He didn't move.

"Well?"

"I can't," Pierre said.

"Why not?"

"I really do have to be up early tomorrow."

"I thought you were just saying that so we could get away from my friends."

"It's the truth."

"What do you have to do in the morning that's so important?"

He shifted his gaze away from her and lowered his voice. "I have to kill someone."

She laughed. "OK, Pierre. Well you have fun with that." She leaned in, kissed him on the lips.

He returned her kiss. He thought about telling her that he was serious about what he said. Decided against it.

"Want to go out again tomorrow?" she asked. "Me and you? Dinner?"

Pierre nodded. "I'll call you."

She smiled, then turned and entered her building.

He watched her as she walked up the wide wooden stairs. Once she was no longer in view, he got his bearings and walked toward the park. He noticed a group of young men half a block ahead. Six of them. Huddled together. One pointed in Pierre's direction.

Pierre kept his pace steady. Not too fast. He didn't want to appear as if he were trying to get away. Not too slow, as he didn't want to appear that he was watching what they were doing.

Three of the men left the group. Walked to the end of the block and turned on Lexington or Park or Madison. Pierre wasn't sure where he was. Only knew that if he kept going west, he'd walk right into Central Park.

The other three men lined up to block the sidewalk. They all faced Pierre. He saw a weapon in one man's hand, possibly a baseball bat. Another man held his hands behind his back. The third stood tall and loose. They all looked the same under the dim false light provided by the street lamps. A tree blocked most of the light out, so the only things Pierre could make out where their clothes and general build. Jeans and gray hooded sweatshirts. Medium height and slight to medium builds.

Pierre stopped six feet from the men. He didn't want to be too far away, should one pull a gun. Didn't want to be too close and find himself in reach of the baseball bat. Yet.

"Evening gentlemen," he said.

"What is that accent, man?" the guy on Pierre's right, the one with his hands behind his back, said.

"French."

"We hate the French." He laughed. "Isn't that right?"

The other guys laughed. The one on Pierre's left took a few steps forward. He used the baseball bat like a cane. The hollow core piece of wood tapped against the concrete sidewalk, then his feet hit, one at a time.

Tap, thud, thud.

Tap, thud, thud.

Pierre slid to his right.

"Don't move," the guy in the middle said as he pulled his jacket open, revealing a handgun tucked deep in his waistband.

Pierre smiled and nodded. He calculated how long it would take the guy to retrieve his weapon and fire a shot. Fortunately for Pierre, and unfortunately for the man, it would take two seconds too long.

"Your wallet," the guy said.

Pierre said nothing. Didn't move.

"Give me your wallet."

"I'm afraid I can't do that," Pierre said.

The guy tilted his head and a confused look crossed his face. He looked to his right and then to his left. Perhaps he sought reassurance from his fellow thugs. Judging by the looks on their faces, he received none.

"What did you say to me?" the guy said.

"You heard me."

"I don't think you—"

Pierre cut him off and said, "I'm going to give you five seconds to get out of my way. Step to the side and I'll forget this ever happened."

The man forced a laugh and looked at the other two guys.

"One," Pierre said.

The man who had stood with his hands behind his back now let them fall. In his right was a knife with a five or six inch blade. He took a step forward.

The guy with the bat lifted it off the ground. Held the thin end in his right hand. Tapped the fat end against his left palm.

The thug with the gun remained motionless. Didn't have the guts to pull the weapon then. Certainly wouldn't be able to man up and pull the trigger when Pierre beat his friends to near death.

"Two." Pierre paused a beat. "Three." He took a breath. "Four." He looked at each man. Stared at one for a second, then moved to the next. He saw the fear in their eyes. They were frozen. They'd never encountered someone on these streets who stood their ground like Pierre. A man, seemingly unarmed, ready to take them on one versus three.

"Time's almost up, Frenchie," the guy with the gun said.

Pierre smiled. He made a face like he was going to say "five," but instead he delivered a kick to his left. It struck the guy with the bat in the chest, just below his sternum. Judging by the cracking sound, he got a piece of the sternum too.

The guy caved backward. He dropped the bat to the ground.

Pierre ducked, spun, and grabbed the bat off the ground. He faced the street. Heard the steps behind him. He whipped to his left, arm out, bat extending from his arm. He caught the man with the knife on his kneecap. The blow swept the man off his feet. He fell sideways, hard, onto his shoulder and his head.

Pierre looked over his shoulder. The remaining man had his hand on the gun and was pulling it from his waistband. It appeared to be stuck, and the guy tugged and jerked to free the weapon.

Pierre stood and swung and struck the man. The bat connected with the guy's left arm, just above the elbow. There was a crack and a scream. The man took three steps back. He let go of the handle of his gun.

Pierre slammed the end of the bat into the man's stomach. The guy bent over. Pierre grabbed the gun and freed it from his waistband. Knocked the man to the ground. He knelt over him and said, "If you are going to carry a gun around, be man enough to use it." Then he stood and fired a shot into the man who had held the knife. The guy's body went limp.

The guy on the ground in front of Pierre started to cry.

"Like that," Pierre said. He knelt over the man. Placed the gun to his head. Grabbed a handful of the man's jacket and brought it up to shield himself from any blood and brain spray. Then he pulled the trigger. The shot echoed off of buildings. Lights had begun to turn on. Pierre decided to run. He crossed Lexington, then Park, and came to Madison. He hailed a taxi and returned to the apartment.

By the time the taxi stopped to let him out, it was as if nothing had happened. The world was down three criminals, and that was a good night for Pierre.

66

Jasmine, Jack and Clarissa sat around the table in Jack's room. They discussed the plan. Watched the clock. Refined the plan. They couldn't put the final part of it together until Clarissa arranged her meeting with Ivanov.

Jack slid the phone across the table. "It's time."

Clarissa picked it up. Grabbed the paper with Ivanov's number. Dialed. She held the phone up to her ear and waited. Ivanov picked up before the second ring.

"Who is this?"

"Anastasiya."

Ivanov cleared his throat. Paused. "You are a hard woman to find."

She said nothing. Looked between Jack and Jasmine.

"Where are you?" Ivanov asked.

"Someplace safe."

"Why don't you tell me and I'll send someone to get you."

"You sent someone last night."

Ivanov hesitated, then said, "I don't know what you mean."

"He's dead."

"What is it that you want, Anastasiya?"

"He said he was going to kill me, then you."

"What was his name?"

"I want to meet."

"Tell me where you are and I'll send a car."

"No deal. We'll meet someplace public."

"Why?"

"I don't trust you."

"Red Square."

"I don't want to be exposed like that."

"There's a place, outside of Moscow, we—"

"No. Has to be in town."

Ivanov cleared his throat. "There are people who might not take kindly to the sight of me."

"I have information you want."

"What do you mean?"

"They never found the documents Boris procured did they?"

Ivanov was silent.

"I have them," she said.

Jack watched for any change in Clarissa's expression. He wondered what Ivanov would say. He held out his hands to get her attention.

She shrugged.

He mouthed the words "hang up."

"I'll call you back soon, General."

She sat the phone on the table. Got up. Walked to the window.

"We should probably leave," Jack said.

"Think he was tracing it?" Jasmine said.

"Probably."

Jack looked at the newspaper spread out on the table. He pointed and said, "What's that?"

Clarissa hovered over his shoulder. The ends of her hair brushed against his cheek. She said, "Russian Fire Theater. They do shows there. The Fire Show."

"Dark and loud," Jack said.

"Looks that way."

"Call him back. Tell him to meet you at the show tonight. You'll exchange the documents with him there."

"What are we going to use for the documents?"

"There won't be any documents."

Clarissa and Jasmine looked at him like he had lost his mind.

"Trust me. Call him."

Clarissa redialed the number. She didn't wait for Ivanov to speak. She said, "Russian Fire Show. You know where that is?"

"I can find it."

"Meet me there tonight. Alone. Eight p.m. It's dark and loud. I'll exchange the documents in exchange for your promise to stay out of my life."

"Deal," Ivanov said.

She hung up the phone. "What's the plan, Jack?"

"It's pretty simple. You're going to tell him that the documents are hidden in the men's room. Farthest stall. Behind the toilet, taped to the back."

"Then what? You're gonna take him out?"

"No," Jack said. "Jasmine is."

"Me?"

"Yeah, you. I can't be in the building. Ivanov knows me. His men know me. He sees me and the whole thing blows up and innocent people will end up dead."

"You really think he'll go alone?" Jasmine asked.

"No, but he agreed to be alone. He'll leave his guys outside. I'll take care of them if necessary."

"Should we go check it out?" Clarissa asked.

"Yeah," Jack said. "We're going to. But first, we need to get our stuff and ditch this room. You got anything at your hotel you need?"

Clarissa nodded.

"We're going there next."

It took Jack less than two minutes to pack. Jasmine a few minutes longer. They left the room and got in the two door white car. Drove a short distance to Clarissa's hotel. They passed by the place where Clarissa had been attacked. Yellow police tape boxed in the crime scene. Jack and Jasmine stared between the trees. Clarissa turned her head the other way.

They stopped in the lot behind the hotel. All three got out of the car. Entered the hotel from the rear. They took the stairs to avoid being seen.

Clarissa inserted her key and opened the door. The room looked untouched. She grabbed her clothes and the submachine gun. Handed it to Jack. Said, "This might come in handy if he brings extra men."

Jack nodded. Inspected the weapon. It was a PP-19 Bizon 9mm. Clarissa handed him two extra magazines. Almost 200 shots. He said, "Yeah, it'll be a big help."

"OK, that's everything."

Jack opened the door. Stopped. There were voices in the hall. Feet shuffled slowly across the floor. He waited. The shuffling of feet had stopped, but the voices continued. They were in Russian and he didn't understand what they were saying. He opened the door, stepped to the side, and looked into the hall with one eye. An old couple stood next to the stairs. They appeared to be catching their breath before taking the next flight.

"We're clear," Jack said. He left the room first.

They took the stairs back down. Exited through the rear. Got in the car and drove north through the city.

The theater was only five miles or so from where they were staying. The drive took close to fifteen minutes. They parked a few blocks away and walked. A sign outside the theater said closed and the door was locked.

"So much for that idea," Jasmine said.

"What now?" Clarissa said.

"Let's go shopping," Jack said.

"For what?" Jasmine said.

"Communications equipment. I want to be able to stay in contact and hear what is going on."

67

Feng woke up at six a.m. Earlier than normal. But today was not a normal day. It was the one day a month he looked forward to. The day he'd get to spend with his granddaughter, Maggie.

Feng had missed the first seven years of the little girl's life. It had been his fault. At least, that's what he told himself. He had raised such a stink over his daughter marrying a white man that she disavowed him. Said she'd never speak to him again, and when she had kids, he'd never see them. She held good on that promise for a long time. He always wondered if he had not been such an ass, would she have remained close to him. In the back of his head he knew that his daughter wanted to get away from him, and he provided the perfect excuse.

But time heals all wounds, or so they say. She did come back and introduced him to his granddaughter. He promised his daughter that he was leaving the business. Just had some loose ends to tie up, and once things were squared away, he'd be done.

And now, that day was close. Retirement was near. Not many gangsters get to say that.

He straightened his tie and grabbed his overcoat. Left his office and walked through the compound. Found his driver and said, "Let's go."

They drove north for an hour to Stamford, Connecticut. Stopped in front of a two story colonial. Feng got out of the car. Walked to the house. Stood under a covered porch supported by two thick white columns.

A thin woman in her late thirties opened the door. She smiled and reached out and hugged the old man.

"Biyu, my loving daughter," Feng said. "How are you?"

She barely got out the word, "Good," before Maggie barreled past her and latched onto her grandfather.

"Hi, Grandpa," Maggie said.

Feng reached down and patted the top of her head. Then he took her hand in his, kissed his daughter on the cheek, and led Maggie to the car. "Where should we go today?"

"The zoo in the park," she said.

"You want to see the monkeys?"

Maggie giggled and made a sound like a monkey, "Ooh-ooh, ahh-ahh, ee-ee."

The old man laughed. He wrapped his arm around the little girl and pulled her close. All the years he'd been involved in crime. The people he'd killed or had been responsible for their deaths. The lives he'd ruined. He didn't deserve this moment with his granddaughter, and he knew it. He knew it and he thanked whoever from above looked out for him and allowed him to live as long as he had and given him this precious time.

"To the zoo," he instructed the driver.

They drove an hour back to the city. The driver let them out on 65th and Feng and Maggie walked to and through the zoo. They spent an hour talking and laughing and making faces at the animals. Then they returned to the car. It was time to have lunch in Queens.

68

PIERRE LAY ON HIS BACK, STARING UP AT THE BLUE SKY. CLEAR, NOT A CLOUD IN sight. The rooftop of the apartment building was easy to get to. He had waited for someone to leave through the locked front door. Grabbed it before it closed. Found the stairs. Took them to the top of the building. He had expected some kind of action or resistance, but it had gone quite well.

His phone buzzed in his pocket. He pulled it out and looked at the screen. It was Bear. He answered.

"It's almost time," Bear said.

Pierre checked his watch. Performed time zone calculations in his head. 11:45 a.m.

"I'm going to the parking lot now," Bear said. "You need to watch the street."

"OK."

"You ready for this?"

"Yes."

"You sure? It's been a while, right?"

Pierre neglected to tell Bear about the previous night's activities. "I'm steady as a rock, my friend. I can do this." He disconnected the call, then stuffed the phone in his pocket. He sat up. Reached into his bag and pulled out two blankets. The blankets matched the cream colored exterior of the building. He covered himself with one of the blankets and stood, hunched over. The rooftop had a four foot high wall. He leaned over the wall and watched the street. His rifle, a Remington 700P Bear had somehow secured, rested next to his right leg. He backed up and draped the second sheet over the rifle.

The street was a little less busy than the day before. Cars passed one or two at a time, but at irregular intervals. The same went for people on the sidewalk. He guessed that there would be a lunch rush at the three ethnic diners across the street.

Pierre's mind wandered while he stared at nothing in particular. He had his sights focused on one thing, and one thing only. A white Mercedes. Until that appeared, he could think about whatever he wanted. And he did. He thought about Marcy. He could have had the woman the night before. Why hadn't he? Was it really because of the job, like he had told her? It was true, he had needed to get up early. Before five in the morning. He was at the apartment building by six, and on the roof by six-fifteen. The job was not an invalid excuse. It could have been Kat, though. What would he do about tonight? He told Marcy he'd have dinner with her. But would he even have the chance? Would they remain in New York after the hit? What if things went badly? He might end up dead himself. Or worse, in jail.

His phone buzzed again. He fished it out of his pocket, brought it up to his face. Marcy. He sent the call to voice mail. He felt a quick vibration against his side, an alert telling him that she had left him a message.

His eyes drifted lazily down the street as he thought about his date the night before.

Focus.

He recognized the car the moment it turned left onto 74th. It approached slowly as it passed the surplus store, then the bank, then the jewelry store. All the parking spots along the street were taken. The Mercedes stopped in front of the diner. Hazard lights blinked in a rhythmic pattern.

Pierre had grabbed the rifle the moment he saw the white luxury sedan. He leaned over the side of the building. Right hand on the trigger. Left hand on the barrel. Center of the rifle balanced on the narrow edge of the four foot high barrier between the roof and sky.

The rifle was equipped with a scope and iron sights. Pierre used both. He aimed just over the roof of the car, at the crack between the rear passenger door and the frame. He lifted his head for a second to get a full view of the street. He had to make sure there were no pedestrians that might cross at the same time he fired.

The area was clear. Only the old man and the driver, who remained seated and looked as though he had no intention of getting out of the Mercedes.

The door opened. At first an inch, then three, and finally all the way. He saw the old man's arm, covered with a navy blue sleeve adorned with pin stripes, reach out and grab the arm rest.

The old man followed. A tuft of silver hair appeared. Then his head. He stepped out.

Pierre's heart rate escalated. His breathing quickened. His index finger trembled slightly. He took a deep breath. Steadied himself. He had to remind himself that he'd done this before.

The old man leaned forward and his head was inside the car again.

Pierre cursed under his breath. Shifted against the wall. Readjusted the weapon in his hands.

The old man reappeared. Stood up straight. He had a smile on his face.

Tis a blessing to die happy and unaware that your life has ended.

Pierre squeezed the trigger, removing any slack. He exhaled. Pulled the trigger all the way.

The muffled sound of the shot was most likely inaudible on the ground. The impact of the shot, however, was felt by one man and noticed by another.

The bullet hit Feng in the forehead. The damage it caused was severe. The man's body flew back a few feet. A cloud of blood hovered in the air from the car door to where he landed on the sidewalk. From the view Pierre had through the scope, he could confirm that Feng was dead.

Pierre leaned back. Took in a full view of the street. The driver, who he had expected to drive off, stepped out of the car. He looked around and then ran to his boss's side.

Pierre adjusted, aimed, and pulled the trigger again. He rushed the shot, but still managed to hit the driver in the back of the head.

The man's large body fell forward on top of Feng's.

Pierre heard a scream. The scream of a child. He lifted his head and saw a little girl emerge from the backseat of the Mercedes. She was short and thin and not even ten years old.

He covered his mouth with his forearm to muffle his yell. Then he pulled out his phone and called Bear.

"Is it done?"

"It's done. But there's more of a mess than we anticipated."

"The driver?"

"Yeah, the driver. But then a little girl got out of the car."

"You didn't—"

"No, of course not. But I didn't expect a child to be present. I can't believe what I've done. Dammit, what have I done?"

"You need to calm down. Breathe deep. Relax. Get off the building. Exit through the back. I'll meet you at the corner of 72nd and 37th Avenue. Through the back, Pierre. Take an alley from 73rd to 72nd. Got it?"

"OK, yeah, I got it."

Pierre hung up. He inched his way up the wall and peeked over again. A crowd had gathered around the bodies. Sirens wailed in the distance. A man picked up the little girl and carried her away from the bloody scene.

Pierre raced across the rooftop, keeping his body low. He reentered the building. Ran down five flights of stairs. Burst through the door leading to the back. He wiped down the rifle and tossed it in the dumpster. He cut down an alley, across 73rd, and through another alley.

69

JACK POSITIONED HIMSELF ACROSS THE STREET FROM THE THEATER. HE TOOK cover inside an apartment building that had a second story window overlooking the theater and its parking lot. Cars pulled into the lot. Some parked. Others left. People from all walks of life headed toward and into the theater. The show was due to start soon.

The sky grew dark, making Jack's job tougher. Fortunately, the parking lot and area in front of the theater were well lit.

He wore a small earpiece. A microphone dangled from his collar.

"How's everything going inside?"

Clarissa responded first. "I'm sitting in the second to the last row, on the right, like he requested."

"I'm watching her from across the room," Jasmine said. "Doesn't appear anyone else is."

Jack didn't like the specified seating request that Ivanov had made. He feared that the General had a plan to execute Clarissa. He laid his fears to rest on one fact. Ivanov wanted the documents and Clarissa promised she had them.

He spoke into his microphone. "It's quiet out here. Haven't seen him or anyone suspicious yet. As soon as I do, I'll let you know."

Five silent minutes passed. Felt like an hour. No cars pulled up. Foot traffic outside the theater had been reduced to none.

A female voice spoke from behind him. She spoke in Russian. He couldn't understand what she said. The rise of the tone indicated she was questioning him.

He turned to face the woman. She looked like an eighty year old battle ax. Tight spiraled white hair, tinted blue. A brown sack of a dress on. Both hands clutched her purse.

"I don't speak Russian. You speak English?"

She narrowed her eyes and lowered her head an inch. "Who are you? And what are you doing in my building?"

"Ma'am, this is a matter of national security. You might not be safe in the hall. Go back—"

"If it was a national security issue, why is an American in the building instead of a Russian?"

"I can't go into detail on that. It's not safe for you here. You should leave."

She took two steps forward. The woman had no fear of Jack or what he might do to her. She said, "You should leave."

"Can't do that."

"Then I'll make you."

"How?"

A smile slowly formed on her lips, starting from the left. Old lips lifted, parting thin gray whiskers. She took two steps back, then turned, then disappeared into her apartment.

Was the old woman going to cause trouble for Jack? Should he take her out? The thought crossed his mind. It would be quick and easy and relatively painless. He shook his head and the thoughts from his mind. Turned toward the window and scanned the street.

A brown Bentley approached from the east. It rounded the corner and rolled past the theater. Stopped at the corner of the road and the parking lot.

Jack leaned into the window, pressing his forehead to the glass. He squinted to see inside the vehicle to no avail. Yellow lights flashed at the front and the back.

That's got to be him. What's he doing, though? Waiting for someone? More men?

A bright light flicked on and a door opened from behind him. He glanced over his shoulder. The old woman stood there, phone in her hand. She spoke quickly and loudly. He had no idea what she said, but felt certain it was about him.

"This is your last chance," the old woman said. "Leave the building. Now."

Jack ignored her. He had to confirm Ivanov's presence.

Two cars pulled up behind the Bentley. The Bentley's driver stepped out of the vehicle. Walked to the car behind him. Stopped at the driver's door. The window rolled down and the man leaned forward. A few seconds later he straightened and walked to the next car. Spoke to that driver, then returned to his car.

The flashing hazard lights cut off. The car started forward, then turned right, then turned into the parking lot. The two cars followed.

The wail of sirens approached.

Jack kept his eyes on the Bentley. The driver stepped out again. He walked around the back of the vehicle. Opened the trunk and grabbed an object. Jack could not make out what it was. The driver moved to the rear passenger door and opened it.

Red and blue lights reflected off the buildings on the other side of the street. The sirens were loud. Close.

Two legs poked out of the back seat of the Bentley. The man did not emerge. The driver bent over. Looked like the two were having a conversation.

Jack looked to the left and right, where the other two cars had parked. Two men got out of each vehicle. Two of them looked vaguely familiar. From where, though? Ivanov's headquarters? Black Dolphin? No, they were the men from Italy.

Three police cars pulled up to the building. Six cops stepped out. Two walked to the other side of the street. Drew their weapons. Aimed at the second story window. The four remaining cops walked toward the door below.

A hand reached out and grabbed a hold of the arm rest on the Bentley's rear door. A head emerged, ducked at first, then full view. Ivanov.

The door below Jack opened. Four sets of footsteps entered. Two sets hit the stairs.

Jack turned and started up the stairs behind him. Grabbed the microphone hanging from his collar. Said, "Ivanov's here with five attached. I recognize two. They are dangerous. I'm dark for a few."

The cops raced up the stairs behind him. He reached the fourth floor. The stairs ended. He scanned the open area. One window in front. One in back. Two doors to his left. Two to his right. Six options. He had to choose one because the footsteps were gaining on him, fast.

70

Clarissa lifted her left wrist and placed it in front of her mouth. She spoke softly. "Jack? What's going on?"

No response.

"Jack," she said again. "Come in? Where's Ivanov? Where are you?"

No response, again.

"Clarissa," Jasmine said. "Jack can take care of himself. Let's focus on what we have to do here."

"OK."

"I'm watching the door. I can see into the lobby."

"Do you see him?"

There was a pause, then Jasmine said, "Yes, he's here."

Clarissa resisted the urge to turn and look. She remained seated. Eyes forward. All other senses on high alert. The air was still. The velvety red curtain hung over the stage. The low murmur of chatter filled the tall and wide room.

"He's in the theater now," Jasmine said. "He's looking around."

Clarissa wondered if anyone came in with him.

"He's alone now, but there are a few guys in the lobby that look suspicious. That might be a problem."

Clarissa stared at the crowd in front of her. What if someone in the crowd was a plant? How did she know that he hadn't marked her should something happen to him? There was no room for thoughts like that. She pushed them to the side and focused. She had to be Anastasiya.

Amid the noise of the crowd she heard the hard soled shoes come to a stop next to her. The scene in front of her passed by in slow motion as she turned her head to the left. She saw the empty seat next to her. The man beyond the seat. She lifted her eyes, adjusted her gaze. Saw the man and instantly the desire to kill him burned hot inside her.

"Anastasiya?" Ivanov said.

"That's him," Jasmine said in her ear.

"Ivanov," Clarissa said.

"General Ivanov," he said.

Clarissa turned her head toward the stage. She refused to be intimidated by the man. A few seconds passed and he sat down next to her with a groan.

"Let's get down to business," he said.

"Not until the show starts," she said.

"Now."

"No."

"I'll have you killed when this is over."

"You tried to have me killed before this began." Clarissa turned her head slightly and made eye contact. "That didn't work out too well, did it?"

Ivanov's face hardened. He narrowed his eyes. Straightened his back. He opened his mouth to speak, but at that exact moment, the lights in the theater dimmed and the crowd fell to a hush.

Jasmine's voice filled her ear again, "I'm going to the hall now. Gonna get a closer look at these other guys." A few moments later she spoke again. Her voice rose and fell, like she was moving quickly. "Only one of them is out here. The others must have slipped into the theater."

Clarissa waited for the entrancing music to begin playing and the actors with their flaming batons and sticks to appear. She leaned in close to Ivanov and said, "Men's bathroom off the main hall. Last stall. Under and behind the toilet. Taped there, you'll find the documents."

Ivanov leaned forward to stand.

Clarissa grabbed his hand. "This isn't over."

"Yes, it is."

Ivanov lifted his hand into the air. A moment later a man stood next to him. Ivanov got up. The man took his seat. Ivanov disappeared. The man grabbed Clarissa's wrist. He held it tightly and said, "Not a word."

71

Jasmine stood near the building's entrance and exit doors. She saw Ivanov emerge from the theater. He nodded at his man in the lobby, then he walked down the curved hall that led to the restrooms.

The man in the lobby waited until Ivanov disappeared past the bend in the hall, and then he followed.

Jasmine followed him. She reached into her purse. Wrapped her hand around a handle. She knew that she'd have to kill two men tonight. At least two. She rounded the curve in the hallway. Didn't see Ivanov. Did see the man from the lobby. He stood in front of the men's bathroom. Blocked the door. They knew that Ivanov wouldn't come alone. Anticipated that he'd have someone either in or outside of the restroom. Outside worked better, as long as there were no witnesses.

She withdrew her hand from her purse. The man turned his head in her direction. He stared at her with cold, dead eyes. The guy was a pro, that much was obvious. Probably had no aversions to killing. That was lost after his second or third year.

She smiled at him.

He stared blankly at her.

She slowed as she neared the restroom.

He turned his head forward, kept his eyes on her.

She stopped in front of him. Turned slightly. Said, "Excuse me, is this the ladies room?"

He shrugged. Feigned disinterest by turning his head away from her. Big mistake.

Jasmine let the handle of the weapon spin in her hand. The razor sharp edge faced toward the door. Her thumb on the back of the blade. She swung her arm upward, in an arc. He noticed far too late. By the time he placed a hand on her, she had plunged the knife into his neck, severing his carotid artery. She pulled the blade out. With her free hand she covered the gash to prevent blood spray. She pulled the knife back and then plunged it into his chest, penetrating his heart.

His gurgled attempts at yelling stopped.

She held him up against the door. Used her foot to push the door open and set his body down inside. She tried to be quiet, but it was of no use.

"What are you doing out there?" Ivanov said from behind the stall door.

Jasmine said nothing. She dragged the dead man into the bathroom and let the door close behind her. Reached behind her back. She brought the pistol forward. Secured the suppressor.

"I haven't found anything in here, Kostya. She set us up. Go tell Dimitri and escort Anastasiya outside."

She walked across the bathroom. Stopped in front of his stall.

"Kostya?"

The stall door opened slightly. She saw his eye peering through, then the door closed and it sounded like the latch slid across to a locked position.

She fired three shots into the center of the door. Heard a groan. She stepped forward and kicked the door open. Aimed the gun at the man who pressed back against the wall. His legs straddled the toilet. He steadied himself with one hand on the wall. His other hand covered his abdomen where a bullet had hit. Blood soaked through his shirt and spread down.

"Just a flesh wound," she said.

"I know," he said. "I'll live."

"No, you won't."

Jasmine lifted the gun, squeezed off three more shots, the first of which hit Ivanov in the forehead. His body slid down the wall. Came to a resting position on top of the toilet. She closed the door. Tucked the gun behind her back.

Stepped over the lifeless body of the man Ivanov called Kostya. Left the
bathroom.

Jasmine walked into the theater. Fire was spinning and flying and rising and
falling on the stage. She looked across the second to the last row. Her heart sank.
Clarissa was gone. She ran out of the theater and through the lobby and past the
parking lot. She stopped a block away. Yelled into the microphone, "Jack?
Clarissa? Where are you two?"

72

THE SECOND DOOR JACK TRIED HAD BEEN UNLOCKED. HE MOVED THROUGH THE apartment, into the back bedroom. He opened the window. Forty plus feet to the ground. Nothing around the window to grab a hold of. No fire escape. No solid drain pipes. If the cops entered the apartment his only option would be to shoot his way out. He hoped it wouldn't come to that.

The radio had been silent for a while. Then two things happened.

First, Jasmine came on, sounding frantic, asking where everyone was.

Second, Clarissa came on. Only, she didn't speak to them. She spoke to someone else. And she asked that someone where he was taking her.

Being trapped in the room left Jack beyond frustrated. He couldn't see who had her or what car they were leaving in.

He lifted the microphone and said, "Jasmine, did you take out Ivanov?"

"Yeah, he's dead, Jack. And another man, Kostya I think he said. Where are you?"

It was the men from Italy that he had seen. Kostya and Dimitri, two of the men who apprehended him and brought him to Russia.

"Jack?"

"I'm in the building across the street. Some old lady called the cops. They're inside. I'm trapped."

"Dammit, this whole thing is falling apart."

"Did you see who took Clarissa?"

"I saw them when they entered, but I didn't see them take her. I'm sorry, Jack."

"Don't be. She can take care of herself. She's already transmitting. These radios are long range. As long as she's conscious she'll lead us there."

Jasmine said nothing.

The front door of the apartment opened.

"Gotta go," Jack said. "Stay out of sight."

He grabbed the sheets off the bed and dropped to his knees in the corner of the room. Covered himself. Used his knife to create a slit he could see through.

The men called to each other from the main room of the apartment. He heard them enter the bedroom next to him. They didn't stay in there long. The door opened to the room he was in. One of the men called out in English, "Come on out, mister. We won't hurt you."

Two distinct sets of footsteps moved through the room. Jack held his breath. He held the submachine gun in both hands. His palms were sweaty. His heartbeat rapid. He slowed his breath. Slowed his mind.

One of the men whistled, like Jack was a friggin' dog and would come out. The men stopped.

Jack waited.

Another cop called out from the main room. "*Obisla, obisla.*"

Jack knew very little Russian. Only a few words. And that was one. Murder.

The men in the room repeated the phrase and spoke in Russian. They left the room. Closed the door. Jack heard the main door of the apartment open and close.

They must have heard about the murder across the street. A Russian General had been executed at point blank range, and that was more troubling than a possible prowler called in by an old woman. At least until a smarter cop arrived on the scene and heard about the man in the building and put two and two together.

"Jasmine," Jack said into the microphone. "Cops are leaving. I'm coming out. There's a back door to this building. Meet me there."

"You OK?" Jack said as he pushed through the door.

Jasmine had her gun out and up and ready to fire. Blood stained her shirt and pants. She said, "I'm OK. I spoke to Frank. He's putting us in touch with his guy here, Marco."

"OK."

"Any idea who those extra guys were?"

"Yeah. Private contractors. Same ones that caught me in Italy six months ago."

Jasmine nodded. Her eyes scanned the building and the dark area between where they stood and the street.

"We should get to the car," Jack said.

They walked two blocks. The streets were dark and empty. The temperature had dropped nearly twenty degrees since they had arrived. The sidewalk had iced over and they found it tricky to secure their footing. They moved from the side-walk to the grassy area and trudged through the day old snow.

They stopped a hundred feet from the car. Stood silent. Scanned the area like an owl scans the ground for his dinner in the middle of the night.

In the background sirens wailed and blue and red lights lit up the night sky. Everyone in the area focused on the scene of the murder.

"Looks clear," Jasmine said.

Jack nodded. "You go first. If anyone pops out, I'll take care of them."

Jasmine set off without hesitation. The woman would walk into a lion's den. She reached the car. Got in.

Jack waited a minute, his eyes constantly on the move. He saw no one. Heard no one. Sensed no one. He jogged to the car and got in on the passenger's side.

Jasmine pulled away. They turned right, away from the theater. Jack looked back through his window and saw a scene of pure madness. A crowd of people in the street. Locals dressed in their lounge wear. The people who had attended the theater, dressed a bit nicer. A few cops stood between them and the theater.

They drove and Jack lost track of time as he thought about Clarissa and what he would do to her abductors.

"Jack?" The voice came from the ear piece.

He lifted the microphone and said, "Clarissa? You OK?"

"Yeah," she said. "Not sure where I'm at, though."

"We're working on that. Going to meet a guy now who can help."

"OK."

"Are you hurt?"

"No."

"Do you remember anything about the ride?"

"Initially, yeah. But then he stopped and blindfolded me. I think we drove for another fifteen minutes after that."

Jack looked at Jasmine. He tried to keep his fading hope from showing on his face. "Can you see where you are now?"

"In a room. It's like a cell within a room."

"Window?"

"Yeah. No. It's covered."

"Anything distinguishable?"

"Um, not really. There is another cell in the room and a man sleeping on a cot in that cell."

"Wake him."

"OK." She said nothing for a few minutes.

Jack drummed the armrest on the door with his fingers. He looked between Jasmine and the road. "How much longer till we're there?"

"About fifteen minutes. We're leaving the city."

"This guy in the SIS?"

She shook her head.

Jack didn't push for more information.

"OK, Jack. He's up. Says his name is Alik."

Jack smiled. "You tell him Jack Noble says hello. Going silent for a bit."

"OK."

They reached a point where the streetlights ended. The road was dark and empty and covered with packed snow and ice.

"You drive well in the snow for having grown up in Atlanta," Jack said.

Jasmine shrugged. "They gave me training."

She turned into a residential neighborhood. Turned right twice and left once. Stopped in front of a one story brick house.

They got out, crossed the snow covered lawn. Went to the door. Jack knocked.

A man answered.

"Marco?" Jasmine said.

"Yeah, come in." He smiled at Jasmine. Furrowed his brow at Jack.

Jack ignored him. Followed Jasmine inside and waited for the man. He led them through the house. They settled around a table in the man's kitchen.

"You got some kind of transmitters, right?" Marco said.

"Yeah," Jack said. "We've been communicating with them."

"Can you still get her?"

"Clarissa?" Jack said.

"Yeah," she said.

"OK, just making sure you're there. Stand by."

Marco motioned to Jack for the device.

Jack reached into his pocket, pulled out the transmitter and set it on the table.

Marco attached a wire to it, connected it to his laptop computer and started hammering away at the keyboard. "Get her on again."

"Clarissa," Jack said. "I need you to get on. You don't have to talk, just keep transmitting. We're getting your location now."

"OK," she said. She left the line open. They heard the sound of shuffling feet. Alik spoke in the background. Clarissa said yes, then no.

"I'm getting it," Marco said as he pointed at his screen. A map zoomed in. At first showing the southwest section of Moscow, then zooming beyond the outer loop. An area called Desna centered on the screen. The map continued to zoom, finally setting on a house in what looked to be an affluent neighborhood.

"Looks like the kind of house a General might own," Jack said.

"You got it," Marco said.

"Can you get the address?" Jasmine said.

Marco struck at his keyboard again and then wrote down the address.

Jasmine studied the screen and memorized the route. "OK. I got it. You coming with us, Marco?"

"I'll pass. This is your mess. But you can come back for a drink later tonight if you'd like."

Jasmine ignored the man. "Let's go, Jack."

Jack stood. Thanked the man and walked out of the house. Looked up at the dark sky. Gray clouds hovered close. He joined Jasmine in the car.

"Want me to put the address in the GPS?" he said.

"No," Jasmine said. "Too risky. What if someone's tracking us? Best to leave it off for now."

The drive was long and dark and boring. They drove on the highway that served as Moscow's outer perimeter. They rounded the city to the south and exited the highway.

Streetlights once again lit the road. Snow had been plowed from the asphalt. It was piled up on the shoulder and sidewalk, as high as six feet in some places.

Jasmine turned left, past a few houses, then turned right. They drove by a long two-story warehouse and into another housing area. The homes were larger. The lots were huge.

"Never thought there were people here that had it this good," Jack said.

Jasmine shrugged. "Just about everywhere, Jack. Someone's gotta have the money."

She slowed the car as they passed a two-story sandy colored brick house on a corner lot. Trees blocked the entrance and obscured the views of most windows. "That's it."

"Keep going."

She drove another block, made a U-turn, then parked the car.

They sat in the dark for five minutes. Watching, listening and waiting.

Jack opened his door. Grabbed the submachine gun strapped around his neck and said, "Let's do this."

73

JACK AND JASMINE CUT THROUGH A WOODED LOT TOWARD THE DRIVEWAY OF THE large sandy colored brick house. The evergreen trees were big and bushy and provided great cover. They stopped at the edge of the lot and watched the house.

A lone man walked past them. He held a leash, and his dog kept perfect pace with him, his large head bumped into the man's knee every few steps. Perfectly trained.

Jasmine waited until the man had passed and said, "I think we're in the clear."

"Stay vigilant. I'm crossing first. Cover me. Wait for my signal before you cross."

"OK."

Jack stepped out of the cover of the trees. Onto the street. Crossed through the pool of light cast by the streetlight on the corner. He reached the driveway and turned to face Jasmine. He signaled for her to cross as he backed into the darkness.

Jasmine arrived a few seconds later. They walked to the rear side of the house. The windows in back were all lit up. The back portion of the house was one gigantic room that stretched from the kitchen, through the dining room, and into a large living area. They saw one man. Jack recognized him as Dimitri.

He sat on a white leather couch. He held a glass in one hand. A bottle of vodka sat on the table. He stared at the flat panel TV that hung on the wall above the fireplace. The man's face was long and drawn and pale.

Jack looked at the TV. "It's the theater. They've got Ivanov and Kostya's face on there."

They continued along the back of the house until they reached the kitchen. Jack climbed four wooden steps to the rear door. Placed his hand on the knob. The door was unlocked. He turned the knob and opened the door. Stepped into the kitchen. He heard Jasmine follow. He pointed toward the stairs across the room. She headed for them. Jack walked silently through the kitchen, then the dining room, and finally behind the man.

"Arms where I can see them," Jack said.

Dimitri stiffened.

"Now," Jack said.

The man held his arms to the side. Extended them. Placed them behind his head, interlocking his fingers.

"Get up."

Dimitri stood.

"Turn around."

The man turned. His pale face drained at the site of Jack. "You? You're supposed to be dead. What are you doing here?"

Jack nodded toward the TV. "Had to tidy up a bit. Took care of the General."

"And Kostya."

"Seems that way."

"What are you doing here?"

"You know what. Here for my friends." Jack gestured with the submachine gun. "Lead the way."

Dimitri sidestepped around the couch, facing Jack the entire time. He turned and walked to the other end of the room.

Jasmine stood by the stairs, her gun drawn and aimed at Dimitri.

He stopped in front of her. Turned. Started up the stairs.

Jack followed, then Jasmine.

They reached the top. Dimitri led them down a wide hallway. He opened the last door on the right. Stepped inside.

Jack went in after him. The room was huge. It looked like they converted the entire end of the house into some kind of prison. He saw four six-by-nine cells in the room. Two were empty. One was occupied by Clarissa. The last by Alik.

"Keys, Dimitri," Jack demanded.

"Screw you."

"Jack," Clarissa said. "He—"

"In a minute, Clarissa." He stepped toward Dimitri. "Keys. Now."

"You'll have to kill me."

"Fine." Jack pulled the trigger. A spray of bullets slammed into Dimitri's chest and head. He twitched and jerked, then fell backward to the floor.

"Jack," Clarissa said. "He's not the one that comes up here."

Jack stopped rifling through the man's pockets and looked up at Clarissa. "What do you mean?"

"Jack, look out," Jasmine shouted.

Jack spun and saw a man barreling into the room. Jack dropped to the floor and worked the gun strapped around his chest into his hands.

The man that entered the room yelled and started firing.

Jack pushed back against the cell bars and squeezed the trigger. Bullets sprayed the room and the hallway beyond. They tore through the plaster and sheetrock and wooden studs.

The man was struck by several bullets from mid-thigh up to his head. He fell back against the wall. Slid down it, leaving a crimson trail in his wake.

"Is everyone OK?" Jack said. A cloud of plaster and dust filled the room. He wiped his eyes with his sleeve and looked around.

"I'm OK," Jasmine said.

"Me too," Clarissa said.

The room went silent except for creaks and crashes where studs collapsed and sections of the wall fell to the floor.

"Alik?" Jack rose to his feet. Turned around. Saw Alik on his back in the middle of the cell, lying in a pool of his own blood.

Jasmine ran to the body of their attacker. Found a set of keys and furiously worked at the locked door leading into Alik's cell. She opened it and both her and Jack rushed to Alik's body.

"No pulse," Jack said.

Jasmine handed him the keys. "Get her out. I'll work on him."

Jack unlocked Clarissa's cell door. "Were there any more?"

"Yes. Two more."

"Jasmine, we need to get him and get out of here. There's more."

Together, they hoisted Alik onto Jack's shoulder. He carried the man's lifeless body down the stairs, through the kitchen, and across the backyard.

Jasmine had run ahead of them for the car. By the time Jack and Clarissa reached the driveway, Jasmine was there.

They placed Alik in the back seat. Jasmine got out and slid in next to him. She worked feverishly to resuscitate the lifeless man.

Clarissa got in the passenger seat. Jack sat behind the wheel. Started the car and pulled out of the driveway, heading back the way they came in.

"Where should we go?" he asked.

"Just drive," Jasmine said.

74

"YOU AIN'T SAID MUCH," BEAR SAID.

Pierre shrugged. Stared out the window. His face pale. Expression blank.

"You didn't know," Bear said.

Pierre nodded. Turned his head and leaned the seat back. "It's probably not the worst thing I've ever done. I don't know why I feel like this."

"Sometimes it just hits the right way."

"Guess so."

"It's been a rough six months for you, Pierre. You've been through a lot. Some things have come full circle. You should take a vacation after all this is over."

"I plan to. Just have to figure out who to bring."

"There a woman back in France?"

"Aye, there is." Pierre paused to light a cigarette. Cracked his window. "She wasn't happy I was leaving."

"They never are."

"I don't think she's waiting for me to return."

"We'll find out soon enough."

"We?"

"I think we need to finish this. Don't you?"

"Charles?" Pierre asked.

"Yeah."

"I'll do it for you and Jack."

"We have to get to France soon. Before he comes to New York. I know Charles is going to be in the mix for the old man's empire."

"Will Frank cover us?"

"If not, I got a friend who will."

"Like your friend in New York?"

"Same guy."

Pierre said nothing else.

Bear kept his eyes on the road. He weaved through the heavy traffic. They drove southwest, into the setting sun. The low angle of the light created a flare on his windshield, making it difficult to see the traffic ahead. They were halfway between Philadelphia and D.C. Frank had told them to come up the next morning, but Bear didn't like the idea of staying in New York after the hit. Especially not in the apartment that Frank had arranged. They were sitting ducks in there.

"I got another friend outside D.C. who's gonna put us up for the night, Pierre. Good cook. Usually has a stocked bar."

Pierre turned his head. Bear looked over and saw the man smiling. "I'm going to need it."

"Me too."

"Have you heard anything about the girl?"

"No." Bear hadn't been in touch with Mandy since they took her and Larsen. He hated putting his trust in Frank and his associates. In some ways the man was no better than those they fought against. The only saving grace he had in Bear's eyes was the fact that Jack trusted him. "But I'll make sure I see her soon."

75

Snow had begun to fall shortly after midnight. The temperatures continued to plummet. The thick steel railing along the side of the bridge was covered with two inches of ice. Long, sharp icicles hung at irregular intervals. Some were short, others long.

The sound of rushing water rose from below. A river raced by, under the bridge. Jack didn't need to get near it to know that the water would provide an icy, frozen tomb for anyone who entered.

"I'm sorry, Jack," Jasmine said. "I think he was gone before he hit the ground. I never got a pulse or—"

"It's not your fault," Jack said. "I went in guns blazing. Clarissa tried to tell me there was someone else. I ignored it. Anger got the best of me. I'm just grateful no one else was hurt."

He felt hands on his shoulder. He leaned over, grabbed his dead friend under the arms and lifted him. Jasmine and Clarissa grabbed Alik's feet and the three of them held the lifeless body in the air.

"So long, Alik," Jack said as he let go of Alik. They heard a splash when his body hit the water. Looked over the railing. Saw nothing. Even if they could, the racing current would have carried him fifty feet or so by that point.

The trio sulked back to the car. Clarissa got in back. Jasmine in the driver's seat. Jack in the passenger's. They drove in silence, heading southwest, toward

Ukraine. Reentering the country should be far easier than leaving it. They were crossing further north than where they entered and they didn't have to deal with people on the lookout for Jack Noble.

They reached the border crossing close to three-thirty a.m. Three lights lit up the two lane road. An old man stepped out of a worn sun bleached wooden building. He walked to the front of the car, then to the driver's side. Jasmine rolled down the window. The guard stuck his head in. He smiled and said, "Passports?"

They handed him their fake passports and waited. Thirty seconds later he handed them back. Walked to the front of the car, then waved them through.

Jack held his breath as they passed into the next country.

Fifteen minutes later, Jasmine pulled over. She grabbed her cell phone and placed a call.

"Frank," she said. "Yeah, we're safe, but I've got bad news. We lost Alik." There was a long pause then Jasmine said, "Jack, he wants to talk to you."

Jack grabbed the phone. Placed it to his ear. "Yeah, Frank."

"Jack, listen. We think we've got a lead on who leaked the information and sold it off to begin with."

"OK. Take them down then."

"Things have changed a lot since you worked for us. We aren't equipped for that kind of thing. I need you and Jasmine."

"What about Clarissa?"

"Well," Frank paused a beat, "I think she's in deep enough already that it won't compromise anything to keep her on board."

"OK."

"Don't tell them about this. I want to brief everyone in person. Where are you guys?"

"Where are we?" Jack asked.

"Near Hlukhiv," Jasmine said.

"Hlukhiv," Jack repeated.

"OK, you guys get to Brovary. Call me when you're close. I'll get you on a flight to Germany, get you fresh passports, and get you home. You'll be in my office by noon."

"Frank, one more thing."

"Yeah."

"How'd that situation go with Bear and Pierre."

"They completed the job successfully."

Jack hung up the phone. He thought back to his long and rocky relationship with the old man. If it had happened two years ago, he might have had a feeling or two. As it was, he didn't give a damn.

"What did he say?" Jasmine asked.

"Drive to Brovary. We're getting on a plane there, then going to Germany. Then home. We meet with him around noon, eastern time."

"What about me?" Clarissa asked.

"You're coming with us."

PART V

EPISODE 10

76

"When will they be in my possession?" the man said into the cell phone he purchased minutes prior.

"Be patient," she told him. "As soon as I've secured them, they'll be yours."

He split the blinds with his index and middle fingers and stared down at crowds hustling along F Street. Tourists who were making their way to the next attraction. Politicians and business people on their way to lunch or a business meeting or perhaps a secret meeting with someone they shouldn't be seeing.

He pulled his fingers back and the blinds snapped into place with a faint clank. He paced across the office. Stopped and leaned against the door. He glanced around the room. It was bare. No pictures or paintings on the walls. A simple wooden desk and a simple plastic chair. It wasn't his primary office, so he had no need for the frills and extras that lined his office in the Pentagon. No one knew of this place. The meetings and business he conducted in the room were not the kind of business and meetings that his superiors would condone.

"How will I get in touch with you?" he asked.

"I'll let you know when the time is right."

He massaged his eyebrows with his thumb and forefinger, starting in the center and slowly working his way out. "This is a throwaway line. After this conversation the phone is going in the trash. Give me your number."

She hesitated. Started to speak. Stopped, then began again after he heard the sound of her licking her lips. The only noise that escaped her mouth was a soft, whistling "S" sound.

He quickly interrupted her. "No names! That's the only condition."

"I'll be in touch," she said.

"Wait—"

The line clicked off and the time display flashed on the cell phone screen. He cursed under his breath and ran his free hand through his thick gray hair.

I've got to get those documents back, he thought.

He turned and reached for the doorknob. Stopped. Walked over to his desk and opened the center drawer. He reached in and grabbed the Heckler & Koch USP Compact 9mm pistol.

He drew the gun to his chest and walked back to the door. Slowly he turned the knob and pulled the door open. He leaned over and peered through the opening, listening for any movement. Then he stuck his head into the hall. His right hand was just out of sight, ready to spring forward and shoot if necessary.

Satisfied the hall was empty, he closed the door and walked back to his desk. Set the gun in the drawer and slid the drawer closed. He scanned the room one more time, making sure nothing was out of place. He grabbed his coat and hat, then left the office.

He was greeted by the warm spring breeze as he stepped out of the building and onto the busy sidewalk.. The overcoat was too much. Not only would he bake inside it, he would also draw unnecessary attention to himself. And unnecessary attention was always a bad thing for a man in his position.

He slipped out of the coat and draped it across his left arm. He pulled the brim of his hat down and lowered his head. At six-three it wasn't quite enough to hide his face completely, but it had to do. He only had to make it a block or so and then he could relax.

An opening in the crowd appeared, and he took it. Merged in with a group of tourists. The group was a curse and a blessing at the same time. There were plenty of bodies and faces, making it harder for someone to notice him. But the meandering group moved slowly, making the walk take that much longer.

Finally, he felt comfortable enough to leave the group and remove his hat. His car was parked at the Pentagon, so he had to either walk or catch a cab back. It wasn't that far, only about a mile, so he elected to walk. It'd do him good, he figured. Although he considered himself in shape for his age, a softening around his mid-section had started a few years back and progressed faster than he was willing to accept.

Twenty minutes later he entered one of the most secure buildings in the world. The guards standing around greeted him by name and smiled and barely paid attention as he passed through the security station.

He nodded as he passed the guard he knew as Jones.

"Have a great day, Secretary," Jones said.

77

Jack sat alone in Frank's office. The room, much like Frank himself, was dull. There was little there to keep his mind off Alik. The scene from the previous night played over and over in his mind. He hated that they dumped him in the icy river, but they had little choice. They couldn't leave him at the General's house. Couldn't leave him on the side of the road. He'd have been found too soon. Sure, his body would probably be found a few miles or a few hundred miles downstream That didn't matter. It gave them time and that they got out of Russia without further incident.

The door handle rattled. Jack tensed. Instinctively, his hands went to where his pistol would be if he had one. He shrugged his shoulders and exhaled. Frank's office was secure and Jack knew he had nothing to worry about, except maybe for Frank.

The door cracked open and Jack twisted in his chair. He nodded at Frank as the man stepped into the office. Jack shifted and followed Frank with his eyes as the man walked past.

Frank stepped around the desk and stood in front of Jack. He placed two cups of coffee on top of his calendar. Offered one to Jack, who reached out, grabbed the cup and brought it to his face. The lid hovered inches from his nose. He inhaled the steam and aroma and then took a sip.

"Thanks for coming alone, Jack," Frank said.

Jack set the coffee down on the desk. He folded his arms over his chest. Rubbed his freshly shaved chin. "You didn't leave me much choice."

"Beard's gone. Looks good."

Jack said nothing.

"When are you going to take care of the hair?"

"Soon." Jack paused for a second, waiting for Frank to continue the conversation. When he didn't, Jack said, "You didn't bring me down here to talk about my grooming habits. What the hell is this about?"

"No, no I didn't." Frank placed his hands behind his head and leaned back in his chair. His eyes shifted from Jack to the ceiling. He opened his mouth several times to speak, but didn't say a word.

"Frank," Jack said. "What is it?"

"You remember I told you we think we have a lead on the leak? For the documents?"

"Yeah, that was a few hours ago, Frank."

"We were wrong."

"How did you find this out?"

"We..." Frank paused. He narrowed his eyes and seemed to study Jack. "Let's just leave it at we were wrong."

"Jesus, Frank. You're about to ask me for my help. If you want it, you have to be honest with me. Who did you think it was and why were you wrong?"

Frank pushed back in his chair and stood. He placed his hands on the desk and leaned over. His face was inches from Jack's.

"Listen to me, Jack. You're going to do whatever the hell I say you're going to do. One phone call and some very important and dangerous people are going to find out that Jack Noble is, in fact, still alive. Oh, and did I forget to mention that those same people also know that you are the one responsible for the documents getting into the wrong hands in the first place?"

"Yeah while they were on their way to North friggin' Korea or the Middle East or wherever the hell they were going."

"Your point? You think this is a lesser of two evils thing, Jack? I can assure you that these people don't see it that way. They get their hands on you and you'll spend the rest of your life in Leavenworth. Or dead. Take your pick."

Jack forced a laugh. "I've survived death once. I'll take my chances again."

Frank pushed off the desk and stood up straight. "This isn't a joke." He pulled his cell phone from his pocket and held it face up in his palm. "What's it going to be, Jack?"

"Just for clarity's sake, what are my options?"

Frank exhaled loudly and shook his head. "Death or prison or you work for me and we get this resolved once and for all."

"What's the resolution you are looking for?"

"Catch whoever leaked the documents."

"Why are we working this?"

"Can't answer that."

"Why not the NSA or Homeland? Hell, the FBI would be better equipped than us to handle this."

"What's your answer, Jack?"

Jack waved him off and looked to the side. "I'm thinking."

"Better hurry."

"Any other incentives? What happens when this is over?"

"I'm pretty sure that I can clear your name if we are successful."

"Only pretty sure?"

"Best I can offer."

Take the offer or leave it? Was Frank bluffing or was he serious? He owed nothing to Jack. They had parted ways years ago. Jack took on a contract every once in a while, but other than that, the two men meant nothing to each other. He knew what Frank was capable of and didn't put it past the man to turn him in. Frank obviously held some contempt over Jack swiping the documents with an intent to sell them.

"I'll do it," Jack said. "After this, you and I are through."

Frank nodded.

"After you clear my name, that is," Jack said.

"You have my word, Jack. I'll do everything I can if you find the leak." Frank looked down at the buzzing phone on his desk. He scooped up his cell and tapped on the screen. His expression went from hard-ass to looking like he was going to be sick.

"What is it?" Jack asked.

Frank waved him off. Kept his eyes on the phone. He swiped at the screen with his index finger. His eyes darted left to right repeatedly. He set the phone down and lowered his head. Covered his eyes with his hand. His head shook side to side.

"What?" Jack asked again.

"Addendum to the previous offer." Frank dropped his hand and looked at Jack. "Find the man responsible, and the documents, and your name is cleared."

"The documents?"

Frank nodded.

Jack shared the same nauseous feeling. After all the work that went into securing the intel and the lives that had been lost, the documents were gone again.

"I thought they were in a safe place," Jack said through clenched teeth.

"They were," Frank said.

"So it's someone in your group?"

"Not necessarily."

"Who had access?"

"Us and them."

"Who are them?"

"Can't say."

"Frank," Jack said.

"Jack," Frank said.

Jack clenched his jaw tighter.

"Look," Frank said. "You're a lone operator. I don't know for sure whose side you're on. You could double cross me on this, and I'll be the one standing around taking the blame, and the bullet. I can't tell you who else had access. Yet, at least. I'm going to have to eventually. Maybe. For now I want you working this on a specific angle. My gut tells me that if, no, *when* we find the man responsible, we will find the documents. I'm sure he wants them back and will have them in his possession by that time. No harm, no foul kind of thing. Got me?"

Jack nodded. Said nothing.

Frank sat down and opened a drawer. He reached in and pulled out a handgun and holster. "You armed?"

Jack shook his head and remained calm despite his muscles tensing at the question, and the sight of the gun.

"Take this." Frank slid the weapon and three magazines across the table.

Jack picked up the weapon. Inspected it. Sat the Glock 17 down and said, "I prefer a Beretta."

"You'll make due with this."

Jack shrugged. "I might need something heavier. H&K MP7, silenced."

"I'll see what I can do."

"What now?" Jack said. "I'm supposed to figure this all out on my own?"

"No." Frank reached into the drawer again and pulled out a card. He slid it face-down across the table.

Jack reached out and picked it up. The card had a local D.C. phone number and the name Rico printed on it.

"Who's Rico?" he asked.

"Your starting point."

Jack got up and turned around. He grabbed the doorknob, pulled it open and walked out of the office. Stopped at the elevator. Frank's footsteps echoed down the dimly lit corridor. He'd have preferred to not see the man again, but he had no choice. A security card was required to operate the elevator, and Frank possessed the card.

"When're you going to get me an access card?" Jack said without turning to look at Frank.

"The day you are on my payroll again."

"So, never."

Frank swiped his card. The doors opened and he extended his arm, gesturing Jack inside the elevator. The men rode up in silence. When the elevator stopped, they got out and Frank escorted Jack through the hall to the lobby. Frank stopped just short of the entrance and held out his hand. Jack grabbed it.

"One more thing," Frank said as he reached into his pocket. He pulled out a cell phone and handed it to Jack. "It's a secure line. You don't have to worry about your calls being traced or hacked. I can track you with it, so if something happens to you, I'll find you. It already has my number, Jasmine's and a few other numbers loaded into it. Be careful about calling other people on it, though."

"Like who?"

"Your girlfriend for one. Get a cheap phone for that. And your hacker pal, Brandon. You don't want him getting a hold of this number."

Jack stuffed the phone in his pocket. "Anything else?"

"That'll be all. Good luck, Jack."

Jack said nothing. He turned and started toward the door before Frank finished speaking. When he reached the exit, he glanced over his shoulder. The empty lobby stared back at him with the presence of a thousand restless souls. The spirits of those that he and Frank, and the men and women who were like them, had been responsible for removing from the living. He knew that this mission would only serve to add to that number. The thought crossed Jack's mind that he could double back and end the whole mess right then by taking Frank out in the hall. Two things stopped him. First, he was certain every inch of the place was under video surveillance. Second, he knew he had to fix the mess he created when he transferred the documents to the old man. If he had done the right thing six months ago and turned the classified intel in, none of this would be necessary.

He pushed through the door and stepped out onto the sidewalk. The air was warm and smelled like beer. Thunder roared in the distance, rumbling and crackling above the city. Gray storm clouds covered the sky, hiding the sun and threatening to open up and soak the city at a moment's notice.

"Jack," the familiar voice called from his left.

He turned his head and saw Bear and Pierre approaching. He started in their direction.

"Take it you just met with Frank," Bear said.

"You could say that," Jack said. "How was New York?" He looked at each man in turn.

Pierre's smile faded and he turned his head and looked up toward the darkening sky.

"We got the job done," Bear said as he tilted his head toward Pierre and slightly shook it. "The old man's gone."

"The world's a better place," Jack said. "What are you doing here?"

"Guessing that we're about to be asked to go to Paris and finish the job."

"Charles?"

"Yeah."

"Wish I could join you."

"I'm sure you do."

"Doesn't Frank know that someone else will step up?"

Bear shrugged. "Who knows why he's doing this. Maybe he just wants to break the circle. Anyone involved in the thing with the Russians. I really don't think he cares about the old man's organization one way or the other except for that. Anyways, we gotta get in there. Call me later."

"Same old number?"

"Yup. It'll ring me."

The men said goodbye, and Bear and Pierre walked toward the SIS head-quarters while Jack walked away from it. He continued on until he found a barren alley. He walked to the bricked-in end and pulled out the phone Frank provided. Then he pulled out the card with Rico written on it. Dialed the number. On the third ring a man answered.

"Hello?" the man said.

"This Rico?" Jack said.

"Who's this?"

"That's not important. Is this Rico?"

There was a pause and shuffling noises filled the ear piece, like the man was leaving or entering a room.

"Yeah, this is Rico."

"We need to meet."

78

FRANK MET THE TWO MEN IN THE LOBBY OF THE SIS HEADQUARTERS BUILDING. After they entered, he walked to the front door and locked it. "No need to go to my office. This will be quick."

"Before you get started," Bear said, "there's still the matter of payment for the old man."

Frank smiled and gestured toward the seating area of the lobby. He crossed the room and pushed one of the chairs close to the square glass coffee table. He placed a briefcase on the table and sat down.

Bear took a seat on the leather couch. Pierre sat next to him.

"I've got accounts opened for each of you," Frank said. "False names. Encrypted online access. You can transfer the money through your computer if you want. ATM cards you can use anywhere. They'll raise no red flags. The accounts are set up that when you make a withdrawal with your ATM card, it will show you in one of fifty random places all over the world. When you transfer money to a different account, it will display fifty random dummy account numbers, none of which are real."

The explanation satisfied Bear. He leaned forward and took the manila folder from Frank. Inside were two ATM cards with paper wrapped around each and secured with a rubber band. He handed one to Pierre.

"The account details are on the paper," Frank said. "Best to commit that information to memory. You don't want to die or get captured with that on you."

Bear nodded. Stuck the card and paper in his pocket. Saw Pierre do the same out of the corner of his eye.

Frank leaned back in his chair. Smiled. "Happy?"

"Happy," Bear said. "Now what?"

Frank gestured toward the briefcase. "Your passports are in there, as are two tickets to France."

"They're clean?"

"Absolutely. Best you can get. Those are guaranteed to get you into any country without any problems. Both are stamped, logged, so forth."

"What are we to do when we get there?" Pierre said.

"I want Charles taken out," Frank said.

"Any particular method?" Pierre said. "Want it to look like an accident?"

"You are working independently," Frank said. "I'd say arrange a meeting under false pretenses. He might be expecting you sooner or later. He might even suspect you in the old man's death."

"You think so?" Pierre said.

Frank shook his head. "I doubt it. Look, you can tell him that you succeeded and Bear is dead. Now you want your money. The old man couldn't pay up. Lure him to a meeting that way."

"I need to think about it," Bear said.

"It's up to you," Frank said. "However you want to do it. Stalk him if you want. Just kill him. It has to look like a hit. That's all I care about."

"Pay?" Bear said.

"One hundred thousand each."

"What about a job after?" Pierre asked.

"We can start with additional contract work," Frank said. "There's plenty of non-sanctioned contracts."

"I want to be left alone after this," Bear said.

"No problem." Frank leaned forward and stood.

"How's Mandy?" Bear asked.

"Safe. You can see her when this is all over." Frank extended his hand. "Anything else?"

Bear looked at Pierre. The Frenchman shook his head. The men stood and followed Frank to the door.

"Call me when you get to Paris," Frank said.

Bear nodded and stepped through the open doorway. He and Pierre walked a block in silence.

"You ready for this?" Bear said.

"Absolutely," Pierre said.

"We have to get to the airport," Bear said. "Flight leaves in three hours."

Pierre nodded. "Guess he didn't want us to spend any time on our own in the city."

"Can't blame him. We're a liability to him. We screw this up and it'll be a huge mess."

"Why's that?"

"This stuff, it isn't exactly in their typical scope of work. That's why he's using us and not his own guys. That's why he used Jack to take out Foster. There's no justification. Word gets out that he's mixed up in this, or anything they contract out, and it's his ass. He gets a little leeway, of course. But only so long as it stays out of the public eye."

Pierre stopped and grabbed Bear's arm. A man bumped into Pierre's back and cursed at him for stopping in the middle of the sidewalk. Pierre glared at the man but didn't react beyond that.

"What?" Bear said.

"Should we be concerned?"

Bear flashed his passport folder at Pierre. "I doubt I'll be using this on the flight back home."

Pierre nodded with a look of understanding in his eyes.

"Yeah," Bear said. "You get it now, don't you?"

The Frenchman didn't reply. He stared ahead, eyes fixed on the skyline. Bear hoped he hadn't spooked Pierre. He needed him to successfully complete this job. After that, Pierre could do whatever he wanted as far as Bear was concerned.

"Don't worry," Bear said. "I'm overly cautious, that's all. As long as we do the job, we can trust Frank."

"I hope so."

Me, too, Bear thought. After all, he knew getting Mandy back hinged on Charles' life being taken.

79

Jack leaned against a large tree in the northeast corner of Lincoln Park. Behind him he could see the traffic moving steadily on 13th and East Capitol St. In front of him he had a view of the entire park and those passing through. As soon as Rico appeared, Jack would see him. Only problem was he had no idea who Rico was or what the man looked like. He kept an eye out for anyone in a suit with close cut hair and the look. The all-knowing paranoid look that Jack and others in the intelligence community had about them.

A man approached from Jack's left. He had dark hair, cut short and speckled with gray. He wore dark sunglasses and a navy colored suit. He was medium height with an athletic build. The guy could take care of himself, Jack was sure of that. He walked slowly and cautiously. His left arm moved. His right arm didn't. His right hand stayed close to his waist.

Jack unzipped his jacket and let it hang open. He kept his hands by his side. He stared at the man as he approached. Nodded. The man nodded back and started toward Jack. When the man was close enough, Jack said, "Rico?"

"Yeah."

The two of them faced off for what felt like minutes but in reality was only a dozen seconds or so.

Jack felt his heart rate quicken. Beads of sweat formed on the back of his neck. He hadn't been able to shake the feeling that Frank might be setting him up. Perhaps Rico wasn't an associate. Perhaps he was an assassin sent to take Jack out. But would he do it in the middle of Lincoln Park in plain daylight?

"Who are you?" Rico asked.

"Nobody important."

"How'd you get my name and number?"

"An associate passed it along. Is Rico your real name?"

Rico ignored Jack's question. "Who is your associate?"

"I'd assume he's been in contact with you recently."

"Does he work for the SIS?"

Jack nodded.

"What is it you want?" Rico asked.

"I'd assume you already know."

Rico lifted his sunglasses and rested them atop his head. He looked to his left, then his right. His hand rested on top of his holstered pistol. He stood just six feet away from Jack. Far enough away that Jack might not be able to hit him before he fired, and close enough that the man would be deadly accurate with his weapon.

"You're really Jack Noble?" Rico said.

Jack took his time answering. He knew that there were people that considered him a criminal and wanted to place him in a reinforced cell three hundred feet below ground. Finally, he nodded and said, "Yeah, that's me."

"Do you know the mess you created with these documents?" The look in Rico's eyes conveyed a mixture of betrayal and anger.

Jack nodded slowly. "You could also look at it like I did you all a favor."

"How so?"

"Think about where those documents were heading before I intervened."

Rico shook his head. He squeezed the bridge of his nose with his thumb and index finger.

"Who do you work for, Rico?"

The man placed his hands on his hips, pulling his jacket back as he did so. His pistol was in full view. "I'm NSA."

"What about before that?"

"Special Forces."

Jack smiled. They had some common ground. "Me, too," he said.

"I've read your jacket, Noble. I know all about you." He didn't seem to share Jack's enthusiasm. "You and I are nothing alike."

"Let's cut the bravado," Jack said. "I want to make this right. I want to get the documents back and get whoever sold them in the first place. Are you going to help me? Tell me what you know."

"I know enough to get you started on the right path."

"Why can't the NSA handle this?"

"Even a group as secretive as ours has to answer to someone. You don't. You get the intel back and take the mole out and it just looks like someone was hit. No one has to know anything else." Rico paused a beat and then lowered his voice. "We do it and there's a paper trail."

The words were enough for Jack to get the big picture. It had to be someone important. Someone that people paid attention to. If the truth got out it would be damning to the country. He understood his true purpose.

"Who is it?" Jack asked.

Rico looked around then turned and waved his hand. "Come with me."

Jack hesitated. He still wasn't sure about the man and his intentions, although he trusted Frank and Rico a little more than he had fifteen minutes ago.

"Come on, Jack. I won't talk here. Not out in the open. Never know who's watching."

"I think we're fine here," Jack said.

Rico stopped and walked toward Jack. He stopped a foot away. "Look across the courtyard. See the man in the jeans, fanny pack and the bright green sweatshirt?"

Jack shot a quick glance at the man Rico described. Turned back and nodded.

"He'd love to know that it's Jack Noble standing here. And he'd take you in and that would be the last anyone ever heard from you."

"Lead the way."

They exited the park to the east and turned left on 13th Street. Walked north and made a right on Constitution Avenue.

"So who is it?" Jack said.

"Who is it what?" Rico said.

Jack held out his hands. "Come on, work with me."

"Do you want to know who sold the documents or who stole them?"

"Both."

"No names until we get to my car."

"Where's that?"

Rico pointed aimlessly down the road. "A few blocks away."

"The suspense is killing me, Rico. At least give me a clue."

Rico stopped and turned toward Jack. "Can I trust you?"

Jack shrugged. "That's your call."

"The thief is a fed. Maybe one of my own. Only a few people knew about the documents. I had them in my possession and I stored them someplace safe. No one had access to them, but that doesn't mean someone didn't figure out a way." He paused, then added, "Obviously, someone did."

"Why do you say *maybe* one of your own?"

"There were only three people that knew about the intel being back in our possession. But they really didn't know what was leaked. So unless someone contracted one of them, it doesn't make sense. At least not to me. They all check out too. Alibis and interrogation. All three of them check out."

"Yet you say maybe."

"I don't trust anyone, Jack."

"You and I might end up getting along after all," Jack said.

Rico smiled and seemed to let his guard down for the first time. "We're going to have to. You're my partner for the next few days." The smile faded and he snapped back into agent mode. "Obviously, whoever stole them knows what they're getting."

"Or were directed by someone who knows," Jack added.

Rico nodded. "Right." He started walking again. "And who, besides us, knows how critical the information is?"

"I'd guess the people that were willing to pay for it in the first place."

"Yeah, but they don't know we have it in our possession."

"Had."

Rico frowned.

"Sorry," Jack said. "Reflex."

"It's fair. I can handle the criticism."

"So who is it?"

"Who would be in a position to know this kind of stuff, Jack?"

"You said only three of your people knew. What about your bosses?"

"Now you're getting there."

"You think it was someone in the NSA?"

"No."

Jack said nothing. He started to think of people beyond the NSA that Rico would report to.

"Come on," Rico said. "Keep talking it through."

"It'd have to be someone pretty powerful. Someone kept up to date on all matters of national security."

"That's right."

"So we're talking maybe the head of an agency?"

"Or?"

"Or the head of a government."

"Not quite that high, but close."

"Shit."

"You can say that again," Rico said as he pulled his keys from his pocket. "This is the garage. You wait out here. Cameras everywhere in there. I don't want to be caught on surveillance with you."

"I'm a ghost. Ghosts can't be filmed. Don't you know that?"

Rico shook his head and said nothing.

Jack looked up and spotted a camera fixed to the building, pointing directly at them. He didn't mention it. "Anything else before you go in? I want to see if I can figure it out before you pull through the exit."

"The Pentagon."

"The Pentagon?"

"I think that's where our mole works." Rico followed the sidewalk next to the building and stepped past the jersey wall at the entrance.

Jack watched from outside as the man walked through the garage. His opinion of Rico had changed quite considerably since they met. The man turned out to be a lot like him.

Rico stopped in front of a late model luxury sedan. The dark garage prevented Jack from making out the model, but it was big and bold and masculine. His eyes met Rico's and the man nodded slightly and ducked into the car. Jack turned to face the street and then the world got hot and loud and turned upside down. He wasn't sure what hit him first, the heat or the noise or the violent blast wind that knocked him off his feet and threw him into the street.

The explosion left him disoriented. It was only instinct that allowed him to bring his arms up to protect his face and head as he barreled through the air toward the faded black asphalt. He landed on his right forearm. Felt the flesh tear from his knuckles and wrist. Pain traveled through his arms. He heard tires squeal around him as traffic came to a halt. He forced himself to his hands and knees and looked back at the garage. Orange flames peeked through the black smoke that poured through every opening in the garage.

Another explosion ripped through the garage. Jack dropped to his stomach, covering his head with his arms. His senses recovered and he knew he had to get to his feet. There had to be a couple hundred cars in the garage. Each loaded with fuel, meaning there would be more explosions.

He took one last look behind him, then began to move away. He tried to run, but his right leg wouldn't allow him to. He looked down and saw his pants shredded below the knee. Blood soaked his leg. Had he taken shrapnel to his leg? He pushed the thought from his mind and continued moving away from the garage. Turned right at the first cross street.

Safe from another blast, Jack leaned back against a brick building. He caught his breath, then bent over to assess the damage to his leg. No bones protruding. No metal penetrating. His knee and leg were scraped from when he hit the asphalt and skidded across the street, but the damage was minimal.

Sirens echoed off the buildings that surrounded him. Police cars and fire trucks and ambulances approached from every direction. Not wanting to be seen in his condition by the police or rescue personnel, Jack opened the first unlocked door he found. He stood in the lobby of an apartment building. Glanced around. Found it to be empty.

He reached into his pocket and pulled out his cell phone. Decided against calling Frank and reached out to Jasmine instead. She answered on the second ring.

"Jasmine, it's Jack. I need you to come get me."

"Where are you?"

"That's a good question." He looked around and found three rows of mailboxes. Read off the address to Jasmine.

"I'll be there in ten minutes," she said.

"I'm inside."

"I'll find you."

80

Clarissa sat at a table in an empty coffee shop on the Georgetown Pike in McLean, Virginia, about five miles from Langley. Sinclair had told her he spent most of his time there now as opposed to their field training location in Newport News, Virginia. None of them were a fan of being under the Langley microscope, but sometimes it was necessary. Or so he had told her.

For now, though, he was late and she was finishing her second espresso.

She glanced over her shoulder at the bored barista who leaned over the counter while reading a magazine. The woman didn't look up or even seem to care that there was a customer in the cafe. No wonder Sinclair had chosen this location, Clarissa thought.

A car pulled up. Clarissa craned her neck to see Sinclair's Audi A8 park in the handicapped spot near the front door. He stepped out of the car with his briefcase in hand and walked to the entrance.

She tensed. He could be carrying anything in that briefcase, including weapons. It was a matter of whether the weapons were meant for her to do her job, or if they were simply meant for her, to take her life. She relaxed as she regained control of her thoughts. Eventually her rational side won out. No way Sinclair would endanger himself by trying to pull off a hit like this. If anything, he'd send Randy. Her eyes instinctively darted back to the vehicle to double check for any passengers. She saw none.

Sinclair stepped into the cafe and smiled at her. She smiled back, remaining seated. He walked to the counter where the barista looked at him with indifference. Clearly she was annoyed at having to shelve her article and serve a customer.

Clarissa checked her cell phone while waiting. No messages. She had made sure to give Jack her number before they landed, yet he hadn't called. No point in worrying, she thought. He's got his own mess to deal with. They'd be together soon enough. Hopefully for a lot longer than this one mission.

Sinclair placed his cup and then his briefcase on the table. He sat down. Took a sip of coffee.

"It's good to see you," she said.

He nodded and smiled. "You too. I heard things got a little iffy in Russia."

She tilted her head and shrugged.

"Friend of a friend told me," he said. "No biggie. You made it out alive."

She spent five seconds trying to figure out who Sinclair might have spoken with. Jack might have mentioned it, but Frank and Sinclair were not on speaking terms, so that wasn't it.

"I'll save you the time," he said. "It was Marco, the man who brought you the guns. He also helped Jack and the woman find you."

"Tell him I said thanks."

"You can tell him next time you see him."

"Hopefully that's never."

"Never say never, my dear."

Clarissa said nothing. She drank the rest of her espresso, then got up and ordered another. The woman behind the counter seemed close to voicing her displeasure, but instead made the drink without saying a word.

Clarissa returned to the table and sat down.

"This whole thing is a mess," Sinclair said. "From what I gather, the documents are missing again."

"Missing?"

"Missing," Sinclair repeated. "Or stolen. However you want to look at it."

"Who stole them?"

"We're not sure. We think it's an agent. Not one of ours. Only so much we can do, you know. No one looks kindly on the CIA messing around on the domestic side. We get a little leeway of course, as long as we keep it quiet."

"You're the CIA," Clarissa said. "I'm just a contractor."

"And the reason we are able to be involved in such a situation."

"So is that all you've got?"

"We know that whoever took the documents originally is not in the CIA."

"Who are they with?"

"No solid leads yet."

"Really?"

"That's what sources say."

"What sources?" she asked.

"A few people we are, um, questioning at the moment."

"You're questioning them?"

"Yes."

She shuddered. "Christ."

"If they know, we'll get it."

"Is that all you brought me out here for?"

He slid the briefcase across the table. "ID, passport, a spare phone, two weapons and some cash. If things go badly, I want you out of the country immediately."

She nodded. Unlatched the locks and opened the briefcase. Everything was as Sinclair had described it.

"Check in with me after you speak with Noble," he said. "I want to hear what he has to say."

"Me too."

81

"WHERE ARE WE HEADED?" BEAR ASKED.

"Kat's," Pierre said.

"Who's Kat?"

"A friend."

"Can she be trusted?"

Pierre nodded and turned his head away. Bear tried not to read too much into the gesture. They were no longer on his turf. He had no contacts in France, or most of Europe for that matter. He had to trust Pierre, the man he blamed for Jack's misfortune half a year earlier. The man who showed up a week ago in Iowa on a mission to kill Bear and kidnap Mandy.

A mixture of panic and rage started to build inside Bear. He tightened his core and his chest and his arms. Took a few deep breaths. Turned his head away from Pierre and stared out the window on his side of the taxi. He tried to figure out where they were. No mental map of Paris had ever formed for him. That would require more than the few visits he had made over the course of his life. All he knew is that they were in an old area full of old buildings and old people.

His mind switched gears and he started to focus on the reason he was sent to France. They had to kill Charles. It had to be bloody and brutal and send a clear message to anyone associated with him and the old man that their time was coming to an end.

After Pierre's reaction to the old man's assassination, Bear started to doubt that he had the right man for the job with him. Jack would have been a far better choice. The hit would have gone down without a hitch. But as his dad always told him, wish in one hand and crap in the other. See which fills up first. Pierre was there and would be the one to go into battle with Bear.

"That's it," Pierre said in French to the driver as he leaned into the empty space between the two front seats.

The driver stopped the taxi and the men got out. Bear walked around back, lifted the trunk lid and grabbed their bags. He walked over to the curb and dropped Pierre's bag on the sidewalk.

Pierre paid the driver and then grabbed his bag. He gestured for Bear to follow him toward an old iron gate that stood at least ten feet tall. It was surrounded on the left, right and top by bricks that Bear estimated were a couple hundred years old. Pierre stopped in front of the gate and entered a code into an electric lock. Bear found it ironic that modern security had been infused into something built centuries ago.

They passed through the entrance and walked through a brick tunnel.

"There's a play area for the kids above this," Pierre said, pointing at the roof above them.

Bear nodded and continued walking. He focused on the light at the other end of the short tunnel. He wasn't a fan of tunnels or being underground or in most confined spaces. He generally avoided those situations and locations, unless on a job. It was only then that he was able to disassociate his thoughts and feelings and complete the task at hand.

They emerged through the tunnel and stepped into a courtyard in full bloom. Flowers swayed in the gentle breeze and the aroma enveloped the men as if they had walked into a mist of perfume. The sounds of children playing and enjoying the warm spring day filled the air. They played soccer and tag and ran around carelessly. The faint sound of children's nursery rhymes carried through the air. Some things, Bear thought, were the same no matter where you went. The names of games and words to hymns might be different, but the structure and the sounds were always the same, whether you were in America, France or some rarely traveled section of Africa.

"It's that building." Pierre pointed toward a five story building with an unimpressive entrance.

They walked up the front steps and past the unlocked door. A few flights of stairs later, they stood in front of Kat's door.

"Perhaps you should wait at the other end of the hall," Pierre said.

"Not a chance." Bear reached past Pierre and rapped on the door. Three strikes, hard and loud.

There was a rattle at the door and a beam of light shot through a glass circle in the center, three quarters of the way up. The light was blocked as a face passed by. Locks were unlatched and the door opened a foot. A stunning black haired woman appeared. Bear took a step back in an effort to appear less intimidating.

"Pierre," she said.

"Hello, Kat," Pierre said in English. "Sorry to show up unannounced, but we need a place to stay for a few days."

"Get a hotel," she said in French. Her eyes darted to Bear and lingered for a moment. The weight of her stare crushed him. She then looked at Pierre and continued. "You got a lot of nerve coming here."

"Why?" Pierre said. "What did I do? Is it because I didn't call?"

She said nothing.

"I didn't think you wanted me to, Kat." Pierre lowered his head and dropped his arms to his side. "I'm here now. Isn't that something?"

"Yeah," she said. "You are here now. With him." She pointed at Bear and shook her head.

"He's essential," Pierre said. "We have to finish something and then he's going back to the U.S. and I'm finished with the life."

Liar, Bear thought. Pierre needed the thrill and the action associated with the job. He was nothing more than a eunuch without it.

Kat took a step back and swung the door open. "Come in."

Bear hesitated a second and then entered the room when Pierre gestured him through the open doorway. The apartment was small and minimally furnished. It seemed adequate, though. He made his way to the kitchen, partly because he was hungry, but also to allow Kat and Pierre a few minutes to talk alone.

He opened the fridge and pulled out an apple. It would have to do. He noticed an uncorked bottle of wine on the counter. He grabbed the bottle and took a drink.

"Help yourself," Kat said.

Bear turned and wiped residual drops of wine from his beard. "Sorry. Long day, you know."

She reached into the cabinet and pulled out two wine glasses. "No, I don't know." She held the glasses at arm's length and Bear filled each half-way. She took a drink, then said, "You shouldn't have come here."

"Not much choice," Bear said. "Had to go wherever Pierre went."

"You shouldn't have gotten mixed up with him. He's ruined."

The words only had half their intended effect on Bear. He couldn't get past her accent and found himself swimming in her stare.

"He'll be all right," Bear said. "He's been doing this a long time. I think the months away from it, coupled with the guilt over Jack, had the biggest effect on him."

"I can't be with a man involved in that kind of work." Her eyes shifted to the left and she crossed her arms.

"Where is Pierre?"

"He left. Said he had to meet someone. Wanted me to keep you here."

Bear chuckled as he took a step toward her. "He really thinks a little thing like you can stop me?"

She backed up until she hit the kitchen table. "I'm tougher than I look."

"So am I." He took another step toward her. Rather than stepping to the side to move away, she braced herself by placing her hands on the table. Her fingers wrapped around the edge. She leaned back slightly. Bear reached out and placed his hands on her waist. His fingers nearly met in the back.

"You shouldn't be doing this," she said. "Pierre is your friend."

"No," Bear said. "I can't stand the guy."

"Me either."

He leaned over and she rose to the tips of her toes. Their lips met somewhere in the middle.

The door rattled and locks began to turn, preventing things from going any further. Bear took a giant step back and nearly crashed into the refrigerator. Neither he nor Kat said a word as Pierre entered the apartment. They smiled at each other and then pretended to be indifferent.

82

"WHERE SHOULD WE GO?" JASMINE SAID.

"Out of the city," Jack said.

"Maryland or Virginia?"

"Where do you live?"

"D.C."

"Go to Virginia." He pulled the battery and SIM card from his cell phone. "Can he track you through your phone?"

"What? Who?"

"Frank."

"Yeah. That's standard operating procedure."

"Give it here."

Jasmine glanced over at him with a confused look on her face.

"Give me your phone," Jack said.

She handed it over and he removed the battery and SIM card.

"What the hell?" she said.

"Someone blew up the man I just met with. I think they intended to blow me up. Frank set up the meeting. Put it together."

Jasmine looked from Jack to the road and back at Jack. "You're not implying that Frank set you up, are you?"

"I'm not implying anything, Jazz. Until I know that Frank had nothing to do with this, I don't want him to know where I am."

"Jack," Jasmine said in a controlled tone, "he's not like that. If he wanted you dead he wouldn't take someone else out in the process and cause millions of dollars of damage by destroying half a city block."

"You don't know him like I do."

She said nothing as she merged onto I-395 southbound.

Jack looked across the highway at the Potomac as they crossed over the George Mason Memorial Bridge. His adrenaline finally settled as they left D.C. and entered Virginia. He saw the Pentagon to the right and recounted his conversation with Rico, trying to make sense of what had happened. Was the bomb meant for Rico, or had it been intended for him? If it were only for Rico, and merely a coincidence that Jack had been there, then it could have been anybody who planted the explosives. However, if Jack had been the target, then that limited the possible suspects.

"Let me call Frank," Jasmine said.

Jack shook his head. "The moment you do, he'll know where we are."

"He probably tracks the cars."

Jack pointed at the exit lane. "Get off here. I'm going to rent a car. You're going to drop this one off at the nearest hotel."

Jasmine exited the highway. She pulled into a shopping center parking lot and went inside a store to purchase fresh clothes for Jack. Then she dropped him off a block past a rental car place. "There's a hotel on Leesburg Pike. I'm going to park the car there. I'll be waiting in the lobby."

Jack changed into the shorts and shirt Jasmine bought, then exited the vehicle. Next to the rental car company was a convenience store. He went in and bought three pay-as-you-go cell phones with five hundred minutes each. He knew he'd only use a fraction of the minutes, but if something went down, and he had to use the phone for tracking, he wanted to make sure it'd last long enough.

He left the store and went next door where he rented a mid-sized sedan. He drove two blocks and pulled into an empty church parking lot. Grabbed one of the cell phones and placed a call, dialing the number from memory.

"Hello?" a man said after picking up on the second ring.

"Brandon?"

"Who's this?"

"Jack Noble. Don't hang up."

Silence on the other end. Then Brandon said, "Everyone knows Jack Noble is dead."

"It's really me, Brandon. A Russian prison isn't enough to kill me."

"Prove it."

"How else would I have this number?"

"Could have found it scribbled on a stall in a ladies bathroom in some seedy bar."

Jack laughed. "OK, how about this then? In 2004 you were instrumental in helping me and Frank Skinner take down a child smuggling ring run by some bad dudes out of South America."

"Lots of people know about that."

"True, but lots of people don't know that it didn't end there and I had to take down someone pretty powerful in our world."

"Jack?"

"That's me."

"Was that you who called me a few days ago?"

"Yeah."

"Sorry for hanging up on you."

"You do me a favor, and I'll forget all about it."

"What do you need?"

"I need a number daisy chained. Can't call it direct."

"How many levels?"

"Ten should be sufficient."

"Number?"

Jack gave him Frank's number and waited. Once Brandon was finished, his call would route through ten different forwarding numbers before it reached Frank, making his call virtually untraceable. Some might call it overkill. For Jack it was being slightly cautious.

"OK," Brandon said. "All set. You got a pen?"

"Go for it," Jack said.

Brandon read the number off and then said, "Anything else?"

"Yeah one more thing," Jack said. "A man was blown up today in downtown

D.C. I only knew him as Rico. He worked for the NSA. Dig up anything you can on him. I'll be in touch in a day or so."

"You got it."

Jack hung up and immediately dialed the number Brandon had given him. There was no point in switching phones. If Brandon was double crossing him, he'd be monitoring the number and get the second cell phone's information.

The phone rang several times before Frank answered. "Who's this?"

"What did you do, Frank?"

"Jack?"

"You know it's me."

"What happened with Rico?"

"You tell me."

"I'm not following."

"Don't screw with me, Frank." Jack's voice escalated into a yell. "So help me, if I find out you are behind this I will unleash a hell you've never imagined."

"Jack, calm down. What are you talking about?"

Jack paused. Was Frank telling truly stumped, or only saying what he had to in order to get Jack to come back?

"Rico's dead," Jack said.

"How?"

"Explosion."

"The thing downtown? At the parking garage?"

"Yeah."

"Christ, Jack. You hurt?"

Jack looked down at his bandaged hand and knee. "I'll live."

"You had nothing to do with this, right?"

"You're asking me? Right now you're suspect number one, Frank."

"Jack, I didn't—"

"Shut up. Who else know Rico was meeting with me?"

There was a pause on the other end. It lasted two seconds. Nothing for most people. But to Jack it was enough to tell him that Frank knew something.

"Nobody that I know of," Frank said.

Jack said nothing.

"I'm going to send a team out to get you guys. Where are you?"

"Nowhere."

The sounds of Frank pounding on his keyboard filled the ear piece. "OK, you aren't that far away. Just stay put."

He was tracking her car.

"Screw you, Frank."

Jack tossed the cell phone out the window. It landed in the middle of the road. Jack watched in the mirror as a heavy duty pick-up truck drove by and crushed the phone. He continued driving till he reached the hotel. Pulled into the parking lot and drove up to the lobby door. Jasmine stepped out and got in the car.

"Where're we going?" she said.

"Nowhere for now."

"What?"

"He's tracking your car. Said he's sending a team. I want to see who arrives and how they act."

"That's not a good idea. They'll spot us."

Jack looked over at her and shrugged.

"C'mon, Jack. You know how this group operates. We're trained to see everything. You think they won't notice an in-state rental car nearby?"

Jack said nothing.

"We'll figure this out, but we need to move. They'll be here soon. Hell, they're probably almost here now. I'm sure he sent someone the moment our phones went offline."

Jack turned the key in the ignition and pulled out of the parking lot. She was right and he knew it. Frank's guys would spot them. Maybe not right away, but eventually. They'd be sitting ducks in the parking lot. And that would spell trouble if Frank's guys were there for a purpose other than escorting Jack and Jasmine back to D.C.

"I'm gonna loop around a couple times," Jack said.

Jasmine shook her head. "You're gonna get us killed."

He ignored her. "Put your seat back."

"Why?"

"They'll know your face better than mine."

Jasmine lowered her seat and leaned back, placing herself out of sight.

The car was easy to spot. Jack saw it in the rear view mirror. Big and black and American made. It screamed government agent.

"There they are," Jack said. "Turning into the hotel lot now."

Jasmine didn't move. Didn't say anything.

Jack made a U-turn at the next light. "Just want to get one look at them as they approach your car."

"Make it quick. Don't stare. If one of them looks your way, speed off."

Jack whipped the car around the median. He drove by the hotel lot, not too fast and not too slow. He casually glanced toward Jasmine's car. One of the men stood just outside the government vehicle. He used the door to shield himself. The other approached the abandoned car. His left arm was out slightly, his right arm inside his coat, likely gripping his weapon.

"You're dead, Frank," Jack said.

"Don't jump to conclusions," Jasmine said. "We need to talk with him."

"I'm not going back to that office."

"We'll arrange it some place safe. Some place public."

"Forget it."

"You've got to trust him, Jack. He's the only person on your side."

"You can put your seat back up," he said. Then he turned his attention to the road and said nothing for over half an hour.

They drove along the George Washington Memorial Parkway, heading west. Merged onto I-495 northbound. Exited a couple miles later on River Road.

"Where are we going?"

"I'm going back to the city." He paused and looked over at her. "You're getting out soon." He slowed the car down and pulled into the parking lot of a golf course.

"What the hell?"

"Get out."

"No way."

"I'll come back for you later. Or you can put your phone back together and I'm sure Frank will come get you."

She refused to move. Crossed her arms and looked away.

"I'll force you out," he said.

"This is ridiculous. We're partners."

"And I have to go take care of something alone."

"You're not going after Frank, are you?"

"No. I have to go see an old friend. Someone that might be able to provide some insight into what is going on."

Jasmine opened her door and stuck one foot on the pavement, then the other. She stepped out and then stuck her head back inside. "This is a mistake."

"I'll see you soon."

83

JACK NAVIGATED BY MEMORY TO THE HOUSE OF ROBERT MARLOWE, FORMER Deputy Secretary of Defense. He doubted the man was as clued in as he had been ten years before when he helped Jack out of a tough spot. Still, he might be able to provide some insight or make a few calls at the very least.

He drove through a dodgy part of town, then past a tree lined park that served as a barrier between the ghetto and rehabbed million dollar townhomes. Little had changed since he had last been there. The trees were a little taller, but other than that, everything looked the same. He found Marlowe's end unit and parked half a block away.

He hoped that Jasmine had kept her phone off. Frank couldn't be trusted, although Jasmine didn't seem to think twice about taking his word as gospel. She'd seemed pretty pissed when Jack left. He hated dumping her like that, but he couldn't risk losing Marlowe as a contact or putting the man in any danger by outing him as a source if he did in fact have some useful information.

Jack's mind drifted as he walked down the sidewalk toward Marlowe's house. He thought about Bear and pulled one of the cell phone's from his pocket. Then he looked at his watch and realized that it was after midnight in Paris. He'd wait until morning to make contact and find out how things were going.

He reached Marlowe's end unit and stopped. He was relaxed and less cautious than ten years ago. There wouldn't be any secret service agents to contend with this time. No need to threaten Marlowe into helping him, either. It'd be like two old friends seeing each other after a decade. A reunion of sorts.

He knocked on the door and waited.

The door swung open and an older gentleman poked his head out. "Help you?"

"Secretary Marlowe?" Jack said.

"Former."

"Don't remember me?"

The man pulled the door open and stepped into the opening. "Jack Noble?"

"That's me."

Marlowe smiled and shook his head as he extended his hand. "You got old."

Jack smiled as he took Marlowe's hand in his own. "We can't all remain as strikingly handsome as you, sir."

"Come on in, Jack."

He followed the older man through the house and into the living room. It looked exactly as Jack remembered it. Two couches with a simple wooden table between them. Two stacks of books on the middle of the table. Perhaps the same ones that sat there a decade earlier. Still no TV or stereo. They passed through the room and headed toward the kitchen. Marlowe pushed the swinging door open and waited for Jack to step through.

"Coffee or beer?" Marlowe asked.

"One of each," Jack said.

Marlowe reached into the cabinet over the stove and pulled down two mugs. He filled both with coffee. He set one down in front of Jack. "Just brewed it not ten minutes ago. Cream? Sugar?"

"Black is fine."

Marlowe turned and went to the fridge. He returned a few moments later with two bottles of imported beers.

"Don't buy the local brews anymore?" Jack said.

Marlowe waved a hand in Jack's direction. "They've gone to the yuppies."

Jack took a long pull on the bottle of beer and then set it down on the table. He leaned back in his chair. Rubbed his forehead and his temples and his jaw with his thumbs. He opened his mouth to speak, but Marlowe jumped in before he could get a word out.

"Word is that you're dead, Jack."

"That's what I've been told."

"Something about the Russians and some God forsaken prison?"

"I did a job, sir. Did the world a favor. Took out a scumbag politician who was hell bent on turning Russia into a military controlled powerhouse. Turns out it went a lot further than that. Anyway, I got caught. His buddy, a General named Ivanov, prosecuted me. Sent me to Black Dolphin. Ever heard of it?"

Marlowe nodded.

Jack continued. "Someone managed to get me out in a creative way. Then I spent six months in Greece. Now I'm trying to clean up another mess I created."

"Something to do with highly classified intelligence."

"You know?"

Marlowe shrugged.

"How much do you know?" Jack asked.

"Somewhere between not enough and slightly more than a little."

Jack took another pull on the beer bottle. He had to feel out the old man and see just how much he knew and where he placed Jack on the blame scale.

"I had no idea what it was when I got my hands on it. Never ask questions. That's the number one rule I lived by."

"Should've broken the rule, Jack."

"When people in my line of business break that rule, they end up dead."

"Maybe you should look for a new line of work."

"I'm done with it, sir. Retired. Just need to clean up this mess and then move on with my life."

Marlowe nodded. He blew on his coffee, sending ripples through the hot liquid and a puff of steam into the air above the mug.

"So what do you know?" Jack asked.

Marlowe thought for a moment. He leaned back and crossed his arms. Brought one hand up to his chin. He looked around the kitchen and then his focus settled on Jack. "I know that someone in a high ranking position is responsible for the information being leaked out. I know that he was pissed as all get it out when it landed in your hands, although he didn't know it was you. His courier was in no state to give an eyewitness account."

Jack smiled. Although he hadn't killed the courier, there was no doubt that he would never recount his interaction with Jack that night.

Marlowe continued. "The documents then ended up in very bad hands and we were on the verge of an attack like no other."

"That was under control," Jack said.

"Be that as it may," Marlowe said, "if they had even hit one or two of those targets, it would have been chaos."

Jack nodded. Said nothing. A twinge of guilt burned inside.

"Then a few terrorists died. A Russian General died. The documents returned to the U.S. and were under the care of the NSA."

"You're pretty clued in for being retired."

Marlowe smiled. "Some people still respect my opinion, on certain matters at least."

"What else do you know?"

Marlowe's smile faded. He leaned forward. Placed one arm on the table. Pointed the other in Jack's direction. "I know that the documents have been taken again."

"Do you know by who?"

"No."

"Do you think it might have been the person who leaked them?"

"It's possible. Or someone working for him. Or someone who had worked for him. Or maybe just someone who knows that he wants them back and knows he'll pay top dollar for them."

Jack studied Marlowe as he spoke. If he was lying, he gave nothing away. Not a single tick of his face or misdirection of his eyes or inflection in his tone. Marlowe didn't show a single tell.

"Sir," Jack said. "I'm going to be direct. Do you know who leaked the intel in the first place?"

"I have a few ideas. First, you tell me what you know."

"The Pentagon. That's it."

Marlowe nodded. Said nothing.

"And it has to be someone high ranking in order to know certain information."

"Such as?" Marlowe prompted.

"That the documents were back in the U.S." Jack shifted in his seat in order to face Marlowe directly. "Where they were being held and how to get to them. And that an agent in the NSA was meeting with me today."

"And then had him killed."

Jack nodded. "I believe I was the intended target."

"I do too." Marlowe stood and unlocked the back door. "I think it's time you leave, son."

Jack pushed back in his chair and got up. Walked toward the open door. He had more questions, but the last thing he wanted to do was draw the ire of Marlowe by pushing too far.

"I've got eyes and ears on the inside," Marlowe said. "I think we're close." He grabbed a notepad and scribbled on it. Tore the paper from the pad and handed it to Jack. "You call me on that number. Twice a day. Eleven a.m and p.m."

Jack took the paper and stuffed it in his pocket. "Thank you, sir. I'll be in touch." He started down the stairs of the back patio. Stopped and turned. "One more thing."

"Yeah?"

"Frank Skinner. He involved?"

Marlowe shook his head. "Don't think so, but I'll double check."

Jack thanked him once more, then left the property. He hurried to his car and started driving toward the outskirts of the city. On the way, he called a taxi company to send a cab for Jasmine with instructions to drive her to the gas station next to the fire department on the other side of the Beltway. He added that the driver was not to tell her where he was taking her.

Jack drove ahead and waited across the street from the fire station. Half an hour later a cab pulled up and Jasmine stepped out, alone. He waited another five minutes to make sure she hadn't been followed and then got out of his car, crossed the street and got her attention.

"Thanks a lot, Jack," she said.

"It was worth it."

"It better have been."

"Wait till you hear what I found out."

84

CHARLES LEANED OVER THE WROUGHT IRON BLACK RAILING THAT SURROUNDED his balcony. The lights of the city created a soft haze that lit the sky hundreds of feet above him before melting into the darkness of night.

He threw back another shot. His twelfth, he estimated. Or maybe his thirteenth. He'd lost track. The alcohol was doing little to distract him. He had the cocaine to thank for that. He figured if he kept drinking, eventually the booze would do its job. He didn't care how much it took. No hangover could dampen the celebration he was having. The old man was dead and the empire was his.

"Alonso," Charles said. "Another drink."

Alonso stepped out onto the balcony empty handed. "Maybe you should take it easy, Charles."

"Why? Afraid I'm going to piss off our neighbors? What do we care? We're out of here in a couple days. Back to New York to take over."

Alonso pulled out a cigar and lit it. Took a few puffs and then joined Charles by the railing. "I was thinking that I'd like to stay here. Take over Europe."

Charles reached for the cigar and took it from Alonso's hand. "You're my right hand man. I need you in New York."

"You'll have plenty of people to choose from there. And with your eye on them, they'll do what you tell them to. Do you really want to send someone here that you don't trust completely?"

"I see your point," Charles said. "But at the same time, I really don't want someone I don't trust within stabbing distance of me."

"You're going to have that whether I'm there or not."

Charles looked up at the sky. Dead center above him it was nothing more than a mass of black. The spot where the lights didn't meet. He knew that he'd have a situation on his hands in New York. There were people in the organization that probably figured he was behind the killing of the old man. Although he was happy about it, it wasn't something that he ever had intentions of organizing. Perhaps at one time, but all that had been smoothed over when Feng put him in charge of Europe and given him free reign to run it as he saw fit. Plus, Feng was old and nearing retirement. Charles was poised to take over soon no matter what.

"What do you think?" Alonso said.

"OK," Charles said. "Only thing is I need you to come with me for the first week or two. Just to watch my back until I get control of things."

"How do you plan to do that?"

"Kill the first one that stands up to me."

"Good plan. Machiavellian."

Charles nodded once and said nothing.

"I'll get us those drinks now." Alonso stepped into the apartment and disappeared into the kitchen.

Charles turned around and looked over the railing, down at the street. Despite the late hour, there were several people out. Were they celebrating as he was? Were they all full of hope and inspiration like him? Or were they, just like him, trying to get drunk?

"Here you go," Alonso said.

Charles sat down at the bistro table near the door. Alonso sat across from him.

"Arrange our flights before you go to bed. I'd like to leave tomorrow if possible."

"Won't happen. But I'm sure we can get out the day after."

"That'll work."

85

JASMINE STARED AT JACK IN DISBELIEF AS HE RECOUNTED THE INFORMATION Marlowe passed on to him.

"The Pentagon?" she said. "Someone in power? You really think this goes that high?"

"Rico shared the same thoughts."

"First of all, we really don't know much about this Rico character."

Her words rang true. The only saving grace Rico had was that Frank arranged the meeting. If Frank turned out to be on the up and up, then so was Rico as far as Jack was concerned.

"The second thing," Jasmine said, "is that it doesn't make sense. Why would someone that high up in the government risk treason?"

Jack shrugged. "People do crazy things for money, Jazz."

"I know that. And will you please stop calling me Jazz."

"Too late," he said with a laugh. "We've been through too much together. It's permanent."

She sighed and shook her head and smiled at him. Her dark eyes reflected the oncoming headlights, giving off the impression that they were aglow. Her expression turned serious and she said, "So what now?"

"Gotta call my contact back in a bit. He's checking on Frank for me. If he says he's clear then you're going to arrange a meeting with Frank. Someplace public, though. I'm not going to his office."

She lifted her hand and pursed her lips like she was about to scold him for his distrust in Frank. If she had, he'd be able to see her point. Jack and Frank had a history together, and Jasmine herself had seven years in the SIS working alongside and for Frank. But it was Jack's history with Frank that taught him to distrust the man.

"OK," she said reluctantly. "I'm on board, for the most part. I'll go on record now as saying that I don't think Frank has anything to do with this. And I think we are wasting time looking at people in the Pentagon. This has double agent written all over it."

Jack started the car and drove aimlessly for half an hour. They spoke little, and when they did it was about nothing important. In the background his mind worked overtime on the puzzle. There had been a time when he brazenly accused a high ranking government official of being involved in a conspiracy. He had been wrong. Fortunately, the man offered up what he knew at the time, just as the same man had done earlier in the day.

He noted how naive Jasmine acted regarding the possibility that someone they trusted could be involved in the disappearance of the documents. In some ways, he wished he shared her simplistic thinking on the issue. If that were the case, though, then another group would get their hands on the documents and the whereabouts of the information might escape the intelligence community completely.

"You got five minutes," Jasmine said.

Jack broke free from his thoughts as her words echoed in his ears. He began to look for a place to park.

"So who is this contact?" she asked.

Jack shook his head. Said nothing.

"Why won't you trust me?"

"It's not about me trusting you. It's about protecting him. No one needs to know but me. His name gets out there, it puts him at risk."

"So in other words, you don't trust me."

"Jazz," Jack reached out and grabbed her hand. "It's not like that. I trust you with my life. You're my partner. I need you to trust me on this. OK?"

"Whatever." She aimed a finger toward the clock on the dashboard. "Make your call."

Jack turned into an empty restaurant parking lot. Pulled around the rear of the building and stopped the car. He reached for the keys but decided to leave the ignition running. A sign of trust. He got out and walked into the field behind the restaurant, fifty feet past the parking lot. Grabbed his cell and placed a call to Marlowe.

Marlowe answered and sounded as if he had been awoken. "Hello?"

"It's Jack. Sorry to wake you."

"I wasn't asleep."He yawned, then added, "Almost."

"What have you got for me?"

"Skinner is clear. He's on your side."

Jack felt a wave of relief flow through his body. "That's good to hear. I'm still going to keep him at arm's length until I feel him out."

"Probably a good idea." Marlowe cleared his throat. "Whoever stole the documents this go around, well, by all appearances that was an inside job."

"We figured that much, sir. But who?"

"Every camera went on the fritz, Jack. Every single one. Out for fifteen minutes. Guys in the security room who were watching the live feeds noticed nothing at all. Not a single thing. Said the place was desolate. One of them called it a ghost town."

"Have they been questioned further?"

"The NSA is in the process of doing that right now."

"What's the feeling? They in on it?"

"I don't know any more than I've told you."

Either the guards were involved or someone highly skilled manipulated the feed into the guard room of one of the most secure buildings in the world. How many people had that ability? That much skill? A handful at most, Jack figured.

"What about the Pentagon?" Jack said.

"That's where things get troubling."

This was the information that Jack anticipated and dreaded at the same time. "How so?"

"I don't know how much I should say over the phone."

"This is a generic line, sir. No one knows about it."

"They know about mine though."

"Can you tell me without naming names?"

Marlowe exhaled heavily and paused for a few moments. "All signs point toward my successor."

"Christ."

"Now Jack, I don't have anything concrete. There's no proof yet. You can't go into the Pentagon guns blazing, or break into his house at four in the morning."

A smile briefly formed on Jack's face, then the gravity of the situation resurfaced. "The Pentagon is the last place I should walk into. And I'll stay away from his house. For now. Keep working it, and I'll check with you in the morning."

Jack ended the call and stuck the phone in his pocket. On his way back to the car, he pulled the phone out, removed the battery and SIM card and proceeded to throw the phone and battery into the woods, then destroyed the card. He'd pick up another cell next time they passed a convenience store.

"What did your contact say?" Jasmine asked as Jack ducked inside the car.

"Frank's clear. NSA is an inside job. Pentagon is legit."

"Good. I believe it. We're wasting our time."

If it weren't for the direness of the situation, he'd have laughed at her ability to be as succinct as himself.

"Call Frank," he said. "Have him meet us at the first place open on F Street between 15th and 3rd."

"Why there?"

"Because I don't want him choosing the location."

"You're paranoid."

Jack said nothing. He didn't have to and Jasmine, of all people, should understand that.

Half an hour later Jack and Jasmine sat on a vinyl bench seat against the back wall of a twenty-four hour diner on F Street. Jack watched the door. A trickle of diners entered and exited. None of them Frank. None of them agents, as far as he could tell. For the most part the crowd was young. People in between bars or filling up before heading home. Friends and strangers. Strangers and friends. Mixed up and intertwined thanks to the false bravado that alcohol afforded them. After a while, Jack began to wonder if Frank would bother to show.

"There he is," Jasmine said, her arm pointing beyond the door.

Jack nodded as Frank entered. The man's eyes scanned the room before finally settling on their table. Jack kept his eyes on the door while Frank walked toward them. He didn't want any surprises entering after Frank sat down.

"Relax," Frank said. "I'm alone."

Jack glanced and him and then returned to watching the door.

"Christ, Jack," Frank said. "You can trust me. What else do you want me to say or do to prove that?"

"Tell me everything," Jack said without taking his gaze off the door.

"It's not an inside job," Frank said. "The theft at the NSA."

Jack lowered his line of sight and made eye contact with Frank. He wanted to watch the man's eye and facial movements as he spoke. "Then who was it?"

"Rogue agent." Frank's eyes were locked on Jack's. His face gave away nothing.

"From the NSA?"

"At least someone familiar with them."

"What else?"

"The leak is inside the Pentagon."

Jack's trust in Frank slowly started to grow. He decided to hold off on divulging the information Marlowe passed on to him.

"Guys," Jasmine said. "We are wasting our time with this Pentagon angle."

"Why's that?" Frank said.

"She's got a conspiracy theory," Jack said.

Frank shifted his gaze to Jasmine and smiled. "I'd at least like to hear it."

Jasmine leaned forward and placed her elbows on the table. "If whoever leaked the first time is actually in the Pentagon, and as high up as you seem to believe, why would they do this again if they nearly got popped the first time?"

Frank lifted a single eyebrow and shrugged and turned up his hands. "He's got balls."

Jasmine rolled her eyes. "Doesn't it make more sense that the original buyer has found a way to turn an agent and has convinced them to procure the information for them?"

"Or maybe had an agent on the inside all this time," Frank said. "No turning needed."

"Ah, c'mon Frank," Jack said. "You're not entertaining this."

Frank whipped his arm around and pointed at Jack. "Jack, we don't have anything to work with. We need to explore all ideas. This is plausible. Think about it. Say North Korea, or someone there, or maybe even someone in the Middle East was involved with the initial purchase. Things happened and they didn't get their hands on what they wanted. But they've been kept up to date on developments and found out that the intel had found its way home. So they contract someone who would turn for money and then issued the command to steal and deliver the documents."

"It adds up," Jasmine said.

Jack leaned back. His hand reached for a cigarette. He had none. He didn't want to admit it, but Jasmine's theory had legs. Maybe Marlowe could weigh in on it. He'd make sure to ask next time they talked. He leaned forward and opened his mouth to speak when the waitress came by with a fresh pot of coffee.

"You guys gonna order something?"

"I'll have three eggs, over easy, and two orders of bacon," Jack said.

Frank and Jasmine declined.

After the waitress left, Jack said, "OK, so tell me, who was the original buyer?"

"Officially?" Frank said.

Jack nodded.

"We don't know."

"Frank, c'mon."

"The only witness we might have had couldn't speak."

"Hey, that was his decision. I gave him the option of walking away."

Frank shook his head. "This friggin' mess."

"What about unofficially?"

Frank's eyes shifted from Jack to Jasmine and then back again. He sat back and said nothing.

"What?" Jack said. "She can't know? Or she does know and you're deciding whether to tell me the truth?"

"Jack," Frank said, his arms outstretched.

"Don't Jack me. I'll walk away right now and you guys can figure this out on your own. You're already barking up the wrong tree with this former buyer garbage."

"It was North Korea," Jasmine said.

Jack turned to face her. Her eyes were dark and her face hard. As he stared at her she seemed to soften, as if she had been holding back a deep, dark secret during the time they had known each other and it had finally surfaced. The question was whether or not this was only the trickle before the dam broke. He broke off his stare and looked back at Frank, who nodded in agreement.

The weight of the situation hit him hard. When it was a ragtag Russian terrorist organization, it was bad. He thought that maybe Muslim extremists had been involved with the initial purchase. That had given him cause to shiver. But now hearing the North Korea was involved left an empty feeling in his stomach that was replaced with an odd sense of validation that he hadn't actually caused more problems by stealing the documents. He'd potentially saved the world.

"The government?" Jack said.

"It's fifty-fifty at the moment," Frank said. "If it wasn't ordered from the top, it wasn't far below him. Even if it was an extremist group, the call would have come from within."

Jack exhaled loudly and shifted in his seat. He glanced around the room to make sure no other diners were paying attention to their conversation. The fact that they were the only sober ones in the place left him feeling a little better.

"Now you see why I'm pushing this?" Jasmine said.

Jack nodded. Said nothing. He was still processing the information.

"I'd be happy to be wrong," she said. "Hell, prove to me that I'm wrong, and I'll dance on the hood of the car. But until that happens, we need to chase this down. It might spread us thin, but we've got to do it."

"Who can help?" Jack said.

"We've got options," Frank said. "Let me take care of that. You keep working your sources. I'll work mine. You meeting with Clarissa soon?"

"I expect to tomorrow."

Frank stood and slid out of the booth. "Call me tomorrow. And for Christ's sake, put your phones back together. I need to know where you guys are."

Jack watched Frank exit the diner and kept his eyes on him until he disappeared from sight. He and Jasmine sat in silence for ten minutes. Finally she spoke.

"We can stay at my place."

Jack nodded. "Let's go."

86

CLARISSA STAYED CLOSE TO THE BUILDINGS, WALKING IN THE SHADOWS. HER dark clothing made her practically invisible. Her hair was tucked under a dark skull cap. Fortunately, the night was cool and the excess clothing was comfortable. Clouds blocked the moonlight, providing another layer of security.

Breaking into the residence of the Chairman of the Joint Chiefs of Staff was risky, but Sinclair believed that was who the unnamed source was. Perhaps with the gentle nudging of Clarissa's 9mm pistol, he'd be more forthcoming.

For a million dollar neighborhood, she found it quite easy to sneak through unnoticed. Still, she couldn't let her guard down. That was how accidents happen and people get caught. For a woman dressed like a burglar and armed to the teeth, that would be a bad ending to a stressful day.

She stopped across the street from the house of General Marcus Prather, Army Chief of Staff. The house appeared still and quiet. The windows were dark, the entrance too. No porch light turned on. Streetlights far enough away that the pools of light they cast didn't reach the house.

She crossed the street quickly, never letting up on her pace. When she reached the house, she pressed firmly against the exterior and slid to the ground. First she had to check for a security system. There was no obvious giveaway that there was one installed. No sign attached to a stake and planted in the yard. That didn't mean there wasn't one, though. Experience had taught her that. She rounded the house and found the utilities. Phone, power and cable all neatly placed one next to the other.

She reached into her bag and pulled out a phillips head screw driver. Opened the phone box. Reached into her bag again and pulled out a pair of alligator clips with an electronic device attached. She clipped the device to the solid blue wire and the blue and white striped wire that connected to the phone company's feed. The device served two purposes. First, various agencies monitor certain phone lines. If she were to simply cut the phone line, it would register a state of permanent lock out. That would be noticed and a Secret Service team would be dispatched. The device she attached cut off phone signal to the house, but left the line in an operable state as far as anyone monitoring would be concerned. The device also relayed the appropriate heartbeat signal to an alarm company monitoring system.

Satisfied the house was cut off, she continued around the perimeter to find the best entry point. It didn't take long. The kitchen window had been left open and it faced the backyard. She'd be exposed for a few seconds as she climbed through the window. However, the houses behind Prather's looked as quiet and silent as his. She decided to take her chances entering through the kitchen instead of picking the lock of the darkened front door.

The house was on a crawl, which left the bottom of the window slightly higher than the top of her head. A nearby lawn chair solved the problem. She lifted and set the chair down, then stepped up, being careful to not let her foot slip through the openings created by the criss-crossed fabric.

She used both hands to force the window all the way open. Reached inside, grabbed the window sill and pulled herself up. Her body slid up and through the opening with the grace of a gymnast on the high bar. A few seconds later she crouched against the wall and reset her bearings.

The information she had gathered on Prather told her that he was divorced and his children were fully grown. That led her to believe that the house would be empty except for him. She prepared herself for the possibility of a third party being present and would deal with them accordingly.

The floorboards creaked as she crossed the kitchen. Despite the updated facade, the house was an older rehabbed building. She knew the General would be able to differentiate between the sounds of his home settling and expanding and contracting, and the sounds of an intruder.

Clarissa continued on, gripping her pistol tightly in her palm. The handle pushed the inside of her sweat dampened glove against her skin.

She cleared each downstairs room, gliding through the house with the stealth of a cat on the prowl. Then she took to the stairs. Up six steps to a landing which curved around, then up another half-dozen steps. At the top she looked left and then right. One door to the right, three to the left. The master, she presumed, was on the right. She headed left to clear the remaining rooms.

The first room she came to appeared to be a guest bedroom. The door at the end of the hall led to a full bathroom. The third door opened up to an office. All three rooms were unoccupied.

Clarissa returned to the top of the stairs. Stopped. Listened. She planned the sequence of events as she wanted them to play out. It would be quick and easy and painless.

She reached into her bag and pulled out a silver tin. Twisted the lid. Scooped out some of the black substance it contained and spread it across her face. She had done this prior to approaching the house, but wanted to make sure that she was covered. Being made later by Prather would bring unwanted attention to herself and Sinclair.

She took a deep breath and started down the hall toward Prather's bedroom. Three quarters of the way there, a loud pop erupted from below her feet. Another faulty floorboard, or perhaps something done purposefully by the owner of the house to alert him should someone be approaching the room. Either way, she saw light flood out from the gap below the door and in the cracks along the side and top.

Two distinct voices began speaking in hurried, anxious tones.

87

CLARISSA'S HEART BEAT AGAINST HER CHEST WITH THE FEROCITY OF A DRUM solo. Her adrenaline spiked. It felt like a fifty pound weight sat atop her lungs. Twinges of panic ripped through her chest and abdomen. Her fingers tingled and began to go numb. She had to get it together. The phone lines might be cut, but who uses a house line anymore? Prather could be dialing the police on his cell phone at that moment. There was no time to waste.

She forced a deep breath into her tight chest. The pain of her lungs being stretched to full expansion nearly caused her to scream. Her hands clutched her pistol tightly. The feelings of panic subsided and her training took over. She took four quick steps toward the door and then kicked it open with her right leg.

She held her weapon with both hands, pointed at the man she identified as Prather and yelled, "Don't move."

Prather dropped his cell phone. He tried to speak, but could only stutter.

Clarissa assessed the room for any potential threats or weapons. It barely registered with her that Prather's companion in bed was another man. She couldn't place him, and he already had his hands up in the air, so she ignored him.

"Throw the cell phone over there." She gestured with her gun toward the closet.

Prather complied and picked up his phone and tossed it.

She looked at the other man. "On your knees."

"What?" he said.

"Do it," she said. "Now. And keep your hands where I can see them."

The man wriggled his way onto his knees.

"Now lie face down. Hands behind your back."

He fell forward and clasped his hands together behind his lower back.

She looked at Prather. "Get up." As he slid out of bed, she reached into her bag and pulled out three black cords. Tossed them onto the bed. "Even though you're an Army man, I'm sure you can figure this out. One for his wrists, one for his ankles, and the third to connect them. Anything funny and *he gets shot first.*"

Prather nodded. He started to settle down. Perhaps he figured because she hadn't shot him yet, she wouldn't. He picked up the cords and began tying the other man's wrists together. Then he moved down to his ankles. Finally, he laced the third cord around the knots near the man's wrists and ankles and drew it tight, hog tying his companion.

"You'll never get away with this," he said.

"Shut the hell up," Clarissa said.

"Do you have any idea who I am?" he said.

"Of course I do," she said. "But you have no idea who I am."

He looked over his shoulder at her as he finished the knot. Said nothing.

"Other side of the room. Face the corner." She waited until he complied with her order and then she moved toward the tied up man. She checked the knots to make sure he hadn't done anything that would allow his friend to escape easily. Satisfied, she turned her attention to Prather. "Now move to the door and wait for me."

"Where are you taking him?" the other man said.

Clarissa flipped her gun in her hand and slammed the handle into the back of the man's head. The blow knocked him unconscious.

"Don't hurt him," Prather yelled as he took two steps toward Clarissa.

She quickly spun the weapon around and aimed it at his head. "One more step. Go ahead. Take it."

Prather stopped and raised his hands, palms out.

"Good boy," she said. "Now turn around. We're going to your kitchen."

"Why the kitchen?"

"Because you have carpet in your bathroom, and blood stains carpet."

He said nothing.

She poked him in the back with the tip of the barrel of her gun, and he began walking toward the stairs. She followed him down the two sets of six steps and through the house to the kitchen. He stopped just outside, seemingly refusing to step away from the safety of the carpeted floor.

"Now what?" he said.

"Go in. Pull out a chair and move it to the middle of the room. Sit down." She watched from the doorway as he performed the tasks in the order she had instructed. After he sat down, she pulled out two more cords. She wrapped one around his chest and the other around his legs, securing him to the chair.

"Can I have some water?" he said.

"No," she said. "This is how this works. I'm going to ask you a series of questions. You are going to give me answers. If you refuse to answer, I'll react in a violent manner. If I don't like your answer, I'll react in a violent manner. If you tell me what I want to know, then I'll get out of here and you'll never see me again."

He lowered his head to his chest and said, "I understand. What do you want to know?"

"Someone in the Pentagon has been a bad boy, General. I want to know who."

"The Pentagon is full of bad people, lady. Choir boys don't choose defense as a vocation."

She squatted down so she was eye level with the man. "Be that as it may, someone has done something wrong, even by your standards."

"What is this wrong deed?" he asked.

"Classified security documents leaked. About six or seven months ago."

He nodded. Said nothing.

"Who was it?"

He looked away, his lips pursed tightly.

She stood. Reached out and grabbed his left pinky finger. "This is where I like to start. It won't affect you much in the days to come, but the pain usually gets the point across." She shifted so his eyes met hers. "One last chance. Who?"

He said nothing.

She lifted his finger up and snapped back. The motion dislocated each bone in his finger. He clenched his jaw and let out a loud groan.

"Then recently," she said, "those documents made their way back and were being kept safe with the NSA. Now, outside of four people at the NSA, no one else knew about them. Except for certain people at the Pentagon. Do you know anything about that, Prather?"

Again, he refused to answer.

She pulled a knife from her bag and in a fluid motion swung it across her body, driving it into his leg above his left knee.

He screamed out in pain and stared in disbelief at the bladed weapon protruding from his leg. Blood flowed from the wound, wrapping around his knee and calf and dripping onto the floor.

"See," she said. "All you need is a mop and the floor's good as new."

He shook his head. "You're crazy."

"So now, we believe that someone inside the Pentagon arranged for those documents to be stolen. Only question is who? And that's where I need your help."

"Screw you."

She smiled. Dropped her bag on the kitchen table and sat down. She retrieved a long steel ice pick from the bag. Then she pulled out a blow torch. "Do you know what hot steel does when it penetrates the human eye?"

"Do whatever you want with me. I'm not talking."

"This isn't for you." She gestured toward the ceiling. "It's for your boyfriend." She looked from his eyes, to his dislocated pinky, to the knife in his leg. When their eyes met again, she could see that he had been defeated.

"When your boss comes to you and says that there's something that has to be done to protect the country, you listen. When he tells you that he intends to test just how strong the web that protects us is, you have no reason to doubt him." His eyes fluttered and his head bobbed backward then forward. He coughed a few times and righted himself. "And then a crazy agent shows up in your house one night and you begin to question what's happened."

"Your boss? Who are you talking about?"

"Learn your government structure, lady. I'm not here to teach a class. Do you want to hear this or not?"

She nodded. Said nothing.

"So a plan was put into place. One of the best guys the Army had was to intercept said intel and transport it to a predetermined location. He never made it. At first we thought it was the web, you know, wrapped around him and did what it was supposed to do."

"But it wasn't."

"No," he said. "Turns out some rogue former agent did a job for some crime boss. Only thing is, our guy is not in a position to talk and tell us what happened."

"What happened to him?"

"Coma," he said. "Still hasn't come out."

"So you're telling me that all this, these documents and the trouble they've caused, were all part of some secret government operation to test the nation's security?"

"Yes."

"And only what, ten people knew about this?"

"Try fewer than ten."

Clarissa leaned forward and studied the General. The man had confirmed he knew something. The question now was whether or not he was being truthful.

"Then how come," she said, "within days of this information resurfacing and being locked down, it goes missing again?"

The General coughed again. Beads of sweat had formed on his forehead and were now trickling down his stubbled cheeks. He cleared his throat and then said, "That's what I'm trying to figure out. I thought once they were returned we were done with this mess. I'm starting to have doubts about my..."

She lifted her eyebrow in anticipation, but he didn't complete the sentence. His face turned bright red and he began clawing at his abdomen with his right hand. His fist clenched his white t-shirt and climbed upward. Finally, he clutched his chest.

"Oh my God," Clarissa said. "General, are you having a heart attack?"

He didn't answer. Couldn't answer. His heart had exploded and in those few short seconds, life had left his body.

"Christ," she said out loud. She pulled the knife from his leg and threw it in her bag. Her hands were covered with gloves the entire time and her hair tucked inside a skull cap. Despite that, she did a quick check to make sure she had left nothing behind. Sinclair would handle everything at the house from this point on. All Clarissa had to do was leave undetected.

She ran through the house and left through the front door. The beeping she heard told her she had triggered an alarm. It was just a matter of how the device connected to the alarm company. She stayed close to the houses as she moved away from the General's. Moving quickly and silently in the dark, Clarissa stayed alert and aware for witnesses. Sirens approached from the distance, telling her all she needed to know about the alarm system and validating her decision to enter the house through the open window.

She stuck to the shadows until she reached her vehicle two blocks away. The cops had approached from the other direction. She escaped like a ghost fades into the darkest recesses of a room.

88

BEAR WATCHED WITH CONTEMPT AS PIERRE DRANK HIS COFFEE. HE HAD NO IDEA how the day would play out. They planned to take out Charles within the next forty-eight hours. Brutally was the description they had settled on. Bear wondered if through the chaos, Pierre might meet his end as well.

The Frenchman set his mug down and smiled. "It's going to be a good day, my friend."

Bear nodded and didn't respond. His gaze traveled past Pierre, focusing on the blue tiled wall. He'd never felt comfortable around Pierre, and that feeling was twenty times worse after the situation with Kat the previous night.

"What did you think of Kat?" Pierre asked.

Had the mere thought of the woman brought this about? Bear hiked his shoulders in the air a couple inches and shook his head.

"She's a good woman," Pierre said. "A shame you can't stick around longer and get to know her."

"Yeah," Bear said. "A shame." His cell phone vibrated in short bursts against the table. A small sense of relief rushed through him, and he scooped up the phone and said, "Excuse me."

He got up from the table and answered the phone as he exited the cafe into a small fenced in courtyard.

"Yeah?" he said.

"You've got six hours."

"Who's this?"

"Frank."

"Six hours for what?"

"Six hours until Charles and his man leave for the airport to board a plane back to New York."

"That's not much of a window."

"Better get started then."

"Why don't we just finish it in New York?"

"No," Frank said. "I want their entire organization to be afraid everywhere they go."

"Frank, we need to think this through."

There was no answer. Bear held the phone out in front of him and saw that the call had ended. "Son of a bitch," he muttered under his breath. There was no time to plan something elaborate. He wouldn't be able to get inside Charles' head and pinpoint a routine. They'd have to go on the offensive and attack. And to do so he'd need a way in. Bear turned and leaned against the metal railing. Through the smoky glass, he could see Pierre at the counter ordering another coffee. Then the plan came to him. He'd use Pierre as bait.

He remained in the courtyard for a few more minutes while he thought through different scenarios. The first idea that came to mind would be to send Pierre in and have him lead Charles to a window. Bear would be positioned across from the building on an equal or higher floor and would take a shot. Too many flaws, he thought. First, he had no idea whether or not Charles would allow himself to be positioned in such a way. Second, Charles might be so pissed with Pierre that he'd kill him the moment the door closed.

Bear smiled. That was it. Use Charles' temper against him. He went back inside and found Pierre sitting at the table, drinking coffee and smoking a cigarette.

"Can I get one of those?" Bear asked.

Pierre pulled out a cigarette and lighter and placed them in the middle of the table. "Who was on the phone?"

"Frank."

"What did he want?"

"Times running out."

Pierre lifted an eyebrow and gestured for Bear to continue.

"Charles is leaving today. We've only got a few hours."

"That's not enough time."

"I've got an idea. But first, what about your contacts here? Anyone that can help us?"

Pierre shook his head. "Those bridges are still burning."

Bear tipped his ash into the tin ashtray and nodded. "Then here's what I'm thinking. We go to his place. You know where it is, right?"

"Yeah."

"You go to the door and act confrontational. Tell him you want your money for killing me. You went to New York to settle up with the old man, but he had been murdered and no one in the organization would pay up."

Pierre pushed away from the table and crossed his arms over his chest. He bit at his bottom lip. After a few moments he said, "He'll know that I didn't kill you."

"That's what I'm counting on."

"Pardon?"

"Charles has a temper. It's legendary where I'm from. He's gonna be pissed to see you. Then, when you start telling him how you want your money, he's gonna get even more pissed."

"He'll kill me."

"I'm gonna be there, Pierre. You stay in the doorway. Keep the door open. As soon as I hear it escalate I'm going to come down the hallway and place a bullet in his frickin' brain."

Pierre stared at Bear with dark eyes. His jaw muscles rippled along the sides of his face. Would he agree? It was his neck on the line, not Bear's, although both men were putting their lives at risk.

"I'm gonna be right there," Bear said.

"What if they're watching the building?"

"Then we'll have a shootout before we even get to the door. And I'll put you and me up against anyone he's got."

Pierre's chin dropped to his chest and his eyes scanned back and forth across the table. The man wasn't a stranger to dangerous situations. However, Bear figured that he didn't get up today expecting to decide whether to put his life on the line or not.

"Let's do it," Pierre said.

89

THE KNOCK ON THE DOOR WASN'T LOUD, BUT IT WAS ENOUGH TO WAKE JACK. HE rolled off the couch and grabbed his weapon. Two narrow windows were placed on either side of the door. He pulled back the curtain on the left and saw Clarissa standing on the porch.

"You found me," he said as he pulled the door open.

She slid past him and took a seat on the couch.

"Let's go to the kitchen," Jack said. "I need coffee."

Jasmine had her coffee maker set to automatically brew at seven a.m. and a full pot awaited them. Jack placed his phone on the table and then walked over to the coffee maker. He pulled down two mugs and filled them both. Set them down, one in front of Clarissa the other in front of an empty chair. He sat down and took three sips. Rubbed his eyes and stretched.

"What have you found out?" he said.

Clarissa sat motionless before shaking her head and saying, "It's down to one of three people."

"Who?"

"I shouldn't even say it."

"Pentagon or higher?"

She nodded.

"That's what I'm hearing, too," Jack said.

"But it might not be what we thought, Jack."

"How's that?"

She proceeded to recount the General's story, including how he met his ending.

He said, "If all that's true then why were they stolen again?"

"We got around to that and it confused him as well. He thought he might be closing in on something. Don't know. Hell, we'll never know now."

"We gotta move on this, then."

"On who?"

"Deputy Secretary of Defense."

Clarissa lowered her eyes and focused on her coffee mug. She picked up Jack's phone and spun it and turned it over in her hand. They sat in silence for three long minutes. Jack went over her story forwards and back, trying to locate any holes or misdirection in the information the General had given her. He couldn't buy the fact that the documents had been stolen the first time as part of a test. That sounded like a good way to get a lot of honest people to pony up and do a bad man's bidding. He'd become party to it himself.

Jack heard the front door open and close. Footsteps approached.

Clarissa looked up. "Jack, I don't think—"

He held up a finger to silence her. "Jasmine's coming. Don't say anything specific. Speak in general terms."

Jasmine walked into the kitchen, poured a cup of coffee and sat down at the table. "Meeting of the minds?"

"Something like that," Jack said. "Clarissa's organization feels the same as I do."

Jasmine shook her head. "I've already spoken with Frank, and we're following up on the foreign terrorist angle."

"You and Frank?" Jack said.

"No," Jasmine said. "Me and you."

"You're on your own, Jazz. I don't work for Frank, and I don't take orders from him or you."

She sighed. "Jack, you're wasting time. Precious time that we can't get back. Every hour that passes, those documents get further away and fall into more dangerous hands."

"Jack," Clarissa said. "My group can work this and you—"

"It's domestic. Legally, Sinclair can't do anything." He turned his attention back to Jasmine. "Get Frank on the phone."

Jasmine got up and went to the counter and grabbed her cell phone. She tapped on the screen, dialing Frank's number and turning on the speaker. She placed the phone in the center of the table and took a seat next to Jack.

"Yeah, Jasmine," Frank said.

"I've got Jack here with me, Frank. He's not down with the plan."

"What's the problem, Jack?" Frank said.

"This is a load of bull. I got a source that leads me to the Pentagon. That's the angle I want to work."

"We did some follow up on Jasmine's theory," Frank said. "It's more than a theory. That's where I want you."

"I don't work for you," Jack said.

The line went silent except for Frank's breathing. It rose and fell, quickly at first and then returned to a normal pace.

"Jack," Frank said. "Either you're on board or I let it be known that your death was faked and you are alive and well and creeping around the Pentagon. I think there are a few people that might be interested in hearing that information. It'll tie up a few loose ends and deflect some blame at the very least."

Jack felt his cheeks burn hot as anger welled up inside him. Frank was lucky this conversation was being held over the phone, or he'd likely have ended up dead. He took a deep breath and regained control of his emotions.

"You and I go back a long way," Jack said.

"You know I don't care about things like that," Frank said.

"Just give me twenty-four hours. If I don't have it figured out by then, I'll go wherever you want."

"Give me a sec," Frank said.

Jasmine grabbed the phone and held it up to her mouth. "You're not considering this, are you?"

"Jack," Frank said. "Take the phone and get me off speaker."

Jack held out his hand and waited for Jasmine to hand the phone over. She dropped it on the table and left the kitchen.

"What do you want, Frank?" Jack said.

"You alone?"

Jack looked at Clarissa and held his right index finger to his lips. "Yeah, all alone. Jasmine left the room."

"You sure about your source?"

"One hundred percent."

"Who is it?"

"I stand by him. Isn't that enough?"

Frank let out an audible exhale and said, "You got twenty-four hours. After that the phone gets switched on and you report to me or I go public and tell the world you're alive."

Jack ended the call and placed the phone on the table. He glanced through the opening between the kitchen and living room and saw Jasmine sitting on the sofa. He thought about trying to convince her to work his angle for the next day, but in the end decided against it. She'd be more of a hindrance than a help at this point.

He turned to Clarissa. "We should get out of here."

She stood and walked past Jasmine to the front door. Stepped outside without saying a word. Jack followed her and stopped at the door. He looked over his shoulder at Jasmine.

"If this doesn't go down the way I think then I'll be back in the morning," he said.

"I'll be gone, Jack."

"Then I'll find you."

She said nothing.

"Good luck, Jazz." With that, he shut the door and headed toward the rental car.

Clarissa stood next to the driver's door. Her face was drawn and she refused to make eye contact.

"What is it?" he asked.

"Sinclair's pulling me," she said.

"Why?"

"I can't say anything other than he's sending me away to attend to another matter."

Jack reached out and placed his hands on her shoulders. She stepped into his grasp and brushed up against him. They kissed for a dozen seconds before she pulled away and jogged to her vehicle.

"You be careful, Jack," she said. "Watch your back."

"Always," he said. "Keep that phone line open."

She waved at him with her cell phone in hand. Wiped her eyes with the sleeve of her other arm.

He waited until she drove out of sight, then got in his car and pulled away. He needed to speak with Marlowe before proceeding and figured he might still be able to catch the man at his house.

90

The apartment building cast a shadow across the street, turning the warm spring day cool. Bear and Pierre stayed close to the building. Bear's plan was to wait for someone to enter or exit the building and then grab the door before it closed. There was a risk in waiting outside, but if Charles showed up, then they'd have a gun fight on the street. It might make for bad press, but that's why they had Frank. He could clean up any mess they made.

"You remember which apartment it was?" Bear asked.

"It's the right side of the top floor," Pierre said. "Penthouse."

Bear shrugged. Looked up. Charles had done all right for himself, he thought.

The door opened and a woman in her seventies struggled to get herself and her dog through the doorway. Pierre stepped forward and grabbed the door, holding it open for the lady. She thanked him in French and walked away from the building without looking back.

"That was easy," Pierre said.

Easier than Bear had expected. "Let's move."

They stuck to the stairs instead of riding up the elevator. They stopped at the final landing and caught their breath and went over their plan one more time.

"Promise me you'll be quick," Pierre said.

"Faster than a ninja," Bear said.

When said to Jack, a joke about the big man's size was sure to follow, or at the very least, a laugh. The phrase did not elicit the same response from the Frenchman.

PIERRE CREPT DOWN THE HALL, every step carrying him further away from the relative safety that having a partner provided. He reached the corner and followed the hall as it angled to the right. The door stood twenty feet away. He stopped and took a deep breath. As he shifted from foot to foot, the cold barrel of his gun brushed up against the skin of his back. The feeling was reassuring in some ways, and gave him cause for doubt in others. He'd have to rely on a clean release, something that was not guaranteed without a holster.

He recalled the last time he had been in the apartment. It was shortly after he had returned to France from Russia. Charles had offered him work and invited him over to discuss details. They hadn't come to a working agreement at the time, and Pierre fell further into his depression as the days and weeks passed.

Now he stood there again, feeling as though he had an opportunity to erase the pain of the previous six months by taking Charles' life.

The air in the hall was still. The skin on his forehead felt clammy. He wiped his brow and took a series of deep breaths, calming and centering himself. Then he walked to the door. Extended his arm. Rapped against the solid wood with his knuckles four times.

The light from the small peephole in the center of the door was extinguished as someone peered through. Pierre braced himself internally. On the exterior he tried to remain as calm as possible, letting his shoulders slump slightly and his arms hang down by his side.

The door opened a bit and Alonso stuck his head out. "What the hell are you doing here?"

"I'm here to collect."

"For what?"

"What do you mean for what? You know what for."

"For wasting our time?

"Where's Charles?"

"Are you crazy? He'll kill you if he sees you." Alonso looked genuinely concerned for Pierre's safety.

Pierre kept the act going. "Kill me for what? I should kill you two. I completed a job and then the old man goes missing just after. No one in New York would pay up. You guys set me up and left me hanging on my quarter million."

"You didn't complete anything. You should leave."

Alonso started to shut the door. Pierre wedged his foot in the opening, preventing it from closing.

"Are you saying I am a liar?" Pierre said.

Alonso shook his head and looked down at the floor. A moment later he lifted his eyes and met Pierre's. "You need to leave. We are about to go. He won't think twice about killing you."

Pierre leaned forward, placing his left forearm against the door frame. He slid his right hand around his back and wrapped his fingers around the handle of his pistol. "Get Charles now."

Alonso stepped back and let the door fall against Pierre's shoe.

Pierre waited and listened. Through the opening he could hear the sounds of the men discussing the situation in the hall. He braced himself for the confrontation.

The door swung open. Alonso stepped up to Pierre and held out both hands. "You need to leave. Now."

Pierre heard the distinct clicking sound of a pump action shotgun being cocked behind the door. In a split second his instincts took over and he reached behind his back and retrieved his weapon.

THE SOUND FOLLOWING the ultimatum to Pierre was impossible to confuse. Bear had heard that sound ever since he was a child and went hunting with his father and uncles. Someone had a shotgun and that someone was about to shoot Pierre. Bear had already positioned himself at the point in the hall where it angled toward Charles' door. He launched himself around the corner, gun drawn and ready to fire.

Pierre stood near the wall. The Frenchman's right arm whipped around, gun in hand. Bear couldn't see inside the apartment, but he did see a man he didn't recognize, but assumed was Alonso, in the open doorway. Pierre fired and hit the man in the stomach. Alonso fell backward and disappeared from Bear's line of sight.

Pierre turned and started toward Bear. The loud sound of a shotgun rang through the hallway and a flash of light filled the shared area of hall and doorway. Pierre yelled and fell to the ground. The cocking sound of the shotgun being pumped followed.

Bear unloaded his seventeen round magazine into the wall and doorway as he ran toward Pierre. He loaded another magazine and switched the gun to his left hand. Fired four more shots. Heard a groan from inside the apartment, but had no way to tell if it was Charles or Alonso.

He quickly inspected Pierre. The damage appeared to be on the right side. He was losing blood at a steady rate. Bear hooked his right arm under Pierre's left and dragged him down the hall, firing occasionally toward the apartment.

When they rounded the corner, Bear hoisted Pierre onto his shoulder. The man had become incoherent and Bear had to hurry. He opted to try for the elevator instead of the stairs. He pounded against the button on the wall next to the stainless steel doors.

Then he heard sound of the shotgun being pumped. Bear adjusted Pierre on his shoulder and extended his arm.

"I'm gonna kill you bastards," Charles said from the hallway.

Bear said nothing. Glanced up at the display above the elevator and saw that it had two more floors to go. He fired a shot down the hallway in an attempt to slow Charles down.

The barrel of Charles' shotgun appeared from behind the wall and began to drop into position. He looked at the display again and saw that it still hadn't moved from the third floor. There was no time to wait. He barreled down the hall toward the exit that led to the stairs. A shot rippled through the air from behind. Bear braced for the bullet to tear through his flesh. It didn't. He hit the door at full speed, barely managing to get his hand on the knob and turn it. He hoped that Pierre's internal wounds weren't severe, otherwise he'd be sending the man to his deathbed with all the jarring and slamming and bouncing.

Bear turned and saw Charles in the hall. He fired without aiming as the door slammed shut. He had no idea if any of the bullets had connected or not. Had no intention of opening the door to find out. As quickly as he could, Bear took the stairs to the bottom floor. He raced through the lobby. The elevator dinged as he approached and the stainless steel doors opened. Bear aimed his gun at the opening, ready to fire on Charles if he were standing there. An elderly couple saw his weapon and cowered back to the corner of the elevator.

"Please don't shoot," the old man yelled out in French.

Bear ignored him at first and continued toward the door. Then he stopped and turned around. The elevator was still open. He stuck his foot in the front of one side of the doors to prevent it from closing. He peered in and found the controls. Pressed the button marked for emergency.

"Do either of you have a cell phone?" Bear held his fingers to his head to mimic the action of using a phone.

The man nodded.

"Police," Bear said, then turned and exited the building. He heard the stairwell door crash open as he left the building and stepped onto the sidewalk. He spun around and fired blindly into the lobby. Sirens approached and Bear craned his neck to see which direction they were coming from. He saw the ambulance turn onto the street and he rushed toward it, waving his free hand.

The ambulance screeched to a stop in front of him. A man and woman emerged from the front. A second man came out from the back of the vehicle.

"Be quick," Bear said in French as he laid Pierre on the ground. "There's a madman inside with a gun. I'll cover you for a second, but I have to go." He knew that the team would be violating half of their training by loading Pierre without first assessing him, but his urging had been met with a rapid response.

The two men scooped Pierre off the ground and rushed him toward the back of the vehicle. The woman got behind the steering wheel of the ambulance and took off before the back door was closed.

Another set of sirens approached. The police, Bear figured. He looked around. Saw a man step out of his car and walk toward a mailbox, leaving his driver's side door open. Bear ran toward the car and jumped in and threw the car into gear. He sped off. He had to get out of the city, then contact Kat, and then find out about Pierre.

91

JACK DROVE THROUGH THE QUIET NEIGHBORHOOD AND APPROACHED THE STREET
that led to Marlowe's house. As he turned, he saw an army of police cars,
government cars and an ambulance parked in front of the man's residence.
Medics wheeled a gurney toward the ambulance. A sheet was pulled over a body.
Jack pulled the car to the curb and stopped. He reached into his pocket and
retrieved a cell phone. Dialed the daisy chained number that led to Frank.

Frank answered almost immediately.

"Did you know who I was talking to?" Jack said.

"Jack? What are you talking about?"

"Dammit Frank, don't screw with me now. Did you have any idea who my
source was?"

"Was?" Frank paused for a beat. "I think I do now. I just got word that
Robert Marlowe was murdered. General Prather, too."

"You swear you didn't know I was talking to Marlowe?"

"Jack, I had no idea. Even if I did, we wouldn't take him out. What purpose
would that serve?"

Jack said nothing. He put the car into reverse and pressed on the gas. Started
back the way he came.

"Why don't you come into the office?" Frank said. "Me, you and Jasmine can
meet and figure this thing—"

Jack hung up the phone and dropped it in his lap. Prather had been an unfortunate incident involving Clarissa. She had told him all about it, leaving nothing out, or so he assumed. She had left unexpectedly that morning. Had she left to take out Marlowe? He tried to recall if he had mentioned the man's name to her. He'd been careful to leave it out of conversation with Jasmine and Frank. But it might have slipped while talking with Clarissa.

He grabbed the cell phone and dialed Brandon's number.

"Jack?"

"How'd you know?"

"Similar number, same exchange. What do you need?"

"I need the mobile number of the Deputy Secretary of Defense."

"Say what?"

"Just do it."

The line went silent except for the sounds of fingers hitting a keyboard. A moment later Brandon read off the phone number. "You didn't get that from me."

"You got it." Jack hung up and dialed the number.

A man answered. "Hello?"

"I've got something you want."

"Who is this?"

"Lincoln Park, at the statue on the east end. Half an hour. You better be there and be alone."

"Wait a minute. Who is this? What do you have?"

"It doesn't need to be said. Don't test me McCarthy. Be there or I'll find your kids." He didn't know whether the man had children or not, but the bluff worked.

"Half an hour, Lincoln Park," McCarthy said. "I'll be there."

It took Jack fifteen minutes to reach the park. He found a metered parking spot and left his car. He stood across the street from the park, on 11th, in a spot where he had a view of the statue. Like clockwork, the Secretary showed up, and he appeared to have come alone. Jack pulled out his phone and called the man.

"Start walking toward 11th," Jack said. "Turn right when you reach the street."

The Secretary looked over his shoulders, turned in a full circle and settled in while looking in Jack's direction. "Where are you?"

Jack had positioned himself where he couldn't be seen. "Just do what I said."

He watched McCarthy walk toward him and stop, then turn right and head north on 11th. After the man had a half block lead, Jack got in his car and drove toward him. He pulled up next to McCarthy and stopped.

"Get in," Jack said.

The Secretary froze. He looked like he was going to shout or run or maybe even piss himself.

Jack lifted his gun. "Get in or this gets used on you and then your kids while your wife watches."

McCarthy opened the door and got inside the vehicle. Sat down and strapped in. "Who are you?"

"That's not important."

"Where are the documents?"

"That's what I'd like to know. You had them stolen from a secure location. Where are they now?"

The Secretary shook his head. "What are you talking about? How do you know they were stolen?"

Jack said nothing. He made a series of turns, going nowhere in particular. He wished he had a place here in the city that he could take the man for questioning.

"Did you kill the General last night?"

Jack laughed.

"You find that funny?" the man said.

"No, I had nothing to do with that. But I'm interested in seeing what you know about Robert Marlowe."

"I just found out. We don't have any information other than he was murdered execution style."

"He was a friend of mine," Jack said. "And he fingered you for the culprit behind the security leak."

Jack pulled the car into a parking lot and turned in his seat to face the man.

"Look," McCarthy said. "You got it all wrong. Yeah, I was involved in the initial test. We all were. But once the documents were back in our possession, I can't tell you how relieved I was. I've been freaking out since they were stolen again, because..."

Jack waited for the man to continue, then said, "Because what?"

"I think I know who did it."

Jack honed in on the man's eyes. They hadn't flinched and still didn't wave. "Who?"

"The Secretary of Defense. Bragg. He's the one that arranged the initial test. And to be frank, I'm having doubts that was a test at all. He used us. All of us, including the President."

"Who's working with him?"

"I'm not sure. Certainly not the man he hired the first time."

"Could it be someone from the same group?"

The man shrugged. Said nothing.

"I can't get into the Pentagon, but I need to finish this," Jack said. "Can you get him to meet you somewhere?"

The man nodded. "He has an office on F Street."

"Call him. Tell him to meet you there and only there."

The man pulled out his phone and placed the call. He spoke quickly and didn't elaborate on any points. After he hung up, he said, "It's arranged. We'll meet in an hour."

Jack drove west, toward the White House. There was a parking garage close to the Secretary's office on F Street and he could ditch the car there.

Neither man spoke during the drive. Jack kept glancing at McCarthy to make sure he wasn't trying to send any messages with his phone. By all appearances the man had settled in and accepted his fate for the day.

They reached the parking garage and Jack navigated through the cavernous structure, winding upward several stories before he found an empty space.

Jack cut the engine and turned in his seat to face McCarthy. "Here's the plan. You're going to show me where the office is, and then you're going in there alone. I'm going to wait out of sight. I'll enter shortly after. From there I take over."

"Then I can go?"

"No. Can't trust you. You'll stay."

"I'll be a witness. Do you want that?"

Jack narrowed his eyes and leaned forward. "You ever threaten me again and you'll watch what I do to your family."

McCarthy's eyes watered over and he shook his head. "I should be armed. Bragg's a dangerous man, and I know he has weapons in that office. I think... I think he conducts alternate business there. Give me a weapon."

"Not a chance," Jack said. "Don't say anything stupid. You'll only be alone for a minute. If Bragg tries anything when I enter I'll neutralize him."

"You'll kill him."

"Not until I have everything I want."

McCarthy lowered his head and shook it. "How did we ever get into this mess? Why would Bragg do something so stupid? Endanger his country like this?"

"For the same reason most men betray their morals and ethics," Jack said. "Money."

Jack stepped out of the car and waited for McCarthy to join him. "You stay close. I better not lose sight of you."

McCarthy practically hugged Jack, he stood so close. They found the stairs and made their way to the street. Navigated their way to the office building where Bragg kept his unofficial office. They entered the building and made their way to the floor above Bragg's.

They had thirty minutes to kill before the meeting. The time passed slowly, leaving Jack to focus on the second hand of a cheap clock hanging on the wall in the floor's lobby. He barely looked in McCarthy's direction and the men said nothing to each other until twenty-five minutes in when McCarthy spoke.

"That's him," McCarthy said. "Entering the building."

Jack walked over to the window and looked down at the street.

"He's inside already," McCarthy said.

"Get ready to go," Jack said.

92

"WE MISSED," BEAR SAID INTO HIS CELL PHONE. "AND TO MAKE IT WORSE, PIERRE was wounded badly. Might not make it."

"I see," Frank said. "Look, you need to get back to the U.S. at once. We can discuss further steps once you are here."

Bear stared up at the sky. Clouds had rolled in and were blocking the setting sun. The orange glow filtered through but did little to warm the cool breeze that blew into his face. He had no intention of doing anything for Frank when he got back to the States. But he wasn't going to say that now. He might never make it to his plane if he did.

"OK," Bear said. "I'll call you after I land."

He ended the call and immediately dialed Kat's number. No answer. He walked until he reached her apartment building. The gate was locked. He paced the area in front of the entrance for half an hour. Then she appeared. Stepped off a bus and walked toward him. He stood next to the gate and waited for her.

"Bear," she said. "Where's Pierre?"

"We should go inside," he said.

She unlocked the gate and they hurried to her apartment without saying a word. By the time they reached the door, tears stained her cheeks.

"Is he dead?" she asked as she pushed the door open.

"Maybe."

"You don't know?"

"I had to leave him with the medics. Charles was coming after us."

She pressed her palms into her eyes and let out a sob. She took a deep quivering breath and said, "Where did they take him?"

"Don't know."

"Where were you?"

"Not sure."

"Why are you here?"

"To tell you about Pierre."

"Tell me why you're really here."

"Come to America with me."

Kat shook her head and turned away. "You should leave."

Bear lifted his hands. Wanted to reach out and grab her. Pull her close. Hug her. Convince her to come with him. Instead he turned and left the apartment without another word.

He made his way out of the compound and hailed the first taxi he saw.

"Take me to the airport," he said.

93

A MINUTE PASSED, THEN TWO, THEN THREE. FINALLY, AT THE FOUR MINUTE MARK Jack said, "It's time."

He led McCarthy down the hall to the stairwell. They walked down a flight of stairs and stopped next to the reinforced door that served as a barrier against the heat and cold and noise between the hall and the stairs.

"Ready?" Jack said.

McCarthy nodded.

"Remember," Jack said. "Don't play hero. Things get out of hand, you run."

"OK."

"Once I enter, you don't have to say a thing. In fact, I'd prefer it if you didn't."

"OK."

"Any final questions?"

"Are you going to kill him?"

Jack shrugged as a slight grin formed on his face. The feeling was there, he only needed an excuse. "Only if he tries to kill one of us."

McCarthy stood there, eyes wide, and said nothing.

"Now go," Jack said while pulling the door open.

McCarthy stepped through the opening and walked toward the office. Jack left the door cracked just enough so that he could see down the hall. McCarthy stopped and knocked on Bragg's office door. Jack didn't see the door open, but he did see Bragg stick his head out and check both ends of the hall. Jack instinctively pulled back but was careful to leave the door cracked in the same position. Letting it close and bang shut would set off a red flag, and surely Bragg was on high enough alert to notice.

Jack prepared to move. The walk would be one of the longest he ever took. The scenarios played in his mind. Would McCarthy double cross him and tell Bragg that Jack was on the way? McCarthy could have been playing him the whole time and be a lot more involved in the plot than Jack knew. What if Bragg had the hallway covered with surveillance? He'd be a sitting duck if that were the case.

Jack shook the thoughts from his mind. The time for worrying had passed. He pushed the door open and started down the hall. As he approached the door, he retrieved the Glock Frank had given him and held it in his right hand. Grabbed the Sig Sauer pistol he took from Jasmine's apartment with his left hand. He stopped in front of the door and listened. The men were shouting at each other.

"I know what you did, Don," McCarthy said.

"What's that?" Bragg said.

McCarthy lowered his voice and Jack couldn't make out his response. Then he heard Bragg start to laugh. It was time. Jack took two steps back and lunged forward, kicking the door open with his right foot. He held both guns at arm's length. Aimed one at McCarthy and the other at Bragg.

"Don't move a muscle," Jack said.

McCarthy threw his hands in the air and backed up until he pressed against the wall, next to a window.

"What the hell is this?" Bragg said. "Do you have any idea who we are?"

Jack used his foot to kick the door into a closed position. It didn't latch, but he managed to get it stuck shut.

"Step out from behind the desk, Bragg," Jack said.

Bragg didn't move. "Get the hell out of my office."

"You're not the one in charge here," Jack said. "Be a good boy like McCarthy and join him next to the window."

Bragg shook his head and reached down toward his desk.

"I wouldn't do that," Jack said. "Considering all the lives that have already been lost, one more won't make a difference. Especially not the life of a traitor."

Bragg lifted his head and stared at Jack for a moment. Then he straightened up and took a step back. He narrowed his eyes and lifted his hand. Pointed at Jack.

"Wait a minute," Bragg said. "I know you. You're that Noble guy. You're the one that screwed up my operation to test our security."

Out of the corner of his eye, Jack saw McCarthy turn his head toward him.

"You mean I stopped you from placing sensitive documents into the hands of terrorists in North Korea," Jack said.

"Koreans? You handed them over to the Russians."

"And I got them back," Jack said. "Only to have them stolen again."

Bragg shrugged. "I don't know anything about that."

"I didn't ask if you did."

"Are you really Jack Noble?" McCarthy asked.

"Jack Noble is dead," Jack said.

"So what do you want, Jack?" Bragg said.

"I want you to go to the President and tell him what you did. Maybe if you beg loudly enough he'll let you disappear instead of having you killed for treason."

Bragg laughed. "If anyone here is guilty of treason, it's you, Jack. I was only trying to make our country a safer place."

"Where are the documents now?" Jack said.

"I should ask you that," Bragg said. "You're probably the one that stole them from the NSA."

Jack took a step forward. "Where are they?"

Bragg stood defiant. "Even if I knew, I wouldn't tell you."

Jack took another step forward, taking care to keep both men in his sight. "Your life means nothing to me, Bragg. I'm a ghost. I'll just disappear. You better friggin' tell me."

"Screw you, Jack."

Jack closed the distance between himself and Bragg's desk. He held both guns inches from the man's head. "Dammit, Bragg. Tell me where the documents are."

"They're right here, Jack," a familiar female voice said from behind.

Bragg smiled.

Jack had let his emotions get the best of him, and in doing so, he missed the sound of a door within the office opening from behind. Not the main office door, but a closet door or one that led to another room. He chastised himself for being so careless.

"Place your weapons on the desk and turn around," she said.

Jack held the guns with only his thumbs and index fingers. Slowly he lowered the weapons and set them on the desk. Then he turned around and saw Jasmine standing at the back of the room with an H&K MP7 equipped with a silencer, aimed in his direction. She held it loosely in her right hand. A briefcase dangled from her left.

"Jasmine," Jack said. "What the—"

"You couldn't leave it alone, could you, Jack?" she said.

"Why?" Jack said.

"I told you from the beginning this wasn't for us to worry about. There are agencies that are made for this kind of thing. You should have listened to me and let me convince you, like Frank, that this had nothing to do with us."

Jack shook his head in disbelief and said nothing.

"But no, you had this redemption thing stuck in your head. Then I tried to steer things in another direction and push the terrorist theory. Even had Frank convinced. But once again," she took a step forward, "Jack Noble argues and gets his way."

"You stole the documents from the NSA," Jack said.

She nodded and gestured with the briefcase.

"How? How did you know where and how?"

"Remember when I told you that I interviewed with different agencies before going to work for the SIS?"

Jack nodded.

"I made a contact in the NSA during that time," she said. "We stayed close and became more than friends. You knew him as Rico."

"He was involved in the theft?" Jack said. "He's the one that put me onto the Pentagon, though."

"He was only involved in a roundabout way. He told me enough. Then he turned out to help you despite my attempts at misleading him."

Jack realized at that moment that the car bomb was Jasmine's doing. "You killed him?"

"And I meant to kill you at the same time, but you stood outside the garage."

Jack reached up and ran his hands through his hair. He grabbed fistfuls of hair in the back and pulled. "This whole time, you've been working against me."

"No," she said. "Not entirely. We had a few common goals. Stop the Russians from pulling off the attacks, for one. Not because I care, but because I got nothing out of it. No money. We were also on the same page as far as getting the documents back. But, again for different reasons."

Jack heard a drawer slide open behind him and then the sounds of metal clanking against wood. Bragg stepped out from the behind the desk and walked past him. Joined Jasmine at the other side of the room. He lifted his arm and aimed his gun at Jack.

"What was that you called yourself, Mr. Noble?" Bragg said. "A ghost, right?"

Jack said nothing. He clenched his jaw and inched backward. His weapons were barely a foot away. Maybe he'd get shot while reaching for them. Maybe not. But it'd be better than dying like a chump with his hands up.

"No, no, no," Jasmine said. "Not another inch."

"Should we kill him here?" Bragg asked.

"Yeah," Jasmine said. "But first you and I have to complete our transaction. After I fire, we need to bolt."

"OK." Bragg walked toward his desk and retrieved a bag. He held up the bag and said, "It's all unmarked."

"What about him?" Jasmine asked as she nodded toward McCarthy.

"He knows too much. Kill him, too. I think we can frame some of this on him. I'll say that he and Jack approached me to do a deal, then things got messy and Jack's partner attacked us." He handed the bag to Jasmine.

She took it from him, then said, "I'll need to make it look real."

Bragg shrugged and lifted his chin, perhaps expecting her to hit him. Instead, she aimed her gun toward the ground and fired a shot into his lower leg. Bragg collapsed and hit the floor with a thud. He cried out in pain and managed to scoot himself toward the wall.

"What the hell?" he said.

"Shut up," Jasmine said.

Bragg groaned and moaned and yelled a half dozen obscenities at her. Jasmine lifted her weapon once again and fired three shots into Bragg's chest. The man fell back and rolled over on his side, silenced.

Jack scooted back and placed his hands on the desk.

Jasmine whipped the weapon around and aimed at Jack, this time with both hands supporting the gun. "Not so fast, Jack."

He brought his hands forward and kept them just above waist level.

She turned slightly and fired another shot, this time hitting McCarthy in the center of his forehead. A cloud of blood hung in the air as the man's lifeless body slumped down the wall to the floor, leaving a river of red in his wake.

"Just you and me now," she said as she turned her attention back to Jack.

Jack said nothing. His mind raced for the correct words to turn the situation around. Nothing came to mind. How had he missed this? How had Frank missed this? Was Frank involved? He decided to ask.

"How long have you and Frank been planning this?"

She laughed. "Frank? He's clueless, Jack. Even more so since he went inside to sit behind a desk all day."

He had to keep her talking. That was the only thing that would keep him alive. And if he could keep it going, he'd eventually get a chance to take her down.

"Why, Jasmine?" he said. "Just tell me why."

"It doesn't matter, Jack. You don't need to know. Not where you're going." She turned slightly, perhaps to brace herself against the emotional impact of killing someone she'd been close to for the past few weeks.

"You don't have to do this, Jasmine. You can disappear. Take the money and the documents and leave."

"I plan to do all that. And I have to do this, otherwise you'll chase me. And I know you'll eventually find me."

"Jasmine—"

She shook her head and said, "Any last words you want me to relay for you?"

Jack knew that was it. She had made up her mind and nothing he could do was going to change it. He took a deep breath and quickly tensed and relaxed his arms. He had to be faster than her. His arms needed to be quicker than her trigger finger. Chances are he wouldn't be successful. Against a thug who had little weapons experience, sure. But against a trained killer, he was as good as dead in this situation.

"Yeah," Jack said. "Tell Bear I said thanks for all the years he stood by my side."

"OK."

"Tell Frank I said screw you for getting me into this mess."

She smiled and nodded.

"And I need you to tell Clarissa that I'm sorry I didn't work harder in the past to make things work. I had every intention of finding her after this and trying to settle down into a life with her."

"You two would have been good together." Jasmine's smile faded. "Now get your hands up and behind your head."

He had to act. He feigned a step forward and swung his hands and body back. At that same time the door to the office crashed open. Shots were fired. Jack felt the sting of a bullet penetrating his flesh. The pain radiated through his chest and shoulder and arm, and he couldn't tell where he had been hit. He fell with his back flat against the desk. Managed to get one of the weapons in his grasp. Rolled backward and fell off the desk.

He glanced to his right and saw blood on his shoulder. He tore at the ripped fabric and saw that he had only been nicked by the bullet.

The room was quiet. He rose up and looked over the desk. Jasmine rested against the back wall, eyes open, gun in her lap. Blood poured down her neck from a bullet hole in the side of her head.

He shifted gaze toward the door and saw Clarissa standing just inside the office.

"Are you OK?" she said.

Jack nodded, then shook his head. He stood and walked around the desk. She met him halfway.

"What are you doing here?" he said. "How did you know?"

She smiled. "You're getting careless in your old age, Jack."

He shook his head, confused.

"Your phone," she said. "You left it on the table at Jasmine's house. I picked it up and put a bug on it. I've been listening in and following you all day since you left Jasmine's."

"Why?"

"Sinclair got some disturbing news that morning I came to see you." She nodded toward Jasmine. "About her."

"Why didn't you tell me?"

"We had to catch her in the act and with the documents. I'd have preferred to take her alive, but as it is I almost got here too late." She looked at the bodies of

Bragg and McCarthy. "I was too late to save them. I'm sorry, Jack. I know this isn't easy to process."

Jack nodded. "I... Yeah." He tucked his weapon and reached for her. Pulled her close. Kissed her.

She pulled back at first, then leaned in. She broke the kiss off a few moments later and said, "We need to get out of here."

Jack collected the documents and the money and followed Clarissa out of the room.

"We need to go up two floors," she said. "There's a service elevator there. Safer than taking the main elevator to the lobby."

They made it outside without incident. Walked three blocks and stopped near the parking garage.

"I believe your car's in there," she said.

Jack nodded. He started to walk toward the garage entrance and stopped when he noticed she wasn't following. He turned and walked back toward her. "Are you coming?"

She shook her head. Tears filled her eyes.

"What's going on?"

"I'm afraid this is goodbye, Jack. At least for now."

"Clarissa, come with me. We'll get this stuff to Frank and then disappear. I've got enough money for us to live on for the rest of our lives."

She leaned in and kissed his cheek. Her tears felt cool against his skin. "Sorry, Jack. I owe Sinclair for this and for him not turning you in. I'm in debt to him."

"Me? What?"

She silenced him with her finger.

"When will you be back?" he said.

She shrugged and shook her head. With that, she turned and walked away.

Jack fought the urge to chase after her. It wouldn't make any difference.

94

Bear got in a cab and gave the driver the address to the SIS headquarters. He had considered calling Frank to tell him he was done, but in the end figured the best thing to do was discuss it in person. He tried to put his thoughts into words on the way there, but same as his time on the plane, he could only think of the woman he left behind in France. He knew that he hadn't actually left her behind. There would have had to have been something between them for that. It was just that no woman had ever made such an impression on him in so short a time. With barely a word, he experienced a connection he'd likely not soon forget with Kat.

As the taxi made its final turn, Bear cleared his head. He pulled out his cell phone and called Frank. "Almost there," was all he said.

The cab stopped in front of the building. Bear paid the man and got out. Waited until the taxi disappeared before approaching the entrance. The front doors were unlocked. Bear received a surprise as he pulled the door open and stepped inside.

"Bear!" Mandy raced toward him with her arms spread wide.

He dropped to one knee and caught the girl as she slammed into him with the force of a sledge hammer, nearly knocking him over.

"I missed you so much," he said.

"Me too." Her hands clung tightly to his shoulders.

He looked up and saw Frank standing a few feet away. Bear pushed Mandy back gently and got to his feet.

"You're off the hook, Logan," Frank said.

Bear said nothing. He looked past Frank and saw Larsen standing just outside the hall.

Frank nodded. "I've got new help. He's going to bring down Charles and that organization, and we'll see where we go from there."

"And we're done," Bear added.

"Disappear," Frank said. "And if you ever need anything, call me."

Bear nodded, then grabbed Mandy's hand and left the building.

"Where are we gonna go?" Mandy asked.

Bear looked down at her and squeezed her hand in his. "We're gonna travel around the U.S. for a month or so. Then I'm thinking we'll go to Europe. France, maybe."

95

CHARLES SAT IN THE OLD MAN'S OFFICE. HIS OFFICE, NOW. HE SMILED AT ALONSO and adjusted the items on top of the antique dark wood desk.

"They're on the way," Alonso said.

"Good," Charles said. "Let's strike fear into their hearts."

He had a meeting with five men in the organization who had risen to some level of power. The purpose of the meeting was to show them that he would be in charge and they were to get in line and do what he said.

There was a knock on the door and the men filed in, one by one. They each took a seat at the long rectangular table at the other end of the office.

Charles stood and slowly walked toward the table. "Gentlemen, glad you could join us today. I'm going to make this quick and relatively painless. You are here today to swear your loyalty to me. I'm taking over."

The men looked at one another. The man named Hessler shifted in his seat and said, "I've got just as much claim as you do. Since you left, I've taken over most of the duties here."

"Vetoed," Charles said.

Hessler stood. "These men support me, not you."

Charles smiled and looked at each man, one at a time. "Is this true?"

No one spoke.

"I'm taking over Charles, like it or not."

Charles reached inside his jacket, pulled out a gun and shot Hessler in the head. The man's lifeless body fell backward and collapsed on the floor. Charles stepped over his body and looked around the room. "I'll ask again. Is what he was saying true?"

The men shook their heads.

"Good," Charles said as he took a seat at the table. "Now let's get down to business. I've left Alonso in charge of Europe. Anyone have an issue with that?"

The room was silent.

"There's been a lot of heat on us these past few days. I think the thing to do is lay low for a while. I, for one, am not going to leave these walls for at least a month. We'll do some intel gathering and start planning our next moves over the next few weeks. Any questions?"

No one spoke.

"Good. Get the hell out of here." He watched the men leave and then returned to his desk where he poured himself a drink. After the attempt on his life, he knew that his time on Earth was limited. The only thing he could do during that time would be to grab as much power as possible. Today was a good start, he thought. A plan formed in his mind. One that would unfold over the coming days and weeks and months in various stages. And anyone who dared to cross him would pay with their lives. Just like Hessler, he thought as he looked over at the corpse on the floor.

96

JACK SAT ACROSS FROM FRANK AT A BOOTH IN A CROWDED DINER. THEY ATE their food and drank their coffee in silence. After the waitress refilled their coffee one last time and left the check on the table, Frank spoke.

"I've got an opening, if you're interested."

Jack chuckled and shook his head. "I'm done, Frank. I'm retiring from free-lancing, government work, everything. I'm gonna travel and maybe settle down somewhere."

"You'll go crazy. Look, why don't you come work for me for a few years. We'll clean up all the messes out there and fix the country."

"Sorry," Jack said. "I can't help you."

Frank nodded. "I figured as much." He took a sip of coffee and turned his head. "I never would have figured Jasmine for a double agent. She was bright eyed and full of vigor when she started. Still seemed to be that way. I'll have to figure out how that happened."

"Let me know when you do, because she had me just as fooled as you. Even now, knowing how it ended, I can't find one single piece of evidence that would have outed her."

"Maybe we're getting too old, Jack."

Jack smiled and nodded. "I think you're right."

A few minutes of silence passed. Jack thought about Jasmine and Clarissa and how he wished that one was still alive and the other was sitting by his side. That wasn't the case, though, and nothing he could do would change it. There was no point in dwelling on it.

"Let's get out of here." Frank grabbed the check and walked toward the register.

Jack exited the diner and waited on the sidewalk. He assessed every person that passed, a trait that was so ingrained that no level of retirement would prevent him from doing it.

Frank appeared a moment later and pulled out a pack of cigarettes. He opened it and offered one to Jack.

"I really shouldn't," Jack said. "But what the hell."

They left the diner and walked and smoked until they found an empty parking lot.

"I've taken care of the rest," Frank said. "You're cleared. You were working for me when you interfered and stole the documents from Bragg's courier. But then you were later attacked and lost possession of them. Everything you've done since has been in an effort to get them back. You were successful, and now the intelligence community, hell the country for that matter, is forever indebted to you. It's cleared through the Pentagon and up to the White House."

"I'm no longer a ghost?"

"Nope. In fact, you can get on a plane using your real ID and passport and go wherever the hell you want."

Jack held out his hand. "Thanks."

Frank grabbed Jack's hand and shook it. "Any time." He let go and walked toward the sidewalk, leaving Jack behind. Then he turned and said, "Jack, if you ever need anything, call."

Jack stood still and watched as his old partner disappeared behind the walls of a concrete jungle. He was free now. Free for the first time in his adult life. He pulled out a phone and called Bear, but received no answer. He'd try again later, he figured.

Jack walked through the city with no destination in mind. He purchased a new cell phone, a permanent one, and then tried Bear one more time. No answer again, but this time he left a message with his new phone number.

Later that afternoon he grabbed a hotel room for the night. A good night's sleep would serve him well and in the morning he could decide on the first leg of his journey.

That night, as he sat in his room eating an overpriced ribeye steak ordered from room service, Jack's phone rang. He answered without checking the number, figuring it was Bear calling him back.

"Hello?" he said, excited to talk to his old friend and catch up on the happenings of the last few days.

"Mr. Jack Noble?" a man with a British accent said.

"Who is this?"

"Is this Jack Noble?"

"Jack Noble is dead," he said.

"You and I both know that is not true."

Jack got up from the table and walked over to the window. He parted the blinds with his thumb and forefinger and scanned the rear parking lot below.

"What do you want?" Jack said.

"I'm calling to offer you an assignment."

"I'm retired."

"Yes, Mr. Noble. But this is—"

"Maybe you didn't understand me because of the accent barrier. Let me spell it out for you. I'm retired. Done. Finished. No more assignments."

The line went silent and Jack nearly hung up. Then he heard muffled voices in the background and decided to wait.

"Sir, I'll be brief. I'm calling on behalf of the woman you knew as Blue Willow in one life, and Dottie in another. She says it will be a great personal favor to her if you will at least come to London to discuss the assignment in person with her. She also says that if you saw what she thinks you saw in Monaco six months ago, then you can figure out what this is about."

Jack sat down and thought back to his night in Monaco. The casino. Seeing Dottie. The encounter with her husband. The attempt on Jack's life. Seeing Dottie being carried out on a gurney after being beaten. Her husband being taken away in cuffs. The man was a billionaire and likely bought his way out of any jail time. And now he was probably threatening her life.

"Is London nice in the spring?" Jack said.

"Lovely," the man said.

"I'll leave in the morning. Give me a number to reach you."

"We'll call you at this number, tomorrow, ten p.m., London time."

The call ended and Jack placed the phone on the table. He got up and walked over to the mirror. Stared at himself for a few minutes and then said, "Retirement can wait a few more days. This is personal."

The story of Jack Noble continues in *Noble Betrayal*. Continue to read an excerpt, or visit https://ltryan.com/pb for purchasing information.

Sign up for L.T. Ryan's new release newsletter and be the first to find out when new Jack Noble novels are published. To sign up, simply fill out the form on the following page:

http://ltryan.com/newsletter/

As a thank you for signing up, you'll receive a complimentary digital copy of *The First Deception* with bonus short story *The Recruit*.

If you enjoyed reading *Noble Retribution*, I would appreciate it if you would help others enjoy this book, too. How?

Lend it. Share with a friend or donate to your local library.

Recommend it. Please help other readers find this book by recommending it to friends, readers' groups and discussion boards.

Review it. Please tell other readers why you liked this book by reviewing it at Amazon or Goodreads. Your opinion goes a long way in helping others decide if a book is for them. Also, a review doesn't have to be a big old report. Amazon requires 20 words to publish a review. If you do write a review, please send me an email at contact@ltryan.com so I can thank you with a personal email.

ALSO BY L.T. RYAN

Visit https://ltryan.com/pb for paperback purchasing information.

The Jack Noble Series

The Recruit (Short Story)

The First Deception (Prequel 1)

Noble Beginnings (Jack Noble #1)

A Deadly Distance (Jack Noble #2)

Thin Line (Jack Noble #3)

Noble Intentions (Jack Noble #4)

When Dead in Greece (Jack Noble #5)

Noble Retribution (Jack Noble #6)

Noble Betrayal (Jack Noble #7)

Never Go Home (Jack Noble #8)

Beyond Betrayal (Clarissa Abbot)

Noble Judgment (Jack Noble #9)

Never Cry Mercy (Jack Noble #10)

Deadline (Jack Noble #11)

End Game (Jack Noble #12)

Noble Ultimatum (Jack Noble #13) - Spring 2021

Bear Logan Series

Ripple Effect

Blowback

Take Down

Deep State

Rachel Hatch Series

Drift

Downburst

Fever Burn

Smoke Signal

Firewalk - December 2020

Whitewater - March 2021

Mitch Tanner Series

The Depth of Darkness

Into The Darkness

Deliver Us From Darkness - coming Summer 2021

Cassie Quinn Series

Path of Bones

Untitled - February, 2021

Blake Brier Series

Unmasked

Unleashed - January, 2021

Untitled - April, 2021

Affliction Z Series

Affliction Z: Patient Zero

Affliction Z: Abandoned Hope

Affliction Z: Descended in Blood

Affliction Z: Fractured (Part 1)

Affliction Z: Fractured (Part 2) - October, 2021

NOBLE BETRAYAL: CHAPTER 1

Jack Noble stood in the narrow aisle of the British Airways 777. He coughed into his hand to clear his throat of the taste of stale air. His joints ached, and his muscles were tight and sore. First Class had been sold out so he had to settle for a seat in coach. The perils of booking a flight at the last possible minute, he figured.

He reached up and grabbed a bag from the overhead for an elderly woman. His shoulder popped as he lowered the bag and handed it to her. She smiled and thanked him. He nodded, turned, joined the crowd pushing toward the front of the plane. For the first time ever, he didn't mind the wait and the throng of people. It gave him time. It gave him cover. He decided to go with the flow and remain a part of the crowd. It gave him a sense of certainty at a time when he was unsure of what he'd find upon reaching the gate.

So after he exited the plane and entered the wider jetway, he found himself surrounded on all sides by other travelers. He was shoulder to shoulder with the two people he'd shared the flight with. Jack thought he remembered the guy introducing himself as Kyle. He was British, bald and heavy, smelled as though he hadn't had a shower in over forty-eight hours. The woman, in contrast, was young and cute and smelled pleasant. She had introduced herself as Hannah. She was from West Virginia, returning to London where she attended college and worked as a nanny. She wore too much makeup, as Jack believed most young women often did. The fact of it was evidenced by the smear of eye liner that stretched from the corner of her eye to her ear lobe. A casualty of the three hours she had spent curled up in her seat, asleep, and getting too close to Jack. Evidenced by the smear of eyeliner on his shoulder.

Good thing I'm not meeting a woman.

He'd spent the last seven hours squished between the man and the woman. What's a few more minutes, he figured. He only spoke to the guy long enough to know he didn't care to ever see him again. Not that he would. And the woman had been pleasant and cute enough that he wouldn't mind bumping into her again. Although he knew he wouldn't.

Who ever runs into flight buddies a second time?

The herd of passengers came to an abrupt stop like hundreds of fallen leaves adrift in the water where the stream bottlenecks. Ahead, people jostled for position as the group merged into a single file line out of necessity. At two or three wide and shoulder to shoulder, they couldn't get through the jetway's exit, or the entrance to the gate, depending on one's point of view. For Jack, the opening meant passage into a terminal at Heathrow Airport. One that he'd walked through at least a dozen times, using the same number of aliases.

Today, however, would be the first time that Jack Noble officially walked through London's international airport.

One by one, people passed through the narrow opening and the line got shorter. Jack breathed deeply, remained calm and relaxed. The young woman had settled in line in front of him. She crossed her arms and tapped her right heel into the floor several times.

"Relax," Jack said. "We'll be through in a couple minutes."

She turned her head, nodded, smiled. The line pushed forward and she followed. So did Jack.

Finally, they escaped the jetway. Jack was met by a burst of stale disinfected air pushed out from a blower above. Moments later the smell gave way to a rush of foul odor as the older man behind him reached out and placed his hand firmly on Jack's shoulder.

"It's good to be home, isn't it?" the guy who might be named Kyle said as he leaned in close to Jack's right ear.

Jack's first instinct was to deliver an elbow to the guy's solar plexus. Instead, he shrugged free of the man's grasp, turned his head to the right, nodded once without making eye contact.

The man pushed forward, bumping into Jack, and continued talking. What he said, Jack wasn't sure. He had tuned the man out while he scanned the terminal in both an effort to gather his bearings and isolate any potential threats. It wasn't hard to do. All he had to do was spot the wave of people. The line coming toward him was maybe two or three people wide. But the one flowing away was seven wide at its narrowest. The way to the exit, he presumed. So he stepped into the walkway and joined them. Assimilated into them.

Not always the easiest thing for Jack to do.

When the opportunity presented itself, Jack broke free from the group. He heard the man call to him from behind and ignored him. He wanted to get as much distance between himself and the guy. Jack knew there would be another logjam at customs. No matter how far a leaf got ahead of the cluster, it would be knocked back into the group as soon as the stream dammed up again.

Although he'd try to get through with nothing to declare, he'd be stopped. He was always stopped. He couldn't recall a time when he wasn't stopped. Even at the age of twelve, traveling with his brother Sean and his parents, he'd been stopped.

Today was special because it would be the first time in over a decade that he'd hand over a passport with the name Jack Noble on it.

The thought already caused a tightening in his stomach.

Had Frank Skinner stayed true to his word? Would the SIS director clear Jack's name from every database known to man? At least those in the known free world?

A few weeks ago, Jack Noble was a ghost. Presumed dead after a shortened stay at Black Dolphin, Russia's notorious maximum security prison. Jack had then been transported to Greece, where he took cover on the island of Crete. It took six months for Ivanov's men to find him. When they did, Frank made the call to bring Jack back to the U.S. It wasn't all for Jack's benefit, though. Frank needed a job done, and Jack obliged. Did he really have a choice? It turned out to be worth it. He had his freedom and a semi-clear conscience.

The slow moving line put him into a kind of trance. He didn't realize he'd reached the counter until the man spoke.

"Passport, sir."

Jack didn't need to look directly at the man with the thin brown mustache to know that the guy was sizing him up. They always did. Could he blame them? At six-foot-two and a touch over two hundred pounds, Jack commanded attention. Police officers and customs agents always watched him a little closer than other travelers. It wasn't that he fit a profile, per se. He had the look of a man who knows how to handle himself and might have ulterior motives. Whether he did or not didn't matter.

The customs agent whistled a basic tune while he waited for his computer to return information. The guy's partner rifled through Jack's carry on. Although Jack knew the agent wouldn't find anything, he felt nervous. What if he had mistakenly placed or left a false passport in the bag? *Impossible*, he thought. He'd never used this bag, and his false passports were scattered among a dozen safe deposit boxes in eight different countries.

"What business do you have in London, Mr. Noble?"

"Visiting my cousin," Jack said.

The agent lifted an eyebrow, beckoning Jack to continue.

Jack didn't. He knew that a simple answer was all he had to give. Saying anymore would open him up to further questioning. If the guy needed more, he'd ask.

"Very well," the agent said. He handed Jack his passport while the other agent placed Jack's bag in front of him, opened. Both men looked toward the next person in line, seemingly forgetting all about the man named Jack Noble.

Which was fine with him. He grabbed his bag, pulled the zipper shut, slung it over his shoulder. He rejoined the throng of people making their way toward the arrivals gate. Once again he found himself in close proximity to Hannah and the guy who might be named Kyle. Jack made the mistake of making eye contact with the guy. He turned away as the man lifted his hand to wave to Jack.

"Jack," the guy called out.

Jack did his best to avoid the man, weaving his way through the crowd to get further ahead. Kyle's girth would prevent him from doing the same with any kind of efficiency.

Jack reached the arrivals gate, scanned the faces in the crowd who were waiting around for loved ones or business associates or for the person they were hired to pick up.

No one waited for Jack, which was what he expected. He was in England to work with professionals. Placing themselves in the airport would link them with Jack if someone dug deep enough.

And when you bring a man in to assassinate someone, you don't want to be linked with that man.

Jack continued to weave his way through the crowd, reached a point where the herd had thinned enough that he could walk without needing to turn his torso to the side in order to squeeze past someone. Finally, he found himself standing outside. He used his hand to shield his eyes from the sun while he searched for the taxi line. He found it and found Hannah standing nearby, frustrated and upset. She had her purse opened and was digging through it, shaking her head. Jack figured she'd lost her keys or her wallet.

Kyle was standing next to her, car keys in hand, thin smile on his face. How had he managed to beat Jack outside? Regular traveler, Jack assumed. The guy knew the ins and outs of the Heathrow like he knew his own house.

Jack approached Hannah and said, "Everything OK?"

Kyle said, "It's fine, Mr. Noble. She just —"

"I asked her," Jack said.

Hannah avoided his stare. Her anger was obvious. Her ears and cheeks were bright red, eyes narrowed, nostrils flared. "I lost my wallet. All my money, my credit card, even my damn library card, it was all in there. I need to be home in, like, thirty minutes. How am I supposed to get there now?"

Kyle twirled his keys around his index finger and whistled, like Hannah was a dog. "I told you I can give you a ride."

She looked up at Jack. The tension in her face lifted, her eyes pleaded with him for help. Jack hadn't liked the guy from the moment the man flopped into the seat next to Jack. He sensed during the flight that Hannah didn't care much for him either. But the look on her face signaled something other than dislike, and Jack wondered if she was scared of the man.

"Where are you going?" Jack asked.

"Kensington," Hannah replied.

"Me too. You can tag along with me."

"Nonsense," Kyle said. "I'll give both of you a ride. I have a car parked right over—"

"Shut up, Kyle," Jack said. "I'm sick of your blabbering. You've got five seconds to get out of my face."

"What? Why? I...?" Kyle's face reddened with embarrassment and he turned around and began walking. Every few steps he'd look back at Jack, hurt.

Jack figured he should feel sorry, but he didn't. Just because he was semi-retired didn't mean he had to go soft and start treating everyone nicely.

"Ready to get that cab?" Jack said.

"Oh, you were serious?" Hannah said.

Jack looked sideways at the young woman.

"Sorry," she said. "I thought you were just being nice. You know, getting rid of him for me."

"I was. But the offer still stands. No point in you being stranded here."

She chewed on her bottom lip while the gaze of her brown eyes traveled up and down Jack's frame.

"I'm harmless," he said.

"For some reason I don't believe that. But, I don't think you'll try anything with me with a cab driver present."

Jack laughed. He liked the girl's confidence. He said, "Tell you what, Hannah. Why don't I just give you money for a cab?"

She hiked her shoulders in the air an inch and pushed her bottom lip out. "That'd work, I suppose."

He escorted her to an awaiting cab, opened the rear passenger door, waited for Hannah to slip inside. Then he reached into his pocket for his wallet. He turned his head to the left as he did so, taking in a view of the long line of taxis and people standing in line, shoulder to shoulder. Amid the wall of faces, one man stood out. He was tall, wore a dark suit, stayed a few yards away from the crowd. His eyes were locked on Jack's. A moment passed and the two men faced off, separated by fifty feet.

The man started walking toward the cab.

Jack stuck his leg inside the open vehicle and said, "Scoot over."

"What? I thought you were going to get your own?"

"Change of plans," Jack said as he lowered himself into the back seat, forcing Hannah to slide over. He slammed the door shut and looked over his right shoulder.

"What are you looking at?" Hannah asked. She turned in her seat.

"You don't have a crazy ex-boyfriend who might have been expecting you, do you?"

Hannah laughed. "No."

Jack didn't figure the man to have anything to do with Hannah, but he knew it was best to know for sure.

The man hadn't broke stride and was now within twenty feet of the cab.

"Go," Jack said.

"What do you want me to do?" the driver said. "We got to wait for our turn."

The man stopped ten feet from the cab. Jack looked over his other shoulder and saw that a black sedan had stopped in the middle of the road. The guy in the suit hopped inside.

"That'll be too late," Jack said. "Go. Now."

NOBLE BETRAYAL: CHAPTER 2

The driver grabbed the shifter like he was reaching for the pull handle on a slot machine. He licked his lips, wrapped his fingers around the knobby end and dropped the transmission into first gear. The vehicle made an audible click and gave a slight jerk as it passed through neutral. The driver eased away from the curb, nosed into the next lane, aided by the fact that the sedan behind them was blocking it.

"Faster," Jack said.

"What is your problem?" the driver said, glaring at Jack in the rear view mirror.

Jack leaned forward and placed his right forearm on the shoulder of the passenger's seat. "Put your foot on the gas or I'm going to kick you out of the cab and do it myself."

"Fine," the driver shouted. He jammed the gas pedal to the floor, sending Jack lurching backward into his seat. He managed to tuck his left elbow in, away from Hannah. Still, his shoulder collided with hers, and she let out a painful squeal.

"Dammit," she said.

"Sorry." Jack stared into the rear view mirror, eyes locked on the driver who seemed too scared to look back at Jack. Perhaps the guy preferred to concentrate his efforts on the road. Jack figured it was the latter considering the man was doing roughly seventy miles per hour in an area designated for thirty.

"You want to tell me what that was all about?" Hannah said.

"No." Jack shifted in his seat, repositioned himself so that he could check behind the cab. He spotted the black sedan about ten car lengths behind.

The driver started to ease up on the gas.

"Don't slow down," Jack said.

"Why not?" the driver said.

"You see that black car back there?"

The driver's eyes shifted from the road to the rear view mirror. His gaze fell upon Jack, then traveled past him. "Yeah, I see it."

"I don't know who that is, but they're either looking for you or for me. I don't know what kind of man you are, but I can tell you this for sure. If they are after me, you want nothing to do with them. Got it? So you better do what I say when I say it. Pick up your speed. Get us as far ahead as you can, then when we are in an area you are very familiar with, I want you to get off the highway and start weaving your way through the city. Avoid traffic at all cost."

"This is London. How am I supposed to avoid traffic?"

"I don't care how you do it, man. Figure it out or we all might be dead."

"How about I stop and get out and offer you up to them."

"Are you really that stupid?"

The driver locked eyes with Jack. The taxi picked up speed, distanced itself from the black sedan. Not for long, Jack figured. But as long as the other car stayed that far behind, the cab driver should be able to lose them if he knew the city well. If not, then all Jack could hope for was that the men would be unarmed.

"Who are you?" Hannah asked him.

Jack shrugged, told her, "It's complicated."

"How so? Seems like a pretty simple question to me."

"Look, Hannah, I don't know if those guys got a good look at you or not. If they did, then the less you know about me the better."

"Why?"

"Because." Jack paused, searching for the right words. "You need plausible deniability on your side in the event someone asks you questions about me."

Hannah narrowed her eyes, shook her head, looked away. Jack caught a glimpse of the anger in her eyes reflected in the window.

He returned his attention to the vehicle tailing them. The car had closed the gap and now paced them from two car lengths.

"Pick it up," Jack said.

"I can't go any faster. One more ticket and I'll have my licensed revoked."

"That car catches up to us and you might have your life revoked."

This garnered a frightened reaction from Hannah, but Jack ignored it.

The vehicle tailing them jerked to the left and sped up. Jack cursed under his breath. Hannah slumped down in her seat until her head was below the window. Fear or street smarts? Within seconds the two cars were side by side. The other vehicle's windows were tinted. Jack couldn't tell how many people were inside the car. He knew there were at least two, so he planned for a third.

Jack reached inside his coat. There was no gun there, though. Not even a holster. He couldn't travel with a weapon. In years past, he'd have had someone meet him at the airport who would have provided him with a pistol at the very least. In some cases he was able to leave from a government installation, which allowed him to travel with a weapon hidden in the false bottom of a bag or suitcase. This time he'd have to wait until one of Dottie's people met him. He had no idea when that would occur. Certainly not in time to deal with the men following him.

For a few minutes it felt as if the two cars were standing still. Then, the black sedan pulled away and exited the highway.

"You can sit up," Jack told Hannah. "They're gone."

"Can you tell me who they were?"

"No."

"If my life's in danger I'd like to know who it might be. Why can't you tell me?"

"Because I don't know."

Hannah righted herself in her seat and said, "You can get off at the next exit."

"Stop a few blocks short of her building," Jack added.

Five minutes later the driver pulled the cab to the curb. Hannah jumped out. Jack pulled out his wallet, handed the driver three ten pound notes, exited the cab.

"What are you doing?" Hannah asked.

"Walking you home."

She crossed her arms, arched her back. "I'm starting to think I would have been better off letting creepy Kyle drive me home."

So that was his name.

"I'm thinking the same," Jack said. "But he didn't, I did. And I need to make sure you get home OK."

She studied him for a moment. "My building has a doorman. He's bigger than you. Try to come in and I'll have him kick your ass."

Jack smiled. He liked the girl's attitude. "Sounds good to me."

Jack didn't have the layout of London committed to memory, but he knew they were in close proximity to Buckingham Palace and Hyde Park. The only reason he knew this was because he saw a sign saying so before they exited the highway.

"This looks like an expensive area," he said.

"It is."

"How's a college girl afford to live in a place like this?"

She smiled. "Well, for one, I live in a tiny little apartment. It's like a master bedroom converted into an apartment. One room has everything. And the family I work for pays for it."

"Who do you work for?"

She turned her head slightly and looked at him out of the corner of her eye.

"OK, question withdrawn," Jack said. "I know where you live, though. I could just follow you."

She stopped, turned toward Jack, grabbed his arm. "That's not funny, Jack. Seriously, don't you even think about following me or popping in on the family I work for when I'm there."

Jack raised his hands in mock defense. "Don't worry. The moment you step into your building is the last time you'll ever see me."

"Is it?"

Jack nodded. "It is."

She pointed and said, "That's it right there."

"Where's the doorman?"

"I lied." She smiled. "Going to walk me the rest of the way?"

"I think you got it."

She extended her hand. "Bye, Jack."

He watched her climb up a set of concrete stairs stained by years of exposure. She pulled out her keys, entered the building without looking back. Jack lingered for several minutes. The air was mild and the breeze light. He scanned the street and surrounding houses, ensuring that no one was watching him or Hannah's building. He'd provided the world with enough collateral damage and didn't want to add Hannah to that list.

After half an hour, he decided it was OK to leave. He pulled out his cell phone, turned on the GPS, punched his hotel's name into the search field. He was staying at the Plaza, other side of Westminster Bridge. A fancy place, but his choices had been limited. The distance to the hotel was less than two miles. Jack decided to walk.

Click Here to purchase Noble Betrayal!

ABOUT THE AUTHOR

L.T. Ryan is a *USA Today* and international bestselling author. The new age of publishing offered L.T. the opportunity to blend his passions for creating, marketing, and technology to reach audiences with his popular Jack Noble series.

Living in central Virginia with his wife, the youngest of his three daughters, and their three dogs, L.T. enjoys staring out his window at the trees and mountains while he should be writing, as well as reading, hiking, running, and playing with gadgets. See what he's up to at http://ltryan.com.

Social Medial Links:

- Facebook (L.T. Ryan): https://www.facebook.com/LTRyanAuthor
- Facebook (Jack Noble Page): https://www.facebook.com/JackNobleBooks/
- Twitter: https://twitter.com/LTRyanWrites
- Goodreads: http://www.goodreads.com/author/show/6151659.L_T_Ryan